HIRO'S WAR

A NOVEL

Rebecca Taniguchi

GAMAN

我慢

PUBLISHING

St. Charles, Illinois

ISBN: 978-1-7370704-0-5

GAMAN PUBLISHING LLC
St. Charles, Illinois

Book Cover Design by ebooklaunch.com
Interior design done by Tami Boyce (www.tamiboyce.com)

for Jan

If you want to see the heroic,
Look at those who can love
In return for hatred.
If you want to see the brave,
Look at those who can forgive.

—Bhaghavad Gita

PART I

1

Seattle

June 1976

"What a bunch of baby-faced warriors," my old lieutenant said as he scanned our photo.

"We were so bright eyed, so determined, weren't we?" I said. "Had no idea what we were getting into."

I handed the picture to Shig, brother of my best friend in the squad, standing next to me in this, our official training camp photo at Camp Shelby, U.S.A.

Shig studied our faces and laughed. "You're the only one smiling, Hiro. Biggest idiot of the whole lot."

I grinned and told him where he could shove the thought. "That may be, but what a team we were. Did ourselves proud. I *was* happy."

"Until you got shafted," Shig muttered.

"Until I got shafted," I said in a low voice. I saw Lieutenant Ando's face darken.

Ruth came into the living room with coffee, and we stopped talking. I had told my wife little about the difficulty I had hidden for years, the shame, the guilt, and I put the picture back on the shelf.

"You need some food to fortify yourselves for the party, gentlemen." Ruth set her tray on the coffee table we were sitting around, and together, we passed around coffee, water, cookies. She whispered to me, "Mind if I stay for a few minutes?" and I patted the sofa seat next to me.

"It's a special gathering," Ando said, "bicentennial and all. So much to celebrate, civil rights growing everywhere, Vietnam coming to a close." He and Shig had flown in from Honolulu to visit before meeting their wives at the Nisei Veterans Reunion in Chicago late tonight. Ruth and I would follow tomorrow.

"Your kind of get-together," Shig said to me. "Always the life of the party, you." He pulled out a spiral sketchpad and began flipping gingerly through the pages, which looked pretty yellowed. He stopped at one.

"Speaking of Chicago," he said, "Ruth, Hiro, I think you might like this." He reached over the coffee table and handed us the pad. "I brought a few of my brother's pencil drawings so we could remember him. Joji—Happi—really had some talent." My pal's given name was "George," pronounced "Joji" by Japanese, but by the time we left Shelby, he was "Happi" to us soldiers.

Ruth and I looked at the sketch and drew in our breath.

"Good grief," I said. "It's us."

"I had no idea," Ruth said softly. "This was when I lived in Chicago, before you boys shipped out."

She turned to Shig. "Your family was there, too," she recalled, and Shig said yes, of course.

"A lot of you in the camps were released to Chicago, weren't you," Ando said. Shig's family was also from Seattle, interned with us at Minidoka, though he moved to Hawaii after the war.

"Happi must have seen the photo of us that I kept," I said, eyeing Ruth. "He based his drawing on it."

I handed the sketch to Ando. "Ruth and I were getting pretty serious by then," I said. "But I don't know when Happi drew this."

"Looks like you two are joined at the hip," Ando said. "Nothing like young love."

I studied the drawing. There I was in dress uniform, Ruth in a pretty suit. I could just make out our faces, but Happi's strokes and shadings had captured the emotion of the moment, the energy and passion and hope.

I stood up and walked to my desk. "You know, I have some of Happi's sketches, too. Always drawing, that guy."

"If he wasn't writing letters home," Ando said, and everyone murmured their agreement.

I opened the desk drawer and felt around until I found the pad in the back. "Haven't looked at this in ages," I said and held it up. "Ando, you remember this?"

"No," Ando said as I took my seat.

"These drawings are from much later in the war." I showed a couple to our group, of our men sprawled out on the ground, dead-tired asleep after battle, of a pretty girl met on R&R.

"Do you mind?" Shig asked, reaching for the pad. "I've never seen these."

"Be my guest." I watched him as he scrutinized page after page. Shig looked up at me and then placed the pad on the table, opened to one illustration.

"Is that it?" he asked. "Where the brawl took place?"

"You mean, *the* fight?" Ando asked.

5

I glanced at Ruth and opted for a bit of nonchalance. "Honey, I don't think I ever mentioned this to you—"

"What's that?" she said, raising her eyebrows.

"A bunch of us got into a scuffle one night, and Happi sketched it afterwards."

"Can I see?" she asked.

Together, everyone examined Happi's drawing of a barroom, dark shaded and angry, bold strokes alternating with fine. In the center, a GI near the bar was taking a swing at an MP officer, while from the corners of the page and room, fellow GIs were running toward the fight. Two more GIs followed, racing toward the growing melee, and MPs surrounded their leader. I could just make out the 442nd's liberty-torch-in-hand patch on the GIs' arms, a different one on the MPs' uniforms.

"This is what set everything in motion," Shig muttered.

I shook my head subtly at him and eyed Ruth, who didn't look like she'd heard.

"You know, at your reunions," she said, "I hear the boys talk about the fights they got into on leave, the bloody noses they got—and gave." Then she looked me in the eye. "But this looks serious, with MPs involved."

"The boys talk a lot at our get-togethers," I said. "After a few beers, maybe too much."

Ruth might not have a clue about the free-for-all and what happened after, but she knew how those reunions had saved me, everyone hashing over the war, one veteran laughing at something one minute, another choking back tears the next, our missing comrades always a presence. Seemed the longer our days went on, the more they were measured by the gatherings we attended at all levels, regimental, battalion, company.

"You kept these drawings all this time," Ruth said. "They must be special, close to your heart, *ne*?"

"This sketchpad is all I have of Happi's," I said.

Ando tilted his head and squeezed his eyes shut, the way he always did when he thought. Sadness covered his face. He looked again at the drawings of the brawl and of Ruth and me. "You know, all these years later," he said, "no one's told me exactly what went on when you were interned together, how you became friends and took on everything we faced. Maybe if we put our heads together, you'd help me understand how one thing led to another, especially after this fight. Who knows how much time we have left to figure everything out, come to peace with it all."

"I knew the camps all too well, but I wouldn't mind learning more about the war," Ruth said.

"Count me in," Shig said.

I looked at the three of them and then focused on Ando. "Come to think of it, there are still a lot of things I damned well don't understand, either." I could feel my old anger rising. Sometimes you had to struggle to forgive your own comrades, as well as your enemy and yourself, and I didn't know what was hardest.

Forgiveness was a bitch.

"Well," Ruth said, thinking, "why don't you do the honors, Hiroshi?"

2

Seattle

May 14, 1942

Someone was shaking me awake.

"Rise and shine, Hiroshi. Time to get up."

I unglued my eyes and saw Wes Inada, my neighbor in our Eleventh Avenue apartment building, standing over me.

My head was throbbing. "Ooooh," I groaned.

I was either still drunk or really hung over. I'd stayed out too late with some of my Caucasian teammates and our girls, and now I would pay for every drink.

"Come on, you old boozehound." Wes Inada pulled me into a sitting position on my bed. He found my glasses near my pillow and handed them to me. "Lucky you didn't break these."

"Thanks." I had only one pair and was blind without them. "Really, thanks."

"You sleep in your clothes?" He laughed. "How drunk were you?"

I looked down at my rumpled shirt and khakis. "Guess I did. And very." Slowly remembering what day it was, I stumbled to the bathroom to relieve myself. The sounds of peeing and flushing bounced off the tiling. I had no towels left. No bath mat. Nothing.

I bent over to take a long drink from the faucet. Water dribbled from my chin down my shirt and chest as I stood up, wishing to God Almighty that the room would stay steady.

"What time is it?" I slumped down on the bed.

"We have less than an hour. How about some breakfast?" he said. "You have any food left?"

"A few eggs."

"I'll boil them up." Wes walked to the kitchen, stepping over one of the beige canvas duffel bags that I'd picked up at Kress five-and-dime, along with the tin cup, plate, and flatware everyone had been directed to bring. I'd already printed "H. D. KOGA" on the bags in big black letters.

I closed one eye to ease the spinning that just wouldn't stop. Two eyes shut were even better. I drifted off for a couple of minutes.

"Eggs are on." Wes returned and handed me a glass of water. "Bet you need this. Drink up."

I knew that Wes had to get moving with his parents and siblings, and I did as told while he gathered what was left of my possessions. I really appreciated he'd left his family to help me.

"Want these shoes?"

"You gonna shave now? We have to pack your razor."

"How long you think we'll be gone? Should I pack your winter coat?"

"Anything else?"

The list of what we could bring—bed linens, clothing, toiletries, basically what you could carry in two hands—had been nailed just a week ago to the telephone pole right in front of our building, just as it had been posted at different times throughout *Nihonmachi*, Japantown, over the past couple of months.

INSTRUCTIONS
TO ALL PERSONS OF
JAPANESE
ANCESTRY

It was an exclusion order, an *exclusion* notice, tailored to each evacuation area by defining its boundaries in every direction. The people on my block and a few around us had to show up at our civil control station, the Christian Youth Center on Madison, at ten am today. After that we would be transported to an assembly center, whatever the hell that was.

"I don't have anything left," I answered Wes. As with all my neighbors, the government had taken away my radio and camera right after the attack on Pearl Harbor, fearing I might be a spy, and Willamette College reneged on my football scholarship before I could start school. Just yesterday a Caucasian snatched my beautiful old Pontiac for next to nothing.

I detected that salty taste at the back of my throat that warned vomit was on its way. I hightailed it back to the bathroom, but my stomach calmed down, and I stretched toward the mirror. *Shinigami ni toritsukamerarete iru mitai,* my mother might have said, *You look like the death god has you.* She remained on my mind as I brushed my teeth and then dug out the dregs in the Pomade can, trying to shape my hair into a semblance of its usual pompadour. I felt the same ache of emptiness and pain I did the morning I dressed for her funeral, what was it, six, seven years ago now.

At first, only those born in Japan, *issei,* were to be evacuated—after all, they had not been given the opportunity for naturalization and were considered enemy aliens who could legally be interned in wartime. But then Uncle Sam decided to give us *nisei* the boot, too. It didn't matter that we were born here; we were now officially "nonaliens."

Nonaliens?

Wasn't it enough to strip me of my rights of citizenship?

But my damned humanity, too?

I walked back to the bedroom, where I had laid out khakis and a shirt for this morning, nice and neat, the way I'd been taught. I put them on and pulled the "I Am Chinese" button off the shirt I'd worn to my going-away party the night before. That button had been my ticket to freedom over the past couple of months, letting me into areas newly forbidden to anyone of Japanese descent. Damned if the Caucasians could tell the difference between us and the Chinese.

Wes came in and handed me a plate of hard-boiled eggs, eyeing the button and then me. "How do you do it?" he asked. "Flouting the rules, getting the girls."

I looked at Wes, not sure what to say. He'd been a couple of years ahead of me in school and had always been a bit of a goody-goody, on the honor roll, the debate team, the newspaper—all the things I could never do and, for that matter, didn't want to. And the way he'd lecture everyone about politics and legal matters was enough to bore me to death. But being a good guy was the whole reason he was here. His mother, knowing I sneaked some beers last night, had sent him to check on me. Since my parents died, Mrs. Inada had treated me like one of her own sons, making me cookies and steaming bowls of chazuke full of rice and green tea, bits of nori seaweed and salmon and wasabi that she had on hand. And this morning Wes was acting like a brother, even while his own family surely needed his help. The clock ticked, and I tried to meet him half-way.

"I dunno," I admitted, knowing that sounded pretty stupid. "Never really thought about it. I guess I bend the rules when I don't think they're right."

Wes stood there, watching me. "You know, that could get you in trouble one of these days," he said. "You won't always be able to get away with things because you're young and all the old ladies like you."

Wes knew how his mother had gathered all the other mothers at our church to help me after *Haha*, Mom, died. I figured he was right, but I didn't want to deal with it right now.

"And the girls?" I changed the topic. "Heck, we all know they go for the dumb jocks like me."

"I don't have a prayer," Wes laughed. He was a senior in college and not even going steady.

"Yes, you do." I talked about my brother Frank, who had left Seattle months before the attack so he could translate for the government rather than be drafted. He was eight years older than me, a pain in the neck sometimes, always telling me what to do, but I knew he really cared for me. He had only recently gotten engaged. I encouraged Wes. "Be yourself. Don't listen to others."

"Hope you're right," Wes said.

I ate the eggs, slowly at first and then eagerly, overcoming the scent of sulfur to fill my belly. We had no idea where we were going or how long we'd be without food.

"You have a tie?" Wes asked.

I pointed to a bag. "Why? I don't need it."

Wes, who wore a suit, his hair neatly parted and slicked back, rolled his eyes again as he fished around and handed me the tie. "I've been arguing about this with Mom and Dad. They keep saying that they have *on* for this country, that we owe it a lot. We have to hold our heads high until this thing passes. But I say this stinks. Why should we play nice?"

"Look, this is rotten," I said. "God knows I'm with you on that. But don't fight with your parents." I tied the damned tie, unsure if my old sorrow or the cloth was choking me. I really had to get over it. "Let's just focus on getting through this so we can get back to normal."

"You really think we're going to get our lives back?" Wes asked. He began pacing the floor, fists clenched.

Someone tapped on the door, and I was grateful for the disturbance. I really didn't have an answer for Wes.

"Abandon all hope, ye who enter here." I opened the door as I recalled a line my English teacher had quoted to my class, about a hell with rings on top of rings on top of rings of deadly sins.

"Hey, you actually learned something in school," Wes laughed as he walked toward me. His mother entered the room. "Dante's *Inferno*, right?"

I said yes, not certain of the name of the work or the author. All I knew is that I hated most everything in school, but I loved that story, just couldn't shake it, full of greed and betrayal, anger and fraud.

Mrs. Inada walked right between Wes and me, grasped our hands, and said, "Getting late. *Iko!*" She was a good half foot shorter than us and looked up at me, clucking.

"Yes, let's go," I said.

With a start, I remembered the photo of my family and ran back to the bedroom. I had wrapped the picture in a folded newspaper, the only one I had ever kept, carrying the first news of the Pearl Harbor attack. I pressed the package to my heart as I brought it to Mrs. Inada. She'd had the picture framed for me, and I watched as she pulled it out and caressed each face with a finger: me and Frank, standing on one side of our seated parents; and then, on the other side, my sisters Molly, who would be evacuated with her husband in a couple of days, and Aiko, a *kibei,* stuck in Japan, her plans to return home after her studies upended by the war; and last, my baby brother, Koichi, on my mother's lap, next to my father, the three of them in heaven.

"They never leave you," she said softly and put her hand over her heart. I fought tears as she leaned over and nestled the photo in among the clothing. She took the newspaper from my hand and placed it on top, patting everything gently before she zipped the bag shut. "I know you and family so long, even before you and Frank live here, *ne.*"

She was right. *Chichi*, Dad, had worked in a Japanese import-export business, and when my parents moved to Seattle, his company gave him a really big house in Leschi Park, a Caucasian part of town, much bigger than most issei immigrants could afford. The majority of issei lived in Nihonmachi, on the shabby fringes of Seattle, south of Yesler, near Chinese, Jews of different nationalities, Negroes, and poor Caucasians. They worked as laborers, grocers, pharmacists, doctors, hairdressers, hotel owners. My family had attended church with many of them, and it was in Nihonmachi where my siblings and I landed after Chichi and Haha died. Once I'd grown up, Frank and I shared this apartment, a few blocks away from our sisters. It took us a while to feel a part of the lively community, drawn tight together under trying circumstances, but we were determined to make the best of things and were soon humming along with everyone else.

"Ready?" Wes held up a narrow tag by the string at one end. He looked as sad as I felt.

"Who can be ready for this?" I took the pasteboard and turned it over and over in my hand. The ID tag, which I'd received a few days ago when I registered, announced in bold black print my reporting time and area, plus a number for my family unit, which was only me. The Inadas may have taken me under their wing, but I was on my own now.

"How about we take these tags down to the morgue? Hook them on the big toes of the corpses?" I tried to make light of the situation.

Wes took back the tag and hung the string around one of the buttons on my shirt. "You have to go by the rules today, Hiroshi. You're going to get your ass kicked if you don't."

I took the hint and with Wes, placed the other tags on my luggage. Then we stood staring at each other. His lips trembled.

"Hey, come on. Japs did this to us, buddy." I patted Wes on the shoulder. "Maybe your mother's right." I nodded toward Mrs. Inada. "We got to do what we got to do for now."

"I don't know. I just don't know," Wes said.

Mrs. Inada trundled down the stairs in front of us to get her daughters and the food she had packed for our trip. "*Musubi*, a little *umeboshi*. Apple slice. All we have," she mumbled. Mr. Inada had gone ahead to our stop with their other two sons and most of their baggage.

Once on the street, I snapped more fully awake as the damp cold hit my face, and I saw the exclusion order hanging forlornly from the telephone pole. The damned notice had come on the heels of President Roosevelt's Executive Order 9066, which authorized the evacuation of anyone in parts of the Western Defense Command who the military thought might be dangerous. The EO, signed on February 19, 1942, two and a half months after Pearl Harbor, never mentioned Japanese by name, but we knew it was meant for us. The postings that followed confirmed that fact in no uncertain terms.

We looked like the enemy and had to leave.

Now I took in the ghostly remains of life, the colors of our neighborhood sucked dead-dull. No one uttered a word as we walked through a steady drizzle past boarded-up stores and hotels, bathhouses and restaurants that had only days and weeks before been thriving businesses, past abandoned houses and apartment buildings. Japanese schools and Buddhist churches were closed up, Japanese newspapers shut down.

"I AM AN AMERICAN," cried a banner across the front of Asahi Laundry. A SOLD sign hung above it.

"Kittens and plants for sale," pleaded a piece of cardboard in Mrs. Shinoda's front window.

"Thank you for your patronage," called a hand-lettered sign on Tanamura Fruit and Vegetable. "God bless you until we meet again. Mr. and Mrs. Tanamura."

"Closed until further notice," announced the poster on Izui Pharmacy.

"Under new management soon," stated the wooden plaque on the Okino Hotel.

Some had unloaded businesses and wares for pennies on the dollar. Others had entrusted their belongings to Caucasian friends in the hopes of retrieving them when they returned. I had battened down my boss's sporting goods store, where I'd worked to save money for college, and I looked forward to the day it might open again.

"Hiroshi!" a voice called my name from the sidewalk. A few Caucasians stood watching us leave, some with scowls, some with tears, and I spotted my friend Paul Johnson, who had taken in my dog, with him now.

"Bou Bear!" I ran over and knelt down to pet my little guy. Bou was a prick-eared Skye terrier that my father had given me for my birthday, the year before he died. Bou had silver-gray fur that fell to the street, with black-fringed ears, and it was love at first sight. Imperfect for the show ring but perfect for me, Bou became my dog and my dog alone, fond of my siblings but devoted to me, our hearts beating as one. His ears stood at attention now as he took in all this tumult, and his big brown eyes looked at me as though asking what had happened. He wriggled and cried and slobbered kisses over my face, licking the tears running down my cheeks.

I looked up at Paul, trying to recover myself. "Thanks again, buddy. Take good care of him, okay?"

"I promise," Paul said. "My parents and I will treat him like he's our own. And we'll all be here when you get back."

I stood up, shook hands, and ran to catch up with the Inadas. Bou and I both stopped to look at each other as we grew apart, my heart breaking in a way I'd never known, even when my parents died.

As we neared our pick-up point, I gasped at the hundreds of people, laborers and doctors and businessmen, teachers and students, emerging from trucks and taxicabs and cars, some driven by clergy and friends from our Christian and Buddhist churches. People herded little ones and juggled boxes and bags of every shape and size, some tied together with string and rope, all marked with family names in big, bold letters. Matsudaira. Ikeda. Takisaki. Kashino. Horiuchi.

Mothers and fathers, grandmothers and grandfathers, all dressed in their Sunday finery, ID tags fluttering in the breeze, sat on trunks and wooden boxes as they caught their breath. The youngest issei and eldest nisei paced up and down, comforting babies and toddlers. Little girls cried for their dolls from Japan, burned by their mothers weeks ago. Off to my right, a daughter cared for her elderly father, lying on a stretcher.

"*Ojiisan,* I don't want to go," a little girl cried to her grandfather, who sat on a pile of suitcases, one hand resting on his cane. He took her by the waist with his other hand and pulled her close.

"*Obaasan,* I'm scared." A boy clung to his grandmother.

Everyone was trying to bear up, the heart of our community already ripped from us, leaving no one to turn to. Our leaders, priests and teachers, journalists and activists, had been swept up by the FBI right after the attack, their homes ransacked. Many still had not been heard from. And the JACL, the Japanese American Citizens League, created several years before to protect our civil rights against the idea of a Yellow Peril, had turned its back on us; its officials, at least one living in Utah, outside the evacuation area, had suggested we nisei form a suicide battalion for dirty jobs while the government held our issei parents hostage in camps.

Even Uncle Sam said nuts to that.

I waved to people I knew, friends and their parents from school and church, shopkeepers, tailors, coaches and neighbors, all looking sad and resigned. Some waved back half-heartedly, while others shook their heads.

Two more days of this, and we would all be gone.

Soldiers roamed around us, holding bayoneted rifles and glowering. What were they expecting? Most of us were American citizens, and our parents were law-abiding, hard-working people.

"What's with all the Army guys?" I spoke into the air as I followed the Inadas, the entire family now, to the queue for buses. Everyone quieted down as we faced the inevitable, like people lining up at a wake to say their last farewells. One of the soldiers politely directed us into the vehicles, his voice soft, his hands extended in help. Blond and ruddy-cheeked, he was probably eighteen or nineteen, and I wondered if we'd ever played ball together. Rain poured down on us, and we looked right at each other until the soldier turned his head away.

I took a seat on the bus, pressed my head against the cold window, and stared into space. Mrs. Inada leaned in from the aisle and handed me a paper sack with the apple slices and rice balls, bits of pickled plum flecking the white. Then she kissed me on the forehead, and I squeezed her hand. Nisei rarely showed emotion in public, issei never. Wes guided her down the aisle.

"Thank you," I said to them.

The bus rumbled to a start, and I shut my eyes, dozing off to the vehicle's rocking. I thought how lucky I was to have friends, and how lucky they were to have parents, even if they had to endure this mess together.

• • •

Barbed wire.

That's all I could see when I awoke.

I stepped off the bus into an enclosure of dirt, guard towers commanding the corners, hundreds of yards apart. Armed soldiers stood in the towers and roamed the area.

"Are they aiming their rifles at us?" Someone pointed up. I squinted to get a better look.

"Good God, they are," I said. Panic grabbed me. I pushed through the crowd and yelled at two soldiers near me. "Are you going to kill us?"

They ignored me as they handed housing assignments to other men, who gathered their families together to sift through mountains of luggage and bundles that grew taller and wider with the arrival of each bus. People who had been uprooted from Seattle days earlier helped us newcomers.

I tried to calm myself, thinking the scene made Nihonmachi look like a paradise. Our parents always took pride in their orderliness and cleanliness, even when surrounded by dirt and chaos, and they drilled it into our heads to do the same. But what was this? A racetrack. A grandstand. Bleachers to one side. A roller coaster to the other. Good grief, our government had hauled us to the Western Washington State Fairgrounds in Puyallup, thirty miles outside Seattle. My parents had taken me here as a little kid, and irony of ironies, I now recalled my father and I standing here ten years earlier, as we joined thousands in welcoming an exciting presidential candidate, Franklin Delano Roosevelt, who promised us a way to prosperity and a better future.

Was this your answer, Mr. President?

Before me stood a shantytown of old buildings and new barracks, lean-to chicken sheds, really, all about twenty feet wide, but of varying lengths. Barracks took up the middle of the track.

"I'm not staying here!" I yelled again at the guards. I came fully awake now, raging mad awake. "No one said anything about a prison."

I looked at the people around me. "Come on, say something!" I said. "This isn't right!" They just looked back at me.

I spotted the Inadas and called out to Wes. "Aren't you going to tell them what you think?"

Wes looked at his parents and then back at me, shaking his head slightly. "Let's get through this for now. We'll have time to protest. And believe me, I will." His face was red.

"Get in line," one of the registrars warned. "We have our orders straight from General DeWitt." DeWitt, head of the Western Defense Command, was overseeing the rushed evacuation of all of us in the western halves of Washington state and Oregon, California, and southwest Arizona—areas where the majority of issei and nisei lived in the lower 48. "Military necessity" was the reason, he repeated over and over, as if it made perfect sense that anyone of Japanese descent near the Pacific would sabotage Boeing or help Japanese invaders.

"We're Americans, just like you," I said to the guards. "How can you turn on us?"

A couple of issei took my arm and pulled me aside. "Hiroshi David Koga, get hold of yourself," one of the men snapped.

"Your father would be ashamed," the other said, barely hiding his disgust at my behavior.

I recognized the men, deacons in our church. In a lower voice, I spoke of the unfairness of it all, as if he didn't know.

"*Shikata ga nai*," the second man said. It can't be helped. Bear up and get on with it.

"Don't make this any worse, for yourself and everyone else," the first man said. "Don't bring *haji* to your family and all of us."

Bring shame? What a crock. But I knew I should tone things down. Making a scene would get me nowhere and could cause more trouble for others. I understood what Mrs. Inada meant. Community and harmony were the center of Japanese life, and we had already been shunned by our country. Stung and hurting, we had to band together and hold our heads high as people worthy of living in America, the land we loved. Who knew what other measures the government could take against us if we protested.

Wes and his family had disappeared into the crowd, and I swallowed my anger and stepped to the back of a line. I waited to receive my room assignment while everyone whispered their fears to one other.

"What's going on?"

"What are they going to do to us?"

"My mother's sick. This is going to kill her."

"What can we do?"

"I hope this won't last long. Let's wait till they sort things out."

The man in front of me was about my age, focused on sketching everything around us, and said little. I kept nudging him ahead as the line moved, so intent he was on his drawing, and the people he followed, probably his mother, sisters, and brothers, waved their thanks. I peeked over his shoulder, impressed with the figures he drew, full of the anger and confusion and frustration I felt. Whether for the pushes or my silent appreciation, he nodded his thanks as we inched along.

Hours later, I learned my new home would be in one of the bachelor's quarters in Area D, where the racetrack, rollercoaster, and grandstand stood. Three thousand issei and nisei would live here, and I would be near the Dipper, beneath the grandstand. I had no idea where my sister and her husband would be assigned; three other areas, A, B, and C, sat way out in the parking lots, with barracks and communal laundry areas, baths, and mess halls for five thousand. I worried about Molly, who was pregnant.

"Can I get some water?" I asked a guard.

"Get your mattress," the Caucasian answered. He pointed me in the direction of a long barracks. "You have your bag?"

I showed him the gunnysack I had just picked up, a standard Army-issue cotton bag that would fit on a cot. I gathered some spit in my mouth and spread it around my tongue as I took my place in yet another interminable line. The funky odor of livestock and manure and old grass filled my nostrils.

"You." Another soldier pointed to me as I neared the head of the line. "Over there." The man waved people into a barracks where hay was piled almost to the ceiling. Men and women and children stuffed handfuls of the straw into their bags to make a mattress. Occasionally they looked at one another, shaking their heads. Off to one side, a woman wept, and her little daughter kept saying to her father, "I don't want Mommy to cry. Do something."

"Are you kidding?" I asked the soldier, anger rising hot again. He looked away.

I spotted Mrs. Oki, an elderly woman from my church, one of the many ladies who had been so kind to me after we lost our parents. I was only thirteen then and needed some mothers pretty bad. Now one of them stood alone, stooped so low her body held the shape of a question mark. A sack hung limp in her hands, and I ran over to her.

"Hiroshi-san." Mrs. Oki patted my arms. "*Arigato*," she thanked me. "This is terrible, but *ganbatte*." Keep your chin up. Do your best. She called on our value of *gaman*, to persevere and endure the seemingly impossible.

I swallowed my anger, stuffed her mattress bag, and walked her over to her quarters. Until then, I didn't know that the government really regarded us as animals. Mrs. Oki's apartment was a horse stall, a horse stall with a dirt floor, one of many in a dark two-block-long stable beneath the grandstand. A single naked light bulb lit the stall. The place reeked of dung and urine. She would share the space with her daughter's family, wherever they were. They had become separated in all the confusion.

I pressed back through the crowd to ask a guard if Mrs. Oki might have a better room. After all, she and the other issei were too old to put up with this chaos. Why not put her in one of the new barracks in the parking lots?

The guard said he didn't work for a damned hotel.

23

We had landed in prison, for sure. I returned to get Mrs. Oki settled, which didn't take long. She carried only a few pieces of clothing and a Bible. Her daughter had her linens. I heard a truck rumble outside and ran to grab cots for Mrs. Oki's apartment, a strong one to support her aged body and canvas ones for the rest of the family. I unfolded her cot and placed her mattress on it, plumping the straw. Before I left, I insisted she take one of my musubi. I munched on the apple slices, which barely quenched my thirst.

A light drizzle fell as I made my way to the bachelor's area and my own apartment, not too far from Mrs. Oki's stall, a palace of maybe twenty feet by eighteen feet, with a wooden floor, a tiny window across from the door, and a wood-burning stove in the middle. The unit was one of several rooms within one of the longer buildings, the walls falling a few feet short of the ceiling, maybe eight feet high. Fissures already ran through the panels of green wood, cheap pine, it looked like to me, and I could hear conversations and coughing coming from the other rooms. Dandelions peeked through the cracks in the floor. Someone had propped up four cotton cots against the walls, and I grabbed one and threw my mattress on it. Searching for my toothbrush, I found the paper with the headlines about Pearl Harbor, and I threw it under my bed, swearing not to read any more news until something changed for the better. I leaned my family's photo against the wall next to my cot. Home sweet home.

I wanted to wash up before dinner, and a soldier directed me to two narrow bathhouses a couple of blocks away, one for women and one for men. Every step jarred my aching bladder, and I joined fifteen other men dancing in line. When my turn came, I walked inside to find a long wooden plank with six toilet holes backed up to another six-holed plank, with no partitions in back of the holes or between them. It looked like prisoners would literally butt up against one another. The place already stank. What could I do? Bashful bowels were banished. I found a free hole and took care of things.

I saw a long queue snaking into the single mess hall that served this area, and I talked with my new neighbors as I joined them in the wait for dinner.

"Hey, didn't I play you in football?"

"We've been here for almost a month. It's just getting worse."

"Tacoma people are coming in soon."

"I hear the old buildings have real toilets."

"Is this our reward?" I looked at my dinner after an hour's anticipation. A couple of mealy Vienna sausages, some kind of potato glop, and a piece of bread had been slapped on my tin plate. What the hell. I took a seat at one of the picnic tables and ate everything, I was so hungry, and I washed the food down with the coffee-water provided. Another long wait allowed me the chance to rinse tableware in water and disinfectant.

I thought I was a pretty gregarious guy, but by the time the dining experience ended, I'd had enough. I headed out to my quarters, catching up with Mrs. Oki on her way back to her stall with her daughter and two grandchildren. As we walked, the heavens opened up, and the earth muddied into goop. I almost brought Mrs. Oki down on top of me as I helped her slip and slide through the muck.

"*Oyasumi nasae.*" Mrs. Oki whispered "good night" to me when we arrived at their door. "Tired, a little tired." She patted my arm as her daughter thanked me, and I bowed my farewells.

Back in my new home, I shook hands with my roommates, and wouldn't you know it, one of them was the same Michelangelo who had dragged his feet in front of me.

"Joji Ishikawa," he introduced himself and then his two brothers. He said their mother and sisters had landed in a stall beneath the bleachers.

"Where'd you go to school?" I asked. I didn't know any of them from Garfield.

"Broadway High," Joji said. That was a football rival of Garfield, both integrated schools on the outskirts of Nihonmachi. "We just moved, so were hauled in with your neighborhood."

Around nine o'clock, we said our good nights, and I fell on my cot, drained from the day. I covered myself with a thin, scratchy Army blanket. The air was damp, and a drop of rain fell from the ceiling onto my arm. I had never been jammed in with so many people as I was right now, yet I had never felt more alone.

Just as I was drifting off, I heard a knock at the door.

"What?" one of the brothers yelled.

"Checking, please," a voice called.

I got off my cot and opened the door.

"Sorry," the man said. He was nisei, probably ten years older than me. "I'm a group leader. We have to count noses every night."

I switched on the lightbulb, and we watched him scan the room.

As he thanked me and closed the door, I thumbed my nose and muttered, "Count this."

Joji joined me, and his brothers grumbled their agreement.

Back on my cot, I leaned over, the hay crackling as I turned my family's picture face down on the floor. For the first time since my parents died, I was glad they were gone. My baby brother, too.

Better they not see this.

3

Puyallup

Summer 1942

"Camp Harmony? Are they kidding?" I said. The government name for our camp made me want to vomit, more than even the food around here.

"Stupid fools," Gordon Nagano said.

"What a load of baloney," Tad Akiyama agreed.

We'd been stuck in our Puyallup prison for a few weeks now, and my new buddies and I were sitting around the mess hall after lunch, complaining about everything. Children ran around unsupervised by parents, who were working at camp-sponsored jobs to make ends meet. Boilers broke down, and showers were nonexistent. We smelled something awful. The hope that we might get out soon, brought by the United States' victory at Midway, had vanished as more and more countries declared war on one another, and time hung as heavy as the stench around here. The stink grew more unbearable with each degree the temperature climbed.

"I can't think of a single one of our rights that hasn't been tossed to the wind, and not a thing we can do about it," Ted Nakashima said, making us recall our civics lessons from school. Even the lousiest students scrambled to point out the living misdeeds of our own government. Like all internees, I was growing more interested in the law as our rights disappeared.

"Due process," I contributed.

"Citizenship," Gordon said.

Voices grumbled around the table.

"Speedy trial."

"Equal protection."

"Search and seizure."

"The list is endless," Ted growled. "Don't give me that 'harmony' shit."

I agreed with Ted one hundred percent, but glanced over at my sister Molly, who was sitting at the table behind us, hoping she hadn't heard the swear word. She and Lawson had landed way out in Area A, where they had six double-width mess halls, but she had obtained a pass to visit a friend in my area today. I waved. My own sister was buying into all that harmony stuff, but I loved her and didn't want to get her upset.

"People are beginning to give in," Isamu Miyata grumbled. In addition to working for money, internees were volunteering for community activities to chip in and to take the edge off the boredom. A few had even begun to argue about the ways we should work with the Caucasian administration versus the ways we should govern ourselves.

"These meals alone are violations of human decency." I picked up a Vienna sausage that I just couldn't stomach, the dregs of Army surplus passing for food every day. But why was everyone looking above my head?

28

"Hiroshi, I need to talk to you." Molly's intense whisper, close to my ear, startled me.

"Of course." I hopped up as I heard the others say they had to be going, too. They looked half sullenly, half sheepishly at my sister, who frowned at them, and they offered to wash my plate and cup.

"Don't lose them," I said. Dinnerware was still at a premium.

I passed my roommates eating with their mother and sisters, looking happier than they did in our tight quarters, and saw a couple of girls hanging out nearby. I waved to everyone as Molly hurried me toward the door. She'd had that same steely look on her face anytime she came and hauled me home when I ran away after Haha died. Twelve years older than me, Molly had become a second mother, and we usually ended my truancy by talking over endless cups of tea as she assured me I was still loved. She always listened to everything I had to say, even helping me when my eyes went bad and I had to quit playing quarterback on the football team. Why not become a guard, she suggested. God, how I loved being part of the team. I mastered the position and played until I graduated.

"Let's chat while you walk me back to my apartment," Molly said in stern voice. She was due in a couple of months and had begun to waddle, and I slowed my steps to match her pace. I bet it was a good mile or more to her area.

"Anything wrong?" I asked in as casual a voice as I could.

"Anything wrong?" Molly stopped walking and turned to me, her face reddening. She tossed her long hair over her shoulders. "Take a look at yourself."

I girded myself for what was coming.

"What's happened to you, Hiroshi?" She didn't yell, but spoke in that low, fervent voice that let you know were in boiling hot water, even though she cared for you. "You make friends with people who sulk and do nothing to make things better. You shove food in your mouth like I never taught you any manners. Look at Wes. He's already writing for the newspaper and doing something to help. One of his brothers is cleaning the mess hall—"

"A cauldron of bacteria and poison if ever there was one," I countered. "And I suppose you're going to bring up all the other do-gooders next."

Molly shook me by the shoulders. "At least people are trying, Hiroshi. But you're doing nothing. Nothing. Even when Koichi and Mom and Dad died, you still cared about things. You were never a smart aleck. Now everything is backtalk and 'Woe is me! Woe is me!'"

I welcomed the silence that followed, but Molly broke it. "Hiroshi, you're not even dating right now, and if there's anything good about the camp, it's that there are lots of girls to go around for all the boys."

Well, that was the last straw. "It's not like I haven't been look-ing around," I defended myself. "I just haven't found anyone interesting."

Molly stopped walking and leaned in. "Do you really think you're attractive to girls, always sullen and whining?"

My lips trembled a little as I thought back to everything we had been through. I'd gotten pretty messed up inside when our little brother died, and after our parents joined him a couple of years later, my heart finally broke, just as my body decided to shoot up and sweat and sprout hairs in new places. My *chinchin* developed a mind of its own, waking me up in the middle of the night, coming alert in the shower, you name it.

And on top of that, my siblings decided I was too much to care for and wanted to send me to an uncle in Japan who yearned for the child he never had. I cried myself to sleep.

Okaasan!
Otousan!
Why did you leave me?
What did I do wrong?

I stopped studying. I threw tantrums and ran away over and over, even when I knew I'd catch holy hell.

Molly's holy hell had saved me. She'd pull me by the ear back home and helped me understand that no matter what troubles I faced, I had to have faith in myself, stick to my beliefs, and bounce back.

She convinced our brother Frank and our sister Aiko to keep me. Our family would stay together.

I watched Molly as she showed her pass to an inmate monitor at the entrance to her area, and somehow got us both in. The monitor escorted us across a city street that ran through this area, and we finished our walk to her barracks, a rushed jumble. The building's vertical wooden slabs grew straight out of the mud, like all the others running down both sides of her street.

Molly stood in front of the door as she spoke, one hand resting on her belly, the other gesticulating. "*Monku,* monku, monku. I've heard enough of your complaints. It's time to finish growing up. I'm going to have a baby to care for pretty soon. YOU are the only one who can get control of you."

"But what of all the injust—"

"Don't you see you still have yourself?" Molly spoke over me. "No one can take that away from you, your real home. Do something useful in your part of the world. Find what you believe in again and act on it."

She handed me her pass. "See if this will get you back in area. You're always good at charming people." For once, Molly didn't wait to hear more of my thoughts and feelings. She patted my arm gently, walked inside her apartment, and shut the door.

I woke up early the next morning and picked up a bat. I'd played all kinds of ball for years, not only in Japantown, but with Caucasians in Leschi Park and with nisei and Italians and Negroes near Japantown.

Within days, I was hitting balls out of the camp, first pretending they represented all the bad government people and nasty Caucasians. *Pow, take that! Wham, good riddance!* Ball teams were forming around camp, but I just had fun playing in sandlot groups and joking with the guys, some of them new pals, some old friends from school. I started flirting with the girls again, too.

I felt even better when the principal from Garfield High came to Puyallup and awarded the current class of seniors their diplomas. I knew this was a way the government was trying to make life as normal as possible or some claptrap like that, but all the same, I was glad to see internees get what they had earned.

Wes Inada must have felt the same way and took time off from his newspaper to stop by after the ceremonies. I explained what I was up to and told him he looked well.

"Like you said to me, Hiroshi, don't fall prey to others' BS, even the government's," he said. "Fight for what you love." He told me of the stories he was following, including one about a fellow University of Washington student, Gordon Hirabayashi, who had joined the Quakers to help families store their belongings. As he worked, he believed his civil rights would be protected, but it soon became clear that he would be interned with everyone else. He made a stink. He broke curfew laws and refused to be interned on religious and constitutional grounds.

I listened to Wes's lecture with interest, my eyes no longer glazing over.

His words had everything to do with our lives.

"You're lucky you never were caught with that Chinese button of yours," Wes laughed. He said he'd let me know what happened to the student, who sat in jail.

• • •

In the days after my chat with Wes, I lent a hand to the carpenters around camp building walls and panels in some of the barracks, happy to be contributing to the resurgence of community, almost seventy-five hundred people now. Visitors, kept outside by barbed wire until recently, were allowed to sit at tables inside a dedicated center, with no supervision. Barbers gave haircuts, a post office and a library opened up, and someone was busy making *geta* for people to protect their feet as they made their way through the mud to the latrines. People regularly stole government scrap lumber, supposedly protected by issei security guards, to make tables and chairs.

The more I sawed and hammered, the better I felt, and I tried real hard not be brought down by news that we were headed to a bigger camp in Idaho, under the jurisdiction not of the Army, but of some new federal organization, the War Relocation Authority, the WRA. Puyallup was, after all, a temporary center, but I had hoped that when we left here, it would be to go home. Would the next prison be worse, on a bigger scale? At least it would be the place we'd be freed from, I hoped, and the sooner, the better.

"I hear the WRA is asking for men to help get the camp ready for us," Molly said. "Why don't you volunteer?"

Molly spoke as rumor inched toward reality, ignoring a recent report that the governor of Idaho had likened all Japanese to rats who should be sent back to Japan, the islands sunk. His comments scared off nisei cleared to assist area farmers, desperate for help after losing men to the draft, and the governor soon changed his tune. Idaho beets were vital for ethanol fuel for the war, and farmers called for nisei hands again.

"You mean, help prepare my own prison?" I said. I could hear the snideness in my own voice. Sheesh. How much could a guy take?

"It would be good to help, *ne*?" Molly encouraged me again. "You might even have a say in how everything turns out. Better than this joint, right?"

I took those last words as tacit agreement that all the "harmony" talk had been a load of rubbish. We had to name the truth for what it was and then act with all the integrity we had.

"Okay, I'll think about it," I agreed. I played with the idea as I worked over the next few days, and I stopped only when an ingrown toenail I'd had forever wouldn't stop throbbing. I just couldn't pound another nail.

I hobbled to one of the camp's issei doctors, who ordered me to an outside hospital for surgery. The excuse we had for a hospital in Puyallup, right behind the grandstand, was too poorly equipped for the procedure.

"Hey, Hopalong," my barracks-mates kidded me as I limped in after the operation. My toe ached like hell.

"Better get the tray service," Joji Ishikawa, the artist, looked up from his sketchpad. He had been a man of few words up to now, so I appreciated his consideration, and his brothers joined in. A tray and commode service had been set up to bring food to the barracks of the sick and elderly.

I told them I didn't think I had to sign up, but I changed my mind when I tried to walk to the lavatory the first evening. Mud mucked up my bandages, and my toe pulsated with pain. A man close to my age brought me a commode within a couple of hours and said someone else would be in with food tomorrow.

"Mr. Koga," a young female voice called at my door the next day.

"It's open," I said. "Come on in."

A pretty girl said hello and handed me a tray, which I balanced on my lap. I smelled her hair as she leaned over me, a fresh, soapy scent, far more pleasant than the putrid aroma of the food. I sure was glad she hadn't brought me the commode. Having to be served my meals was bad enough.

Joji, who was skipping lunch because of a stomachache, took one look at her and hopped off his cot. He stood staring at us.

"And what is today's poison?" I asked, ignoring him. Her back was to Joji, and she focused on me.

"The canned special. Tongue. Boiled potatoes. Green beans," the girl said, apparently oblivious to Joji's presence. She seemed *johin*, my sisters would say, very poised. "Applesauce to finish. Sorry—they ran out of the canned peaches, which I actually like. Seems like every time I go for them, they're gone."

"Not exactly what Mom would make, huh?" I took time to check her out, a little younger than me, for sure, but really good-looking. And that sweet-smelling hair. It fell to her shoulders in waves, and I wondered if she had had one of those permanents, like girls did now and again.

I patted down my own hair, which, of all days, I hadn't combed. I noticed her blushing at my inspection. "So, what's your name?" I asked.

"Ruth Nakamura."

She had a pretty smile.

"School?"

"Broadway High."

I eyed Joji, who had just graduated from Broadway. His principal had conducted a ceremony in the grandstand, a couple of days after Garfield's. I figured he and Ruth must know each other.

As if to confirm my suspicions, Joji grew closer, raising his hand in greeting as he said, "Hi, Ruth."

Ruth jumped at his voice. She turned to him and stopped smiling, caught between the two of us. She blushed and said, "Hi, Joji," before moving to my other side.

Encouraged, I kept my eyes on her and began again. "Garfield here. I was quarterback when we won the city championship."

Ruth said she'd heard of me. She'd even seen me in some games.

Alright then. I added, "Being a quarterback is like wearing a target on your uniform. Everyone is out to get you. You have to be nimble and quick to move the team ahead."

Did her eyes sparkle as she listened? I didn't want to get too full of myself. My family would have none of it, *enryo* and all that, but I kept talking.

"So what year are you?" I asked.

Ruth said she had just received her diploma.

"You don't look old enough—"

"Nice ceremony, huh?" Joji, polite but undeterred, spoke up. "We'll be classmates forever."

Ruth glanced at him and then looked back at me. She said, "I'm sixteen. I've always been a pretty good student. Don't like school, though."

Joji tried again. "Ruth, remember that terrible geometry class we were in?"

I glared at him and turned back to Ruth. "Why don't you like school?" I asked. Despite her age and good grades, I sensed a kindred spirit.

"I just want to get to work. No more theories and formulas I'll never use." She checked her watch and frowned. "Listen, I have to deliver the rest of my trays. But I'll see you tomorrow."

"So long!" Joji called in a weak voice as he retreated to his cot.

I scowled at him and then waved goodbye to Ruth with my fork, a gesture I repeated over the next several days as she brought in trays of Vienna sausage, mutton, Vienna sausage, tongue, Vienna sausage, mutton, Vienna sausage and Vienna sausage and Vienna sausage. Each time she dropped by, I tried to learn a little bit more about her, a no-nonsense girl, smart without being a know-it-all, quick on her feet, a good listener and talker. I liked her, and Joji was usually at lunch when she arrived, so that problem took care of itself.

I thought.

"I like Ruth, too, you know," Joji admitted to me after dinner one night. We sat on our cots as we talked.

"Really?" My sarcasm weighed heavy, and I began to laugh. "Well, thanks for making yourself scarce when she drops by."

"Just giving you a chance," he said, grinning. "Seriously, I had my eye on her in school, you know. I swear she was taking a liking to me before we got hauled to this joint. Even agreed to a date. But then Pearl Harbor was attacked, and everything went to hell."

He pulled out his sketchpad, adding in a lower voice, "If you aren't going to go out with her, put in a good word for me, would you? She seems to like you, listen to you."

Unsure of my own next move, I said I thought she was swell and let several days pass, Joji suddenly opening up about his life in what he called the "ghetto" of Nihonmachi. I didn't know if he was doing this to get on my good side or just felt the need to talk, but I began enjoying the companionship and told him my own story.

"I didn't live in Nihonmachi very long," I said. "But I never thought of it as a 'ghetto' or skid row. Everything's run down, sure, but the people seem real nice. Really take care of each other."

"You're right, but I feel trapped," Joji said. "My dad's a pharmacist and can barely make a living there. But he has no chance of moving out. Caucasians just won't hire issei."

"What about your brothers and sisters?" I asked.

"One sister broke free, a couple of years ago. She's in New York now, a college girl," he said. "I thought everyone else would have a chance. They, we, we're Americans, for God's sake. They've all been looking to get out, but even before the attack, it was hard. Makes you wonder how much education can do for you. Especially now." His voice faded as he made long, bold strokes on his pad. He saw me trying to eye what he was drawing and shut the cover. "I'm not ready to show people my stuff. But soon, I hope," he said.

I didn't mention that I'd already peeked at a few of his sketches and wondered when he'd feel comfortable sharing them with me. Instead, I told him about my own family's experience, which had probably made me feel a little easier in the Caucasian world, at least until the attack. So many of my friends and teammates had been Caucasians, and I'd even grown close to a couple of Caucasian girls, all of them steering clear after Pearl Harbor, of course.

"Speaking of girls, don't forget about Ruth." Joji broached the topic I hadn't wanted to touch. Silently, I cursed myself for creating the opening.

"I like her, too, Joji," I said. "I'd like to go out with her, but that doesn't mean you can't date her."

"Well, just remember, I knew her first," Joji said. "Maybe you could just get me a dance?"

I looked with new eyes at this man, suddenly my competition, and I grew concerned just on a physical level about my chances.

He may not have been an athlete, but I had to admit, Joji was a handsome guy, almost movie-star good looking, tall and big boned for someone of Japanese descent, his face broad and even featured, his thick hair brushed back. Girls always told me I was attractive, laughter lighting up my face, but I wasn't Joji's kind of handsome, not by a long shot.

"I'll think about it," I said, trying to put my best foot forward. After all, I knew how it felt to pine for a girl from afar, and Joji did have a point about being there first.

I mulled things over as I listened to Joji and his brothers talk late into the night about their family, the same ideas discussed over and over with growing worry and concern.

"Wonder where Dad is," Shigeo, Joji's eldest brother, said. Their father, who taught kendo in his spare time, had been rounded up with other issei by the FBI. No one had heard from him since.

"Mom must feel so lost without him," Joji said. "So scared."

"Uncle Minoru, too," Shigeo said. I gathered Uncle Minoru was a draughtsman who loved sharing his knowledge with Joji. A bachelor, he taught judo and had also been rounded up.

"How long you think we're going to be in here?" Eddie, the middle brother, asked. An asthmatic, he began coughing from the hay.

"The longer the war goes on, the longer we're stuck," Shigeo said.

"I should get a job," Joji said. "Bring in some money for everyone."

"Don't worry," Shigeo said. He was working in the mess hall, helping to cook. "You keep drawing. We'll take care of the money for now. This can't last for long."

"You already earned an award, for God's sake," Eddie said. He was helping to deliver laundry to the barracks. "Dad was so proud." They talked about the art prize Joji had won in school last year, their father showing so much emotion that someone might have doubted he was an issei. The man had taught himself to draw and paint, and he helped Joji along in his own efforts. The family had brought Mr. Ishikawa's art supplies to camp, looking forward to the day he would join them.

"Come on," Joji said. "I can chip in."

"You will when you have to," Shigeo said.

"I know you will," Eddie add.

They talked of Joji's hopes for attending art or architecture school and about their own dreams of engineering careers, and their voices murmured into the night, lulling me to sleep.

But one evening none of us slept.

A straight week's worth of Vienna sausage provoked unexpected trouble. I felt ravenous and forced myself to down some meat that tasted worse than usual, and boy, did I pay for it. For the next few hours, I stuck to the commode. Joji and his brothers abandoned the chamber pots they had purchased from the Montgomery Ward catalog, overflowing now, and made a run for the latrines. I could hear people rushing past our door and prayed for everyone's sake that the never-ending problems with the septic tanks had been cleared up.

Between bouts of sickness, I limped out to see what was happening. Flashlights dotted the night as parents and grandparents and children raced to the bathhouses, desperate for toilets. Many had a good hundred yards or more between their barracks and the bath facilities, and lights veered off on their own; bathrooms were full, and nature's urgent call had to be answered, no matter what. Bright searchlights mounted at the top of the grandstand snapped on and lit up the camp. I shielded my eyes and looked up toward the stands. Guards were aiming machine guns down on us.

I heard people crying out as they ran.

"We're going to die!"

"It's the camp's fault we're sick."

"They're going to shoot us!"

"Damned rotten food."

I held my breath, not knowing what to do.

I looked up at the stands again. There seemed to be more guards there now, their guns focused on us.

I didn't know if it was fear or bad food that gripped my stomach, but I had to get back to my commode, and fast. It took a good half hour to calm things down, and then I continued my visits outside, my heart pounding less as time passed and no shots were fired. The herds slowly thinned and then stopped running completely, and the searchlights faded into the dawn.

Joji sketched the scene as soon as there was enough light to see, and this time he showed me what he had drawn. His black pencil strokes and shadows captured people doubled over as they ran in pain and in fear toward latrines, guards cutting through the blackness with their search lights, guns at the ready. I told Joji that I felt the panic and frustration of the evening all over again, and he thanked me.

"The Vienna Sausage Riot," everyone called the emergency the next day.

"They thought we were staging an uprising," people said, dismayed, "being out past curfew and running like that. They called in extra guards."

Others added, "Thank God our stomachs settled down. We could have been killed."

Ruth and I spoke about the "riot" on one of her last tray visits, when I had healed well enough to think about hoofing it to the mess hall again. I knew this would be one of my last chances to talk with her like this.

"I can't believe our own countrymen took aim on us," we both said. We were appalled, but knew that's what we should have expected. We laughed through our anger at the absurdity of the situation.

"Shikata ga-nai, shikata ga-nai." Ruth sounded exasperated. "I know that's what people keep saying. But what's the problem with showing a little anger, righteous anger, at this whole thing?" I had to admit, Ruth had a strength and spunk other girls didn't have, positive without being pie-eyed, grounded and sensible.

"We have to speak up," I agreed as she handed me my tray.

"My parents won't utter a word," Ruth said, "but I keep telling them that the people who say something are making headway. Even the food's improving. It's not a perfect system, but they're helping to govern the camp and get things we need."

I agreed but added, "You shouldn't argue with your parents. Show some respect—"

"Oh, stop that talk," Ruth said, her face flushing. "I know you miss your mom and dad, but that's no reason to tell me or anyone else not to speak up to ours. When you're an adult, you know, it becomes a two-way street, kids and parents. Everyone should listen to each other and work together. That's real respect, mutual respect."

I mulled over the thought and told Ruth she was right, even if she was a pretty young "adult." I liked her ideas. In fact, I wanted to hear more.

The camp had frequent block socials. Would she go to one with me? Area D's mess hall served as the gathering place for Saturday night dances.

"Your foot's okay?" Ruth asked.

I did a jig. "Fred Astaire at your service. I'll be ready soon."

Well, then, yes, she said, that would be grand.

I mentioned my date to Joji after dinner. "Hope you're not upset," I said.

"All's fair in love and war," he said, shrugging.

He thought for a few seconds and then added, "Of course, you could steer her my way for a dance, you know."

"Seriously?" I'd only said I'd think about helping him. I was surprised at his suggestion.

"Just one dance?" Joji insisted.

"Why don't you just cut in?" I asked.

Joji shook his head, and I wondered if, at heart, he was shy, even a little unsure of himself.

What should I do? After listening to Joji and his brothers for weeks, I thought the guy was struggling to grow out of his cocoon, of being the baby of his family, and I was beginning to like him, the way he cared for his parents and siblings, the way he looked so happy and intent when he was drawing, just like Koichi had. I hated to admit it, but Joji made me wonder how my little brother would have turned out.

Heck, if Ruth really liked me, what harm would one little dance do?

I came up with a plan.

"I'll give you one chance," I told Joji. "Stand by the punchbowl."

• • •

The next Saturday, I dressed in my best khakis and shirt and picked Ruth up at her family's unit, just a few blocks from mine, in barracks D-1-1, the first apartment in the first barracks, which made her sort of the girl next door. I knocked, and when Ruth answered, I swore no other girl in camp could look so pretty in a skirt, blouse, and saddle shoes. We took off in high spirits, and we jitter-bugged and lindy-hopped and talked for the first several dances, my foot as good as new.

And then I spotted Joji, chatting with a couple of girls by the punchbowl.

Damn. I was having a great time, but I had to keep my promise.

I began leading Ruth in no uncertain terms through the dancers on the floor.

"Whoa, you're going strong," Ruth said. "Could you slow down a little? I need to catch my breath."

"Sorry," I said. Radios, allowed again by the government, played around the mess hall, tuned to the same station. Glen Miller's "I've Got a Gal in Kalamazoo" filled the air. I slowed our pace but kept my sights on Joji.

"How about a glass of punch?" I said as I steered our way right in front of him. Joji moved toward Ruth.

Ruth glanced Joji's way and drew closer to me as Jimmy Dorsey's "Tangerine" got under way. "Not yet. Let's keep dancing. I love this song."

Ruth practically took the lead as we glided back toward the center of the floor.

I saw Joji watching us and pressed back, pushing us toward the sidelines.

Ruth pressed toward the center.

We twirled around in one spot.

Another song played through.

We danced around in circles.

"You know, I'm getting really thirsty," I said, still committed to my promise and truly getting parched by this workout. And it was hotter than hell in here. "Couldn't we stop for some punch?"

This time, Ruth said of course, and I led us out of the maelstrom toward the punchbowl.

But where was Joji? I looked around as we came to a stop.

I could feel Ruth eyeing me as I poured us a drink. She looked out at the dance floor and then back at me, thinking.

"There you go." I handed her some punch.

"He's out there," she lifted her chin toward the dancers.

I followed her gaze and spotted Joji, cutting the rug with a nice-looking gal.

"Am I that obvious?" I asked, laughing.

"I'm afraid so. Did he put you up to this?"

Joji must have felt us looking, because he waved our way, and we waved back.

"I'm sorry, Ruth," I said and explained that I was just trying to help the guy out. "He's hopelessly sweet on you. Wants another chance."

Ruth rolled her eyes. "You have to understand. Our parents have been friends for years and thought we should date. But I know him from school and I'm not very interested. He's really nice, but, I don't know, he's too quiet for me. Always has his head down, drawing everything in sight. Right before we got here, he asked me to a dance, and I said yes just to make everybody happy."

"I think he has the wrong idea," I said.

"I see now," Ruth said.

Agreeing things would somehow work themselves out, we finished our punch and hit the dance floor, swinging and jiving the night away. We stopped only when the music did.

As I walked her home and we talked about this and that, mostly about our families, one thought fought for my attention.

Should I kiss her?

When?

"My father ran a grocery store," she was saying. "Always gave credit to anyone who needed it. Even Caucasians. But no one offered to help us move here."

"And there are seven of you?" I asked, that kiss on my mind.

"Eight. We had to jam everyone and our belongings into two cabs," she said.

"That stinks," I said, growing angry for them.

She agreed. "But what could we do. I feel really bad for my father."

She spoke matter-of-factly, with no bitterness, and I thought she must have inherited his kindness. We neared her barracks as she finished.

Now?

I got my courage up and leaned toward her lips.

She pulled away, whispering, "Everyone's outside." I looked to see her entire family sitting in front of their barracks to escape the heat. Oh, well. I waved to them all and called, "Good night," and I gazed at Ruth, hoping we would have more chances to dance, to kiss.

We dated others as we courted, of course, but I was growing fond of her. I saw her dancing with this guy and that, but never with Joji, and I caught her looking at me, at least now and then.

Camp-produced invitations to a Sadie Hawkins dance soon poured into my barracks for all us guys. I received a pile of them from the girls I'd been dancing with, and I studied them closely. Invitations were always printed on a single piece of folded paper—even that sheet was hard to come by, things were in such short supply—and they usually carried some kind of ink sketch and cute ditty. But this one was special, covered with water-colored cartoons drawn in Al Capp's style.

I turned the invitations over in my hand as I thought whose to accept. On the front, a scantily clad Daisy Mae, sporting her ever-present polka dot blouse, stood in the foreground of a Dogpatch scene, complete with house and smoking chimney. A wooden sign behind her was carved with the words, "Admit 1 Gal 'n Victim." Inside, the never-ready-to-be hitched Li'l Abner was lying on the ground, clinging fast to a tree stump. Behind him was the cozy little house and a big tag with the hand-printed words

AH HEREBY DE-CLARES MAHSELF
PUFFICKLY WILLING TO BE DATED UP FO' THIS HEAH
DANCE
Signed _____

The words "Sadie Hawkins' Dance" ran sideways on the right, the paper folded so that you could read the words from the front, too.

"Did you get one from Ruth?" Joji said as he examined his own pile.

"Yes," I said. I had returned to her invitation several times, warming to the idea of going with her.

"I didn't." He looked glum.

I told Joji I hoped he'd find just the right gal for the dance, but I was going to accept Ruth's invitation, and he said that was fine by him. Heck, he should have known when I tried to steer Ruth his way.

And then I told Joji how much the theme meant to me, confiding in him memories of my dad. When Chichi was alive, we always read the newspapers together, him teaching me some history and both of us picking up new words, and we always looked forward to the cartoons at the end, especially

Al Capp's. I could still hear Chichi laughing till he cried anytime Sadie Hawkins's father tried to get dates for his homely ol' gal.

"I'm glad you're going with the girl you want," Joji said, and I thanked him.

The evening of the dance, I felt on top of the world, and I knocked with great enthusiasm at Ruth's door. I had donned a Li'l Abner outfit that I'd put together myself, complete with a checkered shirt and overalls I'd borrowed, mattress straw hanging from my back pocket.

"Hi, y'all!" I called as the door opened.

Ruth looked aghast at my regalia. She had turned in the usual skirt and bobby socks for a pretty blue dress and nice shoes, and she even wore a little makeup, from what I could tell. For a moment, I thought she might shut the door in my face. Her mother and older sister stood behind her, peering over her shoulders, little ones peeking from her sides.

I held my breath, waiting forever for Ruth to speak up.

She leaned toward me and whispered, "I had something else planned. But my mother cut up one of my sister's old dresses to make this for me. Wanted me to get all dolled up."

With a roll of her eyes to the moon, Ruth told me to wait and closed the door.

Through the wall I could hear female voices arguing and then laughing and clucking and laughing again, and only when Ruth reappeared did I find out what the commotion was all about.

"Wow! Daisy Mae, as I live and breathe!" I exclaimed. I pulled a piece of hay from my pocket and chewed on it. Ruth was back to the usual bobby socks, saddle shoes, and skirt, but with the extra flair of a polka dot top.

"Ta-da! Here I am," she laughed. "NOW we're a real couple. Let's go!"

She hooked her arm in mine, and for the rest of the night, we were inseparable, dancing and talking until we fell into our chairs to catch our breaths. Our own Harmonaires dance band was in full swing, and when they took a break, a phonograph filled in.

"You're beautiful, Daisy Mae," I said as we sipped some punch. I let my eyes linger longer than usual.

Ruth held my gaze. "And you're as handsome as ever, Abner."

We both looked down, smiling as the moment passed, and I said, "Your mom was a sport to help you change your outfit. Hope she wasn't angry." I didn't mention that I'd heard voices through the walls, something that pretty much went without saying around here. People allowed one another the pretense of privacy.

"Mom's my rock in most matters," Ruth admitted. "She's just old fashioned and is still struggling with English. She doesn't keep up with things like cartoons."

I said I understood, and hand in hand, we returned to the floor for the final round. I breathed in her fragrance as we danced to "Tangerine," that gal with night-black eyes and something-something-la-la-la. The song had hit number one around the time everyone arrived at Puyallup, and though I could never remember the lyrics to any song, this one played so much at dances that I at least had learned the tune. It was my favorite, especially since it was playing when I first danced with Ruth, and she loved it, too. I hummed it now, happier than I'd felt in months.

At the end of the evening, I signed Ruth's dance program, "Mr. Koga," and she laughed and curtsied, glad to know me. I bowed back, thinking how happy I was that Ruth's practicality was hitched to a solid sense of humor. Who could get through life without it.

As we left, she whispered, "You have a good heart."

I stopped in my tracks. No one had ever said anything like that to me before.

"A good heart?" I repeated softly.

Ruth put her fingers to my lips. "Don't make a wisecrack." She pulled her mouth a little to the side, the way she did when I grew too silly or cocky.

She didn't have to worry. For once, I had no words and was on the verge of choking up, and she did most of the talking as we made our way home.

As we neared her barracks, I saw no one sitting outside. My chance had arrived. I leaned down and kissed her, first on the cheek and then on the lips, and I felt the slightest pressure back. I pressed in, my lips lingering before she pulled away and said goodnight. I walked to my barracks, thinking gray skies might clear up after all.

Cheered, I read the newspaper for the first time since we'd left Seattle, feeling Chichi by my side as I learned of MacArthur escaping the Bataan Peninsula, of Hitler attacking Leningrad. The Allies fought in Nazi-occupied Europe, Britain, and Greece; and Rommel maneuvered with cunning in North Africa. Hitler stole supplies from the Afrika Korps to help Mussolini fight Allied onslaughts. Reports of U-boats patrolling the Atlantic near Canadian and American shores brought the war close to home. Blackouts hid lights from possible enemy boats and aircraft. Air raid sirens wailed.

Even without the news, the war was very much with us in Puyallup, a war that had stripped us of the very liberties our country was fighting for, and I knew I had to make a decision, and now. I could stay behind here, or I could do something more in my part of the world to improve things, like Molly said. Lawson agreed, and I was cleared to join the advance crew. About two hundred of us would lend a hand.

That evening, I saw Ruth in the mess hall, talking and laughing with a bunch of people our age, and I started toward her to let her know my news. Out of the corner of my eye, I spotted Joji walking out of the kitchen, a big can of peaches in hand. He stopped at a table near Ruth and waved her over. I stood behind them, just feet away.

"Here." He smiled and handed her the can. "You said you like these, didn't you?"

Ruth looked surprised. "Well, thank you. I do. How did you know?"

He shrugged, saying he had used his connections in the kitchen to get the peaches. "I know we're getting more fresh food these days, but some people still want this kind of thing. Don't let anyone in charge see you, okay?"

She said she'd be careful, and after an awkward silence, Joji said he had to be going.

"Thanks, again," Ruth called as he walked away.

She returned to her friends, took a seat, and set the can in front of her.

Even before Joji was out of the mess hall, people around the table began laughing.

"A can of peaches?"

"Times are tough. But canned peaches for the girl you want?"

"Really?"

I looked over at Joji, walking through the door, and hoped he hadn't heard the sarcastic remarks and laughter. My heart ached for the guy. I didn't want to tell Ruth, but I thought he was incredibly nice to give her that present, to remember what she liked.

Ruth suddenly scowled at everyone, grabbed the can, and stood up.

"Why don't you all just stop it?" she said. I caught her eye as she headed out.

"Hey," I said in a low voice, joining her.

"You saw?" Ruth said under her breath. I said yes and took the heavy can from her as we walked. I didn't know what to say. Joji was getting to be my friend. I hoped she wasn't going to fall for him.

Deciding to let the subject drop, I walked Ruth to her door and handed off the peaches. I told her of my plans to head to the new camp.

"I'll miss you," Ruth said, reaching for my hand. "But I'm glad you're getting out of here, even to another camp. I just hope the next place will be better."

Her mother must have heard us, because she opened the door, dashing my hopes for a kiss. I nodded to Mrs. Nakamura, who nodded to me, and I told Ruth I'd pick her up for our date tomorrow, for what would be our last dance at Puyallup. When I returned to my barracks, Joji didn't appear upset, so I doubted he'd heard anything. I didn't mention a word, but as I listened to him and his brothers talk into the night, I made another decision.

"Here, I want you to have this," I whispered to Ruth after the dance. I placed in her palm the little gold football that I'd been awarded as a member of Garfield's championship team, and I folded her fingers around it. "I want you to wear it on your necklace, close to your heart."

Ruth held it tight before putting it back in my hand. She placed her other hand over mine. "I know how precious this is to you," she said, "and I love you offering it to me. But I'm not ready. Thank you, though."

"Is it someone else?" I barely got out the words.

Ruth caressed my hand. "No, no one in particular. I'm just too young to settle for one fella."

We kissed goodnight at her door, my heart heavy.

4

Minidoka

Summer 1942

By the time I arrived in Idaho, hulks of barracks perched on the desert sands, which the wind blew constantly, irritating my eyes and nose. Large balls of dry sagebrush tumbled all around. A few in the advance crew talked to administration members about things our community needed, and I took up a hammer again to pound and saw and sweat with other nisei men and Caucasian contractors as the semblance of a town came into being.

We hammered planks of untreated wood sideways onto two-by-four frames to create walls. Then we raised the walls and pounded them into place on wooden floor platforms, our new homes.

"Do they really think this is going to protect us?" Satoru Asahina asked as we covered the sides with a skin of flimsy black tarpaper. A bunch of us nisei had ended up by ourselves, away from the Caucasians. "I hear the weather's a bear out here. Hotter than hell in the summer, and colder than Antarctica in winter."

Yeah, and colder than hell, I thought. In Dante's story, the very bottom of hell was ice, saved for the worst of sinners, the betrayers.

"Those little stoves won't do anything," Bill Endo agreed. Each apartment would again have a potbelly stove, feeble against freezing temperatures.

"They're making us work too fast," Satoru said. "Things are so damned sloppy. Why are they rushing everyone in? What's the hurry?" There must have been two or three thousand Caucasian workers, and the camp was nowhere near finished.

"At least it's better than Puyallup," John Nomura said.

"It's still a prison," I said. No matter the WRA's new phrase—Minidoka War *Relocation* Center—no one swallowed the malarkey. Another damned euphemism, designed to disguise the truth, to make it easier to lie.

Heck, we were in Hunt, Idaho, near the town of Jerome and in the county of the same name. We weren't even close to Minidoka, one county away. But the government was building another prison in Jerome, Arkansas, and didn't want the two confused.

I had a suggestion for Uncle Sam: Stop building camps.

We were only a couple of weeks into our work when the first people arrived from Puyallup. I figured that Ruth's family was supposed to come in several moves after that, Molly a little later. I didn't know whose arrival I looked forward to more, and I worried about Molly and Lawson's baby, who was supposed to appear soon.

The day of Ruth's arrival, on a scorching hot day, I quit hammering long enough to run back to my barracks, set up in a recreation hall for now, to change my clothes and brush my hair. Water was still scarce, so I could only hope I didn't smell too bad. I had no idea where I stood with her, but I waited expectantly for her and her family.

The first of several trains rattled into the desert spur late that afternoon, blackout curtains hanging at the windows, and hundreds of people emerged up and down the line of ancient cars, their sweaty faces black with soot from the coal-fired engine. As I looked through the crowd for Ruth, I told everyone they would have to bus a little farther to the camp, pointing to a big cloud of dust hiding the area a couple of miles away. They would then have to check in with the military police, headquartered in a stone building at the front of camp. People would see physicians before getting apartment assignments.

I looked again for Ruth.

No, not here.

Not there.

"Here! Here!" a voice called behind me.

I turned to see Ruth brushing her hair away from her face in the wind, leaning down every so often to wipe sand off the faces of two little sisters.

My heart light, I ran over, only to see her tilt her head toward her parents, standing a few yards away with Ruth's big sister and two little brothers.

I stopped and whispered, "Hi." Did she mean not to show affection?

"Hi," Ruth said. Darned if I could read her, but in those few unsupervised seconds, we grasped each other's hands, and that gave me hope.

Ruth pulled her sisters close as she surveyed the camp, her face covered with grime and fatigue. "Hell's bells," she muttered.

I had not heard Ruth utter anything close to a swear word before, shocking me back to my own first reaction to the endless acres of sand and sagebrush around us. I agreed that it looked depressing. Plus more sand was blowing now because so much brush had been cleared. But I told her that life would improve.

Ruth talked as she got her bearings. "They bused us back to Seattle to cram into these old trains at the King Street station. Didn't even tell us where we were headed."

She bent over to wipe more sand from the girls' eyes. Her older sister moved over to help.

"It was hotter than blazes the whole trip," Ruth said. "Not an ounce of air. Blackout curtains down all the time. Some of the older folks got sick. Two days and three nights of that."

"We peeked sometimes," Ruth's little brothers whispered as they inched closer to their parents.

"We lifted the bottom of the curtain," one added.

"Don't tell the soldiers," the other said.

I leaned down and patted them on the back. "Good for you! You're brave boys." Then I offered Ruth my handkerchief to wipe her face.

"But it's fresh—" she said.

"Please."

Ruth thanked me and dabbed at her face and neck. She said armed guards had escorted people to the few toilets on board, most of which had jammed or broken down completely. Devoid of locks, the doors hung open. She folded my handkerchief and put it in her purse. "I'll return it as soon as I launder it."

"We couldn't budge, so crowded," her mother said. She directed the four small children this way and that, kindly but firmly. "Sleep on wooden bench."

The little ones were getting cranky. "They've had so little food since we left," Ruth explained. "This is crazy."

Ruth's older sister hugged the children, and Ruth had them sing a song to get their minds off their growling stomachs. I recalled my mother's words that you could tell a lot about a person by the way they treated children and animals: *Zenryōna hitobito wa subete no ikimono o shinsetsu ni atsukau.*

Thinking Ruth was doing well, I walked her family and others to the buses, ovens on wheels, for our ride to the camp, and I could feel everyone getting more frustrated as we closed in. An old woman near us wept, saying in Japanese that everyone would be shot dead in the middle of the desert. Despite their own fear, people did their best to comfort her as we stepped off at the camp entrance.

I pointed out everyone's new homes, in a grid of thirty-six residential blocks curving along the lines of the nearby North Side Canal, full of water diverted from the Snake River. "Those barracks cover an area of about one mile by three miles," I said. The entire encampment consisted of more than thirty thousand acres.

"Don't get discouraged. I know it's a prison, but this one will be much cleaner and much more efficient than Puyallup once it's finished."

People looked unconvinced.

I tried harder.

"The new refrigeration is actually supposed to keep food cold. And each block has its own mess hall, larger lavatories with real toilets, and a rec area. And look—no barbed wire." I didn't mention that each block also held a dozen twenty-by-one-hundred-twenty-foot residential barracks, each gable-roofed structure cut up into six tiny apartments and covered in that flimsy black paper. Lavatories were still communal, with no partitions. I knew people would be bumping elbows and bottoms.

"When finish?" Mr. Nakamura asked matter-of-factly, and others joined in, angrily.

"Maybe another month," I said. "Or a little longer. We have to do our best again to make everything bearable, but things are going to be better. You'll see."

I apologized as I stepped over loose boards and showed people where to find the physicians' area and where to register. "The water's not running yet. I'm sorry." I recalled the worst days of Puyallup, when the smell of humans replaced animal odors.

"How *shi-shi*?" Ruth's father whispered to me as others filed into the buildings. Everyone was beginning to rub their eyes, already reddening from the blowing sand.

"The plumbing is going to be real efficient once it's in," I said, "but we have to put up with outdoor latrines for now. We don't even have a sewage system in place." The outhouses again consisted of long boards with several holes in them, water cascading down the floor from a big tank above to wash things away every so many minutes. The flowing water, unfortunately, also splashed on people's bottoms. During a talent show at Puyallup, one skit drew bitter laughter when the actors lined up chairs and repeatedly sat down and hopped up, re-enacting the bathroom ordeal.

Mrs. Nakamura whispered to Ruth and her older sister. I overheard something about one of the girls menstruating and couldn't imagine what she had done on the train or what she should do now. A blush seared my face, and I turned back to Mr. Nakamura, his face reddening.

"*Mechmecha*," he said. "What mess. But we survive."

Most families were assigned to one-room units of no more than four hundred square feet, but by evening the Nakamuras had moved into one of the few double units reserved for the largest families, near where the permanent bachelor's quarters would be, and there was now a little food in the children's stomachs. I was glad they had arrived when they did, because it looked like there wouldn't be enough finished barracks to house the rest of the internees coming in. Ruth and I waved to each other, and I made my way to my quarters, hoping the wait had been worth it.

The next day, I helped Joji's mother and two sisters settle in.

"*Domo arigato,*" Mrs. Ishikawa thanked me. "Joji tell me how nice you are. We still waiting for my boys." She was a petite, energetic woman, her two daughters good looking. But my heart belonged to Ruth, and I was glad the Ishikawas were assigned quarters many blocks away from their Nakamura friends. There would be less chance of Joji seeing her when he visited his family.

"Have you heard from your husband yet?" I asked.

"Get letter, at last," Mrs. Ishikawa said. "He says he is at Department of Justice camp with other issei. Wait for some kind of hearing. I don't understand."

I didn't understand, either, and did my best to make them feel comfortable.

Two days later, I met up with Joji and his brothers in the rec hall. We greeted one another like old chums, and we talked about what we had been up to over the past many days.

When a bell clanged for dinner, I warned them the mess hall wasn't up to speed yet. Shigeo and Eddie went ahead while Joji and I talked.

"Hiroshi, I have to tell you," Joji said. "I asked Ruth to dances a couple of times while you were gone—"

"You did?" I felt my heart sinking.

"Yes. But it's over," he said, pausing. "Over before it began, to be honest. She was really nice when we talked, but she just doesn't take a shine to me. I can't force it. I saw her dancing with this guy and that while you were gone, but I think she's stuck on you."

I felt good, really good, for myself, I had to admit, but didn't want Joji to hurt.

"There are millions of fish out there," he assured me. "Don't worry. I'll be fine."

I slept well that night, still relieved the Ishikawas hadn't landed in an apartment close to the Nakamuras. You never knew.

• • •

"It's a roaring furnace in here."

"The dust storms are terrible. My eyes and throat hurt."

"I have another nosebleed."

"The water ran out. I'm filthy."

"The outhouses stink to high heaven."

"I'm walking up to my ankles in mud when it rains."

"Does anyone have a washboard?"

"I'm thirsty."

The first weeks in Minidoka were long and hot and testy, but once people got acclimated and the water flowed through the pipes that I'd helped lay, everyone revived and took even greater control of their lives than they had at Puyallup.

"Did you see that bureau Mr. Yamashita made?" I asked Molly. She and Lawson had come in on one of the last trains. "Made totally from fruit cartons."

She added, "Lawson grabbed some scrap wood, too. Built a dining table and chairs. Better than what he made at Puyallup."

We looked at each other, proud of the skill but angry at the need for a repeat performance.

The sound of brooms sweeping away the dust became a constant undertone as the days unfolded, and we managed to make a decent life, with schools and a 196-bed hospital, fire departments, and churches. Teachers and medical personnel included issei internees and Caucasians from outside. Sports teams and fields sprang up around camp, and I was soon back to playing ball. Orchestras and swing bands made music as we dreamed and as we danced. Community councils formed, though not without concerns about authoritarian Caucasian control, and there was talk of newspapers being printed in Japanese and in English. Movie theaters brought fun to the barracks. Meals were still lousy and we had to stand in line for everything, but I hoped that would improve. Ptomaine had already broken out in one mess hall.

The WRA wanted us to create a "model town"—when would the government cut the euphemistic crap?—but those of us who could work did so more for our own sanity and dignity than for any government PR campaign. The pay was peanuts, far less than the minimum wage for skilled and unskilled laborers. Even issei physicians earned no more than nineteen dollars a month, much less than the Caucasians who worked with them. But it felt good to contribute while everyone waited to get out.

Especially important to me were those doctors and the improved condition of the hospital, because Molly was ready to give birth. Early one morning, shortly after I'd seen her and Lawson settle in, she began to have labor pains. Lawson and I rushed her to the hospital, but doctors sent her back to their apartment, saying it wasn't time.

"Yes, it is," she whispered as we helped her onto her cot. "I guarantee I'll be back there before you know it."

"Lawson, let me know when she's ready," I said. "I'll do anything for her."

Right after lunch, I heard a knock on my door.

"Hiroshi?"

I didn't recognize the voice.

"Sam Sakura. I'm a friend of Lawson's. He wants you to know that Molly's on her way."

I raced to the hospital, Sam close on my heels.

"I had a nosebleed a few minutes ago," he explained as he kept up with me. He twisted a piece of Kleenex and stuffed it up one nostril, as if to prove his words. "I need to get checked out."

We made good time and approached the nurse's station together. Sam looked around as I asked about Molly.

A nurse offered to bring me to the waiting area outside the operating room and turned to Sam. "You again?" she laughed and called to a nearby colleague, "He only wants you, Sayaka."

"Lovesick," the nurse whispered as we walked. "That's all that's wrong with him."

"Is it the real thing?" I said when I found Lawson.

"You can't fool a woman," he said.

Three hours later, Molly and Lawson were parents, and I was uncle to a beautiful little girl, Virginia Michiko Furuya, Michiko for our mother, always in our hearts.

"Wish Haha was here to see her," Molly said as she held Virginia. "Chichi, too."

I murmured my agreement. "They'd love her."

Virginia had a mop of black hair and the chubbiest little cheeks you ever saw, and Molly let me hold her in the days that followed. What a bundle of perfection and possibilities she was. I let her tiny fingers grasp my pinkie. Wes Inada, who was helping to start *The Minidoka Irrigator,* brought his whole family by to congratulate everyone, and Mr. and Mrs. Inada promised to be devoted surrogate grandparents as they rocked our little one to sleep.

Virginia's arrival prompted me to work even harder to make life good while we were here, and I maneuvered around the growing

tensions between us and the administration and even among ourselves so I could help repair a door or build a shelf.

And then Ruth, of all people, got in my way.

Issei were disgruntled that only their citizen children were allowed to help govern the camp, a rule blamed on the JACL's efforts to mollify the government and emphasize nisei loyalty over
our cultural traditions and rights as citizens. Ruth's father grew
depressed. Our parents had always been our authority figures,
and many, like Mr. Nakamura, were also worried about brothers
and sisters and cousins still living in Japan. So I tried to help Ruth
guide her father toward a job that would at least make him feel
that he was needed.

"Would he be interested in clearing and irrigating land?"
I asked her. At the moment, there were lots of jobs posted at
the placement office. Many issei had been farmers back home,
taking land given up as useless by Caucasians and turning it
into highly productive farms, and they were now cultivating
three hundred fifty acres here, with more planned next year.
We would soon have livestock to raise, too. We sure needed
better food.

"Dad doesn't know anything about agriculture." Ruth did not
appreciate my idea. "And he's too old for muscle work."

"I know that, but some of the positions are desk jobs." I tried
again. "They could use some planning and oversight."

"It's not going work," she said, shaking her head.

"Can you suggest a better idea?" My exasperation flared.

She shrugged. "Not at the moment."

"Not at the moment?" I said. "You haven't made a single suggestion, and you don't even have a job. I'm working my butt off."
I was also frustrated at receiving my pittance of pay late, leaving
me destitute for spending money.

"Look, I've been helping to take care of my brothers and sisters," she answered. "And I'm going to start working in garment
production next week. Bring in some money. Why are you so sore?"

I had to admit, my good feelings about Minidoka were already
wearing thin. The sandstorms never ceased, plumbing problems
were constant, and new people were still coming in from the
Pacific Northwest, sleeping in any free space they could find as
they waited for living quarters. I didn't like pushing souls out of
the mess hall so I could eat breakfast.

"What else can I do?" she continued. "We're just stuck here."

"Why don't you start by keeping up your fighting spirit?"
I said. "Don't act like this place is our only world. It's not. Our
world is out there."

"You're being unrealistic," she said, almost petulantly.

"This isn't like you, not the Ruth I know. Why are *you* so sore?"

"Oh, you're impossible," she said and walked away.

Steamed, I headed to my own apartment, wondering if the
past few months had been a waste of time. I still liked her, but I
decided I'd cool my heels for a while. I went stag or asked other
girls to dances, where I always spotted Ruth in the arms of another man, although never Joji. Sometimes I thought she was looking
over at me, too, but I tried not to notice.

With time on my hands and my pockets incessantly empty, I
began looking for something that would pay more than repair-
ing things. A foreman's job came up in the meat warehouse, a
huge compound that served the camp, close to ten thousand people now, and I grabbed it. The work was pretty grisly, but the pay
was good, so six days a week, I donned government-issued garb
and led eleven men in unloading bloody carcasses from supply
trains. Anytime I wore my work clothes, I wondered if Ruth had
made them.

Everything was going well until the day my boss overworked my crew and just stood there, watching us unload an enormous shipment of meat. I begged him to help and tossed him a big piece. He refused and let the meat fall to the ground.

The next day he fired us all for insubordination.

"Strike!" I encouraged everyone to protest yet another injustice. "Strike!"

We got our jobs back only because the camp would starve without our help, but my enthusiasm waned. I felt under constant scrutiny.

I didn't hear if Mr. Nakamura approached anyone about a job, but I spotted him and his wife helping to build a garden near their barracks. Although issei hadn't stopped squabbling, they were creating beautiful ornamental landscaping on every block, oases to escape the barbed wire, black barracks, and bickering, if only for a few minutes. Victory gardens sprouted up. The Nakamuras were soon hard at work on another garden, too, at Minidoka's entrance, and I saw them placing boulders and locust trees just so.

"Hello, Hiroshi." They waved politely to me whenever I passed by.

"Hello, Mr. Nakamura, Mrs. Nakamura." I waved back, bowing slightly.

I always craned my neck looking for Ruth, but never saw her working in the garden or passing through the gate with other internees, shoppers to go into town on a pass, ball players to take on local teams, members of swing bands and choirs to perform.

Soon the Nakamuras themselves passed through as they joined internees helping area farmers harvest their crops. Issei worked close to Minidoka, often side by side German POWs from their own camps. The Nakamuras worked at one farm, Wes's parents at another.

"Why don't you come with us?" Joji and his brothers wanted me to travel to Montana with them to top beets. Nisei were cleared to help far from camp.

"I can't," I said, disappointed. Getting out of here would be fun. "Darned job is taking up all my time."

With many in our age group scattered across Midwest farmlands, I ate frequently with Wes, also confined here because of his job, and one evening his parents returned from their harvesting indignant.

"German smile at us and call us Aryan. Aryan!" Mr. Inada sputtered as he put his dinner tray on the table and sat down.

"We not German," his mother grumbled. She frowned at us and at her food.

"It's okay. It's okay," Wes calmed his parents and explained the situation. He was taking on his teaching mantle, even with them. "See, Hitler calls Japanese honorary Aryans, because he sees both races as pure. For him, Nordics are the superior race in Europe, and the Japanese are the superior race in Asia."

"We not Aryans!" Mrs. Inada protested. She and her husband ate quickly, and as they left, she said, "Want to be Americans, if country ever let us."

Wes and I said we understood, and after they were gone, we talked over our own situation, the way Japan had given nisei automatic citizenship.

"That's called *jus sanguinis*—law by blood," Wes said, still the teacher. "Germany operates in a similar fashion."

"But we have always thought of ourselves as American citizens, end of story," I said, and Wes said that was *jus soli*—law by the soil.

"So that's the Latin mumbo jumbo behind our dual citizenship," I said.

"You're a quick learner," Was kidded me.

"Have to be these days," I said. I actually welcomed his lessons now. We recalled how the whole situation got upended just a couple of years after I was born, as tensions between Japan and the United States escalated. Suddenly, any issei who wanted their children to have dual citizenship had to register their births with the Japanese consulate. My parents had registered Koichi.

"I think Hitler has an ulterior motive pursuing this whole honorary Aryan thing," Wes added. "Common heritage is a neat way to build an alliance against the Allies, isn't it?"

I began laughing. "So our enemy thinks we're their brothers, and our government treats us like the enemy. That's royal."

As we drank our coffee, I said, "When's it going to end?" The list of insults was piling up again. Most recently, our once-open camp had been enclosed by barbed wire and guard towers—fire lookouts, the administration called them. The boldest internees snipped at the wire. A generator meant to electrify the fence appeared out of nowhere, but the camp swore it had been installed by an outside contractor, without permission. Power was cut. Anger and frustration grew.

Wes thought a minute. "Ever hear about the frog in the pot of water?" he asked.

"What's that?"

"Look, if you put a frog in warm water and gradually increase the temperature, he doesn't notice the difference, and at some point, he croaks one last time. We're the frog here, see."

"Right, right," I said.

"We all have to stay alert." Wes said that part of his job as a journalist was to keep people on their toes by printing the truth and pointing out wrongs, and he was practically breathless as he told me about Minoru Yasui, a nisei who, like Hirabayashi, had purposely broken curfew and evacuation laws to test their legality. He was awaiting sentencing after a cursory one-day trial in his Portland home. Rumors about him were spreading around camp and increasing everyone's frustration.

"The paper is going to start a series about them," Wes said. "Should be interesting. *Habeas corpus* hasn't been suspended, by rule of the Constitution, you know. Only rebellion or invasion can make that happen. So the men have the right to appear in court, in the flesh, and appeal their detention."

Wes checked his watch and said he had a date.

"Really?" I grinned.

"Girl from the paper. Like you said, just be yourself and things will work out."

I congratulated him, and he asked, "By the way, I haven't seen you with Ruth for quite a while. You still dating?"

I hesitated before speaking. "Maybe. We had a little tiff. We'll see."

I didn't want to admit it, but Ruth was never too far from my mind, and I always looked for her at dances, where she was invariably smiling in the arms of another guy.

"I think Ruth still likes you," Molly told me. "Maybe she's playing hard to get. Or is just as confused as you are."

"Women have their ways," Lawson laughed. "Hard to read sometimes."

I wondered what to do.

Should I talk with Ruth during a break?

Cut in?

Had she glanced at me as we sang the opening hymn in church last week?

Why did she sit so far from me at dinner?

So close?

As I worried, more news about protestors increased tensions around camp, some people upset at the brashness of the men involved, others supporting them all the way. Fred Korematsu, a California nisei, had been arrested and convicted because he refused to enter an internment camp. Hirabayashi had just received a ninety-day sentence for his own actions. Yasui, the man imprisoned with us, was about to face the music.

The camp watched him leave under armed guard for his sentencing in Portland.

"He's an Army reservist, for goodness sake," Molly whispered to me as they passed us. "Left his job right after Pearl Harbor to serve. They have to go easy on him."

Yasui had been commissioned a lieutenant after his undergraduate ROTC days and went onto law school. But like so many of us, he couldn't find a job back home and settled for a clerical spot in the Japanese consulate in Chicago.

"Not his fault the Army kept rejecting him," Lawson muttered. "Didn't want a 'Jap,' no matter how true blue."

The next day's headline in Wes's paper said it all.

Evacuation Illegal?

Judge Alger Fee's ruling encouraged and confounded us.

With clear-sighted understanding, Fee declared that all laws connected to the military order of evacuation were unconstitutional for American citizens.

But then he turned around and ruled that Yasui, by taking the job at the Japanese consulate, had given up his citizenship.

What the hell?

The young man was therefore guilty of breaking the curfew law, valid for enemy aliens. Fee gave him a one-year sentence and $5,000 fine.

Yasui sat not just in prison, but in solitary.

The *Irrigator* called on the JACL to step up.

"Good luck with that," Wes muttered. "That group won't have anything to do with dissent."

Long-festering antipathy toward the JACL soon exploded in Manzanar, a relocation camp in California, when a senior JACL figure was beaten there. Thousands of internees joined in protesting the arrest of a presumed perpetrator, and two nisei were shot dead by the military police, nine other inmates wounded, in mayhem that became known as the Manzanar Riot. Martial law was declared in the camp, the newspaper shut down, and some of us in Minidoka feared that could happen here.

How much could we take of the government's inequities?

Of our own internal strife?

As Christmas grew near, I searched for something to lift my spirits. I saw people decorating our mess hall and decided to chip in. I even fashioned a little piece of sagebrush as mistletoe and put it to the test, with varying degrees of success—and no Ruth in sight. Blocks competed for decoration prizes, and gift-giving took place at different times and places, private and public.

"Merry Christmas!" Mr. Matsudaira handed his little boy a wooden bird he had whittled.

"That's really beautiful," Mrs. Horiuchi exclaimed as she thanked her husband for the watercolor painting he had made of the camp, a hazy mix of blue canals and swimming holes and black barracks. Little figures of internees stood beside the waters, enjoying the peace as others swam.

"What is it?" a teenager asked her father. He had sculpted something for her out of greasewood.

"Spirit," her father said. "Free spirit. Cannot trap."

A few days later I visited Rec Hall 21, where young women were distributing presents donated by the Society of Friends—the Quakers—and others outside the camp. The women had already spent days sifting through the gifts to find just the right one or two for each child and then wrapping them up. The children rewarded their efforts with laughter.

I was hoping Ruth might be there, and sure enough, I spotted her.

She was kneeling on the floor as she played with a group of boys and girls.

"Hi," I said in a low voice. I managed a smile.

"Hi." She stood up.

"Want to take a walk?" I asked.

She gestured me to the side, away from the children. "Hiroshi, I'm dating other fellas, you know," she whispered. "My mom thinks I was seeing too much of you."

"How is she, your mom? Your dad?" I tried to keep the conversation alive.

Ruth said her mother was busier than ever with her little brothers and sisters, and her father had begun managing one of the camp's co-ops.

"More up his alley than the fields," I said. "Good idea."

"But you got him on the road," she said, pausing. "Look, I'm sorry I was short with you. My parents were falling to pieces, and I'd about had it with everything."

"I know the feeling," I said. "I apologize, too."

"Hiroshi, I still like you. Really I do. But I need to see other guys right now."

I didn't know what to say. "Okay, I understand." I forced out the words. "I just wanted to say hello. See you around."

I turned to go, and Ruth touched my arm. "That doesn't mean we can't date, can't dance. Just not all the time."

"Do you really mean that?" I said, my heart lighter.

"Yes, really." She said she had to take her brothers and sisters home now.

Not invited to walk with them, I plopped myself on a bench, befuddled as the merriment in the hall came to a close.

Within days, the new year was upon us, and internees learned just how little the potbelly stoves in our barracks could protect us from winter's sub-zero temperatures. Coal was poor quality and scarce, and carrying it by hand was painful and awkward. Wet walks from the bathing areas made icicles out of the most warm-blooded. Schools were hampered by lack of rooms and supplies, teachers and textbooks. Fresh food was hard to come by, and rationing tightened supplies even more. Intestinal flu broke out. Water from our wells was so contaminated that chlorine was used heavily, making the taste unbearable.

But through it all, Ruth and I kept each other warm by dancing together again, and when we were in the arms of different partners, I swore she glanced at me as much as I did her, our looks lingering just a little bit longer whenever "Tangerine" was playing. Sometimes I'd tailor the words and mouth them to her—*my heart belongs to you, dear Ruth, la-la-la*—and she'd smile.

Outside our prison, the war wore on without us, even though the draft age had been lowered to eighteen, the country desperate for men. I heard news of growing successes in North Africa and Guadalcanal with lukewarm enthusiasm, knowing I could not fight anywhere, not even in the brutal battles in Europe. Stories of Jews being hauled by cattle car into Hitler's eastern occupations brought me low, news of their own camps sketchy and heart rending. Surely Roosevelt was right to agree at Casablanca that fighting would cease only when the Germans surrendered unconditionally.

And then it happened.

"Hiroshi!" Ruth ran up to me.

"Have you heard the news?" Molly and Lawson asked.

"What the hell?" cried Joji.

5

Minidoka

Winter/Summer 1943

On a bitterly cold February day, all of us nisei men gathered in a rec hall.

The government had shocked us, and we were responding.

"Up yours, Uncle Sam! You have a hell of a nerve." Sam Sakura waved his fist in the air. He was the guy who had faked a bloody nose in order to see his favorite nurse. I put a finger up my nose to tease him anytime I saw him, but not today.

"How can I leave my parents? They don't speak English," Yoshi Ikari, a football teammate, said. "We don't even have a home to return to."

"They froze my parents' assets. Took every last thing we had," someone behind me called out. "I dropped out of school to earn money for our family. And now this?"

"They want us to fight while our families are imprisoned? Seriously?!" Kenichi Tsukiyama said. He lived next door to me.

President Roosevelt wanted three thousand nisei from the mainland and fifteen hundred from Hawaii to volunteer for service in a segregated infantry unit, most likely in Western Europe. The new unit, the 442nd, was activated on February 1, 1943.

Caucasian officers visited Minidoka with nisei who had been in service since before the Pearl Harbor attack. We listened to their every word.

Several of the soldiers spoke of the Military Intelligence Service, the MIS, which was already training nisei for translation and interrogation duties in the Pacific. The MIS was based at Camp Savage, Minnesota.

"The school moved there from California after the evacuation," the soldiers explained. "We've had to keep a lid on things, given the nature of war, but we've already gathered recruits from Camp Robinson, Arkansas, and from Hawaii."

I was surprised I hadn't heard of the MIS, the first group of nisei called to serve after Pearl, and just a few hundred miles from Fort Missoula, where Frank worked.

But what about us?

"There's another group of nisei," the tallest soldier said, meeting our eyes, "and these are the men who are of most concern to you now." He explained that when the peacetime draft had been enacted in 1940, before the attack on Pearl Harbor, these Hawaii nisei were among the men drafted with other American citizens into the islands' 298th and 299th National Guard. The Guard had been federalized to become part of the U.S. Army.

"These men helped defend Hawaii following the attack," another soldier said. After that, any nisei in the guard, Army Reserves, and regular U.S. Army were transferred into the Hawaii Provisional Infantry Battalion and shipped to the mainland.

The soldiers looked around the room, and the one with the most stripes said in a deep voice, "The men are now serving as the 100th Infantry Battalion at Camp McCoy, in Wisconsin. Just over fourteen hundred men are breaking every training record in existence."

Could we live up to that performance?

It was our patriotic duty to serve our country. The President himself was asking.

The soldiers continued their rally for a couple of hours, and after they left, we talked over our concerns, our anger, our hopes and fears. One meeting turned into another and another, formal and impromptu.

Men continued to voice their worries.

"My father is a language teacher. First they put him in a DOJ prison camp. Now he's in an Army camp. My mom's all alone," a man in back of me said.

"Should I renounce my dual citizenship to prove my loyalty?"

"Can volunteering show I'm a true citizen? Can I keep my constitutional rights for good?"

"Seven years of Japanese school, and I can't speak a word. Do they really think I'm a spy?"

We turned to our parents for guidance, but they hardly offered a united front.

"No one is afraid of Japanese invasion now. Why they keep us here? You should not fight."

"This country give us so much. You bring honor to us."

"442 is *shi shi ni* in Japanese. The shi, the four, is pronounced just like we pronounce the word for death. Bad omen, especially twice."

"The executive secretary of the JACL has already stepped up."

"We will disown you if you fight for government that imprison us. Take all we work for."

"Do not bring shame to our name. Serve proudly."

As we talked and debated, the Army began circulating a questionnaire to us nisei men.

"What's with all the questions? They just asked us to serve." Stan Ohara expressed everyone's thoughts.

The opening questions of Selective Service Form 304A seemed innocent enough, asking where we'd been born and what our religion was, but we began to worry when the questionnaire turned to other topics, like the existence of relatives in Japan, our ability to speak Japanese, organizations we belonged to, periodicals we read.

"Don't you see? They're trying to find out how 'Japanese' we are, damn it all," Ted Taketa said, throwing down the papers. "They just don't trust us."

"Bet Germans and Italians don't have to answer any damned questionnaire," someone else said. Compared to us, only a few Germans and Italians of any generation had been sent to the camps.

Confusion grew when the WRA took the Army form, renamed it "Application for Leave Clearance," and gave it to females and our parents, too.

What was going on?

No one had even asked for clearance, and the last two questions confounded us all.

We didn't know what to make of Question 27: *Are you willing to serve in the armed services of the United States on combat duty, wherever ordered?*

"How's my grandmother supposed to answer this?" someone asked.

"How the hell are *we* supposed to answer?" Joji yelled.

"If we're officially still ineligible to serve, what does a 'yes' answer mean?" Eddie joined in, but began coughing. His lung problems had never cleared up from the hay at Puyallup, and he had visited the infirmary twice since Thanksgiving, first with a cold and then with the flu.

I listened to all the men, remembering that to many outside the camp, we were not just "nonaliens," but "enemy aliens," lumped together with our parents.

Question 28, its three parts strung together, presented us with a ridiculous number of problems.

- *Will you swear unqualified allegiance to the United States of America?*
- *Will you faithfully defend the United States from any and all attacks by foreign or domestic forces?*
- *Will you forswear any form of allegiance or obedience to the Japanese emperor, or any other foreign government, power, or organization?*

Our answer reverberated around the hall as we called out, "What the hell?"

We nisei had never been loyal to any damned emperor. And our parents hadn't even been given the chance to become U.S. citizens, what with all the anti-Oriental laws put on the books over the past decades.

What if they lost their Japanese citizenship, too? They would have no country at all. And they feared our families would be separated if everyone didn't answer the same way.

"I can't say I'm going to serve without telling them what I think," Bob Watanabe said. He bore down hard on his pen as he printed "Only if you restore my civil rights" next to his "Yes" answer about his willingness to serve.

"And let my parents out of camp," Steve Iko added.

"I can't answer 'yes' to either question," Charlie Higuchi said. He answered "No" and "No."

While we men dealt with our consciences, our parents showed what they were made of and loudly protested answering the questions at all. The WRA changed the name of the form again, this time to "Questionnaire," and reworded some of the queries.

"The loyalty questionnaire"—that was what people began calling any version of the form. Soon women were adding their own "No" and "No" to the final questions.

"What do you think?" I talked the matter over with Joji and his brothers. All of us were seething with anger at the entire internment and the questionnaires, but warming to the idea of serving. How else could we prove our loyalty? Mrs. Ishikawa gave her blessing, as did the Inadas.

I hashed and rehashed the matter with Molly, who thought I should serve, and then I turned to Ruth.

"Should I volunteer?" I asked as I walked her home from dinner one evening. We were dancing more and more with each other these days and taking longer and longer walks, no matter what her mother said, and we strolled slowly despite the cold so we could spend more time together, alone. Snow covered everything, making the ugliest facets of our life disappear beneath a peculiar beauty.

"What does your heart say?" Ruth tightened the scarf around my neck. Molly had asked the same question.

"I have plenty of reservations," I said. "But I just can't sit here."

I gathered my thoughts before I said more, emotion overcoming me. "It's the children, Ruth. This is no place to bring up Virginia, no place for us to live." I thought of my sister washing her clothes with a pail and scrub board in the public laundry rooms. Toilets were just now working smoothly.

The cheap pine wood was shrinking, letting dust and dirt into the barracks, plus heat and cold, depending on the time of year. Children ate away from their parents, close family dinners a thing of the past. Women waited until late at night to bathe, hoping for a moment's privacy, and some risked illness by skipping the ordeal. Other camps suffered with worse hospitals and administrative troubles. The bells that called us to the mess halls three times a day rang sour. "Hell's bells," Ruth said. "Literally."

I took Ruth's hands. "It's the only thing I can do to help get this war over with, once and for all. To make our future lives better. I have to serve."

Ruth put her arms around my waist, and we drew close. "Then volunteer, Hiroshi."

"I love you, Ruth." I surprised myself, the words slipped out so fast. "I know you don't want to go steady, but I don't want you to forget me."

Her kiss said she loved me.

But where were her words?

. . .

As March winds teased us that winter would never end, I stood waiting in line for my Army physical. Joji followed close behind, and we felt on top of the world when we aced it.

"Come on, Hiroshi, let's get to the eye exam," Joji said.

"What?" Panic grabbed hold. "Damn it, I forgot." I should have memorized the eye chart, which a lot of near-sighted guys did. No way my vision was correctible to 20/40 with glasses, the Army standard.

"Why don't I help you?" Joji said as we took our place in line.

"It's too late to memorize everything," I protested.

"Forget that." Joji lowered his voice. "I'll stand behind you and whisper the letters. Just look straight ahead, like you're studying the chart." He moved in back of me.

"You sure?" I asked.

"Absolutely."

"Step up." The sergeant giving the test called when I reached the head of the line. I handed him my paperwork and waited. I could feel the heat of Joji's body on my back, he drew so close.

"Okay, read this." The sergeant pointed to the wall.

"A," Joji whispered.

"E."

I repeated the letters in a loud voice.

Joji quickened the pace. "L, T, Y...."

I could barely hear him and repeated what I thought he had said.

Joji paused and then spewed out the rest of the letters, "T, H, P," as the sergeant hurried toward us.

"What's going on?" He scowled.

We stood at attention.

"You there." The sergeant pointed to Joji. "Were you telling him the letters?"

Joji gulped. "Yes, sir."

Hell, we were going to get court-martialed before we even wore a uniform, I just knew.

The man glared at us, his color deepening as he thought.

"Oh, for Christ's sake." He waved his hands. "You want to be in the Army that much, I'll pass you. Both of you. Now get the hell out of here." He signed off on our papers and signaled the next man forward. Joji and I elbowed each other out of the room, before the sergeant could change his mind.

Over the coming days and weeks, we heard that three hundred of us were volunteering from Minidoka, nineteen percent of those eligible, according to the *Irrigator*, and as men began leaving camp, tempers rose when General DeWitt declared that a Jap was a Jap. Weren't his ideas painfully close to those of our enemies? What good were our Constitution and Bill of Rights when the people in charge of interpreting them put blood before soil, race before loyalty? I thought this was the real reason behind our evacuation, not the "military necessity" twaddle he and others incessantly cited.

"Looks like I'm in the Army now," Sam Sakura sang as he ran up to me after dinner one evening. "Damn, just as I was starting to enjoy myself." He had been dating that nurse of his and was just now helping to form a drum and bugle corps of Boy Scouts. "Can't wait to get back to both of them."

"Hey, they called us up," Shigeo and Joji came up behind him. "How about you?"

"Not yet," I said. I had no idea why I had to wait.

"Visit Eddie when you can," Joji said. Eddie had developed pleurisy and been passed over by the Army. He was still in the camp hospital.

I dropped by, the poor guy not getting much better.

I played ball.

I helped issei harvest the newest of their vegetables, the ones we loved, like bok choy and daikon and mizuna.

I even met Joji's father, who finally joined his family. I told him how happy I was to see him, though sorry two of his sons had already left camp. I could see how Joji came by his looks, his father's face square and handsome, silver hair slicked back, gentle eyes behind his glasses.

Mr. Ishikawa explained his absence. "After Naturalization Center, moved to Department of Justice camp. They give me hearing and put me in Army prison camp. Guess they think I dangerous. Then too many POWs come in, and they put me back in DOJ camp. Had to make room for them."

"I petitioned for his release, tried so hard," Mrs. Ishikawa said. "Think it helped."

Mr. Ishikawa leaned close to her, saying of course it did, and added, "Finally turn me over to custody of WRA. Glad to be back with my family, even in prison. Wait so long." He was already working at the camp pharmacy.

I told him I was glad, too, and continued my own wait.

• • •

"Hey, Hiroshi, they've called me up." Wes Inada came by a few days later. "I'm taking off. Stay out of trouble, would you? The Army will kick your butt if you don't." Wes knew what had happened at the warehouse and told me I should keep my mouth shut sometimes. I told him I'd try.

Parties and applause and band music celebrated the volunteers' patriotism, and I waved as they left for Camp Shelby, an old Army training camp in Mississippi that had been reactivated for this war. The 100th had been transferred there for more training, like the Army couldn't decide what to do with them.

I bid farewell, too, to internees getting cleared by the FBI to find jobs or enter approved colleges under a new WRA release program. But I couldn't join them, either, as I waited to hear from the Army. About the only thing that made me happy was spending more time with Ruth, but even that became a problem.

"You see too much of each other," her mother harped on her favorite topic again.

Ruth's father agreed. "You too young, Ruth. Need to see other boys."

Ruth and I were sitting across the picnic table from her parents and pulled apart. Her parents seemed like such nice people, but boy, they sure didn't trust me.

"We're just dancing," Ruth said, indignation rising in her voice.

"I don't have any bad intentions," I added, feeling guilty for no reason. Sheesh, I thought we were past this point. "I just really like your daughter."

I didn't know if it was because of me or the swell of people leaving camp, but Mrs. Nakamura began working with a vengeance to get Ruth out. With our time together growing short, Ruth and I worked just as hard to see each other, and our next dance became a joyful one.

It was *Obon* season, when anyone of Japanese descent welcomed back the spirits of our loved ones for a visit and celebrated their presence through group dancing, *bon odori*. The longer we were in camp, the more traditional Japanese celebrations and shows were being allowed, and full clearance had been given for two nights of dancing and games for all ages in the open fields.

I picked up Ruth at her barracks and waved politely to her parents, who were going to join the festivities with their other children the next evening. We could hear Japanese music wafting through the air as we neared the dance, and we stood watching the festivities for a few minutes before joining in. An inner circle had been created by dancers who had been practicing for weeks in the rec halls, and they now moved on a raised platform around a big wooden tower, a *yagura*, and showed everyone how it was done. Ever-expanding outer circles followed them and danced as one in choreographed motions, gently waving their hands and arms, clapping, turning and swaying. Lanterns glowed everywhere, lighting the way for our ancestors. There must have been a thousand or more dancers, some wearing kimonos or short, loose-fitting *happi* coats, and I hoped that was enough people to allay any fears Ruth's parents had about us getting too close by ourselves. We danced our hearts out, remembering with our community those who had gone before us, and silently I honored my parents and little brother, their spirits with us now, vowing to make them proud in whatever I did.

Bowls of noodles and cups of tea followed the dancing, and Ruth and I drew together as we talked.

"Do you know when you're leaving?" I asked.

"Mom's working with the Quakers now to get me out on the release program," Ruth said. "Schooling, housing, they're arranging everything to relocate me." She said she had convinced her parents not to force her into a four-year college program, but to let her enroll in a business school.

"Where?" I asked.

"Chicago."

"That's supposed to be a great city," I told her. Chicago was nowhere near the Western Defense Command and was full of jobs left vacant by draftees. Many nisei had already headed there, and we were hearing good things about the way Chicagoans treated Japanese.

"You sure this is the way you want to leave?" I asked, worried she was being rushed into something she might not like.

"I'm actually raring to go," Ruth said, reaching for my hand. "Don't worry. Mom doesn't have it in for you. She just wants what's best for me, and I've made my priorities clear. I'm still pretty young, remember. I just want to leave on my own terms."

"Sounds like you are," I said, reassured.

The day came too fast for her departure, and we found a quiet spot between barracks to say good-bye.

"I'm a little scared," Ruth admitted. She was dressed up in a pretty suit, her hair falling in black clouds of curls to her shoulders. She said her older sister's fiancé, a nisei pharmacist in the city, would be her sponsor.

"You'll be fine," I said, trying to boost her confidence. I told her I'd be in the Army soon and would see her on furlough.

We put our arms around each other and kissed until she had to go.

"Well," I said, "I guess this is it. Don't you ever forget me."

Ruth pulled something from an envelope she'd been holding. "Please, take this. I don't want you to forget me, either." She handed me her photo.

My heart leaped. Giving this to me had to be a good sign. We kissed again, and I walked her home.

• • •

I placed Ruth's picture next to my family's and resumed my wait. Soon after she left, news came in about Hirabayashi and Yasui. No one had heard about them since the 442nd was formed, but we now learned that the Supreme Court had upheld the exclusion laws they challenged on the grounds of "military necessity," with no consideration of the legality of the internment. The matter of Yasui's citizenship somehow disappeared in the arguments.

I hated to admit it, but I began wondering if I'd made the right decision to fight. The days dragged by, brightened only by playtime with little Virginia and letters from Ruth. Chicago had become such a mecca that the camp was showing a film about it, and Ruth wrote that she was delighted to get free room and board in exchange for housework at her Quaker hostel, somewhere on the city's West Side. But school was giving her problems.

Can you believe it? I went to enroll in the Gregg shorthand and business school I'd written to, but when the receptionist saw me in person, she told me in no uncertain terms, "We don't allow Japanese." So even here, we are just Japs to some, and they slam the door in our faces. Wish me luck. Now I have to hit the pavement and find work to keep me going. Then I'll look for another school.

Just as I learned the reason behind my own troubles—my warehouse boss had been playing around with my departure day, he was still so angry—I received my notice. As fast as I could, I packed my bag, placing the photos of my family and Ruth side by side, on top of my shirts and slacks. I stood one last time in the Japanese garden at Minidoka's entrance, a testament to the spirit of order and peace and dignity that no prison could kill. An Honor Roll of soldiers from the camp would soon be erected right here, and my heart swelled with pride, knowing that my name would be on it.

I walked out, having no idea the battles I would fight.

PART II

6

Seattle

June 1976

Ruth left the room as I finished my story, and my old lieutenant picked up the conversation.

"You men sure must have been *huhu*," Ando said. "You overcame so much when you volunteered."

"We're dealing with our anger, even now," I admitted. "Relocation centers, my ass. They were American concentration camps. Prison camps."

"I've tried to understand, even make excuses for what they did to us," Shig said. "We were betrayed, abandoned, pure and simple, by our country and by people we trusted. Hard to forgive."

Ando thought for a minute and then said, "Forgiveness doesn't mean overlooking or condoning, you know. In today's language, it's just letting go—"

"Oh, come on," I interrupted. "There's no 'just' about this in any way, shape, or form. To this day I'd like to sock Uncle Sam in the kisser." I still had trouble with some of our own, too, like the jackals, the JACL, who had cooperated with the government in every way they could and expected us to do the same. "There's nothing 'just' about the camps, and nothing 'just' about 'just letting go.'"

Ando looked at me curiously, and I had to laugh to myself. Even I heard the irony of my last comment. There was everything 'just' about forgiveness. I'd heard the lessons in church, about grace and forgiveness for the repentant, about loving your neighbor as yourself, but I was having problems with it.

What the hell was I supposed to do? Hug and kiss all the bigoted bastards, all the people who went along with them?

"At least the JACL is getting better, sticking up for us since the war," Shig said, and we all agreed.

"That's what I was about to say," Ando said. "Another part of forgiveness is the evolution involved. Action by action—"

Ruth called out as she returned with something in her hand, and Ando sat back, looking a little exasperated.

"I have a drawing of my own to share," she said, looking at all of us. She sat down and handed me a yellowed, folded paper that was covered in watercolor sketches, and I let out a short gasp.

"The Sadie Hawkins dance," I said. "My invitation." I examined the cartoons, so cleverly drawn in Al Capp's style, and then passed the invitation to Ando, who studied it and passed it to Shig.

"What's the matter?" I asked Shig. I thought I saw tears in his eyes.

"Joji," he said. "My brother drew this, you know."

"What?" Ruth and I said together.

Shig said, "There must have been a dance committee or something like that. I don't remember. But someone had seen his drawings and asked him to come up with an invitation."

Shig took a drink of water before adding, "I remember how he went to our mother's barracks to use Dad's watercolors and pens. He worked for days on end getting it right. He was so happy."

Ruth and I looked at each other, remembering. Sadness overcame me.

"Sheesh, the guy must have been really hurt," I said to Ruth, "not getting asked by you."

Ruth looked into the distance, shaking her head. "I didn't know," she said. "I just didn't know."

"Guess we can't get too sentimental," Shig said. "Like Joji said, all's fair in love and war. But he sure was sweet on you for quite a while, Ruth."

We sat quietly for a couple of minutes, our hearts heavy for our friend, his young tenderness and his pain.

I had miles to go in my story, and silently, I wondered if the guy had loved Ruth right to the end.

7

Camp Shelby

Autumn 1943

"Ko-*tonk!* Ko-*tonk!*" A tough, sinewy Buddhahead syncopated his chant with each smack of my head against the barracks floor. From the ground, I spied the boots of our squad sergeant as he entered, and I hoped his presence would put an end to the pain.

"Knock it off." Sergeant Ando ran over to us. "Other soldiers may act like this, but not my squad." My tormentor, Kat Kato, and I accepted hands up from the Hawaiians and mainlanders who had cheered us on. "I'm warning you. No more." Our sarge was usually reserved, and I knew he was plenty mad.

I walked over to my cot as I massaged my head, cursing Hawaii and my late arrival at Shelby. The camp had set up a temporary recruitment detachment for us eleventh-hour guys, and I quickly found the only things familiar around here were barracks that leaked, like those in Puyallup, and barracks that were laid out in a military grid, like those in Minidoka. I had to work my butt off to make up in unbearable heat and humidity for the five months of basic I'd missed to become a Government Issue, a GI.

Just as autumn set in, a wicked cold snap killed the season before it could die a natural death, and I was assigned to my permanent group, this 1st squad of the 2nd platoon of the 3rd Battalion's I Company. I took up residence in Barracks 6, one of the many long, weary barracks that made up parts of this old training camp, thinking these guys could deliver a tough 1-2-3 punch. I really wanted to join in unit training, but I didn't know part of that was coming to fisticuffs with my own comrades. "Itemites" was our Army code name, members of I Company, Item Company. I was tussling with my own comrades.

Mak Harada came up to me, laughing. "I tell you, Brah, we're just making sure you haven't missed anything."

"You're too kind," I said. Like all mainland volunteers, I was learning how rough-and-tumble these Hawaii guys were, brought up close together in crowded plantations and in schools filled with children of other plantation immigrants. They even talked weird, in bits and pieces of Hawaiian, English, Portuguese, Filipino, Chinese, Japanese, Korean, the languages of the native islanders and immigrants who had worked the fields for decades, sometimes fighting, sometimes cooperating and enjoying one another's food and company. "Pidgin," Mak called their way of talking, a language for the working people to communicate with each other.

Gibberish, I said.

Why you wen go buss up da jeep?

Da Jerry stay make.

We go buss up some okole.

We give him dirty lickins.

What the hell?

Their speech was indecipherable, but the way they ganged up on people to punch their lights out was clear as day.

"Come on, forget about it. Let's get into town," Mak said. He had celebrated his twentieth birthday by being promoted to buck sergeant, right under Ando, and had gone out of his way to make me feel comfortable. I guessed he was stepping up to the plate, now that he had three Fuji-sans, sergeant stripes, on his sleeve.

"You sure you no come?" Mak turned to my old pal, Joji Ishikawa, whose cot stood across from mine. I didn't know how the Army assigned us to units, but a lot of us in this one had names in the H-I-J-K range, and Joji and I were together again.

"I can't," Joji said. The three of us had been invited to a Saturday luncheon by some *haoles* in Hattiesburg. That's what Mak and the other Hawaii boys called Caucasians, *haoles,* and sometimes not too kindly. Evidently the haoles were lords of the sugar and pineapple plantations, the Big Five owners running first the fields and then the rest of island society with an iron fist. And now haoles in the Army were the bosses as martial law took hold of Hawaii, *habeas corpus* suspended.

Joji added, "Send my regrets. I haven't seen my brother in ages. We're going to down some beers at the PX." Shig was now a staff sergeant in Canon Company.

"If no can, no can," Mak said, shrugging. "Okole maluna."

"What?" I said.

"It's okay. Bottoms up. Word for word." Mak grinned, pushing us out the barracks. "Let's get the bus."

I offered Mak a cigarette as we began walking through camp. We lit up, coughing a little as we got used to the smoke.

"Head okay?" Mak asked.

"I'll live," I said.

Mak said, "Kat, he can be one nasty Buddhahead."

"Son of a bitch, that's what he is," I said.

Mak, from rural Molokai, eyed me as he took a drag off his cigarette. "Look, I know us guys from Hawaii rough around edges compared you kotonks, yuh. But we good guys. Kat just has big chip on shoulder. He'll come around. Don't let him bother you."

I rubbed my aching head. "Is that a suggestion or an order?" I kidded Mak. I was still feeling my way around, not quite sure how I should deal with him, as my friend or leader. He was a real nice guy, soft spoken and almost gentle beneath it all—like any soldier wanted to be described like that—but he was disciplined and made sure you toed the line, too.

"Both," he said "Way Kat beat up on you, make me feel we starting all over again." Mak said my fellow kotonks had arrived in our segregated area of Shelby a couple of weeks before the Hawaiians. Mainland nisei who had been drafted before the war were already there and had filled many of the spots of non-commissioned officers who would train the 442nd. When the Hawaiians arrived, all hell broke out.

Weren't only haoles supposed to be 442nd officers?

Were these non-coms volunteers, like them?

Fisticuffs broke out between hotheads on both sides.

Kotonk! Hawaii boys laughed that our heads made the sound of a coconut when they smacked them against the floor. We were standoffish and didn't even buy our pals a drink.

Buddhahead! We looked down our noses at the backward Hawaiians, more like our grandparents and more Buddhists among them than we had.

"I sort of understand how you see us," I admitted to Mak.

"How's that?" he asked.

I told him how most of us had grown up in small groups, in cities and farms spread out along the West Coast. Caucasians were at the top of our social ladder, too, but we couldn't help but intermingle with them. And we went to schools full of them. "Lots of other immigrants and Negroes, too," I said, "especially in the cities. We all did our best to learn the King's English from our teachers. We had to."

"Don't even know what 'King's English' is," Mak said. "You just talk snobby. Act funny."

We paused in front of a barracks to watch what I thought was a training exercise, with men in our 1st Platoon. "And here's another big problem," Mak muttered. He told me we were watching Lieutenant Raymond Lewalski, a ninety-day wonder fresh from Officer Candidate School, not a West Point graduate. He was shouting at five or six of his men.

"You left camp without a pass last night, damn it all," the looie bellowed.

Mak whispered, "This guy real mean to us, yuh. Lost cousin in Pacific couple months ago and don't want to work with us. 'Japs,' he call us."

"Sheesh," I muttered. By now, we could deal with all the bullshit from Caucasians training in other units at Shelby. All of us, Buddhaheads and kotonks, gave as good as we got, and they backed down after we'd bloodied a few too many noses. But our own officers? After months of training?

Suddenly a squad sergeant stepped forward. "Sir, that is not true," he growled. "We did everything by the rules."

"Like hell you did. Now give me fifty," Lewalski yelled.

"Guy better watch it," Mak whispered to me. "That's Rocky." Everyone knew Rocky Yamada was a professional boxer from Kauai and built like a tank, one of the biggest guys in the whole regiment. He stood solid while the rest of the platoon poured out of their barracks, tempers rising.

Rocky stared Lewalski straight in the eye. "No," he said. "No more your shit. No can blame me or my men." He rolled up his sleeves. "We do this here or outside camp." He clenched his fists at his sides.

"Get the hell inside," Lewalski said in a stern voice. "All of you."

The men quickly obeyed, and Mak and I took off. Threatening an officer could result in court-martial.

"How we gonna fight under some these guys?" Mak said. "Lives depend on each other."

I agreed. We truly loved the best of our Caucasian officers, the ones who worked diligently and respectfully by our side, who believed in us. We would do anything for them, and there were many. But damned if there weren't others like Lewalski who were blatant bigots or goldbricks and still gave us trouble.

Weren't we on the same side?

. . .

Once at the stop, we boarded the bus, and Mak asked, "You go into Hattiesburg yet?"

"Nah. I've stayed close to camp," I said. "Overnight GI."

Mak directed me to a seat at the front. "This your day to learn, yuh. Never thought this the way we start the war, eh. Nisei-nisei. Haole-nisei. Haole-Negro. Nisei-Negro."

Mak sat back and said, "100th at Shelby before us. Mostly away on war maneuvers when we got here, but managed to give us some advice. Here's one tip. Don't sit in COLORED section." He tilted his head toward the back. "You think you're doing right, but you take away the few seats reserved for Negroes, and then they can't get on bus."

I watched a Negro board at one stop and then another, both in uniform, fascinated to see other non-Caucasian GIs. I knew there was a sizable contingent of Negro soldiers at Shelby, but I had seen few of them, Shelby was so damned big and so damned segregated. The men looked quizzically at us sitting in the white seats while they moved to the back. I squirmed in discomfort, but the ride passed quickly, and with a sigh of relief, we stepped off the bus and walked around town, killing time before we headed to our luncheon.

"So where do we belong?" I asked as I took in the town. Signs for "WHITES ONLY" and "COLOREDS" screamed everywhere, inside and outside theaters, bathrooms, luncheon counters in the five-and-dimes.

"Depend on who looking at you," Mak said as we walked into a store. A few Caucasians turned to glance at us before going about their business. No Negroes were in sight.

"Go take drink." Mak pointed to two water fountains, one for Negroes, one for Whites.

I ran water into my mouth from both. "No one's coming to get me." I wiped my lips as I darted my eyes left and right.

"Oh, but wait long enough and some haole will," Mak said. "Some stare and sneer, yuh, call us 'Japs.' But when I sit in colored section of movie theater one time, up in balcony, other haoles escort me downstairs to white section."

Mak lowered his voice. "Haoles call balcony 'Nigger Heaven.' Some Negroes can't even read the signs around here, they given so little education, yuh. But they sure get bigotry jammed down their throats."

Saying to hell with it, Mak took a drink from both fountains and added, "Haole soldiers won't let Negroes into USO, fight like hell, so now Negroes have own. Like us."

Earl Finch, a local resident, had established an Aloha USO for nisei after a few too many fist fights between us and the

Causcasian soldiers, mostly 69th Division men training at Shelby. He'd even invited nisei to barbecues at the ranch he shared with his mother, slipping a little cash to soldiers who needed spending money on their furloughs.

"Separate but equal," I said, remembering my history lessons.

"Not so equal, seems to me," Mak said.

I knew I had more to learn, but I eyed my watch. "Hey, we better get moving."

Minutes later, we welcomed the sight of the Allens' house, just outside of town, spacious and white, complete with portico. Green lawn, swaying trees, and late autumn flowers colored the scene.

"Some fancy, eh?" Mak said. "Lucky, come here."

The Allens had, like Earl Finch and many other Hattiesburg residents, extended their hospitality to nisei soldiers several times. Word at Shelby was that the brass had persuaded the townspeople to overcome any prejudice they held and be extra cordial, with varying degrees of success. Our higher-ups wanted us to succeed as red-blooded Americans, and we enjoyed the resulting kindness.

Sally and Jimmy Ray Allen made us feel right at home, just like our parents would. And what a meal they had prepared: fried chicken and mashed potatoes, collard greens, grits, and sweet potatoes. We had no trouble gobbling everything up, once Mrs. Allen explained that it was just fine to pick up the chicken with our hands. But at the end of the entrée, she placed little bowls of water in front of everyone. Mak picked up his bowl and took a sip, but I waited, assessing the situation. My sister had trained me in the basics of what you might call "etiquette," even if we didn't own fancy things, and I whispered to Mak, "I think it's a finger bowl. Put it down."

"Hah?" Mak said, still sipping.

I tilted my head toward Mrs. Allen, who smiled at us as she dipped the fingertips of one hand at a time into the water and then dried them on her napkin. I began shaking with laughter, afraid I would pee in my pants if I didn't let out some air, and Mak guffawed.

"Just don't know," Mak said to our hosts. "Gotta learn, eh."

The Allens broke up, saying no one was born knowing these things, including themselves, for goodness sake.

Mak and I dug into the pecan pie and coffee that ended the meal with relief, and we felt so good that we joked around with both Caucasians and Negroes on the bus ride back to camp. A couple of Negro soldiers told us that they and their comrades were from the Midwest, unfamiliar with the Jim Crow attitudes that ruled both the South and the Army, and we grew serious as they talked. Even their blood banks were segregated.

Most other Negroes had been sent to Fort Huachuca in Arizona, they said, where the segregated 92nd and 93rd infantry divisions were training, the only Negroes allowed to prepare for combat since war was declared.

"Negroes mostly get assigned to support and service, at any base. Thousands and thousands of us building, cooking, digging, helping the infantry," one of the soldiers said. "We're service. I'm with munitions. 316th Ordinance Ammunitions."

"153rd Chemical Decon," the other man said.

This back-of-the-bus treatment was the order of the day, in the Army and in town, no matter your background, they added. They were generally discouraged from entering most parts of Hattiesburg, and their USO was situated in the Negro business district around Mobile Street. "It's where we feel comfortable, a home away from home."

We told them of our Aloha USO, and as we came to our stop, we shook hands and wished one another well.

Mak and I spoke little as we walked the rest of the way to Shelby. Mak broke the silence. "Read about slavery in school, yuh, the way families broken up, people whipped, but I never knew how it still affects everyone. No wonder hardly any Negroes come work at our plantations. Probably think they in for more of this, yuh."

"So you never saw a Negro before now?" I asked.

"One. Just one."

We fell into thought again, and this time I spoke up. "Even the words Caucasians use make us feel inferior. Japs. Niggers."

"Beats me what it takes to be an American sometimes, even a full human being," Mak muttered. "I wonder if our fighting will help any of us."

A couple of days later, the brass summoned all us nisei soldiers, having been told by townspeople that we were spending too much time with the Negroes. We shouldn't upset the applecart, our top officers said. We'd have our own troubles when we returned home after the war. We should focus on our training.

• • •

Tough as we thought we were, our squad looked like a motley crew in the field, most swimming in outsized uniforms cut for Caucasians, bumping into each other, and slipping in mud. Everyone was having difficulty keeping in formation and completing the longest tasks, but I thought my school years had left me with some dexterity. I began sensing the flow of maneuvers and kept my eye on our Sergeant Ando, gesturing for others to do the same.

"Watch your sides," I said. This was a little like a football game. You had to keep focused, have your eyes everywhere, have every wit about you.

"Come on, give me your rifle." I lent a hand to the smaller guys, more than half the squad. They clearly struggled on our twenty- and thirty-mile hikes, but not one of them would give up. We marched and marched. And marched. In the light of day and in the dark of night. "Here, let me take that backpack a while." When we were fully loaded, our equipment weighed close to sixty pounds. Rifle and trenching tool, grenades and bullets, sleeping roll and backpack, first aid pouch and canteen, plus rations out in the field—the lightest men carried half their weight.

"There you go!" I followed Ando's every move and pushed men up hills until they trekked under their own steam. Ando wasn't the biggest guy himself, more wiry than beefy, but every ounce was muscle, and he didn't miss anything. He was a couple of years older than most squad members and seemed much more mature, but just as full of piss and vinegar. I guessed he was one of those people born knowing what to do, firm without being overbearing, like a father who respected his children.

My new buddy Mak brought up the rear, making sure we stayed a tight fighting unit.

I learned from Ando's moves, and I learned from Mak's, and I watched other men.

"Joji, see what happened after you did that?" He had run ahead on his own, almost impulsively, in a maneuver in which we were approaching the enemy. "You left Mak far behind, with the rear open. The enemy could shoot our asses to kingdom come."

Joji said he understood and would do better. But the next day he goofed again. And this time Ando was watching.

"Think before you act," Ando said. "And remember, uncalled-for heroics can get us all killed."

"It's hard out there, sir," Joji said. "I was trying to show what I could do."

"But remember everyone else. You're part of a team." Ando spoke sternly, and after he left, I told Joji about my quarterback days, how it took lots of practice to be nimble and quick in thought and action.

We had one more exercise to finish that afternoon, and as I was getting ready, *Whump!* I felt a shove from behind. I spun around and saw the tall, knotty musculature of Kat Kato waiting to pounce again.

Well, screw that.

Whump! I pushed back as hard as I could, just as I saw Ando approach.

"We're training for war," Ando ran between us, yelling. "We have to function as one force, from squad through division. If you don't work right, the team doesn't work right. Everyone's lives depend on it."

Ando turned to go, and then added, "This is the last time. If you don't clear this up yourselves, I'll do it for you."

We shouted, "Yes, sir," and I watched Kat skulk away. Why was he being such an asshole?

After dinner, most of the squad returned to our barracks, and Joji took a seat on his cot.

"Thanks for helping me out," he said. "Hard to take sometimes, but I need it."

"You do the same when you see me screwing up, okay?" I said. "We're in this together."

Joji stretched out and handed me a cigarette. As we lit up, he pulled out a sketchpad and began drawing. I looked over and could see a picture emerging, our sarge getting us lined up to march in proper formation, men tossing their cigarettes and tucking in oversized shirts as they obeyed orders.

"Looking good," I said.

"Drawing helps me think, sort everything out I'm feeling," Happi said. "I'm not too good on my feet."

"So why don't you try sketching some of our moves?" I said. "Maybe they'll make more sense then. You'll see what's happening. Sometimes our football coach used to map plays for us."

Joji liked the idea and said he'd give it a try. He held out his pad and said, "Want to see what I've drawn since we landed here?" He flipped a page to a pencil sketch of our barracks in the center of all the barracks around us, together forming what the Army called a hutment. Ten privates stood outside our quarters, talking and laughing as two sergeants looked on. I couldn't make out the faces, drawn for effect, not recognition, but I sure felt the spirit. Joji had somehow taken an ugly-ass Army camp and made it feel good, full of the growing camaraderie of our men.

He added, "Of course, you haven't seen the earlier stuff, what led up to this." He let me turn the pages back. I stopped at one, of two nisei hammering each other, with the words "Damned Buddhahead!" and "Asshole Kotonk!" in clouds above their heads. I studied the strokes and shadings that his pencil made, trying to figure out how he did it.

"Guess things have gotten better, except for some hold-outs," I said.

He flipped the pages forward to one sketch. "I'm not too good at faces yet, but here you are."

I looked at his drawing. I had to admit, it looked only a little like me, though his shading and strokes gave a strong sense of the anger and confusion I held inside. I told him how good he was at capturing the emotion.

"I'm going to get everything together someday," Joji said. "Real good likenesses to go with the feelings."

"Still want to be an artist after the war? Architect?"

Joji said both and asked, "What about you? What are you going to do?"

"No idea about a job yet. I just want to get back to my home and family, get married, and have kids. Who knows how I'll make money."

"Speaking of marriage," Joji looked up. "What's with Ruth?" He pointed to her photo, which I'd pinned up above my cot.

I could feel myself beaming. "Just heard from her today." Only Molly had written as much as Ruth, her last note letting me know that she, Lawson, and little Virginia were among the growing number of internees released. They had settled in Chicago.

"Let's hear," Joji said. "Do you mind?"

"I'll leave out the mushy stuff." I pulled Ruth's letter from its envelope, handwritten on airmail parchment and smelling faintly of lavender. I breathed in the perfume as I read.

No 5 Eleanor Club
430 South Ashland Boulevard
November 15, 1943

Dear Hiroshi,
Sorry it's been so long since I wrote. We have been really busy getting ready for Thanksgiving and I have lots of news.
First of all, I moved! I heard about the Eleanor Clubs around Chicago through the WRA and am now living in one that gives me a room for a reasonable price, plus two home-cooked meals a day. Bathroom and shower are shared, but that's okay. I've met

lots of working gals like me, saving our pennies, here and at a church nearby, and I'm already talking to a couple of them about getting our own apartment someday. They are from Bainbridge Island, rounded up weeks before we were, and just got released from Manzanar. One of their cousins was also released from Gila and is studying to be a nurse at the University of Wisconsin at Madison, just over a hundred miles from Chicago, and we hear a few internees have settled in Milwaukee, too, so things are look-ing up for us in this region.

My other big news is I'm working as a mother's helper for a Russian professor and his wife. They have only two children, so what can go wrong. And now I can start saving to pay for what-ever school I find.

I've seen Molly and Lawson a few times. They spent a couple of weeks at a hostel run by the Japan Mutual Aid Society, and then the Friends helped them settle into a little apartment on the north side, a few blocks off of Michigan Avenue which is the main drag here. It's pretty difficult to find a decent place to live, even in Chicago, so they've been very lucky. Seems we're relegated to just a few neighborhoods between Caucasian and Negro areas. And I have to say, whenever I go to any of those neighborhoods, I get choked up when I see a flag in the window of issei with sons in the service. I've even seen a couple with four blue stars for four sons. Let's hope none of them turn to gold, for a son lost in battle.

Virginia is the most darling little girl you could imagine, with long black hair and big brown eyes and the loudest laugh you ever heard. You'll be amazed at how much she's grown and how beauti-ful she is.

"So that's the news from Ruth," I said as I folded the letter. I didn't read her closing words in case I choked up.

I have been saving my ration coupons for sugar so I can send you
some cookies and candy. I miss you so, my sweet. I do think distance
has made my heart grow fonder. I have had time to think.
Are you still planning to visit for the holidays?
Until then,
Ruth

"She's a good gal," Joji said when I finished. "I'm glad you two are getting serious."

I thanked him as he held up his own letter, from his mother. He could barely get the words out. She and his siblings were being released from Minidoka, though his father was being held back for some reason. And Uncle Minoru was stuck in an Army camp.

"The ladies and Eddie are headed for Chicago. First step to me designing a house for them someday," Joji said, choking. "Worried about my father and uncle, though."

It looked like Joji needed some time to recover himself, and I stood up and took Ruth's photo down from the wall. I had taken to lending the picture to any man I thought needed his spirits lifted, and Susumu "Poi" Hirano, a few cots away, was the lucky recipient tonight. I was still getting to know the Buddhahead, a sharp and funny guy, a little more heavyset than most of us—too much poi, he joked—but I could see he needed cheering. His girl had just written him a "Dear John" letter.

"Thanks," Poi said. He kissed the photo once I had pinned it in place. "Here's to girls who are true blue."

He turned to me and said, "Sounds like a toast, doesn't it? I think we need a beer to seal the deal."

"Okay, who wants beer?" I called. We corralled squad members, and I ran over to Joji, who was already sketching a couple of our maneuvers, and told him a beer would do us both good. He joined in, and we all toasted everything, girls, life, girls, victory, girls. I danced around the PX as I hummed "Tangerine," beer in hand.

Only Kat hung back, staring at me like he wanted to kill me.

What the hell.

8

Camp Shelby

December 1943

By the time holiday furloughs beckoned, soldiers were calling *Kotonk!* and *Buddhahead!* in jest, and with all our might, we accepted as our motto the Hawaiians' cry to give your all in a game of craps.

Go for broke! Men shouted during exercises.

Go for broke! Soldiers yelled at the bar.

"Come on, kotonk, show us what you got," Mak called me into the squad's circle a couple of mornings before we all took off for Christmas. The day was a rare one in the Mississippi winter, dry, refreshingly cold, and "sunning out," I heard the Buddhaheads say. We stood in front of our barracks, and high spirits abounded, everyone eager to see families and friends.

"Let's go, Hiroshi," the squad pressed me.

I waited as Poi Hirano ran to the center of our circle, back to his old self. We had completed training at squad, platoon, company, and battalion levels, and this morning we were showing one another what we could do as individuals, the way we would show the Jerries.

Poi called Mak into the circle to demonstrate how *jujitsu* could protect a guy. Poi's legs became flying scissors and grabbed Mak across the chest and behind the knees, throwing him right to the dirt.

"Take that, you Jerry bastard!" we yelled. We were intent on using lessons learned from our parents, enemy aliens that they were, to defend our country.

From the ground, Mak sputtered as he turned onto his back, holding his crotch. "Hey, you try *karang* my *alas*?"

Everyone roared. Several ran to give Mak a hand up. His face was flushed from the force of the fall, and red dirt covered the thick brows that arched over his eyes.

"Brahs hurt family jewels," Mak explained the obvious as he stood next to me. With half our squad from the islands, I had no shortage of tutors in their pidgin, the easiest words becoming ours, part of being in the 442nd. We kotonks began understanding sentences with skipped verbs and words like "dat" for "that," "beeeg" for "big," "t'ree" for "three," and "da kine" for anything you wanted. We followed the Buddhaheads in calling ourselves AJAs sometimes, Americans of Japanese Ancestry. "Nisei" sounded too Japanese now.

"Come on, Sarge, your turn," the men called for Ando. He stood across from me.

"You, too." Mak pressed me toward the center, but I hesitated.

I knew what was coming. We had seen our sarge perform his *seoinage*, where you twist under your opponent's front, lift him, and throw him over your shoulder by one arm. That's what they wanted Ando to do to me, to get me *huli*, flipped.

"Show what us kotonks got!" Joji nudged me.

"Thanks for the vote of confidence," I laughed. "Are you leading me to the slaughter or what?"

"Come on," he yelled again. "Give him all you got."

I looked at Ando with caution.

"Hiro!" Mak called out to me.

"Hiro!" Poi echoed him.

I stopped for a second. Buddhaheads were giving everyone nicknames, some that captured a guy's looks or personality, some that were shortened versions of our names. Whatever—Sam, Shorty, Stink Eye, Musubi Head, Mutt, Gramps—they were part of belonging to the 442nd, and I had just been called "Hiro," one of the fold now. Silently, I vowed to live up to the sound of my new name.

"Hiro, get your butt out there," Mak hollered. He gave me a good shove, and I felt Ando sizing me up. I had several inches and at least thirty pounds on him.

He waved me toward him, and I took my cue. What the hell. I ran around the inside of the circle, motioning my buddies to raise their voices as I neared the center.

"Okay, let's give it a go." Ando bowed. I rubbed my hands together.

We squared off, waiting, assessing.

Suddenly Ando spun around, leaned his back against my torso, and grasped one of my arms. Sensing the flip coming, I grabbed my sarge around the waist and lifted him in the air. To prolonged applause and whooping, I let Ando down nice and gentle, and we slapped each other on the back and shook hands.

"Son of a gun," Ando grinned. "Good work."

I wondered if I'd done right.

"You wiry buggah, you," I tried out my best pidgin. "You caught me by surprise. I didn't know what else to do."

"You were perfect," Ando said. "Moved on instinct and got me off my feet. Good job."

I breathed easier, knowing that Ando wasn't angry.

After a few hours out on the training fields, Ando called an end to exercises and told us to clean things up. Everyone joked as we worked, only Kat holding back as he looked stink eye at me again.

He pushed me.

Damn.

Before I could even make a move, Ando pulled us aside.

"Look, this has nothing to do with you outsmarting me earlier, Koga. So listen up, both of you."

Ando turned to Kat. "You know us Hawaii men can't get back home. So I'm visiting Jerome at the new year," he said. "And guess what? You're coming with me."

Then he focused on me. "And so are you."

I returned to our barracks in a funk.

"That's tough," Joji said of my situation. "Spending time with your sarge instead of making out with your girl."

"Guess it's Kat's turn to cut the rug," Mak said.

I lit a cigarette as we talked. Girls from Jerome and Rohwer, the nearest internments camps, had visited Shelby for dances since everyone arrived, but the brass, afraid nisei couldn't fight the enemy if we didn't stop fighting each other, started busing the Buddhaheads to dances in the camps, too. The more the men saw the conditions we had volunteered from, the more smoothly training went. The Buddhaheads even understood why so few of us, around twelve hundred, had shown up at Shelby, compared to their nearly three thousand.

"I'll just go for the ride," I said.

"Eh, come on, let's head out," Mak said. We'd planned to hit the town and were soon drowning our sorrows at our USO in Hattiesburg.

The place was packed, loud and smoky and beery, and we had to push and shove our way to the bar.

"Who you going gaga for tonight, Joji?" I called as I bought us a round. The guy was always falling in love with any creature with a skirt and gorgeous breasts, and most breasts looked pretty damned exquisite. The girls loved him, not only handsome, but gentlemanly, but it sounded like something more was in the works.

"Come on." Joji encouraged me to join him on a visit to ladies of the night. "What's there to lose?"

I thought the answer was obvious, but just said, "Don't feel like it right now, okay?"

"'Saving yourself' for Ruth?" he laughed, but when our eyes met, he stopped.

Next day our squad performed a few exercises outside the barracks, and Joji and I laid final plans for our furlough as we cleaned up our gear. I was still going to visit Chicago with him and Mak, but would leave early for Jerome.

"Hey, maybe you'll be in great shape for our last maneuvers, spending all that time with our sarge," Joji laughed. Maneuvers would be held in the surrounding De Soto National Forest after the holidays, the final exercise that put us to a realistic test of war. God knows what was in store after that.

Joji saw how disappointed I was and stopped his joking. "Look, Ando and I met up on furlough in New York, you know, before you got to Shelby. He's a really decent man, and fun. He even met my sister, the one who broke out of Japantown. We all went to dinner and had a great time. You'll be okay."

My spirits revived. Maybe this wouldn't be the end of the world.

"Hey, did they find anything in your short-arm inspection?" I kidded Joji as we worked. Like any other soldier who'd been to a brothel, he'd had his precious parts checked out by medics.

I lifted a snake from the ground with a rifle and said, "This guy's not so short!" before throwing it away from us.

"Eh, screw you." Joji made a face. "At least my dick don't have poison ivy all over it." Joji socked me in the stomach, and we scuffled for a couple of minutes. Soon after I landed at Shelby, I had, without knowing it, handled poison ivy before taking a leak one day.

Never made that mistake again.

Someone called Joji into the barracks, and he gave me the finger as I called, "Up yours."

I finished clearing the equipment with a couple of other privates, a little annoyed that Joji hadn't stuck around to complete the job. The guy sure had come out of his shell, volunteering and stepping up to the plate, but sometimes I felt I was as much a big brother as a friend, one who needed to nudge the kid now and then to see things through.

Work done, I leaned against our barracks while I had a smoke, cleaning my glasses with the end of my shirt. I didn't see Mak waving at me just a few yards away until I put them back on.

"Hey, kotonk," Mak said as I walked over to him, "you blind with no specs? How you pass test?"

I told him about Joji and the eye chart, but Mak's laugh didn't make up for his obvious concern. With his promotion, he had to think of the safety of every man in our squad.

"Look, I would have done anything to be in the Army, but I sure as hell wouldn't endanger our buddies," I said. I was coming to admire Mak as a leader as well as a pal. He had even learned to give orders in clear English. The guys from the most remote areas of Hawaii seemed to speak the most incomprehensible pidgin, so this was a bit of an accomplishment.

"Anyway, the Army's given me a million extra pairs of glasses in case mine get blown off."

"One," Mak said. "You get one extra pair. You sure that's not a problem?"

"Don't worry," I said.

. . .

After chow, Joji and I decided to get a beer, and he told me that he had been called a new name, too. "Happi," he said.

"Hoppy? Like you're a rabbit?"

He laughed. "No, like *hapa* haole, because the Buddhaheads think I look half Caucasian, hapa haole." He was silent for a few seconds before he added, "Tell you the truth, I'm not too hot about the sound of it, like a happi coat. Like I'm dancing with the dead."

"Oh, come on, Blockhead," I said as we pushed our way to the bar. "Remember a lot of the coats have *kanji* for long life on them. And we have fun at those dances."

Seeing he still looked down, I added, "And think of the hops in a good beer." I gestured to the brews around us. "The sound's the same, and all good things come with it. That should make you, well, hoppy-er, yes? Happi-er."

"I like that," Joji-Happi laughed. "Happi it is."

. . .

The next day we repeated our exercises, and Happi called from the barracks as Mak and I finished clearing the field.

"Hey, get in here." Happi propped open the plywood covering a barracks window. We had just repaired it, along with the door, which had become dislocated from its hinges. We didn't know who had moved into all the new barracks built since war was declared—many to replace tents, no less crumbling buildings—but it sure wasn't us. "We have something for Ando."

"What you guys eating?" I asked as we walked inside. Everyone was stuffing something in their mouths, laughing and wiping crumbs from their lips as they chewed. We never had enough food and grabbed at the chance to eat anything.

"Cake—it's Ando's cake," Tiny said between bites. No imagination in that nickname. Taro "Tiny" Hayashi was all of four foot ten inches and confounded even the best of Army tailors. He'd skirted by Army rules when the number of nisei signing up on the Big Island overwhelmed recruiters, who threw up their hands and tossed out the physical exam. Ten thousand Buddhaheads had volunteered to show their patriotism and, yes, for some, to escape the confines of the plantation while doing so. Less than a third made the cut. "Come on, eat up."

Mak and I snatched cake from this hand and that as we learned of the squad's plot.

"We're going to put one piece back in the box, seal it up, and tell Ando he has a package waiting for him," Tiny said.

Tiny positioned the cake just so, and everyone helped tape the box shut. I carefully placed it on a shelf above Ando's cot while Happi acted as lookout at the window, licking his fingers.

Half an hour passed and no alert.

Then another half hour.

"He's coming," Happi whispered from the window. "Act relaxed."

Everyone hit their cots and pulled out books and letters from home, pretending to read as Ando entered.

"Oh, Sarge, you have a package." Poi sounded casual as he spoke up. "Got it from Red Cross."

Ando beamed. "Oh, boy, Christmas will be here before you know it. What did I get?"

I watched Ando, guessing what passed through his mind as he took the pastry box from the shelf. *Doesn't feel heavy enough to be cake, right? Hmmm.*

Looking puzzled, Ando opened the box.

There lay a sliver of golden cake.

Ando turned to us as we burst out laughing.

"Some *ono*, Sarge," Tiny said. Really delicious.

"Hey, guys, thanks for saving me a piece." Ando eyed the treat.

"Mele Kalikimaka!" Buddhaheads called "Merry Christmas" to our sarge.

"You give one bad haircut if we're not nice, eh?" Mak said. Ando, who had an impressively thick head of hair, had become the squad's unofficial barber and improved his aim with every trim, shaving closely around the sides of the head and leaving as much on top as the Army allowed. He left my pompadour intact.

"Yeah, well, I'm gonna down this now, just in case your 'nice' runs out." Ando munched away as we surrounded him. I knew being a squad leader must be tough, and not everyone could walk the line between being a sarge and one of the guys. Ando was doing a good job.

After dessert and dinner, in that order, Ando told us to relax and get plenty of sleep. A bunch of us hit the PX, more crowded than ever as we neared furlough.

"Hey, good to see you." I spotted Wes Inada, now a staff sergeant in the 2nd Battalion's Company E. "What you doing here?" I clapped him on the back as Happi handed me a beer.

"Looking for a friend, before we head out," Wes said. He told me one of his brothers, Glenn, had landed in Company M, the other in the MIS, and then introduced his buck sergeant, Bert Noritake.

"I hoped they'd make me a medic," Bert yelled over the hubbub, "but your friend here is great to serve with." He had his sights set on becoming a doctor after the war.

Hearing those words, Happi pulled a sketchpad from his pocket as he told Bert that he wanted to learn anatomy to improve his drawing. The Buddhahead said he'd already been studying the subject in college.

"Don't know how much longer we're here, but I'd be happy to give you some pointers," Bert said.

"Fantastic." Happi thanked his new friend.

Back in our barracks, someone thought that a game of craps was in order, and the Buddhaheads grabbed money that their parents had given them, bills overprinted with the word "Hawaii," twice in small bold letters on the front, once in large outlined letters on the back.

"If Hawaii gets invaded, the Japs won't be able to use the cash anywhere else," Poi explained as he set up a make-shift craps table. "But it's good enough for us."

Happi lent him a hand, and the Buddhaheads gathered round, their fists jammed with bills. As I watched, I wondered how many thought of the money as *senbetsu*, farewell money given for a trip, even if the journey brought us to war. Those guys might be backward, but they sure were lucky. Cake. Cash. Wow.

Poi rubbed his hands together as he got the game under way, and men placed bets with the dice thrower. We glanced at each other as I backed away from wagering and positioned myself just to watch and join in the calls. It had taken a little time for Poi and me to get to know each other, but we really hit it off after discovering we had both cheated on our Army tests. The Buddhahead was about as deaf in one ear as I was near-sighted in both eyes. Friendship sealed, we plotted ways to have fun any chance we had.

Men yelled louder and louder as the game continued late into the night.

"Hot roll comin'!"

"Press it up!"

"Whole lotta crap!"

"Hot shooter!"

The room grew feverish.

"Yo-leven!"

"Yo-leven!"

Suddenly a man cried, "GO FOR BROKE!" And then another.

"GO FOR BROKE!

We called out as one.

"GO FOR BROKE!"

"GO FOR BROKE!"

"GO FOR BROKE!"

Everyone knew the time was coming.

Our motto would soon become our battle cry.

"Time to get some sleep," men said as the game broke up. "Have to get up for training."

The squad worked as hard as we ever had the next morning, and we pushed away thoughts of furloughs as we devoted the afternoon to catching up with our brothers in combat.

The MIS interested us, of course, especially because many 442nd men had real brothers and close friends in the outfit. But MIS actions were kept secret, and we felt satisfied with our assumption that they were translating and interrogating the Japanese enemy in New Guinea. Bougainville. Tarawa. Rabaul.

We focused our attention on the 100th, which had left Shelby weeks before I joined the 442nd. We knew their performance would influence our own future and might even mesh with it, and soon. We had to start living and breathing battle, battle, battle.

Much of our information came from newspaper clippings and letters from the Buddhaheads' parents, who feared their sons were being used as human shields.

We pieced together the bits of news, which said otherwise.

After the 100th landed in Oran, Algeria, just as Mussolini's government fell and the Italians became our allies, a single officer, Major General Mark Clark, head of the Fifth Army, agreed to lead the nisei. As members of his 34th Division, the "Red Bulls," they joined the Allied fight against the Germans attacking Italy's boot.

The nisei acted on their motto, "Remember Pearl Harbor," as they battled over steep, rocky mountains from Salerno toward Rome. Although support from the Italian Resistance grew strong, the Germans dug in and hurled everything they had at the men.

Awards for the nisei piled up while rations grew scarce and casualties mounted, and the 100th became known as "the Purple Heart Battalion." As they took on the peaks and frigid cold of the Nazis' defensive Winter Line, rain froze into snow, which the men sucked to slake their terrible thirst. They shivered in summer uniforms, no heavier weight available in their small sizes, as they forged ahead to the final defense fortification, the Gustav Line, anchored in their sector by the German stronghold of Monte Cassino.

A 1500-foot-high monastery stood at the top of Cassino, providing ample spots for enemy observation posts. Walls were ten feet thick. The Germans, ensconced on the peaks of surrounding mountains, had cleared trees, buildings, and anything else that might provide a hiding place for troops approaching the mount. Barbed wire and mines filled the rivers and the fields. Irrigation ditches were flooded. A towering cement wall loomed above the riverbank.

Allied commanders called for a frontal assault.

The men of the 36th Texas Division struggled to cross the swift Rapido River on their way to Cassino. German interlocking gunfire mowed them down, their boats shattering beneath them. Soldiers who made it to land were picked off like so many flies.

A call came into the 100th to relieve the Texans. Our brothers donned new winter uniforms and marched onward to aid their fellow Americans.

Desperate to fight alongside our comrades, we knew there was nothing we could do to help, and we pulled ourselves away from the newspapers to meet our own responsibilities on the homefront.

Our friends and families were waiting for us, and we headed out for the holidays.

9

Chicago

December 1943

Mak, Happi, and I stepped off the train into the concourse of Union Station, where thousands of model bombers flew suspended overhead. Allied flags hung from the steel columns. In the Great Hall, sprawling murals supported the war bond effort. Soldiers rested on long wooden benches, pushed one another to get to their transfers, collided as they searched for the USO café. Servicemen were visiting Chicago or training here for war, at Navy Pier, Fort Sheridan, or the Great Lakes Naval Training Station. The air buzzed with eagerness and apprehension.

We joined in the hustle and bustle, Happi slowing our pace as he pointed to the room's broad arches, imposing columns, high barrel-vaulted ceiling. He stopped as soldiers jostled past us.

"What the hell you looking at?" Mak and I asked.

"Everything. Daniel Burnham designed this, you know. Uncle Minoru said he made the whole city plan of Chicago. After the Great Fire."

My buddy was so fascinated, so excited by it all that I wanted to let him know I was appreciating the experience, too. But all I could see was some fancy carving on the tops of the columns, and the skylight was, well, sort of curved, and really, really big. And blacked out for the war.

I looked around for something I could comment on and spotted sunbeams on the floor. "Beautiful light, isn't it?" I tried.

"Amazing," Happi said, pointing up to some windows. The sun was shining through the latticework. "So carefully designed."

"What the hell. You guys gone *lolo*?" Mak shifted his duffel bag from one shoulder to the other as soldiers bumped into us. "Come on. We're in everyone's way."

"Okay, okay. Sorry," Happi said as we walked toward a grand staircase, our pathway to the outside. "Wow," he gasped as he stopped. "Italian marble. Travertine. One group of stairs falling into the next."

"Come on." I pushed him up the stairs. "Yeah, it's a really big staircase. Let's run up it."

Outside, bitterly cold air blasted its welcome to the city. Rubbing my ears, I pulled out a letter Ruth had written and scanned her words as we figured which way to turn. She had given me the address of the new local field office of the War Relocation Authority, on West Jackson, right near Union Station, in case we needed help. Issei and nisei who had been released were no longer in its custody, but the WRA was offering assistance as people relocated from the camps, homeless and broke. A Friends' office a few blocks north might help us, too.

"I think we go this way," I said, pointing east toward the city's towering buildings. "Want to take a bus? Walk? What?"

Public transportation was free to servicemen, but we decided to hoof it.

We crossed one of the bridges over the Chicago River, the damned wind howling until every last appendage froze, and we saw cars puttering along the streets, but only a few, assuredly because of gas rationing. Streetcars followed the old cable car "loop" around the city's business section. The El train grumbled overhead.

"Like elevated flumes back home." Mak lifted his chin to the tracks above, explaining how a series of chutes, on the ground and in the air, floated sugar cane to the mill for processing.

Soot from the diesel trains pulling into Union Station was bad enough, and now I noticed how dingy the coal fires made the air. But not even the grime darkened our enthusiasm, we'd heard so much about the city, so kind to issei and nisei.

Oh, boy, and then Happi's architecture tour really picked up.

The Monadnock building.

The Rookery.

The Great Fire.

The Columbian Exposition.

Neo-classical this and neo-Gothic that.

The guy didn't stop talking, all the while admitting he knew only a little about a whole hell of a lot. I barely took anything in and stopped to gaze at State Street, on my own list of things to see. Bright red trolleys clanged down the middle of the street, and colorful signs announced department stores and theaters, plus jazz clubs where Negroes from the South Side played for Caucasian audiences, Ruth said. Restaurants offered all kinds of foods, at least as much as rationing would allow these days. Pedestrians bustled about, mostly older businessmen and servicemen and women. This was the life of freedom and happiness that I was fighting for, the one I'd come back to.

Happi insisted we walk up Congress toward the lake, and I was clueless why he begged to stop in the Auditorium Theater.

"Hey, look," Mak said. He pointed to a marquis that spanned the top third of the building's enormous stone arch.

Chicago's Own
Service Men's Center
Chicago Commission on National Defense
Mayor Edward J. Kelly Chairman
Everything Free

An electric American flag, its stars and stripes created from colored bulbs, flashed in waves above the marquis. Servicemen dashed in and out. The wind from the lake stung our skin.

"This is it," Happi said as he looked all over the front. "The biggest American building of its time. Adler and Sullivan, I think. Late last century. Electricity and air conditioning and everything. My uncle talks about it all the time. His favorite."

We followed him inside and grabbed cups of hot coffee, taking the chill off.

"What's that?" I asked. I swore I heard bowling balls rumbling down alleys. Pins clattered to the floor.

"Oh, no," Happi whispered as we walked around. He told of the descriptions he had read of the gilded theater and lobby. "Look at it now. One big snafu." That was the term we Army guys used to describe any Situation Normal All Fucked Up. "This was the first mixed-use structure in America, theater and offices and hotel. But I don't think bowling was on the list. My uncle's going to die when I write him about this."

I watched Happi take it all in as we stood in the seating area. Sailors and soldiers bowled on stage beneath medallions of composers, the theater curtain high above everyone's heads. Some of the men were staying in the building's makeshift barracks, some at nearby hotels, we heard.

"You can still see arches, the gold stenciling." Happi studied the walls and ceiling. He grew quiet, covering his ears as he took everything in.

"Music," he whispered after a few minutes. "Frozen music."

"What the hell?" I asked. It was like my buddy had entered another world.

"My uncle told me some philosopher said that music was liquid architecture and architecture was frozen music. Take away the changes, and I bet you'd see that, feel that," he said.

"For true?" Mak said. He crossed his eyes at me and made a "what the hell" motion with his hands.

Happi said, "I know, I know. I'm learning. Those are other people's words and ideas. But I really want to know about it all and understand. The way art can express life and rise above it. Show something bigger than ourselves."

I loved that Happi had this real passion of his, but I didn't comprehend anything. I glanced at my watch and mentioned that it was getting late.

"Please, just one more minute," he said. "I know everyone's waiting for us."

He looked around. "The theater acoustics are supposed to be amazing, near perfect." He looked down, thinking, and added, "I want to come back here after the war. Draw every damn thing in this city. Hear the symphony right where we're standing."

He turned to me. "Do it for me if I don't make it back. Please."

I had to admit, Happi caught me off guard with that last comment, and I took a chance reaching out. "Don't worry," I said in a low voice. "We're all scared. You have to face your fear directly, call it what it is, and then get on with it."

"Okay," Happi said. "But you gotta understand, art helps. It really does."

"We're all coming back," I said. "And now, we have to go."

We zipped up Michigan, pausing for just a few seconds at the Art Institute, and again crossed the river, now winding near the Wrigley Building. Happi commented on the Tribune Tower across the street, studded with architectural artifacts from around the world.

"Go!" I laughed. We hoofed the last leg of our journey up Michigan Avenue to the Water Tower.

"Did you know that survived the Great Fire?" Happi pointed to the tall structure.

"Time to see your family!" I said. Happi's mother and sisters were renting a couple of rooms in a greystone on the 1300-block of Lake Shore Drive, east of Molly's apartment, and after consulting Ruth's letter again, I told him to head a few blocks north to the drive.

"See you tonight, okay?" I called. Happi waved.

Mak and I walked west to Clark and Division, shivering with the wind.

"You brought up near water, like me, eh?" Mak said as we walked. "Funny, no scent of sea here, close to lake."

"Fresh water," I said. At least the air was cleaner away from the congestion of the Loop.

As we neared the address Molly and Lawson had sent to me, we began seeing a Japanese face here and there, the neighborhood full of drab greystones, a few stores, and a couple of restaurants, the signs in English. I spotted a few nisei coming out of a three-story building with Molly's number on it, and I ran inside. It seemed a lifetime since I'd seen my family, and then, behind barbed wire. I bolted up two flights of stairs with Mak in hot pursuit, bursting in after one knock.

Hiroshi!

Molly!

Hiroshi!

Lawson!

Virginia!

Everyone hugged and spouted stories over one another, and Molly and Lawson made Mak feel right at home. Virginia was the most beautiful little girl the world had ever seen, baby-fat chubby and long haired. I squeezed her until she squealed.

"I swear she looks like Haha," I said.

"I do, too," Molly said.

I looked around as Molly and Lawson made sandwiches. The apartment was the size of a big closet and in need of fresh paint, but by golly, it was theirs for now. We huddled around the dining table, eating and talking of Chicago and Shelby and Hawaii, Seattle and Minidoka. Molly said that our brother Frank had been transferred from Fort Missoula to Santa Fe, another Justice Department camp, because Italian and German POWs now outnumbered issei at Missoula, and we worried about our sister Aiko and our grandparents, living in Tanna, just over the mountains from Hiroshima. Aiko had planned to be back home by now, and we knew even if she did make it out, she'd be immediately imprisoned. Kibei—nisei who took some time away from home to study in Japan—were the most suspected of espionage by the government.

After Mak called me "Hiro" a couple of times, I explained my new name, and Molly said she hoped I'd live up to it.

"I'll do my best," I said and turned to Lawson. "So when's your chance? When are you getting called up?"

Lawson's face dropped. "Actually, I received orders for a physical a couple of days ago. And another yesterday. I didn't pass. Heart murmur."

The table fell silent. "Sorry," Mak and I said together.

"Is it bad?" I asked.

"They don't think so," Lawson said. "But they don't want me on the battlefield."

"Hey, men are needed on homefront, too," Mak encouraged him. I agreed, but knew that a man not in uniform these days had to find something else to make him feel he was pulling his weight.

Lawson made a face and cleared the plates with Molly. He had already given notice at the restaurant equipment factory where he worked, thinking he'd be inducted immediately, and he didn't know if he could get his job back. But even women were making torpedoes at International Harvester and cargo planes at the Pullman factory, and he'd heard nisei were applying, too. There had to be room for him somewhere.

"You can work in defense-related jobs?" I thought back to the government's fear that we would sabotage the Boeing factory in Seattle. Besides the businesses Lawson had mentioned, I knew Chicago had steel mills that might call for sensitive hiring.

"Even munitions," Lawson said. "You just have to figure out how to make your way. We're not Caucasian and we're not Negro here, and we have to get around the people who see us as 'Japs,'" Lawson said.

I said that sounded a lot like Hattiesburg.

"A lot of Negroes traveled north to find work here, you know," Lawson said. "I'm sure it's better than the South, but things are still tough for them."

Molly added, "We've had our own problems, but Chicago is giving us a start to get our lives back." She said close to seven thousand AJAs were here now.

Lawson and Molly arranged homemade cookies on a plate and set down cups of steaming coffee—they'd been careful using their ration coupons and eking out supplies—and conversation grew spirited once more. We talked through the afternoon, and I checked my watch a few times, wondering when Ruth would get here after work.

"Sure hope we don't have any air raids," Molly said as we moved onto dinner. They'd had one a couple of evenings ago, she said, with sirens going off and block wardens running around to make sure everyone had their shades drawn and lights off.

We talked about tonight's dance at the Aragon, and I eyed my watch as we ate.

Had I misunderstood something?

Was Ruth okay?

Just as we finished, we heard a knock at the door.

And there she was, at last, just as beautiful as I remembered.

I waltzed Ruth into the room as we kissed and she apologized for her tardiness. Molly brought the food she had put aside for her.

"I have to tell you why I was late," Ruth said between mouthfuls and looked around the table. "I just quit my job."

"Huh?"

"What?"

"Why?"

I sputtered, "I thought you were excited about it."

"I was. But the kids turned out to be horrible brats," she said, "and the parents blamed me for everything, even when the children tore the whole house to pieces when I wasn't there."

Molly scowled. "You said a couple weeks ago that they weren't paying you on time, right?"

"Not just that, but they made cracks about me being Japanese. My mother said I should quit, and I agreed. I walked out this afternoon."

I cringed just a little at the mention of her mother, hoping I would get in her good graces someday. But I asked, simply, "Do you have another job?"

"Even better," Ruth said. "I just found out that I'm starting business college next month, at last."

Applause went around the table.

"I struck out on my own this time," Ruth said. "I just sat myself down and called every number in the phone book. Walked all around Chicago. Finally I found a school that would take me."

"That's terrific," I said, admiring her tenacity. "What's the program like?"

"Just what I was looking for. Real training in accounting, shorthand, business things like that. Very straightforward. And I'm still talking with a couple of gals about getting our own apartment."

Molly looked at the clock and said we should get moving. "Could the men please clear?" she said as she motioned Ruth to come with her to the bathroom. "We have to paint fresh stockings on our legs."

"Can I help?" I said, knowing the ladies would draw lines up the back of their legs to look like the seams of nylon stockings. Since trade with Japan had stopped, any remaining silk was being used for parachutes, and nylon had been commandeered for rope and rubber. Not hearing anyone accept my help, I let my imagination suffice.

Ruth was the first ready for the evening, emerging from the bathroom in those new stockings and a deep emerald dress that floated and fluttered around her ankles. My heart skipped a beat.

"She's lovely," Molly whispered as she and Lawson went in to wash up. They moved into their bedroom to change while Mak and I took over the bathroom, reappearing in our dress uniforms. Lawson walked out in a black, slightly worn jacket, slacks, and tie, Molly in a pale blue, floor-length blue dress that she'd made, lovely enough to gain entry to the Aragon Ballroom, where semi-formal gowns were expected. We were primed to go.

"You look so beautiful," I told Ruth as I offered her my hand. Smiling, she took it.

Molly dropped Virginia off with a neighbor, who was also putting up Ruth for convenience's sake. We swung by and picked up Happi and his sisters, his mother just beaming as she told everyone to have fun. Eddie, still bothered by lung problems, didn't feel up to dancing just yet and wished us well. We spilled out of the El near the Aragon.

"I can't believe it, but this place knocks my socks off," I admitted to Happi, who needed no more encouragement to wax eloquent about the Moorish exterior arches and diamond-shaped brickwork. But the outside was nothing compared to the ballroom. The dance floor looked like a moonlit court-yard, encircled by white towers and arched apartments and passageways. At the back of the room, Duke Ellington's band performed on the broad golden-curtained stage, the air pulsating with the beat of jazz. How could anyone not get in the mood for love? Silently, I vowed to let go of Ruth tonight only if I had to.

Lawson disappeared on the floor with Molly, Mak found an attractive nisei partner, and Happi danced with his sisters and the girls hovering around him. All the while, Ruth and I floated beneath the twinkling stars and clouds painted on the ceiling high above us. Damn, I was happy.

"May I cut in?" Happi tapped on my shoulder, smiling as he turned to Ruth. "I hope you'll dance with me now, even though Hiro's here."

Ruth said of course, and I watched them waltz around the floor, surprised at my own lack of jealousy. I'd come to trust them both.

During the last band break, Ruth and I sat close together as we sipped punch, and I hoped she was in the mood as much as I was.

"So," I started.

"So," she said, locking eyes with mine.

"Here we are."

"Here we are."

"So, are we good?" My heart beat hard.

"I have to be honest, Hiroshi," Ruth said as she drew closer, "I've dated a few fellas here."

Oh, no. After all this time, had it come to this? Ruth struck me as so mature now, so sure of herself, but was I out of the picture?

"But I've thought a lot about you," Ruth said.

"And?"

She squeezed my hand. "No one measures up."

And then she kissed me, right on my lips.

I held the kiss.

Did this mean she was my girl?

I kissed her.

Again.

And again.

Was she really mine?

We stood up as the music started, growing close again on the dance floor.

"I'm so glad we're together. Hiroshi," Ruth said, and I echoed her. We held each other tight as we got back in the swing, dancing until the music stopped.

After kissing Ruth goodnight, I went back to Molly's apartment and told Mak that things were looking up. The evening had gone well for him, too, and he said that the girl he'd been dancing with, Masako Fujihara, was a dental student at Northwestern. Could you imagine that, a female dentist? She had sailed by herself from Honolulu on one of the last Matson civilian cruises before the Pearl Harbor attack.

"On the *Lurline*, eh?" Mak laughed. "They made it into a troop ship after Pearl Harbor, you know. All us Buddhaheads sailed over on it, same damned ship. But no state rooms for us." He added that he was escorting Masako home the next day and would have lunch with her. Her apartment was a long walk from Molly's, in a more haole area of town.

By the following afternoon, Christmas Eve, I was getting my courage up to ask Ruth to go steady again. Molly and Lawson got the idea and took Virginia out for a walk, leaving us alone.

Seconds after the door shut, I drew Ruth close. "Talk to me, would you? I want you to be my girl, but I'm still not sure you want that."

This time I had purchased a necklace myself and hung the football charm on it. I placed it in her palm once more.

Ruth looked serious. "I've been through a lot since I got here, Hiroshi."

"Of course."

She looked at the charm in her hand.

Well?

She clasped my hand, both of us holding the charm. "I just needed time. You're my fella. I'd love to wear this."

My whole body and soul lit up, and I helped Ruth with the clasp. That's when pent-up passion overcame me. I ran my lips over the back of her neck and then kissed it up and down, enveloping her in my arms, and she didn't pull away. My hands brushed her breasts and she waited for a minute, pressing into my chest, before she turned to kiss me. I touched her breasts again. I grew firm in my commitment as we hugged, and I pressed against her.

"I think I'm falling in love with you," she whispered.

"I love you," I said, my heart gladdening with the words I had been waiting to hear. We ran our hands over each other. Her heart beat hard against mine.

After several very heated minutes, she pulled back. "Whoa." She exhaled decisively as she adjusted her clothes and hair. "We better stop. Everyone's going to show up before we know it."

"Right," I said. I calmed myself down and glanced outside. "Tell you what. Why don't we take a walk. It's snowing a little. Wouldn't the cold feel good?" I sure as hell needed it.

Arm in arm, we strolled several blocks along the streets and returned through the alleys in back of the greystones, familiar passageways for Chicagoans. We pressed into each other's bodies and kissed now and then, snowflakes dissolving on our faces and on our tongues. We met up with Mak near the brick backside of Molly's building, and I saw he had his camera.

"Hey, would you take our picture?" I asked.

Snow spun lightly in the air as Ruth and I posed in front of the brick. We held each other close, Ruth's suit melting into my uniform.

I prayed that Ando had a damned good reason for dragging me to a camp for my final days of leave.

10

Jerome

New Year's 1943-1944

Where the hell should I sit?
I scanned the seats as I boarded an Army bus to Jerome.
Out of the corner of my eye, I saw Kat looking around, too.

"Over there, both of you." Ando came up from behind and directed us to a seat on the left. Kat took the window, me the aisle, and Ando plunked himself on the aisle seat across from us.

Kat and I sat stiffly next to each other, and I breathed easier only when the bus rumbled forward and some Buddhaheads pulled out their ukuleles. Everyone was soon joking and singing songs of the islands and of our parents' homes in Japan. Ando joined in several choruses, and then I did, too, while Kat napped, or pretended to. Our sarge kidded that I should consider living in Hawaii. I was already more like a Buddhahead than a kotonk and right now knew a few words to "My Little Grass Shack" and "Lovely Hula Hands." We laughed, knowing that I'd forget the lyrics and tunes soon.

During a lull, Ando turned to me and Kat. "Okay, time to get going."

I elbowed Kat, not too hard, to wake up, and he sat upright.

And then we waited.

Honest, I hadn't felt this way since being hauled into the principal's office for goofing around, for socking some bully, or for walking Caucasian girls home, in my own Leschi Park neighborhood, mind you. I really wasn't guilty of anything bad, and I really didn't know what to say to the guy in charge.

Ando studied the floor and thought for a long time before he looked at us again, saying, "You both know why you're here. You're the only two in our squad at loggerheads. But I know you're good men. First thing now is to get to know each other better. Koga, you first."

Ando looked pretty concerned, so I took this seriously and began talking about my parents and siblings, my love of sports, my life in Puyallup and Minidoka. I even took out the photo of my family, creased from being folded up in my pocket, and showed it to Kat.

"So name everyone." Kat showed some interest. "I got lot of brothers and sisters, too."

I pointed to my parents and then to Frank, Molly, and Aiko.

"And who *keiki?*" Kat asked. He pointed to my little brother, who sat on our mother's lap, his ears sticking out of his head like sugar bowl handles. Everyone wore somber faces except for that kid, who laughed as he held his crayons and coloring book in his hands. God, I loved him.

I hesitated before I answered, trying to squelch the pain rising up. "Koichi," I said in a low voice. "I came down with spinal meningitis, and then he caught it. I don't know why, but I lived and he died, in the bed next to me."

"Sorry. That must have hurt bad," Ando said.

"Mom died just a year later, from TB," I said. "She'd been sick a long time, in and out of hospitals and sanatoriums. I think Koichi pushed her over the edge. And Dad followed her a year after that, like he'd been wounded twice and just couldn't make it."

I didn't tell them how empty, how utterly hollow and alone and sad I felt as I sat in church, saying the Lord's Prayer and 23rd Psalm for my own parents, and so soon after Koichi. Mom had always prayed with me at bedtime about Matthew, Mark, Luke, and John hovering around the corners of my bed, four angels surrounding me, and I used to imagine Koichi and Frank, Molly and Aiko with them.

Kat spoke up. "Real hard, eh. I sort of lose father, too."

"Sort of?" I asked.

"Real bad drinker. Just walked out on us one day." He explained that his parents and five siblings had moved a couple of years earlier from their plantation to Palama, a tough area of Honolulu, full of all kinds of immigrants.

Now it was my turn to sympathize. "I'm sorry, too, Kat. Never knew that kind of treatment."

I thought I saw Kat's eyes well up as he added, "Real hard on Haha, but we pitch in to help. And Nu'uanu YMCA really help neighborhood kids get along. Had good fun. Played ball. Even snuck craps."

"You guys sure are teaching us the game," I laughed.

"Big brother joined National Guard to get out, make money," Kat said. "Defended islands after Pearl Harbor, but then shipped off islands with other nisei soldiers in secret. What if Japanese made land invasion? Could you tell who was American, who was Japanese national? Men re-formed as the 100th. He's in B Company."

I nodded, not surprised Army recruiters had skipped over that part of the 100th's story when they came calling at Minidoka. I told Kat I hoped his brother was safe, and he thanked me. "Haven't heard from him since Cassino began."

Ando expressed his concern, too, and after a few minutes, conversation moved to happier topics.

"What about your girls?" Ando kidded us. "Everyone says you have steadies. Both of you."

Kat perked up. "Hisako. Beautiful. Real gentle. Lives just two block away. We gonna get married."

I chimed in with stories of Ruth, competing with Kat for who had the best girlfriend.

"You both lucky, eh? Steady girls so young. I'm still working on it," Ando said.

After a few minutes, Ando added, "One of the reasons for this trip is for you to meet my teacher, my sensei, from Japanese school, yuh. In fact, we're spending a couple of nights with him."

"He's at Jerome?" Kat and I were both surprised. Ando said he'd fill us in when we got there.

Ando asked me, "You're Christian, ne?" and turned to Kat, "And you're Buddhist?" We said yes, Kat muttering that he rarely went to church, and Ando added, "Eh, doesn't matter, anyways. I think you'll like Sensei, even learn something." He turned to me, saying, "Both of you."

Wondering what the hell that meant, I joined in the talk about this and that as the bus rolled along, Kat and I easing into our seats as we chatted. I could see relief on Ando's face, so I guessed all was going well, at least in his eyes. I'd wait and see.

Wetlands and trees soon announced our entry into the swampland of the Mississippi River Delta, hotter than blazes in the summer, Ando said, with mosquitoes, malaria, and snakes, and blasted cold in the winter. We knew by now that all ten WRA relocation centers had been built in God-forsaken inland areas, two even on Indian reservations in Arizona, our families joining with other displaced, non-Caucasian Americans. The truck climbed to the top of a ridge and began its descent on the other side, allowing a solid view of Jerome.

"See, Kat, standard Army layout." Ando and I pointed to the blocks of black tar paper barracks. Ando said the camp ran around ten thousand acres.

"Bad memories closing in," I said. The thought of entering all-too-familiar territory brought me low. I hoisted my duffel bag and stepped off the bus with the other soldiers.

"Understand," Ando said. "But I think the trip will be worth it."

As we walked, our sarge pointed to the waters around the grid of the camp. "Nasty snakes swim there. Venomous. Why add guard towers?"

Another bus pulled in, and I watched everyone as they stood still and took in the prison, thinking that no matter how well things were going, I'd rather be in Chicago with Ruth. But since I was here, I joined in the quiet choruses of *Shinnen Omedetou*—a wish for a Happy New Year given before the year begins—as soldiers split up to see friends and families.

Ando, Kat, and I approached the entrance, where two Caucasian privates asked in clipped sentences what our business was at the facility. I hated needless decorum, but I just couldn't believe the soldiers ignored Ando's sergeant stripes.

"Ando-san!" A pleasant-looking middle-aged woman scurried toward us and shook Ando's hand, and the two bowed. She ran her papers under the guards' noses, told them she was our hostess for the holiday, and turned her back on them.

She must be someone important.

"I am Mrs. Suzuki," she introduced herself to me and Kat. "I am on the YMCA and USO boards and arranged the camp dances with your commanders. Ando-san set up your stay, and I have been asked to escort you to dinner."

"Domo arigato," Ando thanked her.

"*Dou itashi mashite,*" she said. You're welcome.

Everyone exchanged pleasantries as we passed row after row of black barracks over to Block 39. Mrs. Suzuki sounded downright chipper as she told of the auditorium that residents had just built and the Boy Scout camp they had created down the road. It was the same old scene to me, but not to Kat.

"They look just like my parents, brothers, sisters," he said of the people scurrying around. "You from same kine place?" He sounded taken aback.

"Unfortunately," I said as we joined the line for chow. Twenty minutes later I added that the wait vied in length with Minidoka's. But once inside, we enjoyed the decorations that filled the mess hall, cardboard pineapples and plastic leis, drawings of palm trees festooned with ornaments. And what a spread of Japanese treats awaited us, plenty of rice, miso soup, tofu, stews, and *tsukemono*, pickled vegetables, more of the food we loved than any of us had seen in months. Maybe some good grub would help make up for being here.

"Believe me, we have had our fill of Vienna sausage," Mrs. Suzuki said, "but this is special holiday fare, all made by us."

A gray-haired man approached Ando. "Toshio!" he bellowed. I eyed the man, bright eyed and ruddy faced, and guessed he must be Ando's sensei.

Ando put his tray down and bowed to the man, fist in palm.

Raising up, Ando asked, "So how you?" That was the way they asked after you in Hilo and other parts of Hawaii, just skipping the verb and stringing the words together melodically.

He turned to us, beaming. "Sorry. I forgot my manners, I'm so excited. Men, I want you to meet my sensei, Jiro Mizuno." Everyone bowed to one another and shook hands. "I didn't get a chance to talk with him when I attended a dance. He is one of many Hawaii folks at Jerome."

"Really?" Kat and I asked. All of us moved close together as we inched ahead.

"Blocks 38, 39, and 40 are all Hawaiian," Mrs. Suzuki said. "About eight hundred people, a good ten percent of the camp, far, far from home."

She turned to Kat. "You are from Hawaii, ne? You are a feisty lot, I must say, always getting into scraps. But you are wonderful cooks, especially with vegetables. You always win our contests—"

"We are not just a feisty lot," Sensei interrupted her, laughing as he cut the air with a couple of karate chops. "We are unusual, too." Turning serious, he explained that the nisei among them, mostly kibei, like him, had actually been arrested legally under Hawaii's martial law.

"I hadn't thought about that," I said.

"But that's only where story begins," Sensei said. "When the government ship over its first group of prisoners from Hawaii, all of a sudden it realize nisei would come under different jurisdiction on mainland, able to appeal imprisonment under *habeas corpus*. So guess what? It shipped them home."

"Seriously?" Kat said.

I was shocked. "So why are you here?"

"Darn if they still send a few more, anyway," Sensei said. "I one of them."

I reminded everyone of the fate of Yasui, Hirabayashi, and Korematsu and wondered if Wes was aware of the situation. I asked Kat, "You Buddhaheads know about this?"

"Think everyone knows about round-ups, sure," Kat said. "And camps back home. But not whole situation here."

I was going to ask about the camps in Hawaii, but Mrs. Suzuki and Sensei moved us along in line. Kat and I eyed the food we were nearing. We'd only eaten a snack since we left Shelby.

I could hear Kat's stomach grumbling, and whispered, "Soon."

Kat muttered, "Not soon enough."

We went to our table with full plates.

"*Itadakimasu*," Sensei prayed as soon as we took our seats, knowing we were hungry. We quickly bowed our heads, grateful for the meal, and dug in.

As we ate, I listened to Ando tell of his life since he and his teacher had seen each other, how he had worked in Honolulu to earn money for college, how he had spotted the Japanese planes flying in for the attack, how he had been allowed on base to help with the clean-up, though followed by guards everywhere, even the bathroom.

Sensei told how he was rounded up, just like issei on the mainland, as though the government had been waiting to pounce, and he spoke of his many prisons, beginning with Kilauea Military Camp on the Big Island, the Immigration Office and Sand Island in Honolulu. "First issei treated like criminals at Sand," Sensei said. "Horrible. Strip-searched, had to dig and re-dig holes if guards suspect something wrong. No razors. Stood naked for showers."

"They were humiliating you, our leaders," Ando said, his voice low.

"I haven't heard anything like this," I said.

Sensei continued his litany of camps. Angel Island in California. McCoy in Wisconsin. Army camps at Fort Sill in Oklahoma, Livingston in Louisiana. Santa Fe Justice camp. "Along the way, treatment get better than Sand, thank goodness."

145

"McCoy?" Kat asked. He told Sensei that's where the 100th had trained at one point.

"Internment camp before that," Sensei said. "I heard some prisoners and boys looked right at each other when 100th come in."

We stopped eating, our appetites dulled by the thought, and I asked Sensei if he'd happened to meet my brother at Santa Fe.

"One of translators must have been him," he said. "They worked close with issei from Hawaii and mainland, from Latin America. Some protestors transferred from Tule Lake, too."

He leaned toward me. "You know, Tule Lake is camp where government sends issei, nisei it thinks are out of line, not loyal, like mainland no-no internees. And people who say they want to return to Japan."

I thought of the people at Minidoka who had answered "no" to the last two questions on that damned loyalty questionnaire, about our willingness to serve our country, about our loyalty, and I hoped they were okay. We were hearing of mistreatment, violence, uprisings at Tule Lake, rougher than any other camp.

Sensei took a sip of tea and told us to get back to eating. We needed to strengthen ourselves. We obliged, and he continued his story. "Then I was told I was going to be released to WRA custody, to Jerome. And while I wait, new program starts so my wife and children can volunteer come Jerome, too."

"That's sort of nice and sort of strange," I said.

"Just the beginning of strange," Sensei said. "They got here before me. Then they had to petition so I could join them. Can you believe? Lolo, Uncle Sam." He added that he felt bad for the loudest prisoners who landed in Jerome, men who met up with their families and were then whisked away to Tule Lake.

Once we had finished eating, Sensei offered thanks for the meal, pronouncing it quite a feast. *"Gochiso sama deshita."* Mrs. Suzuki excused herself to take care of Sensei's wife and daughters, who were staying with her while we slept in their barracks, and we headed to Sensei's unit, its cramped, rough-hewn quarters like Minidoka's. Personal touches included a tablecloth hung between the sleeping areas of the parents and children. A hotplate and utensil shelf served as the kitchen.

I watched Kat as he took it all in, frowning. "Our houses back home are really simple, real modest, but this is ridiculous. How could the government make you live like this?" he sputtered.

"FUBAR," I said, deciding to clean up the abbreviation for Sensei's ears. "Messed up beyond all recognition."

"Come, boys. Always cold here, fuel so hard to get." Sensei gathered us near the pot belly stove that stood in the middle of the room. He and Ando had just lit a couple of pieces of wood. "You must be bone tired, yuh, so let's relax, talk story, and then off to bed. Big day tomorrow."

We sat on the floor, and Sensei tossed blankets and pillows to us for comfort.

"I talk too much already," Sensei said. "What about you, Toshio? What else happen in Honolulu after the attack?"

Ando said the boys in the University of Hawaii's ROTC had helped guard the islands and then re-organized as the Hawaii Territorial Guard for additional defense work with their haole comrades. But within days, the nisei got the boot. "Same reason that the 100th was shipped away. If Japan invaded, the government feared it couldn't tell nisei from Japanese nationals," Ando said.

"And that's where I come in," Kat blurted out.

"How's that?" I asked. He sure didn't sound like a college boy.

"A few men stepped up and taught the students there was another way to serve, with shovels, not rifles," Kat said. "One of them was Hung Wai Ching, head of my Nu'uanu Y, yuh. He worked on a morale committee to help everyone of all races. Next thing I know, the students formed the Varsity Victory Volunteers. Hung Wai Ching wanted some street-smart kids to round them out, and I got to be part of the team."

I looked at Kat with new respect as I recognized a different kind of toughness in him. The guy had had such a rough time of it at home, but he still had the spirit to join in.

"We built roads, bridges, sewers," Kat said. "Mrs. Roosevelt herself saw us, and next thing we know, the VVV's broken up and President calls for 442."

"And that's where I come in," I said, and everyone laughed.

"Right you are," Kat said. "All of a sudden President says patriotism has nothing do with race or ancestry. All about heart and mind. Very insightful eh?"

After sharing more stories and more memories, we called it a night.

"I never knew about your camps," Kat said to me as we turned in. "I'm sorry."

"I didn't know about Hawaii, either," I said. "You, Ando, everyone."

We said *oyasumi nasae,* and I hoped our truce would last.

• • •

"Time for *mochitsuki,*" Sensei said the next morning, rubbing his hands together. "Rice steam all night. Now pound."

The New Year was a big holiday for all us Japanese, no matter what religion or belief, and I felt grateful to be joining in the annual celebration of rice, pounding it into *mochi* cakes for all to enjoy.

"Mochitsuki is special for all of us this year." Sensei's words brightened our walk past the dark barracks and reminded us just what the holiday meant. "Act of beating rice helps people think about past year's blessings, cleanse, and prepare for year to come."

I felt Ando looking at us, hoping we were grasping Sensei's lessons, I bet. Sensei spoke to our hearts. I was keen to learn.

Sensei added, "Long ago, rice was the most precious food for Japanese, served only at special times. Grains of first crop were offered to the gods. Tradition developed so when we make mochi cakes, each grain rice represents a beautiful human soul. Pounding cake shows many, many souls coming together. Priest offers mochi cake to gods on behalf of whole community."

We rounded a corner toward the festivities, and Sensei slowed our steps as he continued. "Samurai warriors prepared mochi cakes before battle. You, too, do this and act by best ideals of Bushido code, remember all the moral values you have received from ancestors and family and country."

He spoke of the Golden Rule, held precious by all the world's religions, to treat others as you would be treated, and he said never to forget that perseverance and kindness and community made everyone's lives better.

Sensei turned to me. "Buddha and Jesus are not so far apart," he said. "Doing for others, having compassion, are always important."

"But what about 'Thou shalt not kill?'" I asked the question that was never far from my mind as battle neared, and I knew it was not far from the minds of others. "Love your enemies?"

"We have the same principle." Sensei said. We drew close to hear his words. "Look, discrimination, camp, war—of course your first reaction is anger. Even Jesus showed anger, yuh, righteous anger. But you know this is tough time for all. Confusing."

Sensei paused before saying, "One thing is clear: this is national emergency. Put America first, not your own pain and anger. Time to fight for your country and family. For good in the world. Fight so ideals live. Fight for justice for all. *Iza to yuu toki ni wa, kuni no tame ni tsukusu koto ga ichiban to-o-toi kot da.*" In an emergency, the noblest action one can take is to serve one's country.

"*Yamato damashi.*" Sensei appealed to the old Bushido spirit of valor and honor in our souls.

"But aren't Japanese soldiers hearing that call, too?" I asked as we picked up our pace.

"Hai, hai. But you must not let go of your center. Fight with compassion, not hate. Then stop. Follow the Middle Way. That makes all the difference."

"But how can we kill if we follow our guidelines?" Ando asked. I guessed he had traveled here for a reason, too.

"If you don't fight, you go to one extreme. If you love to kill, you go to the other. Buddha would not want either for ordinary person. Understand?" Sensei said.

I had to admit, those were the first words about the topic that made any sense to me, but they were a lot to take in. I'd have to think more about them.

Sensei stopped our walk and met our eyes. "This very important lesson. You are called to defend good and the lives of others. That is Middle Way here. Buddha says ruler must defend land and people. You are soldiers in that defense. You still follow Noble Eightfold Path in national emergency. Maintain calm, clear mindfulness, stay attentive to what's around you, strive for good."

Ando asked, "What of right speech? We cuss too much, eh?"

We all laughed. Sensei said, "All these are principles, not hard fast rules, ne. Guidelines. I know you soldiers swear like pirates. War is horrible. Who blames men for cusses? But do not belittle. Do not be mean. Be free of greed and vindictive anger. Show restraint and discipline. Words and actions reflect what is inside you. Both matter very much."

Sensei patted each of us on the back as he steered our way to a crowd gathered in a circle outside a barracks.

"*Yoisho! Dokkoisho!*" everybody was calling. "*Yoisho! Dokkoisho!*"

In their middle were two nisei soldiers, each wielding a *kine*, a big wooden mallet, to pound sweet steamed rice. The rice sat in an *usu*, a wooden mortar that had been improvised from an enormous upended log.

"*Yoisho! Dokkoisho!*" the crowd yelled their encouragement.

One brave soul after another risked their fingers turning the *mochi* as people of all ages stepped up to pound, sprinkling a little water between turns until their efforts produced a soft dough.

"Go help turn the mochi," I kidded Ando and then Kat.

"Oh, no, you first," Kat said.

The rice transformed, everyone went into the barracks to make mochi cakes for tomorrow's *ozoni* soup and for the traditional New Year display, *kagami mochi*, "mirror rice cake."

"Come, help me," Ando waved us toward him. Together, Kat and Ando placed a smaller mochi cake atop a larger one on a wooden stand, their white a symbol of purity, their elasticity a sign of strength. Then Ando and I topped them with a tangerine. Traditionally a bitter orange, a *dai dai*, was used to represent the passage of generations, but the tangerine stood in for it now.

We talked about other symbols of abundance and long life used in the displays back home, like fern sprigs, *kombu* seaweed, and images of cranes and lobsters and squids. But such holiday items were in short supply, and we were grateful to make do with what we had.

Sensei brought us over to meet his wife, who had worked with others for days to prepare for the holiday, and he hugged their little girls. We thanked them all for letting us stay in their barracks, allowing us more time to talk with Sensei than a stay in the camp's USO would have.

Afterwards, we took the kagami mochi we had made to Sensei's barracks, where he placed it in front of the family's *Butsudan*, a small black shrine with a golden altar and statue of the Buddha inside. Sensei said he had made it from scrap wood. The shrine stood on a little table next to the kitchen area, and quietly, he and Ando bowed as they put their hands in *gassho* and murmured, *Namu Amida Butsu. Namu Amida Butsu. Namu Amida Butsu.* Beside me, Kat put his hands in gassho, too, bowing his head as he murmured something unintelligible.

I admired Kat for his effort and asked Sensei what the words meant.

Sensei asked Ando what he thought.

"I'm still learning," Ando admitted. "Today, this is what I think. We open ourselves to eternal compassion, the real nature of existence, where we are all truly alive."

"Today, that is good," Sensei said, taking obvious pride in his student.

Huddled by the stove, we talked into the evening about everything, war and peace, men and women, God and Buddha. As the time came to leave for the New Year festivities, I lifted my chin toward the spot where the family hung its clothes, near the sleeping area. Several men's shirts had numbers stamped on the back of them, and I asked Sensei what they were.

He walked over and picked out two. "This I wore at Sand Island," he said, holding up one shirt and then the other, "and this I wore in mainland camps." He showed us the different identification numbers on the backs. "Easy to reduce us to a number, yuh."

I told him about our family unit numbers, and a shiver ran down my spine as Kat and Ando added that even on their plantations, escaped Japanese contract workers were hunted down by groups of owners banded across the islands as "Runaway Jap Number 15" and "Runaway Jap Number 5."

"Are you upset, Sensei?" Ando asked as we put on our jackets. "When I think what you've gone through, what a lot of my men have suffered in the camps—"

"You are right. You are still learning, " Sensei said in a soft voice.

He looked at Kat and me and then back at Ando. "You think the Buddha kid about suffering? The way to end it?

"Some patches are rougher than others, like now," he said. "This is probably the first time you face serious difficulty. *Ganbatte.* If your heart is full of bitterness and anger, how can you engage in right effort and all the principles that flow from it? Your mind will grow clouded and distracted from your task. Energy becomes divided, weak. You cannot go forward with compassion to face ever-changing life. And that you can count on. Everything changes. Do not cling to the past. Do not worry about the future. Be present."

He stood before his family shrine. "If you do not keep yourself on the path, how can you honor those who go before us?"

I thought of all the changes I'd experienced since Pearl Harbor, one after another after another, and hoped I'd overcome some of the bitterness I'd felt.

As we left the apartment, Sensei said to Ando, "Close light, eh?" and Ando turned off the light bulb.

We walked over to Barracks 23, where the Buddhist services for the camp were held, and Ando admitted that he didn't know how he could be a compassionate human being and kill, and Kat and I said we felt the same way.

"Only you can learn," Sensei said. "And when you come home, you forgive."

Confused by his last words, we entered the barracks, overflowing with holiday reverence and cheer and celebrants. Ando bumped into a couple of friends of his family from Hilo. Kat saw someone he knew, too, a pal from elementary school.

Together, we brought in the new year with all its hopes and dreams, helping to ring the temple bell one hundred and eight times, the number representing the earthly desires to be overcome by followers of the Buddha.

"*Akemashite omedetou!*" People wished one another a Happy New Year as 1944 opened.

"No fighting this year?" I turned to Kat.

"Only enemy," Kat said. In a lower voice, he said, "Someday I explain why I act like jerk. But not now."

11

De Soto Maneuvers

February 1944

"Auwe, will this ever let up?" Poi Hirano grumbled into the forest. He marched just a few feet in back of Ando, who shushed him, and I followed close behind. Our squad was making its way through the ice-muddy swamps of the De Soto National Forest that surrounded Camp Shelby, in this, the final exercise of D-maneuvers.

As an orphaned, "separate" unit, the 442nd, like the 100th, had to be attached to one division or another for combat, even for practice fighting, so we were working in these exercises with the 69th Division, the same haole bastards we'd stood up to at camp and in town. An uneasy peace had taken hold, bolstered at a literal gut level when the haoles traded their rice for our potatoes, thanks to the maneuvering of our company cook.

I could tell Ando was pleased with the way we had worked together with the 69th men as "comrades," learning from mistakes in the field, and we rallied now to take on this last maneuver, which pitted us against the 69th "enemy."

Cold-cold-cold. I focused my thoughts with the mantra as we slogged on, Happi close on my heels. The thick woods smelled of pine, reminding me a little of Seattle's forests, and a freezing February rain drove down between the needles and branches. Sleet storms had pelted us for days. Our uniforms clung to our arms and legs, chilling flesh and bone and soul. I could barely feel my face or fingers.

Could I even squeeze the trigger? I shivered as pellets of water dripped from my helmet and trickled down my neck. Even the hair in my nostrils grew brittle with cold, yet the smell of damp pine and wet earth seeped through.

"They're giving us only the information we need," Ando repeated whenever we asked what we were doing. "We have to focus on the task at hand."

I kept a general image in my head of the three 442nd infantry battalions spread out in parallel paths as we searched for the defensive positions of the 69th. But my focus was right in front of me. Our 2nd Platoon was following the 3rd Platoon, and our 1st Squad marched in back of the 3rd Squad. Formation had to be fluid in battle, and we were on high alert. The men flanking our platoon were getting "killed" and "wounded." We forged ahead.

Where did the 69th lurk?

There?

No, over there?

"Every damned bridge is blown out," Happi whispered.

The streams below had also been ruled "inaccessible" to the men carrying supplies, even our engineers. I knew Ando worried about having enough rations for at least a couple more days, and I bet that Kat, who had volunteered for a carrying party, struggled with others to bring us rations and supplies. I had heard a saying at Shelby, *An army moves on its stomach,* and wondered how many men dreamed of food, like I did, as we learned just how far we could march on empty bellies and sips of water. Ando praised us for eking out the little we had to sustain ourselves and sharing with our buddies.

Darker dark and colder cold taunted us as night descended, and my stomach growled with hunger.

When would we eat, even get some rest?

Our platoon sergeant, a tech sergeant from Kauai, ran from his position in the midst of our three rifle squads. He took a stand between two trees, and with one hand, signaled to Ando and the other sergeants leading our squads. We could stop for *kau-kau.*

But chow was all we had time for.

A runner raced in with the next order.

We were to march into the night.

Ando sat apart from us as we gulped down our C rations, cans of wet meat and processed cheese that seemed edible only when we were starving and that we damned well better get used to. We didn't talk much for fear we'd alert the enemy to our presence, so I just watched our sarge take off his wet boots, rub his ankles, and put on a dry pair of socks. Like most of us, he carried his spares against his stomach.

He was getting to be a good leader, Ando was, after a real fast climb up the ranks. The whole squad said that before I'd landed at Shelby, he had mastered everything he'd been taught as a private and had impressed his own sergeant with the common-sense way he rolled his pack blanket tighter than the other men had. As training grew tougher, he offered a suggestion for avoiding a sniper's bullet if you'd been wounded and hit the ground. Why not roll to the side, out of his sights, Ando had reasoned. That would make the guy take time to get you in his scope again, and in battle, time was everything. Next thing he knew, he was a corporal, and then a buck sergeant, and now a staff sergeant, leading our whole damned squad as he followed the command of our platoon sergeant.

"What you thinking?" Happi whispered as we ate.

"Right now, about him," I tilted my head toward our platoon sergeant as he came over to talk to Ando. "Now I know how important his position is."

"Me, too," Happi said, both of us seeing in the field things that we had learned about in camp. The platoon sergeant had to keep the squads in good shape, see that everyone performed their duties, and relate to the three other platoon sergeants in the company. Plus he had to answer to the platoon's commissioned lieutenant, the Caucasian "looie," above him. Lucky for us, our looie was one of the officers who really trusted nisei, and he let our squad and platoon sergeants go about their business by leading, not prodding or interfering. In fact, he usually marched out front of the platoon, just in back of our scouts. Our platoon sergeant and Ando were the men we interacted with the most, and we wanted to do our best for them all.

Left by himself again, Ando waved us together. He met our eyes as he whispered in as loud a voice as he dared. "I'm sure there's a good reason behind our orders to march ahead. I want you to forget about sleep, right now. You'll have plenty of time for that later. We've trained for this. Now is our chance to prove ourselves. Let's show them what we can do. Go for broke!"

"Go for broke!" Mak and Happi whispered, raising their fists. Hearing our battle cry ignited us, and I echoed the words with the rest of the squad. Adrenaline pushed fatigue away. We shrugged into our backpacks, picked up our rifles, and marched again into the blackness, reaching out at times to touch the backpack in front of us to insure we were still all together. We strained through mud and muck and crossed icy streams and marshes. The sound of boots sucking the mud lent a strange cadence to our march.

"You okay, Tiny?" Mak whispered. The squad tightened formation as we crossed a deep stream. While other men waded waist high in water, Tiny came close to drowning.

"Hey, give me your pack," I whispered. I took it for a while, and then passed it silently to Happi, who carried it to another crossing. My buddy was acting quicker on his feet these days, with more direction and follow-through, and I saw Ando nod his approval.

"Give me rifle," Mak said. He held it above his head, with his own rifle. Another soldier took a turn, and then me.

"T'anks, eh?" Tiny said. "*Okole* frozen." He added in a lower voice, "Think *chinchin* shrink. Nothing now."

A muffled laughter of recognition ran through the squad, and we sloshed and slogged on. We saw nothing but black at times, and I swore I could smell and hear the darkness. At other moments, just enough light came through the trees to let us discern shapes and forms.

We trudged on. Even after all our months of training, our legs ached as we marched without rest.

The forest brightened with the dawn, and our squad, our platoon, and our company came to a standstill. Forward observers had caught sight of elements of the 69th's rear, strong and tight.

New orders rushed in by radio and by runners. Phone lines had been cut by the enemy.

Charge the rear!

K Company would battle on our flank, moving toward the weak center to attack. The 2nd Battalion's G Company had climbed to the area and would circle wide to the right to create a squeeze.

Our looie and platoon sergeant gave the signal to prepare to charge, and Ando motioned us to crouch as we waited. My heart pounded, some force tingling deep down in my being. I swore I heard others' hearts beating as one.

Charge!

Ando waved us forward.

Faster than swamp snakes we pounced, swooping down on the sleeping soldiers of the 69th. We zigged this way and zagged that way, shocking the enemy soldiers awake and capturing them in their stupor.

Get up, you ugly asses. We pointed our rifles in their faces.

You're dead as a doornail.

Make (mah-kay)! The Buddhaheads added their pidgin for the deceased.

No can move.

No can.

We planted boots on their chests.

Damn, this was a big capture.

These enemy soldiers made up not just the kitchen and motor pool of their battalion, but the command post, the damned CP itself.

You take that, and you steal the soul of a unit.

Enlisted men and officers alike held up their hands in surrender. Orders came for the 442nd to split forces, some to oversee the POWs, others to regroup for a sustained attack on the rest of the 69th. Men who had been held as a pool of replacements were called in to finish the fighting.

"Beat damned circles around us," 69th soldiers said. They congratulated our brass, including our battalion commander, Colonel Matthews, who had guided us with fatherly wisdom and genuine respect through training. Then the haoles stood to the side, their faces still showing surprise.

We walked around, cooling down from the heady surge of attack and success as we waited for the replacements to come in. Lieutenants and sergeants waved men over to the breakfast the 69th kitchen crew had risen early to prepare. The men in this area were getting real food, not the rations we were sucking down. Better be prepared for the worst of war, our commanders said.

"Come on, let's eat," everyone said. "Victor gets the spoils, eh?" Gladly, we snatched eggs and beans and bread.

"Look at that," I muttered as I wolfed down the food. We watched a group of 69th men standing yards away, scowling at us. Even their commander was there.

"Assholes," everyone whispered as we ate.

"This is just a war game."

"We're on the same side for real, don't they know?"

Replacements marched in to wrap things up, and we focused on savoring the victory we had won.

• • •

Back at camp, we cleaned and re-cleaned our rifles, sometimes with our eyes closed, and the tales about our exploits grew.

We got 'em the hell up, we got 'em the hell up, we got 'em the hell up on that morning, Happi sang, and we joined in. The accolades pouring in from the 69th encouraged taller tales and we pushed aside thoughts of the sour soldiers.

We knew time was running out. Trips into town were plenty, beer flowing and men glowing as we ogled the girls. Only a few soldiers swung out of control, hauled back to camp by MPs or disciplined by their sergeants or lieutenants, and one of them drew our squad close together in anger, aware for perhaps the first time just how tight and pumped up a unit we had become.

A private in our 2ⁿᵈ squad returned to his barracks so plowed late one night that he stumbled and grumbled up the stairs to his barracks, directly across from us.

"This is Sergeant Ando. Quiet! My men are trying to sleep," Ando yelled out the window. We jumped to his support, half awake.

"Eh, fuck you!" the man growled.

Amid mutters of "The guy should shut the hell up" and "Screw him," Ando let the show of insubordination go as we stayed close.

"The guy's bombed," he said. "Let him sleep it off."

"Jerk tried to borrow my jeep yesterday. Wanted booze," Vic Abe, a jeep driver housed with us infantrymen, said as he made out the soldier's features. Ando often rode shotgun on Vic's special weekend driving assignments, even learning to drive the jeep himself.

Kat added, "That's Yoyo Wasuke, yuh. Buddhahead, but strange guy."

"You know him?" I asked. Kat and I were still feeling each other out, but getting on better terms.

"Just from the Y back home. Kept to himself a lot even then."

"Glad he's not in our squad. Bad enough we have to fight next to him," Ando said. "Let's get some sleep."

"We're with you, Sarge," Happi said as we headed back to our cots. "We'll beat the snot out of him if he does that again."

• • •

In the days that followed, we drank and we danced, Happi took a few anatomy lessons from Wes's friend, Bert Noritake, and we played endless pick-up games of touch football. Joining in the fun was First Lieutenant Jack Stewart, a man the Buddhaheads in the

100th had loved even before the war, when he served with them at Schofield Military Barracks in Honolulu. Second Lieutenant Brad Donnelly came by, too, much to our delight, the Georgia native always ready to crack a smile, reassuring us that there really were some good haoles and Southerners. Both officers respected us for our tenacity and courage, appreciating how different we were from the Japanese nationals, those *boburas* we *all* hated, and we hoped they would fight alongside us, wherever we went.

We used the time to catch up on correspondence and the news, too, the war growing more complicated and more personal by the day. January 1944 had seen the reinstitution of the draft for AJAs, men leaving their families behind barbed wire to serve, just as we volunteers had, except the action was compulsory now. I could only imagine the debates going on in the camps. Monte Cassino turned into hell on earth for the 100th, the men of Company B mowed down as they tried to maneuver long ladders to climb the monastery's wall. Kat said he'd just heard from his brother, a member of that company. The guy was shaken to his core but in one piece.

The battalion had been oversized when it began, with six companies, not four, because the government had jammed in all the nisei available. Now only five hundred men remained.

"We can't let up," Ando said. It seemed a lot of Army time was spent waiting, but Ando tried to keep us focused and hungry for action, making us work hard in daily exercises. We stayed in good shape, and General George Marshall, Army Chief of Staff, inspected the entire 442nd and declared us in fine fettle.

So fine, that on the Ides of March, we were ordered to prepare to ship out to Hampton Roads, Virginia, where we would board Liberty ships headed overseas. More than one hundred fifty men from our 1st Battalion had just left to replace soldiers in the 100th, and the rest of us were primed to show what we could do.

What began as thirty or forty soldiers grew into hundreds as we gathered together in the realization that we were actually shipping out, and several began singing a new 442nd song that some boys in L Company had written. During the summer, they had guarded German POWs working and singing in the peanut fields around Shelby, and the Buddhaheads had borrowed the Germans' "lai-lai" for the chorus.

"Come on, Hiro, you can at least sing the lai-lai-lai," Happi kidded me.

"Let's give it a go," I laughed. I tried to keep up with the words the men around me were singing, all to the tune of the Coast Guard's *Semper Paratus*, and I lala'd and lai-lai'd with the best of them. To think "Tangerine" had prepared me for this.

Four forty-second Infantry
Something-something Hawaii nei
Fight for you and
Red, White and Blue
Something-something to the front and back to Honolu-lu-lu-lu
Lailalailalalalailailialala!
All hail our combat team!

After twelve months of training and training some more, we rushed around to ready ourselves for the real thing, tensions mounting as yet more men from our 1st Battalion shipped overseas to replace 100th casualties.

Grabbing supplies became a contest with other units shipping out.

"That's mine!" Happi pushed a Caucasian aside as they both made a grab for tourniquets.

"Damn it, that's our tank!" Another soldier picked a fight.

We built our own crates to pack everything.

"You're handy with the tools," Ando complimented me as we hammered.

"You, too," I said. "I picked it up in the camps."

"My father taught me," he said. "He builds flumes on our plantation."

New uniforms came in, haole sized, not a bad fit for me, but other men scrambled for tailors to nip and tuck, sometimes with riotous results.

"You one big *mahu*." Mak laughed at Poi, who had donned a particularly form-fitting tailoring job.

"Up yours," Poi said, punching Mak's arm.

Buddhaheads traveled on their own and tagged along with us kotonks on long-weekend furloughs to say goodbye to family and friends and girls. I journeyed by myself to see Ruth, but only for a few days, and our parting about tore me to pieces. Mak had given me two copies of the photo he'd taken of us at Christmas, and I gave one to Ruth.

"I have one, too," I said. We sat close on the little sofa in Molly's apartment the afternoon I left. "I'll keep it next to my heart until the war's over." I patted my breast pocket.

She placed her copy just inside her blouse. "I'll make pockets so it's always near mine."

We kissed long and deep, and I made her promise that she would find someone new if I didn't make it back.

She put her finger to my lips. "We just committed. Don't talk like that. Concentrate on life. You're going to make it back."

"And we're going to get married?"

"We're going to get married."

"And have a million kids?"

She waited before responding. "Why don't we start with one?"

. . .

Back at Shelby, another pastry box for Ando appeared at our barracks, and once again we awaited his return from a meeting.

"Hey, Sarge, there's a big cake box for you," Happi called out the barracks window as Ando approached, late in the afternoon.

Ando looked up. "Hey, bring it out here. We can get some fresh air while we eat," he said, apparently remembering our first stunt.

"He's smartened up," I said to Happi. Our squad rushed out, and Mak handed Ando the box.

"Hey, it's heavy." Ando sounded surprised. He raised his eyebrows as he placed the box back in Mak's hands, opened it, and removed his birthday cake for all to admire.

"No can eat without you this time," Mak joked, bending over to pat Maui, a little blonde puppy who had adopted us and vice versa. *Happy Birthday* was written on the cake in frosting, along with the names of Ando's sisters.

I think we all appreciated the difference between this and Ando's first cake. Before, we were showing that we accepted him as one of guys and as our leader, knowing he was learning to walk the line between the two. Now, we were his trained team and headed overseas, and who knew if any of us would live to see another birthday.

"Hey, let's get a photo, yuh," Ando said. "I have to show my sisters that I got the whole cake this time."

We gathered around him, and he held the cake up for the camera. Then we hammed it up for one more shot before he sliced the confection and we set about gorging ourselves. Maui scarfed down the little pieces offered to her as the Buddhaheads patted her head and called her their little poi dog, their mutt.

"No relation," Poi kidded.

I laughed, thinking of my own little dog back home. I hoped Bou was okay.

Mak and me, Happi, Poi, and Kat figured we'd grab an early dinner, and as we walked toward the mess hall, we noticed a platoon's worth of soldiers undergoing inspection by their sergeant.

"Must be the new draftees," Kat said as we watched from a few yards away. One last group of nisei had joined the 442nd before everyone shipped out. They'd been pushed through a super-crash course in combat training so they could go overseas with us.

"Aren't those men from the 69th?" Happi asked as we walked closer. Several Caucasian officers were looking on, snickering and glowering. In the middle was their commander, the same Caucasian colonel who had scowled at us after we beat the 69th in D-maneuvers.

"I think we're still considered attached to the division," Mak said. "Guess they're checking things out."

We drew near the officers and saw "Fowler" stenciled on the colonel's uniform, clean and neatly pressed. He towered over everyone, and gray touched the brown curls of his hair. The officers spoke loud enough that the sergeant could hear them pointing out a boot that needed cleaning, hair that lacked trimming, a shirt that should be tucked in more tightly.

"There are guidelines for a reason," the colonel grumbled. The other officers voiced their agreement, and he nodded his thanks.

"Glad we're not shipping out with them," a captain said and spat on the ground. The group turned toward the 69th's area of Shelby and began walking.

"Still have our country club," someone else said. The officers laughed while Fowler glanced back, pursing his lips as he eyed the nisei.

"Guy just won't let up," I said.

"Country club's not for us," Kat muttered. "Glad we're not shipping out with them, too."

"To hell with this crap," Happi said. We were already upset. We had just learned that Colonel Matthews, who had earned our trust and respect as our battalion commander, was being transferred to Washington because he was too old to deploy. And the haole officers we knew and loved best, Stewart and Donnelly, would fight away from us, leading different platoons.

"Why the long faces?" Ando said as he joined us. "Come on."

Ando began running as he called, "Last one there has to drink beer from my helmet."

"You're on!" we yelled, and we raced as fast as we could.

PART III

12

Seattle

June 1976

"Time for a break." Ruth called us from our memories to lunch, and as she set out platters of sandwiches and salads, I told Ando I wanted to turn the tables on him for a moment.

"Why didn't Hawaii have the number of nisei interned that the mainland had?" I asked. "You had so many stresses."

Ando tilted his head to one side and squeezed his eyes shut as he thought. "I can still feel the racial tensions even before the war, plus a lot of bigotry from the military haoles coming in," he said. He looked at us. "Navy commanders ran drills and patrolled waters for months before the Pearl Harbor attack, but a lot of locals thought they were trying to protect installations more from the local Japanese than possible invaders."

He took a bite of his sandwich. "I even remember a haole swabbie making slant eyes at me the day before the attack, while we were watching UH play Willamette in the football stadium.

He shook his fist and told me, 'Go home, Jap.' I was afraid he was going to come over and throttle me. Right there, in the land of my birth."

"You never told me that," I said. "That's maddening."

"Lots of that was going around," he said.

"By the way," I added, "I almost attend Willamette." I told him how the school had taken away my scholarship, and Ando shook his head, saying that we were destined to meet, one way or another.

"Some of the military's bigotry backfired, of course," Ando said. "Commanders set their airplanes wingtip to wingtip for easy guarding, in case Japanese workers attacked from surrounding cane fields." He looked around the table. "The planes ended up sitting ducks when Pearl was attacked."

Ando stopped to eat more, and I told him that I was amazed to still be learning about him and our Buddhahead comrades, the suffering they had also endured and overcome.

Shig asked, "But why the low numbers?"

Ando wiped his mouth and said, "Our governor, Poindexter, was pretty panicked, like that General DeWitt of yours. He declared martial law right away. But cooler heads prevailed." Ando mentioned several names, Fielder, Loomis and Burns, men who had worked long and hard for harmony between the island's many races.

"General Delos Emmons took over as military governor. He just wouldn't be pushed around by Washington when it came to incarcerating us. He fended off each and every demand for our mass evacuation."

Remove anyone of Japanese descent?

No way. They made up a good forty percent of the population, and he needed them for labor.

Ship them all to Molokai?

No. Ships were vital to the war effort and should not be taken up transporting issei and nisei to prison.

"People pulled together. Even the boys from Willamette, they guarded one of our munitions depots in the days after Pearl." Ando looked my way.

"So what of the prisoners sent to the mainland?" I asked. "People incarcerated at home?"

"Some people think Emmons allowed just enough to mollify Washington," Ando said. "Tough for those singled out, but one way out of a bigger problem."

Ando dug into his salad. "By the way," he added, "it was Emmons who paved the way for the VVV that Kat spoke of." He explained that once the nisei were kicked out of the territorial guard, they wrote to Emmons that they still wanted to contribute as loyal Americans. He said of course, and Hung Wai Ching picked up the ball, along with Charles Loomis, head of the Y at UH, and Shigeo Yoshida, a school teacher and activist. "Those men believed in the nisei, gave everyone the boost they needed. Not sure we'd have had a 442nd without them."

We finished eating and turned to the war.

13

First Push, Italy

July-September 1944

On May Day—Lei Day in Hawaii, the Buddhaheads said—we shipped out from Hampton Beach in a flotilla, uncertain of where we were headed.

"Has to be Italy," men said.

"The 100th's still there," others added.

"Could be France. Lots going on there."

"You never know with the Army."

The days at sea grew long with all the zigzagging to avoid German U-boats, and when we weren't playing a guessing game, we were puking our guts out.

"Outta my way!" We stumbled on wobbly legs, pushing one another aside to reach the ship's railing. Happi and I leaned over and offered our meals to the gods of the sea.

"Ooooh," Poi groaned with seasickness.

"Stop. Stop. Never do nothing bad again," Kat moaned. Mak and others promised the same.

Someone upstairs must have been listening. Sunbathers soon outnumbered the sick, and we took to exercising on deck. Buddhaheads gambled their money away in endless games of craps, their vows of righteous living forgotten, and boxing matches became a constant source of entertainment. I took on Rocky Yamada, the boxer who had stood up to Lieutenant Lewalski, and the officer cheered him on. Soon after his confrontation with Rocky, Lewalski had admitted he was wrong and joined the ranks of haoles who had faith in us and earned our respect. In my corner, Ando yelled his encouragement, though I doubted he had wagered any money on the match. He was a careful guy in all things, including his cash. I pummeled Rocky, and men cheered us both.

Italy was soon revealed as our destination, to no one's surprise, and we pieced together words and phrases of Italian from the little books the Army gave us, dreaming of wine, women, and song.

Scusi (SKOO-see) Pardon me
Por favore, Signorina (Payr-fa-VO-ray, seen-yo-REE-na) Please, Miss
Come si chiama (KO-may see-kee-AH-mah) What is your name
Voglio passare la note (VOHL-yo pahss-SA ray la NOHT-tay) I want to spend the night
Il Petto (eel PEHT-toa) Breast
Mostratemi (mo-STRA-tay-me) Show me
Grazie (GRAT-zee-ay) Thank you
Ho fame (O-FA-may) I'm hungry
Ho sete (O-SAY-tay) I'm thirsty
Portatemi (par TA—tay-mee) Bring me—

Dell'acqua (Del-LAHK-kwa) Water
Da mangiare (Da-mahn-JA-ray) Food
Vino (Vee-no) Wine

But we thumbed through other pages in silence.

Sono ferito (SO-no-fay-REE-to) I am wounded
Arreste il sangue! (ar-ress-TA-taay eel SAHN-guay) Stop the bleeding!
Scottatura (Scoht-tah-TOO-rah) Burn
La sutura (Lah-soo-TOO-rah Suture
La medicazione (Lah may-dee-cahzee-OH-nay) Surgical dressing

We poked the phrasebooks in our pockets until we needed them.

After stopping amid the wastes of war in Naples and in Anzio, we bivouacked at Civitavecchia and merged with the men of the 100th. Our brothers had spent their own May Day collecting flowers on the bloody beaches of Anzio and were now coming together with the 442nd as our 1st Battalion.

This action made us not just a regiment, but a self-sufficient, all nisei regimental combat team, with our own band, engineers, medical unit, field artillery, service company, and antitank group. General Clark thought so highly of his 100th boys that he allowed them to keep their entire unit name, so we would fight together as the 100th Battalion (Separate)/442nd RCT, attached to Clark's 34th Division. The Buddhaheads frequently called the 100th "One Puka Puka"—that was pidgin for 100, "puka" meaning "hole"—and we followed suit.

As we regrouped, we talked with our new team members, learning that Cassino had finally been won by Polish Lancers in mid-May. The monastery had been bombed into oblivion by the

Allies in case Germans were using it as an observation post. The 100th battled on.

"After all our fighting, we didn't even get to march into Rome," we heard the 100th men grumble. They felt miffed that they had not participated in the Fifth Army's triumphant entry into the ancient city until the celebration was over.

"They let the haoles march in for the cameras, for the papers," the men said.

"Only Caucasians can be conquering heroes."

"We fought our asses off."

"And no recognition."

"No one even knows."

We felt bad for our brothers, but nothing stopped the tensions that grew between us as we began to work together.

"Can't they stop bossing us around?" Happi and others spoke up. The 100th veterans were trying to show us the ropes as we exercised our way back into condition after our long break from training. We trudged up and down hills steeper than we had ever climbed and wondered what we would do for protection on the barren land around us, so unlike the forests near Shelby. But we waved away our older brothers.

"We can handle ourselves," Kat growled.

Some in our outfit belittled the 100th men as a bunch of draftees. In turn, they complained that we were brash and didn't appreciate the path they'd cut out for us.

"How the hell we going to work with those guys?" soldiers in both groups asked.

Time was growing short to find out.

The Allies were moving from Rome northward to the Arno, and we were to join the drive. To begin, we would relieve the men of the 36th Texas Division and most of its related units, who were pressing the Germans northward from Rome, and fast. Then we would clear any Jerries blocking the Allies' way to Livorno, or Leghorn, where enemy supplies were flowing in. Once the Jerries were gone, the next move to the Arno could proceed.

"Okay, here's our first mission," Ando told us. He pointed to a map. "The 2nd and 3rd battalions are going to surround the Jerries and clear the road through Suvereto and Belvedere. That's where a crack German motorized battalion is firing from the tops of the hills, slowing the Allied advance. Then we'll march further north. The 100th will attack northwest of Belvedere and meet us in Sassetta."

Ando stopped and looked at us directly. "Expect a torrent of fire."

Squad members eyed each other as he spoke. Mak, Happi, Poi, Kat, they looked as scared as I felt. My palms began to sweat. I put on a brave face.

"Go for broke, men," Ando said. "This is what we've trained for."

We soldiers in the 2nd and 3rd battalions dressed proudly in our new olive drab uniforms, our ODs, and marched fifteen miles from Gravasanno to our jumping off point.

The 2nd Battalion plunged ahead at 0630, moving close to the Jerries. Our 3rd Battalion set out at 0900, advancing on the 2nd Battalion's left. The terrain sat wide open, with little to hide us.

In our company's area, calm prevailed, and we passed our 1st Platoon as Lieutenant Lewalski gave a pep talk to the men, who raised their fists with enthusiasm and then fell into line.

Ando led us forward. I followed, with Happi right behind. Mak brought up the rear, Poi and Kat in front of him.

"Doesn't even seem as bad as Shelby," I whispered to Happi as we marched. We were attracting only small arms fire, but thought we heard artillery way out in the 2nd Battalion's area.

Our company led the 3rd Battalion into Suvereto with barely a scratch on anyone. Italians lined the streets, calling to us, their heroes, and offering us wine and cookies.

Viva Chine'ese!

Viva Chine'ese!

Oh, no. We pulled out our phrasebooks and pointed to ourselves as we yelled back, *Giapponese! Americano! Giapponese! Americano!* We tasted the treats and asked, *Dove Tedeschi?* Where had all the Jerries gone? The Italians, obviously perplexed, waved toward the hills.

Calling *"Grazie,"* we walked through the village. Just as we approached a hill on the outskirts of town, someone pointed up. "Hey, I see some Germans."

Everyone ran over to look, like a bunch of idiot tourists.

The vacation ended abruptly.

The air exploded in fire.

Brrrrrrrrp! German fire sprayed us without mercy.

Ratatatatat! We answered their volleys, firing in the direction of the hill.

We zigzagged as we dodged bullets, taking cover in an olive orchard. Leaves flew down on us. The smell of cordite and blood, burned flesh and fear filled the air.

Our platoon sergeant ordered our squad into reserve while the 2nd Squad ran ahead. Automatic weapons hit us from the north, from Belvedere. We hit the ground and fired back, to little effect.

The Jerries had the upper hand, literally, and pinned us down. We called on our training to control the panic taking hold and ran between any cover we could find.

The 2nd Squad was ordered down. Only the mortar squad was to advance so it could shell a machine gun emplacement spraying the platoon. The 2nd Squad took heavy fire as the men retreated, and we covered them before following ourselves, one man at a time.

"Run!" Ando waved us down. "Go!"

"Run for it!" I yelled to Happi. He took off toward some shrubs by the side of the road and fired for the first time, helping to cover the next man. Kat reached the side and joined in.

Mak and I had been assigned the Browning Automatic Rifle, reserved for the biggest men, and we all knew that lugging that heavy sucker around was like wearing a bull's eye; the Germans aimed to kill the carrier fast. But right now all Mak had was an M1 Garand, and he shot freely. I made it to the side and scrambled to set up the bipod on my own BAR. I helped cover our men. Poi ran down last, always solid, that guy, just like Mak, forever sure on his feet and looking after the men around him.

The mortar squad shelled the hell out of the Jerries and then began their own retreat. We covered them.

Mak spotted a Jerry machine gunner watching the squad's movement and shoved an antitank grenade on his rifle. He found flat ground, knelt, and dug the rifle butt into his shoulder. He fired.

Thwack!

The man disappeared.

Vanished.

Mak stared for just a second, his face showing shock, remorse, resolve. He checked on our men and rushed to the next skirmish.

Our battalion fought for hours as bad news came in about the 2nd Battalion. Less than a quarter mile into their march, the Germans had pounded the men from a ridge above, the Jerries' Panzers joining with their artillery to unleash a fury of fire. One company, advancing far, bore the brunt of the attack.

We made little progress in the chaos of garbled communications, incessant pounding, shuddering earth. The world was ablaze, the air thick with explosions and screaming and gunfire, smoke and sweat and blood.

No amount of training could have prepared us for this.

One Puka Puka raced in from reserve.

The battle-tested soldiers knew they had no time for reconnaissance and whipped up a plan. Recognizing they were outnumbered, they marched ten miles into enemy territory and directed two companies to block the exit and entrance to Belvedere, a third to attack the enemy.

The 100th ripped apart the Germans' right flank in a rear-end assault, clearing the way ahead for us. One hundred eighty Jerries died on the spot, fifty more were taken prisoner, and useful equipment came into American hands.

At dusk our battalion received the go-ahead to move out, up the hill toward Sassetta, our original objective, and we climbed the road single file. We had seen our first dead and wounded, men with their bellies ripped open and arms and legs torn off, calling, "Medic! Medic!" As we walked, we took in the aftermath of battle in all its gruesome reality: the sight and smell of smoking tanks, wrecked jeeps, bodies burned and maimed, all soaking up the demonic orange hue of the fires of war. Mak and Kat were somewhere ahead of us, and I walked with Happi and Poi behind Ando. We stopped at the sight of a German sitting on top of his Panzer, slumped over the turret. Ando turned to us, his face ashen.

After covering several miles, we settled near a gorge for the night. Vic Abe circled around with his jeep and pulled over to talk to Ando for a couple of minutes. The two had been friends since Ando's first day at Shelby, when he was so sick from traveling that he couldn't make it to the mess hall, and Vic had brought him soup. They stood near me now, and I heard Ando admit how difficult it was to shoot if you saw the guy's face, his eyes and mouth.

We were learning what we were made of, what we needed to overcome or build on. If we didn't master the lessons, we might as well go home—or be sent home by a bullet.

"Saved our butts, the 100th did," Ando admitted over rations.

We murmured our agreement and finished eating in silence.

Mak checked his ammo clip after chow. "Shit," he said.

"What is it?" Ando asked.

Mak pointed to the spot where a German bullet had sailed between two rows of ammo.

Ando gasped as he looked. "One eighth of an inch the other way, it would have struck the primer and ripped you apart. You must lead good life, eh?"

Mak undid a couple of buttons and opened his shirt, making sure the *senninbari* wrapped around his waist was in one piece. The wide cloth was a talisman of good luck. His mother and her lady friends back home had sewn 1,000 red stitches on the belt to protect him in battle.

"Damned thing works," Mak said. Other men who wore a senninbari, literally, "thousand person stitches" or "thousand-stitch belts," patted their torsos.

We all dropped to the ground, desperate for sleep, and only a few bothered to dig foxholes. Happi offered to take guard duty as the squad rested. I saw him feel inside his pocket for the most recent letter from his family, and then his sketchpad.

"Wonder how our friends are doing," Happi said of Wes and Bert Noritake, both in the 2nd Battalion. Happi began to sketch in the fading light.

"Hope we hear soon," I said. "Wes has been a good friend since the day we got evacuated."

"And Bert's a good man, really helping me," Happi said. He put his pencil away, giving into a very long day.

He handed me the pad. "Here you are."

I recognized my likeness right away—those lessons were paying off—but was taken aback at the exhaustion that covered my face.

"I look that bad?" I asked. I looked like I'd aged five years since Shelby.

"Everyone does," Happi said. "Welcome to war."

The next morning, Ando told me that he had fingered his *ojuzu*, his prayer beads, as he drifted to sleep, wondering how he could be a compassionate man as he killed.

"I felt so cold, I pressed against the guy next to me to get warm," he said. "Woke up next to a dead German."

I shivered up and down my spine, and then began to laugh, uncertainly, uneasily.

Focusing on ways to improve our fighting skills gave us new confidence, and over the next few weeks, we learned to battle shoulder to shoulder with our 100th brothers. Our Buddhaheads even learned that the heaviest pidgin spoken over the phones and radios could confound the enemy, and I knew they could take that lesson to the bank. Heck, when those guys spoke quickly, they lost me.

Refreshed, we faced our next battle as a team. Hill 140 stood smack in the middle of the Allies' path to the port at Livorno, and the Germans honeycombed the slopes. Some of the meanest troops the Nazis had, the 36th SS Regiment, had established observation posts in the nearby coastal town of Rosignano Marittimo to the west and in the village of Castellina to the east. Once again, we faced an enemy with the literal upper hand, aiming down on us from the hills.

Before we could take a shot, the Germans set off the Fourth of July fireworks.

Our 3rd Battalion sweated and strained as we relieved the 100th Battalion in broad daylight, climbing through a ceaseless spray of bullets and mortar and artillery. I looked over at Kat, grunting under the weight of equipment as he returned fire. I glanced at Happi, shooting at anything and everything. Mak glowered as we battled on. How many were dead? How many wounded? We lost count. Friends fell. Cousins fell. Brothers fell. A single shell downed a whole machine gun squad in L Company. One hour, three hours, five hours of bombardment beat us down, including our battalion commander.

By dusk, our regiment's executive officer had taken temporary command of our battalion and moved us to a strategically better position. I didn't remember falling asleep, I was so damned tired.

The next morning, as the 2nd Battalion made headway east of the hill, we were ordered to protect the men's left flank. That meant we had to climb the reverse slope, which ran west toward the sea and was full of Jerries. The head of our company, Captain Grand, positioned us further forward than usual, calling on platoon and squad leaders to get us ready to fight like hell once we drew fire, which we assuredly would, given the sparse cover around us. Ando told us to give it our all. He knew we could do it. He drove us so hard toward the top that every tendon and muscle in our legs protested, despite our months of training.

Halfway up, chaos broke out. The Jerries threw everything they had at us, letting loose their screeching Nebelwerfer rocket launchers, screaming meemies, they were called, and with good reason. The fiendish sound pierced our eardrums and ran through to our core.

"Damned buggahs," Poi cried as he fired.

"Jerry assholes." Happi took aim.

Mortar sneaked up on us, silent until it hit the ground. We hugged the earth and prayed as bullets, dust, and rocks flew everywhere. We snaked and crawled, struggling toward washouts off the field of battle. Reverend Akira Morimoto, our somewhat portly battalion chaplain, left the safety of the field hospital to run around the battlefield without a weapon, praying with both the wounded and those who battled on.

Ando led our squad to the side to join the rest of our platoon, but something grabbed hold of me, and I didn't know if I could go on. I really didn't. I began crawling, behind everyone. And then I froze. I rose to a crouch, but froze again. Bullets whizzed past my ears, and bombs ripped the earth. Artillery shelled us from the Germans' 88-mm guns. Ando and the rest of our men lay on the ground and aimed their rifles toward the source of fire. I didn't budge.

Kat belly-crawled out and pushed me to the ground, hard.

"Get going!" He smacked me on the butt. "You can do it. Back to the squad." Bullets kicked up storms of dust and stone, biting into my skin and blinding me. I couldn't move.

Kat hollered again. "We're a team. Move!" He began scrambling back, and I followed, slowly, and then quickly, through the hail of bullets. Together we belly-crawled and zigzagged the rest of the way to our squad and platoon, firing wherever we could. I fought shoulder to shoulder with Kat and Ando, Happi and Mak and Poi. I swiped at bits of stone and dirt digging into my skin.

"I'm with you," I hollered over to Kat. I fired from the eroded earth. "I got it. I got it." I saw Mak and Happi spraying the area with bullets, Poi covering a soldier as he ran, and I knew I was one with these guys.

I understood now.

I felt it, deep in my gut.

We battled on.

Cries for "*Mutter! Mutter!*" and "*Okaasan!*" filled the air.

Squads of men, platoons of men, moved in support of one another, and Lieutenant Lewalski in the 1st Platoon took a direct hit, not far from us. Blood spurted from one of his arms, and he called, "Medic!" into the battle. All the medics were tending to other wounded, and one of them shouted over the din for Lewalski to be strong. The lieutenant held up his arm to slow the bleeding, but blood soaked his ODs. The lower part of the arm hung from the elbow.

I spotted Tiny Hayashi struggling through the barrage toward Lewalski. Tiny raised his torso as he applied a tourniquet to the lieutenant's wound and took artillery fire to the face. Covered in blood, he fell back without a whimper.

Captain Grand took flak in the final barrage.

Chaos and valor and pain ruled the field.

How many would we lose in a single day?

Suddenly Ando leaped up and fired like a madman. I'd never seen him shoot like that, like something in him had cracked. He wouldn't stop firing at the enemy, closer and closer and closer.

We battled through the storm, and the Germans grew still. We must have worn them down to nothing, supplies and energy gone.

Amid the stench of death—of explosive powders and smoldering weapons, of sulfur and bloody bandages and singed flesh—the rescue of the living began. Men carried Captain Grand out on a stretcher, we soldiers saluting him, Grand saluting us, as he passed along. Tiny was evacuated unconscious but breathing, and Lieutenant Lewalski teetered down the hill next to Sam Sakura, a medic now, who held Lewalski's bandaged arm, what was left of it. His men knew only a million-dollar wound would take Lewalski away from them and called,

"See you on May Day in Hawaii." He said in a weak voice, "See you then!" and "Aloha!"

Our squad settled on the ground for a few hours rest, and I clapped Kat on the back. "Thank you."

"Anytime, you bastard," Kat said. "You'd do the same for me. Or the next guy."

I knew he was right.

I was ready now.

• • •

Later in the afternoon, Jack Stewart, now Captain Stewart, took command of our company.

Lieutenant Colonel Martin Edward Fowler, called in from the 69th, became head of the 3rd Battalion.

I eyed my buddies, worried as I remembered how the officer had scowled at everyone back in training, how he had derided our new men.

That night, the 2nd Battalion climbed undetected to the top of Hill 140, now called "Little Cassino," but met hellish German resistance the following morning. Our battalion fought on their flank, struggling up the reverse slope, inch by inch. King Company got battered as the battle wore on.

"Isn't that Fowler?" Happi said as we negotiated a bare ridge.

"What the hell?" Mak said.

There was the colonel, running along the ridge to direct us. Was he being brave, or did he not trust us to do our job? He seemed such a stickler for Army rules and details. Most commanders directed from further back.

"Can't figure the guy out," Kat muttered.

We hunkered down to our task.

A few units of the 36th Division remained in the area, and with their support, we cut the Castellina-Rosignano road, seized the high ground, and routed the enemy.

Not wasting a second, Ando called Kat and me over to help him process POWs, reconvening our Jerome trio for a few minutes, and I swore the prisoners looked downright relieved to be off the battlefield and in our hands. The Army was known for treating its prisoners well, for honoring the Geneva Convention, and we nisei always took as many POWs as we could. We lined up the Germans for evacuation to our battalion collecting area, and we heard them calming a baby-faced soldier who was visibly shaking.

Amerikaner.
Gut.
Nett.
Sie weden dich nicht toten.

"Strange, we were just trying to kill them," I said as we watched the Germans march away. "And now we're being kind, protecting them."

"Someone has to uphold our standards, on and off the field." Ando looked into the distance as he thought. "I just hope I can."

"What do you mean?" Kat asked.

"Something happened to me today," Ando said in a low voice, squinting as he thought. "I crossed some kind of threshold. I've seen too many of our men go down—"

"We all have," I said, thinking Ando still seemed comfortable confiding in me and Kat, months after our time with his sensei.

Ando continued, "Yesterday, I couldn't shoot a Jerry if I could see his eyes, his mouth. Today, I don't care. I'm shooting to kill, close up. I'm shooting to kill, far away. My mantra everywhere is *kill, kill, kill.*"

Ando looked at us as he added, "I just hope I can stop once the war is done."

"I don't think you have to worry," I said. "Look how we're caring for the POWs."

"Maybe that's what your teacher meant, eh," Kat said. "You know, about fighting with compassion. We don't enjoy killing. We'll stop when we don't have to fight anymore."

I thought Kat had a good point. We were killing only to defend what was right and good. We'd stop when we could.

. . .

A few weeks after Hill 140, the Jerries hit our platoon sergeant in the neck and arms, and after his first replacement took a bullet to the eye, Ando moved up to the position. Mak stepped up to squad leader, and I became buck sergeant, bringing up the rear. We were soon tested by our captain, himself new to his position.

Captain Stewart told Ando to take our platoon on a reconnaissance mission to determine how many Jerries were out there.

Ando ran back to us, knowing from Shelby that Stewart trusted nisei to do the job right, with no prodding. A pleasant-looking man, Stewart towered over everyone physically and mentally, and he accepted our loyalty and commitment as a matter of fact.

"Captain Stewart said there could be lots of Jerries," Ando said. "On your toes, everyone."

We grabbed our rifles and took off, eager to show what we could do. I patted the pocket where I kept my photo of Ruth and me, which everyone in the squad knew well by now, and I hoped she would bring all of us luck.

The vineyards around us stood barren from bombardment, the branches gnarled and dried in the dying light of dusk, and we spread ourselves out, moving silently as we held our fear in check. We looked for direction from Ando and Mak, our squad point for the platoon. Happi walked a couple of men in front of me, turning now and then to make sure we were all together. Poi and Kat marched in front of him. The only living creature we saw was a dirty old goat grazing here and there.

Twenty minutes into the patrol, we were inching toward a canal when our scout pointed into it, and we raised our rifles. Slowly, silently, we approached the canal, which looked man made and dry.

It was loaded with sleeping Germans.

Our fire shattered the quiet.

Germans jerked awake and blasted back.

Bullets filled the air.

Happi hit a Jerry, who fell dead. My pal hesitated just a few seconds as he stared at the first man he had killed. I hefted my BAR in one hand so I could grab Happi around the shoulders with the other. "You got to do it," I shouted. "That's the way." We plunged ahead.

Two, three, four nisei soldiers fell. We grew furious.

I repositioned my BAR, but couldn't find the bipod, which I had detached. I raised the rifle to my shoulder, but my arms were rubber from constant battle. I couldn't hold the damned thing steady enough to fire.

I shot from the hip.

"Hiro, use me," Ando hollered, using my nickname for the first time. He patted his shoulder as he ran over. I thought quickly, not wanting to make my sarge a target with my BAR. But Ando apparently didn't care, and I decided the risk was worth it.

He hunched in front of me, and I dug the butt of my rifle into his shoulder. What a team we made. I felt like I was entering a zone of mental clarity I had not known, sensing which way to fire, which way to work with my sarge. We blasted Jerry after Jerry, the rest hightailing it faster than deer chased by coyotes.

Our patrol made it through the areas Captain Stewart had set as boundaries, and Ando reported back: twelve Jerries dead. We dropped into foxholes to sleep, if only for a couple of hours. We had given our all, and it was good enough. Happi took out a letter and held it close before dozing off.

"Could have gotten us both killed," Ando said to me before he took cover in his foxhole. "But we did it."

"Whatever it takes," I said.

The RCT measured the next several weeks in battles for the towns and ridges between us and Livorno, and it looked like we might leave Italy not only alive, but victorious. Town after town, ridge after ridge, we aced our battles against the Germans, who were pouring everything they had from the top of the steep hills. Pieve de San Luce. Pastina. Lorenzano. We took the ground with our sweat and our blood.

The Germans made their final stand in Luciano, a vital high spot looking down on the road to Livorno. Ando and Mak, Happi and Poi, Kat and I, we fought tight with our men through two straight days of frontal assaults, land mines, bombs. Rocks and shrapnel flew all around. Artillery rained down so hard, so long, we prayed we wouldn't suffocate or bleed to death. Medics learned to wait until dark to find the wounded, and Reverend Morimoto, far less portly and much more pensive, joined the grave registration officer at night in retrieving the dead. Hunger hounded us, and we eked out K rations, lighter than the canned C rations and never enough to fill us. Water was scarce, and even drinking from a stream demanded caution. Halazone tablets prevented any living creature in the water from killing us, the chlorine taste bringing back bitter memories of Minidoka. But we answered every volley and fought house to house, taking as many Jerry prisoners as possible.

Our capture of the hill town allowed the Allies to enter the seaport below, and we thought that Lieutenant Colonel Fowler was actually doing well. His time with us on the frontlines seemed increasingly well thought out, and he even consulted with some of our men before retreating to the rear to think and to plan.

We forged ahead, gathering information on the enemy along the sniper-infested banks of the Arno, the minefields that maimed and killed.

Maybe we could trust the guy, after all.

14

First Push, Italy

July-September 1944

Our R&R in Vada marked our final merger as the 100th Battalion/442nd RCT, a single orphaned unit, and as though to baptize the union, engineers rigged up a tent shower for us. A tube sucked water from a nearby stream and brought it to four showerheads, to everyone's delight. We threw our filthy clothes into numbered bags before a whistle called in four men at a time for a two-minute scrub, so we all got a hot bath. Fresh ODs made us feel halfway human, no matter how big they were for us, no matter how war weary we felt.

We heard no word of a cessation in battle around here, but our spirits rose as several enlisted nisei received field commissions to Second Lieutenant. News in *The Stars & Stripes* and around our encampment also cheered us as it indicated the war in the Pacific was going well. Allies had won the Battle of the Philippine Sea, seriously damaging Japan's carrier capability and nailing 400 enemy planes. Saipan, Guam, and Honshu had been attacked decisively. Tojo's cabinet fell, leaving the government in the hands of Emperor Hirohito, who wished to end the war, according to some.

With the filth of battle washed away and some good news under our belts, we managed to laugh a little as Tommy and the rest of our cooks set about making *gochiso*, tasty food. They even scrounged up some chickens, vegetables, and rice in local houses and farms and made chicken *hekka*, a favorite stew of the Buddhaheads. Hungry kids hung around camp, begging for something, anything, to eat, our rations, our fortified chocolate bars, little candies, and we gave them whatever we had, knowing they were suffering. We showed them how we pickled vegetables in our helmets, using the bouillon cubes from our rations. I saw children wrapping up a piece of meat here, a ration portion there, and figured they were taking everything back to their families.

Duffel bags emerged from hiding. Footballs and baseballs and bats flew out. Mustering some of their pre-combat piss and vinegar, Buddhaheads pronounced everything good fun and told us kotonks how much the warm ocean and sand around here reminded them of home. Medics brought around a little blonde poi dog that they had adopted in Luciano, and we all felt good as we patted Lucy and gave her treats.

"Come, go beach," Mak said. We got Happi and Poi on board and packed up some rations in case we couldn't find any food, so scarce in war; even the fruit on the trees would not yield easily, hanging tight to ripen more fully for the locals after we left.

I had to admit, the beach was stunning, with really white sand that backed into a forest of pine trees. Poi left his ukulele with us, grabbed some rations, and went in search of a little fishing, and the rest of us stripped down to our skivvies to swim; there were too many people around to skinny-dip. I removed my glasses, but could make out a few bella signorinas standing and watching us from yards away, and I waved as we waded in. The ocean was warm and salty, and I dove and surfaced, spouting water and wriggling like a fish, I felt so happy and free and glad to be alive. Happi began showing off for the girls, who were still eyeing us. I joined in, rolling over into my backstroke while Kat tried his butterfly, which came off more like a flailing fish. He saved his dignity by easing into a breaststroke while Mak dove deep for a headstand, waving his legs above the water.

Refreshed, we headed back to where we'd left our clothes, dried off, and got dressed before walking over to the signorinas, who sat in a circle now. They looked pretty young, maybe fifteen or sixteen, but boy, were they knockouts, with long black hair, fair skin, and really big bazookas. They glanced our way as we grew near and then turned back to each other in laughter, and Kat kept whispering, "Wanna touch da *chichis*. Wanna touch da *chichis*." Didn't we all.

We said "*Buongiorno*" and "*Americano*" as we pointed to ourselves, but that just sent them into more chirps and twitters. That's how groups of females sounded, I thought, like a bunch of birds. We joked around, gesturing madly with our hands, and they batted their eyelids and pouted enticingly, all the while making sure we could see their cleavages, and how. And then the flock of them just flew away, chirping themselves into the distance.

"What teases," Happi muttered, laughing. "Now I can't pet the *pettos*."

"They're too young, anyway," I said.

Happi looked at me, thinking. "Could be our sisters under different circumstances, right?"

"Yeah," I said, all desire disappearing with his observation.

Disappointed but determined to enjoy ourselves, we took off
our shirts again, this time to just lie in the sun, warm our aching
muscles, and bake away as much of the damned war as we could.
I loved the feeling of emerging from the sea, my body still sensing
the swimming and floating, my skin tingling from the salt, and I
closed my eyes as the breeze blew across my flesh and the waves
lapped the shore. Everyone must have felt the same way, and we
dozed in the beauty of it all, Happi letting go of his pencils and
pads as he slept. We awoke with a start, as Poi dripped cold seawater from lobsters on our hot stomachs.

"How the hell you get those?" I asked, shivering from the
shock. My eyes adjusted to the full assault of sunlight. My face
felt tight and burned, so I was glad he'd gotten us up.

"Traded my cigarettes and some rations with a fisherman."
Poi grinned. "Come on, let's eat. I got enough for everyone."

We sped back to camp.

"How about a few potatoes?" Happi begged Tommy.

"That pot would be great," Kat said as he grabbed it. "Promise
to return it."

"This one, too," Mak laughed as he took it.

"You buggahs better save me some food," Tommy said, waving
a spoon at us.

Cleared to return late, we found a vacant farmhouse on the
way back to the beach and left more cigarettes and rations for the
wine we took. *Cambio*, we called it, exchanging when we could,
rather than just stealing things. Then we found a new spot in the
sand and foraged for wood for a fire and seaweed for our dinner.
Happi and Poi filled the pots with seawater, and together, we created our feast, burning our fingers as we cracked the hot lobsters
open with rocks and gobbled up steaming potatoes with seaweed.
I didn't think I'd ever had a better meal.

As the stars came out one by one, we found more wood for the fire and lay back in the sand, smoking cigarettes and swigging wine.

"Can't believe how tight we're fighting now," Poi said.

"Why didn't the government just leave everyone the hell alone? Why did they have to tear us from our homes?" Happi asked.

"Fear," I said. "That's why. Panic. Sort of like on the battlefield. If you don't get it under control, everything gets all muddled up."

"And look now. We lost so many guys," Mak said, lighting a cigarette. "Let's just kill every damned German. I want to go home already."

"What else can we do to prove our loyalty?" Kat asked.

As conversation wound down, I listened to the ocean and felt the wind blow over my sunburned skin again, and thoughts came that I could not express to my comrades, mostly about how Kat had saved my butt, how I wasn't feeling as scared shitless as I used to. We had all been trained to function as one, and without so much fear, I was sensing the interconnection on a new level. The grand ideas of proving your loyalty and saving the world from evil were always there, but when bullets flew and the earth exploded around you, you fought for yourself and your comrades to make it through alive. We relied on one another's spirits and hearts and courage. We trusted the men around us. We truly were part of one another.

I thought back to the lessons I'd heard in church, all the stuff about "Fear not" because God was always with us. Maybe I was beginning to understand, God being in me and making me feel like this. God was in the other men, too. Maybe it was like that "frozen music" stuff that Happi had talked about, the feeling of rising above it all while being part of it, too.

We didn't leave the beach until the fire had died down and the wind picked up, and we slept better than we had in weeks. The next morning we attended our battalion's memorial service for the men we had lost, growing somber when Morimoto called the name of each of the forty-six KIAs from our 3rd Battalion, and we prayed for the hundreds wounded, too. The numbers didn't begin to include the casualties from our other battalions. The 442nd band played a few hymns and patriotic songs, and some men formed a choir to share the solace of music. Soldiers prayed on the battlefield to anyone who would listen, God, Buddha, Jesus, and silently, we did so now.

Bad news hit me hard as we met up with men from our other battalions.

Wes Inada had been seriously wounded on Hill 140. The damned Jerries had blown his leg off, and he was headed to a hospital in England.

I worried about Mr. and Mrs. Inada, all their sons in the service. I hoped the other two were doing better than Wes. I hoped they were holding strong.

"What about Bert Noritake?" Happi asked.

We didn't hear a word.

Mail call turned our attention to cheerier matters. V-mail and packages poured in, in huge batches, and we lunged for them all. Happi was beside himself to learn that his father was getting out of Minidoka, released to their family. Seemed his application for leave clearance had been questioned because it was full of pen marks scratching out words he had printed next to his answers—not enough to send him back to a DOJ or Army camp, but enough to hold him in suspicion.

"I don't know if they could make out what he wrote, but I bet Dad was telling them to go to hell," Happi muttered. His parents had appealed the decision for months. "There's a chance Uncle Minoru is getting out of his camp, too. Maybe he can join everyone in Chicago. Hope they'll all meet up with your sister and Ruth."

"Of course they will," I said as I tore open Ruth's most recent letter.

June 20, 1944

My darling Hiroshi,

I worry about you so, now that you are in battle, somewhere far away. I read about the war in the newspapers and pray for you every night. I know God will watch over you. Take care of yourself, darling, so I can hold you in my arms again, once this horrible war is done. And I hear some people think it will be over soon!

Our news must seem so mundane and self-centered, after all the fighting you have been going through, but I bet you still want to hear what's been happening at home. Virginia is getting bigger and prettier by the day, and she's learning lots of new words. She'll be two years old in a couple of months. Can you believe it? Molly is very busy taking care of her and has made lots of friends in a church she and Lawson have started attending. He finally found a new job at Curtiss Candy, where many nisei work. He says the company is even making malted milk tablets for K rations, so think of him when you eat them.

Recently Chicago had quite a stink with our old catalog company, Montgomery Ward, whose board didn't stop a strike as the War Labor Board had ordered. I guess the store's chairman, Sewell Avery, really doesn't like the growing power of the unions and wouldn't cooperate, even though the government said he was impeding the flow of essential goods. So the government took control of the store, and The Chicago Daily News showed a photo of two National Guard MPs carrying Avery, seated on their hands. A tempest in a teapot, compared to the war, but quite a big thing here.

My parents are going to be released later this month and think they are going to settle in Minneapolis. One of our cousins is studying to be a translator with the Military Intelligence Service in Fort Snelling, not too far away. The school just moved there to bigger quarters, I hear, so I hope the whole area is friendly to AJAs. And guess what? My mother actually asked after you and hopes you are doing well. How about that?

I'm studying hard and once I graduate, I hope to begin full-time work at a milliner's that I've spoken with, Goldstein-O'Connor Millinery Company, at 18 South Michigan. It will be grand to work at a real job and earn some serious money!

I miss you so, and I think of the way we danced under the stars at the Aragon, the way we held each other close, the way we kissed good-bye. I have sewn pockets inside all my clothes, and our photo is next to my heart, always. I know we will be in each other's arms soon.

Affectionately,
Ruth

I leaned back, lost in the memory of the way Ruth's body felt when we danced, the way our lips met so naturally, so fully. Laughing that Mrs. Nakamura finally seemed to like me, I showed Happi a little of what I wrote back to Ruth, focused only on the fun times.

We're finally having an R&R in a beautiful part of Italy. My pals and I went swimming in the ocean near our camp, and Happi tried to make up to a group of pretty signorinas. They would have none of his advances, and he drowned his sorrow in wine, which is really delicious here, and he and a bunch of us made a really great feast right on the beach, with fresh lobsters and the works. Other guys set off grenades in the water and concussed the fish to bring them to the surface, so a lot of us are eating like kings.

I love hearing all your news so don't worry about being mundane. Normal life is what we're fighting for over here, and we can't wait to come back home and get things back to normal again, and even *better than normal. And I just know the war will be over sooner than you think.*

Over chow one night, Ando said that he'd received a letter from Sensei, who was about to be transferred because Jerome was closing, the last camp to open and the first to shut its doors. Sensei didn't know where he was headed, and he actually hoped it wouldn't be back home. Hawaii had stopped sending issei and nisei to the mainland soon after we visited him, confining about twelve hundred of them in the broiling hot gulch of Honouliuli, along with German Americans and thousands of POWs from Japan, Okinawa, Korea, Taiwan. Prisoners cursed the place as *jigoku dani,* hell valley.

· · ·

On August 1, we prepared for battle once more, and Ando introduced us to a new member of our platoon. Ben Honda was a strapping Buddhahead who had just been transferred from our heavy weapons company M because he'd gotten into a brawl in town with some Italians. He'd received a summary court-martial.

"Ando thinks Ben Honda's a snafu guy," one of our men said.

"Heard Sarge doesn't want him in the platoon," another added.

"Stewart's making Ando take the guy."

"What squad's he been assigned to?"

"Third. They're making him a BAR man."

"Taking his friend's place." The last carrier, shot dead by the Germans, had apparently been Honda's good pal back home.

As we headed out, we heard Honda talking to Ando. "I'm really not a bad guy," he said. "I'll keep my nose clean."

We'd see about that.

. . .

The Germans had been pushed to the south side of the Arno, and our next orders were to chase them across the river. The 100th was reassigned to IV Corps to cross around Pisa, and we were assigned to II Corps to cross near Florence.

Mak grabbed his rifle and took the position of 1st Scout to probe our path along a steep slope toward the river, about three miles toward enemy territory. I helped lead our squad in Mak's stead, with Happi following close on my heels, Poi bringing up the rear. We kept Mak within our sights as much as we could.

Just as we thought the path was clear, we saw a German pop up at Mak's side.

Mak and the Jerry fired at each other, and Mak tumbled head over heels down the slope. The German took off. We raced after the bastard, following Mak's path.

We spotted our buddy at the bottom of the slope, propped up against a tree, covered in blood.

"Medic! Down the hill!" we yelled, knowing we couldn't stop to help.

"You'll be okay, Mak!" Happi called.

"We'll get them for you," I shouted. I couldn't see well enough to know if he was checking his senninbari, but I wondered if it had protected him from a worse fate.

We caught up with the Jerry bastard as he neared his platoon, and we routed the enemy. But we returned to our company minus three casualties. Mak accepted evacuation to a field hospital, and I continued to lead the squad, soon as staff sergeant.

I looked at the new stripes on my sleeve and ran my fingers over them, filled with pride. I would do my best for our men.

But before I could be put to the test, I, too, was sent away. The constant shelling had concussed my ears so badly that I landed first in a field hospital and then in a fixed hospital, in Naples, half deaf. And then our man of God fell. Chaplain Morimoto's jeep tripped a triple-layer teller mine, the car torn apart by an explosive designed to destroy the strongest tank imaginable. The three men riding with him were blown to pieces, and Morimoto suffered shrapnel wounds all over his body. Everyone vowed to keep him in the safety of the rear when he returned.

Wounded soldiers poured into my hospital, and I even met up with Wes Inada's younger brother, Glenn, from M Company, who was here for surgery on his arm. He told me Wes was going to make it and was heading home. His assistant, Bert Noritake, had taken his place.

"By the way, do you happen to know Ben Honda?" I asked.

Glenn laughed. "Sure as hell do. One of our messengers. Real rabble rouser, that one. Always making trouble and getting put on KP duty."

"What about that fight he got into?"

"Oh, yeah, we all heard about that. See, he'd gone into Vada with his sarge to buy some cabbage and such, and when they headed back, they came across a street fight—a bunch of Italians egging on their pal, who was beating the shit out of one of our guys. So Honda and his sarge went over and pushed the Italians away and pulled their friend off our guy."

"So what's the problem?" I asked.

"Honda's wasn't done. He started pummeling the Italian fighter."

"And—"

"Everyone ran the hell away, but Honda kept at it. And then an MP came by."

"Caucasian?" I asked.

"Of course," Glenn said. "Thing is, Honda had already been court-martialed for a scrap back at Shelby, and our captain blew his top. Really let him have it. Court-martialed him on the spot. But Honda begged to stay in the Army."

"So he got put in the infantry as punishment," I laughed. "And handed the BAR." Sheesh, what the hell had I done wrong?

Two court-martials meant the guy was pretty well washed up as far as the Army was concerned, we agreed. I'd have to keep my eye on him.

Other wounded soldiers coming in told us news of the war.

As the Germans retreated, men said, they bombed all the bridges along the Arno except for Ponte Vecchio, Hitler's favorite. Our troops geared up to break the Gothic Line.

Everyone knew the Jerries had been digging into rock and reinforcing everything with concrete along that line, from the Apennines in the west and central parts of Italy over to the Adriatic Sea on the east—from the Arno to the Po Valley. The brass wanted us to break our part of the line and send the Jerries running from Italy.

But what the hell?

Men sat up in their hospital beds to hear.

"Get ready for your next assignment," our commanders said. "We're heading to France."

15

The Vosges, France

October 13-18, 1944

As soon as I heard our regiment was shipping out to Marseilles, I went reverse-AWOL and joined my men in the war-torn buildings of the University of Naples, our staging area.

"Son of a gun," Ando welcomed me back. "Glad you're here. All better?"

"Alive to fight another day," I said, admitting my ears still rang a bit. "With our men, where I belong."

"About time you showed up." Kat and Poi laughed and shook my hand.

"Where the hell you been?" Happi grabbed me by the shoulders.

Everyone caught me up on what had happened while I was gone, and Happi sounded downright somber when he said that no one had heard from Mak yet, that our good chaplain was stuck in the hospital. "Lots of new guys around," he added.

"Speaking of which," Ando said to me, "let's get to know some of them."

Happi went back to talk with our old guys while Ando and I made our way to the replacement depot, the repple depple. Nearly seven hundred new AJAs, mostly kotonks, were being processed there, and we shook hands with all the new men in our company, quietly assuring and assessing them. I had to admit, the war seemed to have worn well with Ando, at least as a commander. He walked and talked with a greater aura of authority. But he wasn't what you'd call a stoic, like our old platoon sergeant had been, the kind of guy who buttoned up and seemed pretty much unapproachable. On the contrary, Ando just adored our men, and they adored him. I hoped I was achieving the same.

For their part, the greenhorns caught us up with news back home. Two soldiers from Heart Mountain internment camp told us of fellow internees who had recently been sent to prison for resisting the draft. Why should they fight for a government that had taken away their rights?

People in the camps were arguing about the men, of course. They could ruin the reputation of nisei and upset us soldiers as we fought. But I was shocked to hear that Minoru Yasui had helped lead the JACL's opposition to the resisters. His own case had been pushed aside, and he'd even informed on the protesters to the FBI.

I sensed how complicated the situation was and knew I had to focus the men on battle.

"Resistance is their rightful choice," I said. "Service is ours."

Ando voiced his agreement, and for the time remaining before we shipped out, I joined with our other squad sergeants to get our men in shape and hear their concerns about battle.

"Where are we headed?"

"Why did everyone leave Italy so fast?"

"Are we trained for this?"

Ando gathered our platoon together. The Allied drive in Europe, he said, had shifted to France and Operation Dragoon, which had, since D-Day, moved quickly up the Rhone from the south of France. Troops were now linking up with Patton's Third Army to form a solid wall of Allied forces stretching from the Belgian port of Antwerp to the Swiss border.

"We have a good command of the air," Ando said, "but the Jerries have dug themselves into the ground near their home. We're heading into northeastern France, into the mountains and forests that border Germany. We're going to rout those buggahs."

Wondering just what kind of fighting that would take, we packed our equipment and set sail on September 27, the swells of the sea bringing us low once more.

Three days later, we wobbled off our transports, grateful for terra firma. Trucks drove us ten miles to our staging area, Septemes, where we received new socks and boots and ODs—and a breath of fresh air. The Army was trying so hard to find right-sized clothing that it had sent along WAC uniforms.

"Give me some lovin'." I squeezed into a form-fitting blouse, put my hand behind my head, and kissed the air.

"No, no, over here, baby." Poi and Kat beckoned in falsettos as they modeled a jacket that tapered halfway down their torsos.

Happi laughed, sketching us all.

Sobering us were the other offerings, bazookas and Thompson submachine guns, designed not for the distant, barren hills of Italy, but for more close-range fire. We sensed the kind of combat we would face here and said, "Bring it on."

"Here's where we fit in, men," Ando said. "As part of the Allied push, we'll be fighting within a smaller operation, called Dogface.

And this time we'll be attached to the 36ᵗʰ Division, the Texas Division. The men are now part of the Seventh Army."

As he gathered his thoughts, we old-timers told our new comrades our history with the men of the 36ᵗʰ, all of us fighting under the umbrella of General Clark's enormous Fifth Army in Italy. The Texans had found their way to France after we relieved them during our last campaign.

"We'll be working with a couple of other outfits, too," Ando continued, apologizing in advance for murdering any French names.

Here was the set-up.

The three outfits would start by lining up north to south outside the German-infested forests of the Vosges—"Vo-jes," he pronounced it, so we guessed that was about right.

He moved his hands down an invisible ladder as he spoke.

"Up here in the north will be the 45ᵗʰ Division.

"We'll be here in the middle.

"The 36ᵗʰ Division will be here in the south."

Together we would drive eastward to the ancient city of St. Dié, then over to Strasbourg, across the Rhine River, and into Germany.

Boom-boom-boom.

"Got it?" he asked.

I, for one, thought things were getting pretty complicated, and we breathed easier when Ando said that was all for now. We should focus on our own initial objective.

We would move eastward into the forests, take the hills around Bruyères—"Broo-years," he said—and free its villagers. There we would meet up with a battalion of the 36ᵗʰ men and forge ahead.

• • •

Cold, pouring rain set in as battle neared, and we felt bad for the men of the 100th and 2nd, our lead battalions, who set off in open trucks to Chamois-devant-Bruyères, a three-day journey. They'd feel like shit before they even began fighting. Our 3rd Battalion was hauled in rickety forty-by-eight train cars from France's last war with Germany, designed to hold up to forty men or eight horses. We enjoyed the cover, and along the way, we hung out open doors to wave to French bikers and pedestrians, who waved back at us. We arrived on Friday, the thirteenth of October 1944.

"Eau de chevaux," I laughed as we disembarked, dry but reeking of old horse piss.

Two days later, we sat in reserve as the lead battalions kicked off in icy rain and mud and muck near the hamlet of le Void de la Borde, named for the Borde folks who had lived there for generations. One of our officers was descended from people in Alsace Lorraine and said the name could be loosely translated as "the edge of doom," but not to worry about it. What did bother him was the unusual cold for this time of year.

"Eh, forget da kine talk," Poi said. I echoed him and brushed away the Friday-the-thirteenth arrival, too. But secretly I didn't like the sound of either one. Ando said to ignore the scare talk, but he looked apprehensive. Happi looked downright frightened.

Were we fools to worry? General Hugh Bristol, our new division commander, assured RCT leaders that no Germans lurked in the hills that surrounded the valley of Bruyères on three sides, code-named Hills A, B, C, and D. Another mound, Hill 555, stood smack across from A and B, in the Helladraye section of the forest. Taking the hills would be a cakewalk, he said. Then we could liberate the village's thirty-five-hundred inhabitants.

"Does that make sense?" Happi asked.

"Is he sure?" Kat asked.

Although small, Bruyères was an important center for transportation and communication and a major road intersection, its high ridge road leading to the German stronghold of Belmont, about seven miles to the northeast. The village's railways linked two important cities, Épinal and St. Dié. Nazis had held the town for four long years, taking for themselves the best of everything available, food, wine, women, houses.

It was beyond reason that the Jerries would hightail it.

We discovered all too soon who was right.

Rain soaked us and fog hovered eerily over the ground as we waited for news of the men forging ahead. What happened to them would dictate our next action. Communications wires were difficult to lay by hand or by truck because of the tough tree roots that gnarled the forest floor and minefields that lay hidden in thick mud, so we gathered close to Ando, who spoke by radio to our company Command Post. CP spoke with Battalion HQ, and HQ spoke to Regimental and Division. Runners and messengers came and went. Bits and pieces of news made their way to us, feeding the worst of our imaginations and worrying us into the night.

Companies of the 100th and 2nd battalions divided themselves into two columns as they entered the forest, not knowing where the enemy lurked. Hill 555 was their first objective. From their dug-in positions on Hills A and B, the Germans announced their presence with a storm of terror. Our men crawled through icy mud and hails of bullets and mortar as they gained ground, even as their tanks stalled in the freezing muck. They cleared their sectors of Hill 555, but were pummeled by a new Jerry onslaught. They reorganized to move toward the hills and attack.

As we waited to join the fray, the cancer of apprehension spread everywhere. We heard that our new general, rumpled and impatient and covered in sweat even at the beginning of the campaign, was breaking the rules of war and common sense, endangering himself and his division command by constantly running willy-nilly to the frontlines.

Advance! Advance! Attack! he bellowed to battalion commanders.

To soldiers.

To anyone who would listen.

Advance!

He threatened court-martial to any who dared to disobey.

"The man sounds nuts," Kat muttered.

"Does he have any experience in the field?" Poi asked.

"Bastard's going to kill us," I said. "Who needs the enemy?"

We had come to appreciate our battalion commanders visiting the front, assessing the action for themselves, directing, and listening to the men familiar with the field. But we knew they needed to go to the back, too, to think and to plan, to protect us and their command.

But our division leader did not plan.

He did not think.

And he didn't trust his own men to get the job done.

Nothing was fast enough for him.

The last story coming in scared the bejesus out of us.

Bristol had spotted a platoon from the 100th waiting in reserve.

"What are you doing, just sitting there? Why aren't you helping the other Japs? Attack that hill!" he yelled as he pointed to houses at the base of Hill A.

The platoon leader deliberated. Even the greenest soldier knew those houses were full of Jerries. And to be called Japs. Shit. But what choice did he have?

The soldier commanded his men forward and then ordered them to stay back and cover him while he ran ahead.

Within minutes, the platoon leader lay dead, a good part of the Jerry squad destroyed by his angry men.

"Was that suicide or murder?" the intelligence officer of the 100th cried when he heard the news.

Early on the third day, we crossed the edge of doom, the threshold, into the dark, wet forest. Artillery barraged the hills that we needed to win. Lieutenant Colonel Fowler stayed a safe distance toward the rear, strategizing. He called for a thick smoke screen to cover the 2nd and 3rd battalions as we crossed an open valley to Hill B, and we were grateful. The cover allowed the 2nd to begin a full frontal attack while we diverted attention on another slope.

As we fought, three 100th Battalion companies continued to battle for Hill A.

German fire pummeled all of us.

"Keep going!" Ando called in our sector.

"You can do it!" I shouted to a frightened replacement soldier, and I stayed close by his side to show him the way to maneuver, this way and that.

During a lull in the fighting, Ando signaled us to stop, and I walked over and talked to him, offering a couple of ideas about strategy. Ando always listened to his squad leaders and treated us with respect, even if we didn't always agree.

Ando joined in my concern not just about General Bristol, but about the new kind of fighting we faced. The Jerries here did not give way as quickly as they had in Italy. No, in these forests, they just came back for more, digging in and slamming us from the rear or on a flank.

Just as we jumped off again, a bullet whizzed by my head and struck Happi. My heart jumped as I saw my pal fall to the ground, cradling his bloody arm.

"Press on it, press on your arm," I yelled. Kat and Poi called, "Medic! Medic!" I helped Happi stem the bleeding, the smell and the wetness of his blood covering my hands and uniform. Bullets fell all around as I held my buddy. Dirt kicked up. I could barely breathe. Ando signaled everyone ahead.

"Get going," Happi shouted. "I'm okay. Go."

A medic took over, and we fought on.

Two hours. Three. At the end of the fourth hour, everyone in my sector scrambled for cover. I traced the fire to a machine gun nest and let loose on it. Then I hopped over the brush and ran up to the foxhole to make sure I'd destroyed it. The hole was unusually deep, and a dead German soldier leaned against one side, flesh hanging from his chest, blood covering his uniform. His eyes were open but unseeing. I looked for the machine gun, but guessed the man's comrade had escaped with it. Instead, I spotted a blood-smudged photo next to the dead man's hand, of a long-haired blonde woman and little boy, his wife and child, I was sure. He must have pulled the picture from his pocket as he died.

Germans began firing again, and I signaled my men to take cover as I jumped in the hole.

Silence returned.

I held my rifle tight.

Not a sound.

I looked at the man again, wondering all kinds of things. How the hell Hitler could call the Japanese honorary Aryans. How that little boy would grow up without a father. How it could be me lying there.

Ando moved us ahead, and I shook myself and led my men forward, Kat a few feet behind me, Poi bringing up the rear. Artillery barrages and bullets poured down on us, and some soldiers fought hand to hand. I ran toward Ando as he struggled with a German, kicking and choking and punching each other. The German slumped to the ground just as I got there.

"Back to our men," Ando yelled. His voice was raspy, his face gray.

By mid-afternoon, we had attracted enough attention away from the 2nd Battalion that it could take hold of Hill B. We moved ahead toward Bruyères.

A messenger brought news of the 100th, which had blown the machine gun nests at the base of Hill A. Men hopped from tree to tree as they battled up the hill's slopes to reach the top.

Soldiers consolidated their positions.

Hills 555, A, and B were under control.

K Company took battalion reserve and covered Item Company's flank as we moved toward Bruyères. We picked off snipers and cleared a roadblock with our engineers. Company L made it into the village, expecting to meet up with a battalion of Bristol's own men, the 143rd, "his boys," we had heard him say. His boys.

Inside and outside the village, we waited for the men.

Where were they?

Where?

A runner raced in.

The Texans had battled from the south and gotten slammed. Bristol had underestimated the number of Jerries in their sector.

What the hell?

It wasn't only us suffering the general's incompetence.

Worn out and hurting, the soldiers joined in fighting house to house, and everyone in the RCT knew what they were going through. Hearts pounded as they kicked in doors and searched every room, every last corner, for Nazis. They pressed rifle to rifle, strangled, and stabbed.

As survivors emerged, spent but alive, our platoon moved into the village, along with K Company. Our men patrolled the area, close by our 1ˢᵗ Platoon. Battle was at an end, but snipers still fired from the buildings around us.

Every nerve stood on edge.

Was a sniper over there?

There?

Zap.

A bullet hit Lewalski's replacement in the 1ˢᵗ Platoon, just within our sight. He was a Buddhahead who had just received a field commission.

We looked up at the building where we thought the fire had come from.

Out of the corner of my eye, I saw a man from our 3ʳᵈ Squad running in the lieutenant's direction, hauling his BAR.

"Honda!" his squad leader called. "Get back. You're going to get killed!"

Honda raced, spraying the building with bullets while men grabbed the lieutenant and dragged him away. Sniper fire ceased.

We mopped up, collecting one hundred thirty prisoners in the fields and gardens.

In the eerie silence that follows the violence of battle, I walked with my squad through Bruyères' cobble-stoned streets. We passed old stone houses, many pockmarked by bullets or gaping with holes from mortar and artillery. People peeked from behind curtains and shutters.

"You okay?" I pulled alongside Ando, who limped a little. He was totally pale now, his uniform soaked in blood.

"Yeah, yeah, yeah," Ando said, almost to himself. He tossed his helmet to the side of the road and sat on it. "Just a couple of blisters."

"You killed that German with your hands, didn't you." I squatted next to him.

"I want to puke," Ando whispered.

"Tough, sir," I said. No kind of fighting proved worse than hand-to-hand combat.

I saw Ando's hands shake as he took out his ojuzo beads, and I left him to recover and joined our men.

As troops gathered in the center of town, a few villagers emerged, and a good-looking boy of fifteen or sixteen approached us, gesturing with his hands and speaking in broken English.

"You no Japonais?" he said. "Certainement?"

We pointed to our liberty torch patches. "*Americains.*"

The boy introduced himself. "Giles Montaigne. Resistance. Resistance." He had a pleasant face, real cordial, with thick black hair brushed straight back and that kind of prominent nose some of the French had, Gallic, I'd heard it described. The kid was rail thin, his jacket threadbare, his shirt cuffs frayed, but he held himself with dignity. We offered him our rations and candy bars. "*Pour vous,*" we said.

Ando walked over to us, and Poi and Kat and I gathered around him with the rest of the platoon. Ando seemed quieter than usual, but the color had returned to his face. He made gestures of friendship to Giles and made his contribution.

As Giles said, "*Merci! Merci!*" to everyone, he handed Ando a bottle of wine and pieces of dried beef and chicken. His eyes sparkled with tears. "Please, eat. We keep for when free."

Ando said, "Merci," and we passed the treats around. A little dog approached, its ribs showing, and I shared my food with him as I thought of Bou.

"Honda, you're one gutsy buggah," Ando said as he handed him a piece of beef. "Just have to be careful, eh."

"He's my friend, close to my family back home," Honda said. "Couldn't see him *make*. He'll be okay now."

We all told him he'd done a great job, and I promised myself to get to know him better. Honda had a bad reputation, but the guy looked tough and true to me, willing to risk everything for a friend and comrade.

As we ate and laughed and motioned to our new French friends with our hands, I could hear a few soldiers singing to the villagers. Ando's face softened as we heard the strains of *Aloha O'e* from one direction, *Hawaii Pono'i* from another.

But jeers drew close, and we turned to see collaborators being dragged out of houses, villagers gathering to spit on them and shave their heads.

16

The Vosges, France

October 19-24, 1944

"Good God, how are we going to make it?" I muttered to Poi and Kat the next day. We crouched as we looked up at the tower atop Hill D, the next objective of the 2nd and 3rd battalions. We were fighting at the front of the regiment, just east of Bruyères, with the 100th in reserve.

"Hill's full of Germans," Kat said. "I don't care what Bristol says." We'd all seen what that asshole had done not just to us, but to "his boys."

"Fodder, that's what we are," Poi said.

Just days into this campaign, the cold, wet forest was eating us up. I had lost count of the killed and wounded, and our own squad was short Happi and Mak now, plus another man. I worried about them in the hospital, and I worried about the men in the field, our numbers depleted and ailing. My throat was sore, my body achy and chilled.

I blew on my fingers for warmth as we assessed the situation. Not only did the Germans infest the hill, but the tower gave them a commanding view of the territory immediately below and of the entire region.

We took off with Ando and the rest of our men, battling with all our might up, up, up the hill through a storm of bullets and artillery and mortar.

The Germans threw everything they had at us. Our infantry fired and the 522nd Artillery blasted away.

We amazed even ourselves.

Two hours of German pounding and pummeling is all it took.

We made our way to the top.

But then, without a moment's rest, Bristol ordered us to leave. He didn't give us a second to consolidate our position to insure we held the hill.

Now we had to clear a railroad embankment a couple of thousand yards more toward Belmont. Yet another mound, Hill 505, loomed just across from the rails, giving the enemy easy view of our movements.

"What's the bastard doing to us?" I cried to Ando.

"Is the guy nuts?" Poi asked.

"The man doesn't know what he's doing." Kat scowled. Even before we left Shelby, every one of us had learned that things had to be fluid in war, that soldiers had to change course on a dime to respond to whatever was happening. But men shouldn't give up the ground they'd just gained. "Bastard didn't keep a single reserve unit on the hill," Kat spat. "Not one man."

The Jerries infiltrated the rear of Hill D at night and grabbed it back. Their comrades increased pressure on the rear and front elements of the 2nd and 3rd battalions. We battled a counterattack of tanks and artillery while soldiers from other companies struggled to win the hill again. Fighting grew dirty. Some German soldiers were young teenagers, others, men in their 40s, and many weren't even Germans, but Poles and Danes and men from who knew what other nations the Nazis had occupied. The Geneva Convention was tossed aside. Germans fired at one of our medics waving the Red Cross flag while he tried to save his buddy. They shot at him again when he was lying on a stretcher.

That pushed our men over the edge.

Companies F, L, and H recaptured Hill D. Usually we took as many prisoners as possible. Today we took none.

We spotted Colonel Fowler running here and there, forward and back again, near the front. He looked like was trying to maintain his cool as he talked on the phone and directed battalion movements.

"Wonder if he's as upset as we are," Ando said during a pause in battle. "Must be hard to command under that general."

Kat and I agreed. From everything we'd seen, we thought Fowler liked to play things by the book. He had to be pissed.

The next day, Bristol repeated his mistake, this time with the 100th. He advanced the men so fast to capture Hill C that they had to return to several sectors to clear hidden clusters of the enemy, risking their lives twice.

Now get off the hill! Bristol yelled.

The flames of hell spread wide.

Germans who had survived the re-taking of Hill D attacked one of the carrying parties bringing us food and supplies. Forward observers spotted more enemy troops heading in from Belmont toward Bruyères. A taskforce of riflemen and tanks combined with airpower to push them back. Jerries pounded us from everywhere else as we neared the railroad embankment.

We fought like crazy men. Enemy automatics covered part of Hill 505, and Jerries over in Belmont aimed self-propelled guns, SPs, on the area. Barbed wire and mines lurked everywhere.

"Shit!" Kat cried. A bullet hit him in the shoulder. Blood soaked his shirt. He grimaced as a medic and I pulled him out of action. We held up our hands to each other in farewell, not knowing when we'd see each other again.

I wondered if he would catch sight of Mak in the hospital. Or Happi.

Our company and Company K, the Kingsmen, battled on, soon just northeast of Companies E and G. Our flanks went unprotected. The 179th, from the 45th Division, and the 143rd hadn't been able to keep up.

Taking security on our perimeter, Ben Honda caught sight of twenty men coming toward him through the fog. He couldn't tell if they were our own troops or German. His squad sergeant stood ready with his rifle while Honda called from their hiding spot, "Stop! Halt!"

Two of the soldiers stepped forward and looked toward their ridge through binoculars.

Honda called, "Buddhahead?"

Silence.

Honda rose to a crouch with his BAR and tried one more time. "Buddhahead?"

Silence.

Honda let her rip as he ran over, blasting the Germans.

The dead men were officers, and the other Jerries surrendered on the spot. Honda walked them over to Captain Stewart before rejoining our platoon.

Pupule guts, men said as word of his actions spread. The guy had crazy courage.

We inched ahead toward Hill 505, bullets flying, praying every prayer we knew and making up our own. Fog grew thick. Night descended.

"Stop!" Ando yelled to the platoon.

"Don't move!" I ordered our squad.

"Stay still!" Calls moved up and down the line.

We froze in the middle of a minefield. Engineers struggled to clear the area.

I shivered in the icy rain and rubbed my throat, so raw I couldn't swallow. We had fought continuously for five straight days. I drifted off to sleep, rifle in hand.

"Come on, Hiro." Ando shook me awake. "Get ready to move." I saw he was limping a little, but he was already leading the way.

I roused myself and my men, and sheer will and adrenaline propelled us ahead. I caught sight of Poi, his face determined. We joined a fury of fighting in a frontal attack on the Jerries across the tracks, on Hill 505. We took the hill and pushed the Jerries toward Belmont. A soldier from Company K captured German defense plans to infiltrate the area and handed them off to a new taskforce, which cleared the ridge overlooking the village. Air support thundered in. The 141st and 143rd advanced to our north.

We dared to feel relief.

And then Bristol outdid himself.

I really thought he was going to annihilate us all.

Bristol advanced the 100th too far, too fast, rushing the men in to support the second taskforce and take the ridge between Belmont and Biffontaine, near a junction known as Croix Thomas, completing the regiment's control of the high ground.

The men raced beyond the protection of our battalion and the 2nd's.

Communication became impossible.

They were isolated, a soldier's worse nightmare.

The Jerries, who were non-existent according to Bristol, pummeled the men without mercy and cut any remaining phone wires.

We were called in for the rescue, along with the 2nd Battalion and a taskforce. Details struggled to bring in supplies, their maps outdated. Vicious German bicycle troops attacked, the Nazis intent on completing the 100th's isolation. Men died.

The FFI, the French Forces of the Interior, stepped forward.

"They've known these forests since they were born," Poi said. "They'll get the job done."

The 100th escaped with their lives, but our faith in the general was gone, completely non-existent.

Yet we still had to obey his orders.

• • •

Attack Biffontaine, down in the valley.

Bristol's next command continued the horror.

Attack!

Men cried, "What the hell?"

"*Bakatare!*" Poi yelled.

The village was a little farming community of no strategic consequence.

But what could anyone do?

As soon as the 100th was rescued, the men were ordered to lead the charge.

We were to move in and support the 100th once again.

The 100th spread out over the hills and attacked the village, descending on three sides.

The Jerries were waiting.

They surrounded our men.

We maintained tight communication as we moved in. We glanced down into the village as we arrived. White stucco cottages, capped with ochre tiled roofs, painted a disturbingly quaint picture, complete with smoke curling from chimneys.

Did Bristol give even a thought to strategy?

We battled on.

We tried to rally what men remained.

"Give it your all!" Poi yelled.

"This has to be it!" I called.

"Dig deep!" Ando waved everyone forward.

We joined in fighting Jerries hand to hand, house to house, cellar to cellar. I looked into the eyes of the man I killed, smelled his flesh and his stink and his blood. I rested for just a few seconds outside with Ando and Poi, spent from combat.

Then we grabbed German weapons and supplies to replenish our own stocks.

Villagers cared for the worst of our wounded in the warmth of their homes, laying them on their best bed linens without a second thought, giving them the little food they had. The 100th's intelligence officer, one of the smartest, most experienced, and revered men in the whole damned regiment, was evacuated, close to bleeding to death. An OCS graduate of Korean descent, he had at first been told by the Army that he would be assigned a mechanic's job; when he volunteered to lead the AJAs, he was informed that Koreans and Japanese didn't mix.

So much for that crap.

We battled Germans on every side as we advanced, fighting fatigue and cold and hunger as much as the enemy. Our company stood no larger than the size of a couple of platoons, officers almost nonexistent. Under heavy fire, our engineers cleared the main road so we could move in men and supplies.

Squads intermingled. Ben Honda raised a bloody fist to me as we fought close. "Assholes!" he yelled. I raised my fist back at him.

After two days of fighting, Biffontaine was ours. We were relieved by Bristol's 141st, advancing toward St. Dié, and his 143rd, moving through the Les Pouiers-LaChapelle valley.

Soldiers looked out with the thousand-mile stare, from nothing into nothing. I was close to joining them.

Bristol's promise of ten days rest could not come soon enough.

17

The Vosges, France

October 25-28, 1944

Bruised and bleeding, weary and sick, we marched into the meadows between Belmont and Biffontaine. I didn't know where they got the energy, but our engineers brought up a fifty-five-gallon tank they'd rigged to a wooden platform for showers, and we took turns bathing for the first time in weeks. My mud-caked, sweat-soaked ODs walked off on their own, leaving my body to stink by itself. My God, the water felt good, even if my cuts stung and my bruises throbbed. I scrubbed as hard as I could bear, hoping to clean my body and soul of all the muck and killing and maiming that infested the forest. I revived a bit, but the list of our casualties weighed on my mind. Matsuura. Saito. Minaai. Some were gone for good. Others, like Happi and Mak and Kat, might return to fight.

And now we were losing Ando, too.

"Wasn't blisters that caused my limp," he said as he accepted evacuation to the field hospital "My Achilles heel is torn to shreds." He fingered his ojuzu, assuring us, "I'll be back as soon as I can."

I was feeling pretty stranded as we said our good-byes, but I focused on getting everyone clean and rested. Fresh uniforms were on their way. We divided our sleeping quarters between a barn, a farmhouse, and tents.

My men insisted I take a bed in the house, and I slept better than I had in weeks, though fever wracked my body. I awoke the next morning to men's voices outside.

"Come on. There's a lot of farms around here. Let's see what we can find."

"I'm starving."

"Let's go."

A few seconds of silence followed, making me think they had left, but then I heard whispering—and a knock at my door.

"Why the hell you still in bed?" Mak laughed as he walked over to me. "It's late, asshole."

"Wow!" I stood up to shake his hand and welcome him back. "I can't believe you're here."

"Your hand some hot," Mak said. "Go back to bed. You look bad."

"And you look like a piece of shit, you ugly buggah," I said as I lay back down. Damn, I was glad to see him. We talked until fever got the best of me, and I dozed off for a while. When I awoke, Mak and a few other Buddaheads were bringing me soup made from the cabbages they'd found, a treat after a steady diet of dried crackers and hash. My fever soon broke and my good spirits returned.

"Hiro, good to see you," Ben Honda said when he dropped by. I was just getting going.

"Ben," I said and raised my fist, remembering the last battle. He held his up, bandaged pretty heavily.

"Just want to tell you, eh, I'm going to be a good soldier for you and Ando," he said. "I'll show you."

"You're a good fighter," I said, believing him. "And true. That's what counts."

"Got nothing on you," he said. "Pupule guts, that's what you got. Pupule guts."

I said I'd heard the same about him as he pulled out a P38, a luger that he'd taken from the Germans he'd brought in. I ogled the piece, the souvenir all soldiers wanted, and for the next hour or so we talked about our families and how we'd ended up here. He was another plantation boy, from someplace I couldn't begin to pronounce, and he told me more about that fight in Vada, how he couldn't just leave one of our own men, an American GI, to fend for himself. As far as he was concerned, he'd taken the fall.

"That must have hurt," I said. "You stood up and still got screwed." By the time he left, I was thinking every outfit needed some bad boys in it.

Early the next morning I was up and at 'em, and I told Mak I was glad that he and I were a team again, especially with Ando out of the picture.

Mak's face fell.

"Not exactly," he said.

"Huh?"

"They assign me to lead 2nd squad for now."

I couldn't hide my disappointment, but admitted to myself that I was glad we didn't have to jockey for position. We agreed we'd continue to work together, just in different capacities.

News came in that Kat's wound was superficial. But he was being pulled out of the infantry to fill in as a jeep driver. I sure as hell would miss him.

What else could I do? I spent the rest of the day horsing around and helping to unpack ukuleles and footballs and baseballs from storage. After chow, I enjoyed some playtime with Lucy, the medics' sweet little dog, and I went to bed content, looking forward to a good, long R&R.

. . .

"Get up," Captain Stewart voice roused me from a deep sleep. "Everyone, up!"

"What?" I mumbled as I stretched for my glasses.

"We've been ordered back on line. Some of Bristol's men got isolated. They're surrounded by the Germans," Stewart said. He raced out to let others know.

"What the hell time is it?" I asked.

"The hell-o-two-hundred," Stewart called as he ran.

Poi Hirano, nursing a bad sore throat, had taken the bed across from me and came awake. "What the hell?"

I oriented myself as consciousness grabbed hold. It was just thirty-six hours or so since we'd been relieved.

I heard men grumble as they awoke.

"What the hell?"

"Our mail hasn't even caught up with us."

"We just got here."

The discipline of our training soon kicked in, and we ceased our complaints as we slapped on equipment, grabbed rifles, and hefted backpacks. Poi and I got our men moving to the assembly area. Our battalion would jump off with the 100th right behind us.

Word spread that the 2nd Battalion had already marched into the forest to reinforce units of Bristol's 36th Texas Division. Other units were falling in—chemical weapons, tanks, tank destroyers, artillery, the works. The general meant business.

Rain pelted us, icy cold and sharp, stinging our skin and plastering our uniforms to our bodies.

"What happened?" I heard men talking as I wiped my face.

"Beanies got themselves trapped," someone said. That was the name we used sometimes for the Caucasian soldiers. They seemed to like beans a lot more than we did and were shaped like a beanpole.

"How many men?"

"A few platoons, sounds like."

Rumor gave way to fact, and we learned that the trapped Beanies numbered two hundred seventy-five men from the 1st Battalion of the 141st. They'd been moving north of us, fighting along a thickly forested portion of the ridgeline road from La Houssière to Biffontaine, when they got squeezed. Their mission had been to prevent the enemy down in the valley of La Houssière from climbing up to the road and capturing such strategic junctions as La Croisette and Le Baignoire des Oiseaux. Their objective was a highway that would take them right into St. Dié.

A German pincer move stopped them cold.

They were trapped.

"So where are Bristol's other men? Why can't they help?" our guys asked.

"Does Bristol think we're machines? Why can't his men take care of this?"

I walked around with other squad and platoon leaders, handing out squares of toilet paper from our ration kits and telling everyone to put the paper on one another's backs. Men needed something light to follow into the night.

"Let's line up," Stewart said. "I know you're more tired than you've ever been. Everyone is. But a bunch of American soldiers are trapped out there. We have to get them."

I told my men to dig deep.

Soldiers took off as one, the clack of rifles, the rustle of ODs, the sucking of boots in muck all too familiar, the ache of our leg muscles extreme. I could barely see the man in front of me, toilet paper be damned, and I felt the weight of a hand on my backpack. I turned around and saw Walter Inouye grasping it for safety, the man behind him doing the same to Inouye's back. I reached out to the man in front, lengthening the chain.

Another pull on my back threw me off balance, and I slipped to the ground when Inouye fell on me as another soldier toppled over on him, domino after domino. I slid my way back up and extended a hand to the men around me. Once everyone was on their feet, I scraped the mud from my ODs as best I could and wiped the muck from my lips and cheeks with a sleeve. I used an index finger to clean my teeth, a big mistake. The taste and grit of wet earth filled my mouth.

"Fall in, keep going," I whispered.

We slogged on, the forest closing in as we entered its caverns once more. My nerves twitched at the creak of a branch.

Our platoon followed the first platoon, veering to the right to climb a sharply inclined road, an even harsher slope to the left. Dawn lightened the forest, and the Germans spotted us and fired. Damn it to hell. We ran off road and fought tree-to-tree as we climbed, and I inched along on the most extreme left position, struggling not to lose my footing. I waved our squad toward my position and advanced. Poi kept the men together.

I examined the underbrush around us as we walked, so thick I didn't think anyone had gone before us. But as I peered through the fog, I made out bodies lying all around, in rain-filled fox-holes and on top of the ground, and I heard my men gasp. Rifles were stuck barrel-first into the earth near each body, American helmets sitting on the rifle butts. I spotted the T-Patch of the 36th Division on the dead men's uniforms, and chills raced up and down my spine, chicken skin or *torihada*, the Buddhaheads would say. *Kimochi warui*, parents and grandparents might add, a most uneasy, unpleasant feeling. Would this be our fate, too? We slowed our pace as we took in the graveyard. Tripwires laced the bushes.

We picked our way through, no time to retrieve the bodies of the T-Patchers. We had the living to rescue.

Deeper into the forest we marched toward the Beanies. Bullets killed and wounded on every side. By 1400 our battalion neared the 100th. The 2nd battled on our left.

Captain Stewart was leading our first platoon when the Jerries pinned them down. I quickly assessed the risk of trying to free them. I knew my men could do it, and I felt myself entering that zone of clarity again, sensing which way to move with little thought or effort. I led my squad over and fought close on the platoon's flank, racing to free them, right in the sights of the enemy. I maneuvered my men around to attack, ran fifty yards up the hill as Poi and the rest of our squad covered me, and then I covered them as they climbed. I traced the fire hitting Stewart to a machine-gun nest and directed the squad's fire at the Jerries. Stewart's men escaped, and my men found higher ground on the right.

Yow! A bullet ripped across my bicep. My mind worked in slow motion as I watched blood pour out. Training kicked in, and I pressed on the wound and then moved my fingers and arm. I kept fighting and told my men to keep firing. Damned if we would withdraw.

Bullets flew, artillery and mortar pummeled, and bombs slammed into trees. We hit the ground. German tank fire blasted us. We fired back.

Where were our own tanks?

The company fought tight together, and I spotted Mak running around, pushing his men in the 2nd Squad hard, checking on everyone near him, and now, near me, too. One indentation in the earth sat silent. Mak called, "You okay?" as he crawled over to see what was amiss.

Mak returned to my sector, sputtering. "Yoyo Wasuke, practically pissing in his pants." Little ruffled Mak, but he was angry now.

I remembered the drunk asshole who had told Ando to fuck off back at Shelby.

"Deal with this later," Mak said as he ran onto other matters. We had both seen enough fear in even the best soldiers to know it could work to save a man's butt or get him and everyone else killed. If it didn't look like a fellow would work out, he should be sent to a position in the back, like the chaplain's office or some kind of administrative job.

We dug deep. K Company fought on our flank, bloodied by the worst of the Jerries' barrages. Showers of bullets filled the air as German tanks closed in, within two hundred yards, a hundred yards, seventy-five yards. We rushed a bazooka team into action and destroyed a tank and a half-track. The Jerries withdrew into the growing darkness, and we collapsed on the ground to rest. Mak maneuvered his way over and said that he'd sent Yoyo to the rear, to protect him and the men he should have been fighting with.

During the lull, I heard my men whispering.

"I was scared shitless when Hiro went for Stewart's platoon."

"Me, too."

"Thought I was a dead man."

"But he knew what he was doing."

"Always protects us."

"Would never get us killed."

"Saves our asses, the guy does."

I said a silent prayer for wisdom. I was always careful to weigh the risks, however quickly. I would get our men through the war alive.

• • •

Fighting returned with the dawn of October 28. Stewart put the 1st Platoon in reserve, and our platoon took point, followed by the 3rd. A few hundred yards into our march, we ran into a manned roadblock. Snipers hid in the brush. The Jerries bombarded us. I felt the earth shudder and called to any and all powers to watch over us. I fired whenever I could, covered my men when they needed it, and sought cover for myself, roadblock after roadblock, barrage after barrage. Poi was constantly on top of our squad, encouraging and protecting. Sometime after 1400, the forest grew quiet.

We marched into La Croisette Junction as night descended, spent but knowing we could approach the road to take us to the trapped men from here. The 3rd Battalion settled down alongside the men of the 100th, who were resting after their latest ordeal. One Puka Puka had been pulled into a sucker play earlier in the day, running after Germans who appeared to retreat but then turned and hammered them. The 2nd stood to our north, on Hill 617, clearing Jerries and covering everyone from that angle.

Our energy depleted, we ate in silence, and I used the time to think. It must have been four miles or so directly from the fields where we began to the spot where the Texans sat trapped, but the territory we covered was expanding as we circled around hills and zigzagged to avoid minefields and artillery barrages and grenade blasts. Our tanks stalled in the mire, and like yesterday, bazooka teams attacked German tanks. Our artillerymen, usually accurate, tapped every bit of their considerable brainpower to compensate for the foggy, mountainous terrain, which forced them to aim at a higher angle than normal. Sometimes their ammo flew over the Germans.

Just as I finished eating, a runner told me I was wanted at our company Command Post, our CP. I hopped up and made my way to Captain Stewart, sitting with some other officers under tent material, the ground too hard to pitch it properly. He said Lieutenant Colonel Fowler wanted a ration detail to go out tonight to replenish water and food and ammo supplies.

"Can I take it?" I volunteered immediately.

"I was hoping you'd ask," Stewart said. "You sure your arm's good enough?"

I rubbed my wound without thinking. The medics—including Sam Sakura, that lover-boy nosebleed imposter—had patched me up quickly after action stopped. They were smart and brave, those guys, moving closer to the front than other aid units did. Their speed kept wounds from getting infected and saved lives.

"Just a graze. I'm sure I can do this." I recognized a power that hit me in the gut when I was doing right, something that kept me centered and alert and confident no matter how tired I was, that made one action flow smoothly into the next. I felt no separation between me and my men. I was ready to take on more.

"Bring twelve men, including yourself, and report to Battalion CP. Tell them to carry just rifles and ammo belts. There'll be a ton of supplies to carry back," Stewart said. I knew that Battalion CP was located nearby, as Fowler had moved up between Companies I and K, just in back of the foremost of the frontlines. Command wanted to be accessible so they could communicate quickly and see the situation for themselves as they prepared for tomorrow's actions. Formation held tight. No more men would be cut off.

"Get some men from K Company, too," Stewart said. "We're in this together." The Kingsmen sat right next to us, while L Company stood on the battalion's left flank, too long a distance to walk in my search for volunteers.

I prepared to leave and asked, "Any news of the Texans?" I saw a field switchboard near Stewart and assumed he was in constant communication not just with our field phones, but up the chain.

"They've moved to higher ground, where it's safer," Stewart said. "But the German's 716th Division is ready to pounce. It's really touch and go. We have to get to them."

Things looked grim. Men were falling dead as they struggled to break out of the trap, and the wounded grew desperate for medical care. Gone were food, water, ammo, radio batteries. Fog hampered supply airdrops from the 405th Fighter Squadron, the packages landing in trees, unapproachable gullies, enemy hands. Rations and medicine were being jammed in shells and shot toward the men. Artillery couldn't be fired for fear it would fall on the T-Patchers. Stewart said the press had dubbed the isolated men "the Lost Battalion," and Hitler himself was watching the standoff. He had sent in some of his last crack shooters, vowing to kill every single American. Cameramen from the U.S. Signal Corps were embedded in our troops and recording action.

"Be careful," Stewart said as I left. "Germans are all over the place."

I ran back to our platoon and told Poi to watch over our men. Like everyone else, he had thrown his trenching tool aside, defeated by the roots gnarling the ground. Even on a good night, if a man could dig a hole deep enough to lie in, he had to cover up with logs and branches and mud to protect himself from tree bursts. I saw men crouched beneath trees and prayed a blazing rain of wood and shrapnel wouldn't kill them.

"You going to be safe, Hiro?" he said.

"I'll see you in a few hours." I grabbed my rifle and ammo belt and slapped Poi on the back. Fog lay thick in the forest, and the evening grew dark and cold. Manpower stood so low that soldiers from the rear were joining in the fighting. The kitchen itself served as a staging area for replacements coming in and for wounded returning from the hospital.

I walked through I Company. "We're running out of supplies," I said to one group after another. "I need volunteers for a detail." Weariness covered everyone's faces. I didn't know if the men had any more to give, but we needed rations and bullets and water if we were to escape this forest alive.

"Okay, Hiro, I'll come with you," a young private said.

"Come on, guys, do our company proud." I apologized and pleaded and encouraged. I received yeses from two more privates.

I headed toward K Company, huddled at the base of the hill next to ours. The two hills meshed together, and I ordered my three men to stay at the front of the common area until I returned with more volunteers.

Men sat in shallow foxholes or on their helmets as they downed rations with their squads, too drained to talk.

"Hey, put your boots back on." I spoke to a young soldier rubbing his bare feet. "Your feet are going to swell up like damned balloons, and you'll never get them back into those boots."

"But my feet are throbbing, Sarge," he said.

I watched the boy clench his teeth through the pain. "Think you have trench foot?" Standing too long in water and wet socks could cause flesh to rot, causing excruciating pain. Trench foot had sent many soldiers to the field hospital, incapacitated.

"No, I don't think it's that bad."

"You sure?"

"Yes, sir."

"You have a pair of dry socks?"

"Yes, sir."

"Then put them and your boots on or see a medic. You have to walk to keep up. Everyone's depending on each other. You could get yourself and your buddies killed."

I had to be tough to get men out alive. I felt against my belly to make sure my extra socks were there, dry and warm, and made the rounds a few times, ending up with five more men, four privates and a sergeant.

Nine down, including myself, and three to go.

I wandered back to I Company, where another private stepped up.

"Two to go," I said.

"Please, we just need two more men." I talked to groups of three and four soldiers, hoping I didn't appear desperate as the clock ticked. The men were battling to stay alert, stay awake, their energy gone.

Back in K Company, I approached yet another group of men, pleading.

I accepted another volunteer, another private.

"One more. Just one man to go." I made the rounds yet again. And again.

I saw a buck sergeant check his watch and then raise his hand. "I'll go," he said.

I smiled. "Sure you have the time?"

We both laughed, and I told him he'd bring up the rear.

I gathered my men together and ordered them to walk in tight formation, silently, in blackness so absolute that I could barely discern the silhouettes of the trees surrounding us. Only the crackling of branches and thud of boots on the icy ground broke the hush of the forest.

We stopped at Fowler's tent, sagging and open. A lieutenant stood outside and directed me in. Fowler sat on the ground, studying a map with a couple of officers I didn't recognize.

"We have to get the coordinates straight," Fowler said, his voice tight. He ran his hand over his head. "We were off by a thousand yards this morning because of the damned maps. It looks like we've cut the German line north of La Croisette. We've cut the road that runs over the ridgeline."

Fowler was reputed to have an amazing sense of direction that had guided our battalion through the maze of the forest this far. Bad maps would drive the man crazy, and with good reason.

Fowler traced the road from Hill 617, where the 2nd Battalion was covering us, down through the Houssière Valley. "We're getting close. Both slopes of the road pinch right here so the road's too narrow for us to march on." He pointed to a spot. "So tomorrow we climb down to attack the slopes and cross the junction. Once we get back on the road, we have to run like greased lightning. That's the same ridgeline where the T-Patchers got caught, and you know the Jerries will have us in their sites. But there's no other way."

Suddenly aware of my presence, the colonel stood up. "Here for the supplies, Sergeant?"

"Yes, sir. I have eleven men waiting."

"The supply trucks aren't here yet. Head down the road and meet them as they come up." Fowler pointed toward the area where the 100th had fought.

That was a crazy order.

Were our own commanders beginning to act like Bristol?

To go down right now would be suicide.

I'd heard Fowler listened to GI input sometimes. I had to speak up.

"Sir, could we wait? Or try a different route? The 100th was slammed near where we're going, just a few hours ago. A tank got taken out close by." I told him the Germans had that trail zeroed in. They'd hear the trucks and see us.

"Our men are going to get desperate real fast." Fowler frowned. "We need those supplies now. Get going."

I hesitated, thinking I had been wrong. This guy wasn't what I'd hoped he'd be.

He was pulling rank, pure and simple, and rushing things.

"That's an order, Sergeant. 2000 hours sharp." He returned to his meeting.

Before I could say more, a call came in from the general, and I heard him yelling for the battalion to get moving before his boys died. I heard Fowler mutter, "Oh, shit," as I left.

I gathered my men, feeling like I was leading lambs to the slaughter. My thoughts raced. Everyone could get killed if we followed orders, and we could be court-martialed if we disobeyed—and with Bristol constantly threatening soldiers with just that, we took the idea more seriously than ever. I could speak up again and dare a court-martial on my own, but that wouldn't save my men from going out on the mission. I would just be replaced, and the detail would move on.

"What do you think?" I asked the men themselves. They discussed the situation quickly and quietly. They came to an agreement.

"We have to go."

"No choice."

I said okay, then, and used the little light coming from the tent to check my watch. It was time. I felt for my photo.

I led my men toward the trail, my heart beating out each inch, each foot, each yard as we marched in silence.

One yard. Two yards. Three.

Four. Five. Six.

My counting measured the depths of the darkness, in back of the frontlines.

One hundred ninety-nine. Two hundred.

Kaboom!

Bright orange flames exploded into the forest. I felt myself fly through the air. My body slammed to the ground.

Black.

Black.

• • •

Okaasan!

A soldier crying into the night for his mother stirred me awake, and I felt around my body. My glasses had disappeared, and I searched my pockets for my extra pair. I put them on, only to make out the fog of smoke that stung my eyes and filled my nostrils. My ears rang. How long was I knocked out? Was I wounded? Where were my men?

I rose up on my elbows, my back aching like a son of a bitch. I smelled the metallic scent of blood and felt a small, ragged patch of open flesh near my spine. I stood all the way up. I began walking, trying to see.

I made out part of a boot, a severed ankle sticking out. I looked this way and that. I listened. Was that one of my men calling into the forest?

"Anyone there?" I whispered.

"Over here. Here." I heard a voice a few yards away.

I followed the sound and found a soldier from the detail.

"Where you hurt?" I knelt next to the man.

"My leg," he said. "I can't get up. I really tried. I can't."

I felt around. Blood covered his left leg, positioned at an unnatural angle.

"You see anyone else?" I pressed on the wound to stem the bleeding. I didn't have any first aid materials to make a tourniquet.

"No one," he said. "No one. It's like everyone vaporized."

"We have to get you to an aid station," I said. I helped the guy stand up on his good leg, bent down, and hefted his body over my shoulders.

"Tell me when it hurts too much," I whispered.

"No, you tell me," he said. "You're wounded, too."

I strained my eyes as I got my bearings and inched down the hill, away from the front.

Okaasan!

The soldier's cries started again, first strong, and then softer and softer, following us through the forest.

"Poor guy has to be one of ours," the soldier said. "No one else is out here."

My heart was heavy.

I knew he was right.

An icy rain cut through the pine needles and dripped from the boughs, the forest itself weeping for the young man.

I found a narrow dirt trail and followed it for ten or fifteen minutes before catching sight of medics. They sat beneath a collapsed tent awning painted with a red cross centered in a circle of white, protected in a gully.

"You okay, Sergeant?" a medic asked. He lifted the soldier off as he said to me, "There's blood all over your back. Is that yours or his? Let me take a look."

I turned to go. "Later."

I raced through the forest back to the battalion command post, swearing every goddamned swear I knew and then making some up. I didn't wait for permission to address the colonel.

"Why the hell did you have us go out there?" I confronted Fowler head on. "I told you the Jerries had the trail zeroed in." My heart raced. I didn't care if Fowler was a colonel. Ten of my men had vanished.

"Don't you talk to me that way, soldier. We need supplies. Now. Details are always risky."

"But not like this!" I screamed. "I'd rather starve than see my men killed! Don't you listen to anyone in the field? The Jerries are all over the area. They know that trail. We were dead ducks before we began."

"Now you listen here, Sergeant. I gave you an order. You followed it, and some men died. This is war."

"War, my ass. You're supposed to listen so you don't get us killed."

A couple of other officers approached, their faces alarmed. Fowler was purple.

"You get back to your unit this instant, soldier." Fowler shook his finger at me. "You're way out of line, and I'll have none of it."

"Why don't you search for the bodies of my men, you bastard?" I stormed out. Images of Fowler back at Shelby, rattling a new nisei sergeant, scowling at the men who had just defeated his outfit, flooded my mind.

Should have known back then, damn it all.

I walked through the night toward my squad, breathing hard. I heard the soldier calling for his mother again, the voice drifting and fading.

I found my squad. Men said the cries had started a couple of hours ago, about the time we got barraged, I figured.

I fell to my knees. I didn't give a damn if a tree burst hit me with blazing wood and metal.

The young man's cries stopped, and the forest echoed in silence.

18

The Vosges, France

October 29-November 17, 1944

A detail taking a different path brought provisions to the troops, and we eked out our rations as we shivered with chills and fever. I told no one how I had berated the colonel, and I vowed never to go against my conscience again, if I could at all help it. No more of my men showed up. Company command said too many dangers lurked in the forest to search for them. They would join the growing number of soldiers looked for only when safety prevailed.

At dawn the next day, Bristol appeared out of nowhere in our sector and pushed us over the edge.

He kicked a platoon radioman in the butt and told him to get fighting.

Company I was still pinned down with Company K at the base of two hills that would lead to the lost men, and we watched in horror from a slight distance.

Our radioman tried to explain that phone lines had been cut, that he needed to reach our lieutenant by radio, but Bristol was already storming over to Lieutenant Colonel Fowler, who had just arrived.

"*Charge, I tell you!*" Bristol yelled at Fowler. "Get your men to fix bayonets and run up that damned hill."

I think Fowler cracked right in front of us, once and for all, throwing military decorum to the wind while trying to keep a semblance of order within his grasp.

Already more than half a foot taller than Bristol, Fowler pulled himself up so that he towered over the general, screaming, "Those are my boys you're trying to kill! Goddamn it, I'll give the orders to them when we've prepared a battle plan. They're not getting blown to pieces because of you." He reached for the general's lapels, but put his hands down.

Bristol shrunk away, mumbling something about court-martial, and Fowler passed us as he stormed out, red faced and cussing. For just a moment, I swallowed my anger at him, I was so grateful that he had stood up for us. I nodded to my men as we refocused on the hills in front of us, thick with Germans and trees and shrubs.

The earth shook with explosions as fighting intensified with the day. More cooks and clerks and cleric's aides picked up arms and took their places by our sides. We took heavy losses as we maneuvered one inch here, another inch there. We called for fire from the 522nd Artillery, but the steepness of the slope and denseness of the trees threw calculations askew. Tanks stuck fast in the icy mud, and the Jerries' interlocking fire and mortar and artillery froze us in place. We pressed ourselves into the earth as the thunder and lightning of battle threatened to annihilate us.

General Bristol raced around the front, screaming orders at anyone he came across. He bumped into our company's reserve platoon, the 3rd, and bossed the men around.

"Flank the enemy!" he yelled.

The men ended up in the 100th's area. The Jerries blasted them.

Bristol, his two stars sparkling, brought his new aide to the front. The young man's silver bar flashed on his helmet and on his shirt collar. Men wondered why the general hadn't taken precautions. Obvious targets for the enemy, he and the first lieutenant stood reading a map on the hood of Bristol's jeep.

Shots rang out from the Jerries' position, and the aide collapsed forward.

Bristol caught him and lowered him to the ground, the young man's blood splattered over the general's hands, his uniform. Bristol moved to the rear, leaving the aide's body for others to pick up.

• • •

Two hours later, Bristol commanded the 522nd Artillery to fire at a hill he had marked on the map.

"Isn't that right in the middle of the T-Patchers?" one of our artillerymen asked. The depth of their smarts matched the accuracy of their aim. Knowing the general was shaken, our men held their fire. They returned to providing support for our battalion as we slogged on.

"Move!" Someone pushed me aside just as a blazing branch fell right where I'd been fighting. I turned and saw Ben Honda, running away from me toward the enemy.

Just as I was absorbing the fact that Honda had saved my damned life, shrapnel pierced my back. Men insisted I get help. I argued, but couldn't stem the bleeding. I left for the aid station, and then the field hospital, where I found Ando, champing at the bit to get back to combat. Together we heard news of battle from soldiers carried in.

Fowler came through with new orders, much like Bristol's, but issued with thought and planning.

"Charge the slope!" the colonel commanded I Company, in sync with K Company. Tank fire would cover everyone.

Men looked up the steep hills as bullets poured down on them. They had had enough.

Fowler roused the men in K Company.

Ben Honda stood up in our sector and ran ahead, right into enemy fire.

Then another soldier rose.

And another.

Fowler ran with the men, his pistols drawn. He fought like a madman. He was a big guy, making him an easy target.

"Go! Go!" Soldier after soldier charged through a blizzard of machine-gun fire, a storm of mortar and grenades.

"Nazi bastards!" men yelled.

Ben Honda wiped out two machine gun nests, and then picked off two snipers.

Captain Stewart grabbed the BAR off a fallen soldier and charged with the men. They cleared the Jerries from their foxholes and the trees. Men on the American side fell, men on the German side fell, and our soldiers fought on, jumping from tree to tree, climbing and firing and advancing. Jerry defenses crumbled.

A machine gun hit Honda in his face, arm, shoulder. His BAR shattered. He begged to get patched up so he could fight on, but had to accept evacuation.

Companies I and K reached the top, where our regimental commander lay wounded. What Germans were left ran for their lives.

Our men glanced down the slope, carpeted with bodies, German and American, and ran ahead to find shelter for the night. They stood close to the Texans, but could go no further in the dark.

As I got bandaged up, I caught a glimpse of Ben Honda being rushed in, and Ando ran over to check on him, one of his men, covered in blood. Wounded soldiers coming in were breathless as they described Honda's bravery, saying he had started I Company's charge up the hill and kept everyone going. Ando beamed like a proud father. Sometimes you just have to have faith in someone, he said quietly to me, to let the good inside them shine.

Chaplain Morimoto prayed with everyone, and by chow, my back felt good enough that I walked over to eat with Ando. A little French boy approached him and handed him a hard-boiled egg, saying "*Pour vous. Merci. Bonne chance.*" They hugged, and the little boy waved as he made his way out.

"Been feeding him?" I asked, already knowing the answer.

Ando said yes. "I'm supposed to get out of here in a couple of days. Let's hope that the luck he wished me goes for everyone. We sure need it."

I agreed, telling him I'd keep him company this evening; the doctors were insisting I stay the night. As we ate, I caught movement in the corner of my eye and turned my attention away. I pointed to a soldier being brought in. "Whoa, isn't that Mak?"

Ando and I rushed over. We couldn't see Mak's foot, covered in dirt and splinters and blood. The smell of his singed flesh and sweat filled the area around him.

Mak gasped that a tree burst had cut into him. Like most other nisei, he didn't scream or cry, but he squeezed my hand hard as he croaked, "*Itai.* Itai." It hurts. Ando rubbed Mak's arm and told him to heal fast. Mak passed out. Help moved in.

I looked at my buddy and I looked at Ben Honda, near each other now, both in bad shape. Unable to settle down, I paced the area and spotted bodies piled up to the side of the hospital, like logs I had seen outside Seattle. Boots dangled from feet, and death exuded its rotten fruity stink. I covered my mouth and nose and turned my head away.

I had to help the living before everyone ended up like that.

Well before dawn, I hitched a ride back to the front with Kat Kato, who was bringing up supplies in his jeep. We held our hands up in greeting, but I begged him not to slap my back. We tried yelling our news to each other as the barrages around us grew strong. We gave up as we entered the main battle area, where I joined our men.

Those who could walk moved ahead, our battalion fighting abreast the 100th. One Puka Puka followed a telephone line that was supposed to lead to the Beanies, and we advanced through the junctions of Baignoire des Oiseaux and Col des Huttes. Our company took point for the battalion, and our platoon combined forces with our 1st and 3rd platoons, together reaching the size of a squad.

At 1400, two scouts and a couple of other soldiers from the 1st approached the outer defenses of the Beanies, and we followed as close as was safe. The 100th blasted through from the right flank. Suddenly our nisei spotted a hollow-eyed soldier staring from behind a tree, a few hundred feet away. Our men stood still, fearing the soldier was German.

The soldier in back of the tree held his position, looking gray and afraid.

"Want a smoke?" one of our men ventured.

The two hundred eleven remaining T-Patchers, bearded and weary, emerged from trees and from craters in the earth. Tears welled up, lips quivered, and hands stretched out for water and cigarettes, some offered in gladness, some in begrudging and utter exhaustion. The Beanies hugged us as more of Bristol's soldiers moved into the area. Cameramen continued to film.

But we had no time for celebration.

Bristol called his lost boys down for hot chow and showers and ordered the men of the 100th Battalion/442nd RCT to battle on. We formed a perimeter defense line and advanced along the road the Beanies had set out to win seven days before.

• • •

Just hours later, what was left of our company encountered a skirmish, and a load of shrapnel pierced my right thigh and knocked me on my butt. My skin ripped apart, pain searing up my leg. My head throbbed in commiseration.

Kat was nearby and hauled me into his jeep. We raced through a blizzard of bullets to medics, who stopped the bleeding before getting me to the field hospital.

Ando came up and held my hand tight. "You don't look so hot," he said.

Forty-eight hours later, I ached not from pain, but from grief as news came in.

Captain Stewart had tripped a Bouncing Betty, killing him instantly, gruesomely. Lieutenant Donnelly immediately transferred from our weapons platoon to become acting company commander. Just days on the job, Donnelly got hit, badly. Mits Oyama, Company I's clerk, took charge of the few men left.

Morphine made me lose track of time, but at some point, Vic Abe swung by to pick up Ando.

"Heal fast," Ando said as he left.

Next thing I knew, there was Ando again, in the cot next to mine, his head heavily bandaged.

He'd gone on recon patrol along a ridgeline, he said, searching for Jerries hurling artillery at our men. The patrol took out four Jerries before Ando ordered the men to stay back while he probed the forward slope by himself. A bullet pierced his helmet and cut across the top of his head.

"Crawled back to our company, darn it all," he said. "Let them know where the Jerries were hiding."

Hurting but proud, we both drifted off to sleep, only to awaken to confounding news.

"Bristol called for a dress review," the newest patient told us. He had come in with trench foot and took a cot across from us. "Yelled at our commanders for not having everyone there. You should have heard Colonel Carpenter." Carpenter was our regimental executive officer, filling in for our wounded commander.

"What did he say?" we asked.

"'All the men are what you see,'" he said. "He was steaming mad."

We all wondered if the damned general had any idea of our losses. Did he even know the 100th had already been called into reserve, somewhere in the Maritime Alps?

"Your old company commander was there, you know," the soldier said.

Ando said he'd heard Captain Grand was due back from the evac hospital. We all loved him.

"Guy just stood there, silent, gulping back tears. So few men left."

The soldier frowned. "Bristol went around pinning medals on everyone, but we were all sick. Bone tired. Could barely stand at attention."

I wanted to give Bristol a medal, too, right up his damned ass.

Soon after this, I was evacuated to a hospital in England for a growing infection in my leg, and I heard that the 442nd was relieved on November 17, after patrolling the front and flanks of troop movement toward St. Dié. Bristol marched into Germany.

Men coming in for treatment told me that the 442nd was joining the 100th to patrol the French-Italian border and get some rest after the hell of the Vosges. Mak and Ando went reverse AWOL, and I could just imagine their bandages flying in the wind as they raced to our troops.

Happi could sketch a good picture of that, if he ever got back.

19

Champagne Campaign

December 1944-February 1945

I measured my time in the hospital by the number of dark dreams that haunted my sleep and by the number of letters from Ruth that cheered my days. One nightmare repeated itself over and over.

I have entered a forest, its ceiling a black mangle of pine branches that admit no light, about as far from heaven as you can get. When the Jerries blast their ammo against the trees, the tops fall in hot splinters and blazing shrapnel. Tree bursts, everyone calls them, bloody tree bursts. They join the incessant, frigid rain to create a world of fire and ice, the very bottom of hell. The Jerries have their backs to the wall, closer and closer to the fatherland, and their soldiers fight around the clock like fools.

The air crackles with freezing cold, crazy cold, as though the natural order has gone awry with war's destruction, and fog and mist cover the world. My men and I don't even have winter-weight ODs to warm us. We shake with cold and fear. The dirt trails, trodden by the boots of Allies and Germans, are a mire of muck, and Jerries hide in the tall grasses off the roads, their bunkers camouflaged with twigs and logs. Men shoot at everything, everywhere. We can't see the enemy or know where he was. The Germans let us pass by and then pop up to blast our rear to kingdom come. We take a shot, the Jerries fall, and then new ones pop up. When we find open ground, we halt. It is wired to kill.

The dark hills are honeycombed with Jerries, topped with Jerries, all of them firing down on us. We run up and down, up and down, up and down, winning the territory, seeing it revert to the enemy, and winning it back again.

And out of the mist emerges Major General Hugh Bristol, waist high in the icy brush, the belt of his trench coat trailing behind like the tail of the devil himself. Advance! Advance! Advance! he yells to anyone and everyone. Advance!

I become lost in the forest, dense fog hovering everywhere. A voice cries out through the black in desperation and pain, strong and then faint, strong and faint.

Okaasan!

Okaasan!

I think of my family, but they are not here.

I look to my friends.

They have vanished.

Off in the distance, just outside the forest, I hear cheers of celebration and music of bon odori.

I want to join everyone, but my legs are frozen.

I open my mouth to cry for help, but my voice is gone.

Gone.

Gone.

Everything gone.

I always awoke in a sweat after this one, comforted only when I read Ruth's words. They gave me hope that goodness and sanity would one day reappear around the world. I always held her latest letter close, reading it again and again.

4100 Drexel Boulevard
Chicago, Illinois
November 29, 1944

My darling Hiroshi,
I worry every time I receive a letter from you on Red Cross statio-nery as I am afraid you have been wounded and are in the hospital. And now I have had two such letters in a row. Are you all right, sweet-heart? You never say anything about being hurt.

We follow news of the war religiously, and we have twice seen a newsreel of the Lost Battalion rescue in the theaters. Thank goodness the men were saved, and people are hearing about the bravery of your outfit. We are also heartened by General MacArthur's return to the Philippines and the Leyte Gulf. His work with Admiral Halsey to de-feat the Japanese naval and air fleets should make the Japs surrender soon, I hope and pray. When will they? This kamikaze horror has to end. Taking what is left of their aircraft and crashing them into our ships shows how desperate they are. How many more islands must we take? Must we fight on the ground in Japan itself?

The only news I have is that I've settled into a really large apart-ment with the two girls that I met at the Eleanor Club, Beatrice Fukuda and Akiko Kanno. I'm now on the South Side, where quite a few of us AJAs live. The previous tenant had to rush off to war so we were very lucky to grab the place. Our neighbors grew a Victory garden last year and we're going to give them a hand come spring. The only drawback here is the stench that floats into the neighborhood from the stockyards on killing days, but we say prayers for the poor cattle and count our blessings.

Did I tell you that Beatrice's sister got accepted into the MIS as a translator? She began her training at Snelling last month. Her cousin just enrolled in the WACs, too, so it's not just in civilian life that women are showing their moxie.

I love my job and am saving as much money as I can, waiting for you to come home.

I miss you more with each day and look forward to holding you in my arms again, to dance and laugh and kiss. Get you and your friends home as soon as you can.

I sent you a box of candies and cookies so keep your eyes peeled.

Love,

Ruth

My letters to Ruth tried to reassure her of the good job we were doing so we could get home soon.

December 10, 1944

My dearest Ruth,

Now that we're taking a break from battle, your letters are catching up with me, and I have time to read them and think about all the good times we've had together. I can't wait to get home and see you for real not just in my dreams. And I just know we'll be back home pronto.

You mentioned the Lost Battalion rescue, and I have to tell you, that was sure a proud moment for all of us. We are even hearing that the man in our company who led the charge up the hill has been recommended for the Medal of Honor. Can you believe it? The highest award in the country! That news really gives us a boost, after all the hard work we put in. Plus the fact that this guy used to be a real troublemaker and no one thought he'd amount to anything. Guess he just needed a place to show his guts the right way. Anyway, we're all waiting to hear if he gets the MOH and hope that the medal isn't downgraded, like so many of our awards are. The officers who know us well, right on the battlefield, make the recommendations, and then officers way high up who don't know us or anything that happened just knock the awards down a notch or two. But I hear the 442nd brass thinks this one will stick.

Our outfit has left the Vosges and is enjoying some R&R in the French part of the Alps. Everyone is looking forward to some good food and wine. That all depends on what is available, of course, but anything beats a steady diet of rations, that's for sure shooting. I promise I won't get into trouble. No flirting with the mademoiselles. Why would I want to anyway? They can't hold a candle to you.

I have to run now. I will write more later, my darling.
Avec amour,
Hiroshi

Three dozen nightmares and eleven letters later, I escaped the hospital and navigated my way to our men via a series of trains and trucks, eager to join with them again. On my last rail, I bumped into Nobu Sakai, a Buddhahead from a Waimea sugar plantation, high up on the Big Island, and we agreed to finish the journey together. Nobu served in our 1st Platoon and had been laid up for weeks with trench foot, even before the rescue.

Nobu and I laughed it up in our relief to be alive and free, on our way to see our buddies. But on the second day of our journey, his feet swelled so he had trouble getting his boots on. I began carrying him wherever we ventured, on the train and on all our stops. We disembarked for good in Menton, where the 100th's HQ was receiving flak.

"Come on," I said to Nobu. "Piggyback."

"You sure?" Nobu said. "You're still limping yourself."

"To hell with it. I'm fine. Hop aboard."

We knew the 442nd was stationed somewhere around here, also receiving flak, and after talking to several soldiers, we learned that the 2nd Battalion had just left the valley of L'Escarene to relieve our men high up in the Sospel area. The men told us that GIs froze their balls off way up there, on patrol and in negotiations with the mules that carried their rations. The 3rd Battalion was now in regimental reserve down in L'Escarene, and happy for it.

As we neared our encampment, we saw soldiers struggling with mules, too, but the 3rd Battalion's new situation looked pretty damned nice. The slopes of the area overlooked Monaco and the surrounding villages, the men closer to fun. And parts of I Company had lucked into staying in a schoolhouse. We found our way there, and after making sure Nobu was settling in with his own men, I found my buddies and backslapped everyone in sight.

"It's about time, eh?" Mak called out. Poi joined in, and then Kat.

"Hiro! Son of a gun!" Ando, his head still bandaged, ran up to me. "You're back!" He clasped my hands. "We were afraid you'd gone stateside."

"Beat you by a day," Happi welcomed me back. "Froze my ass in an open truck to get here."

"Our buddy's in loooovvvve," Mak said as he grabbed Happi by the shoulders.

"Really?" I grinned.

"Nurse at my hospital," Happi said. "What a knockout. Black hair, emerald green eyes. Gentle hands."

We met the last comment with oooohs and aaaaaahs and a few rude gestures.

Ando excused himself for a moment, and conversation resumed.

"So you going back to her after the war?" I asked, trying to imagine what Happi's nurse looked like. It was great to see my pal smiling so much. The guy was actually blushing.

"Hope to. We promised each other we'd write every day."

Our platoon members gathered round to hear one another's news, but as we talked I was surprised to feel a tension I couldn't quite put my finger on, a sense of unease about the way things were going on the homefront and in the war zone, about changes in command and in soldiers, about the prospects of war and the prospects of peace.

Buddhahead reports brought us high and low.

Martial law had been lifted while we fought in the Vosges.

But anyone the government saw as "dangerous" was still trapped in camp. Roosevelt had even signed another executive order, this one to seal the deal.

Haole soldiers stationed on the islands were tearing up Buddhist temples and statues all over.

News from the mainland was just as *hamajang*, a real mess, men said.

Mitsuye Endo had just won her Supreme Court case, making illegal the internment of citizens deemed innocent by the government.

More people were released from the camps to go home, to attend school, to find jobs, but others stayed imprisoned.

And the very same day as the Endo decision, the Court found Fred Korematsu still guilty.

What the hell?

At least the JACL had supported him this time, but the idea of military necessity continued to rule the day. We were at war with Japan when he disobeyed the directives.

Other areas posed their own challenges, even Chicago.

I worried about my family. About Ruth.

Mak said that girl he'd danced with, Masako, had written that she'd been forced out of her apartment by her very nasty landlady. The rental had been arranged earlier by her dental school, and the landlady had known only that her new tenant would be a student, not an AJA. She was a downright bigoted bitch, he said, and turned on Masako immediately, rifling through her things when she was in class, moving her belongings into the hallway, refusing to cash her checks so she'd be delinquent.

"Masako's classmates—all real nice haoles, eh—they got her moved," Mak said, adding her new place was near Molly's. "Her brother and one of his friends moved in to share rent and help, yuh. They just graduated from law school and were looking for jobs. But then FBI haul them all away in paddy wagon. Accused them of being spies."

"What the hell?" I said. I imagined any sudden activity by three unknown "Japs" would scare the shit out of the government.

"They didn't even have a WRA to help, yuh," Mak said. "Took them all day and all night to convince agents they not doing anything wrong. Really students."

I had to admit, I was curious to see the WRA in a new light, and we all wondered what it would take to turn the tide in Hawaii and on the mainland, once and for all.

"Maybe Honda will help," men said. The guy was still in the hospital, and everyone was waiting to hear about his Medal of Honor.

"He wins that, and we'll all get recognized."

"Brave buggah, that one."

"Get what's coming to us."

"Think it was Fowler who recommended him?" someone asked.

"At least had to go through him, I'd think," someone else said.

Men stopped talking, and I could feel their discomfort growing.

Everyone in our company knew it was the colonel who had ordered my ration detail out into that black night.

But we knew, too, that he had directed us well in battle, and he had charged up that bloody hill by our side.

What should we make of this man?

We fell silent, confounded by his contradictions.

Ando came back in the room and broke the quiet. "Well, men, I have a little bit of news."

We perked up, hoping for some straightforward cheer.

"The command structure is changing these days," he said, pausing as he looked around.

Could it be Fowler was going back to the 69th?

Ando continued. "Colonel Carpenter has agreed to become head of the Regiment. And Lieutenant Donnelly has just returned from the hospital. He's going to resume his position as acting company commander. First lieutenant now."

Everyone cheered. Carpenter had a good reputation, and we all loved Donnelly.

"And one more piece of news," Ando said. We quieted down.

Was there still hope?

"Lieutenant Donnelly has offered me a field commission."

We called out, "Congratulations!" and *Omedetou!* and Mak and I shook Ando's hand, not sure of our own positions, now that we were all together again.

"It's about time they promoted you," Happi said.

But Ando surprised us again.

"Tell you the truth, I don't know if I'm going to take it," he said. "Like I told Lieutenant Donnelly, I'm not even a college boy."

"What did he say?" we asked.

"The battlefield's my university."

"So?"

"I told him I want to stay close to you guys, my men."

"And?"

"He said I can still be close, just as a lieutenant."

"He's right," everyone said.

"I'm going to beat the hell out of you if you turn this down," I said. "You deserve it."

"When's this going to happen?" we asked.

"Christmas Day. 0900 hours. At General Devers' post." Devers commanded the Sixth Army, active in this area.

"You have to take it," I said.

"Not a doubt," Mak said.

"I really don't know," Ando said. "I still have a couple of days to think."

Offering final words of encouragement, we left our sarge to his deliberations and filled those days with holiday celebrations. We even helped our 2nd Battalion throw a Christmas party that they had long planned for the children of L'Escarene and the surrounding area. Happi and I remembered how much it had meant to the kids in Minidoka when people inside and outside the camp cared enough to give them presents, and we ended up surrounded by a good share of the boys and girls, ours from an orphanage. We handed out toys that our 2nd Battalion comrades had asked their parents to rush from home, plus candies that everyone had saved from their rations.

When we returned to camp, mail call brought our own gifts of letters and packages, and to my delight, Ruth's box of goodies caught up with me, plus a new note, which I poked in my pocket. I passed the cookies and candies around, making sure Nobu got his fair share, and we all wondered if Ando was going to take the damned field commission or not.

. . .

We awoke Christmas morning, and our platoon gathered together.

"I don't see him," men said.

"Think he's gone to General Devers?" everyone asked.

"Maybe sisters sent him Christmas cake," Mak laughed. "He's hiding, eating whole damned thing himself."

"I bet he's taking the commission," I said.

"I think he is, too."

"Me, too."

"Tell you what," I said. "When he gets back, let's salute him."

We kept watch as we waited for both our leader and our Christmas luncheon, and just in time, Ando's jeep approached.

Our platoon stood together to honor our new lieutenant. The men, including Mak, asked me to call "Atten-hut!" and I proudly ordered them as Ando walked toward us, his brass second lieutenant bar holding pride of place on his garrison cap and collar. We saluted him smartly and then gathered round to congratulate him and give him a hard time.

After a while, Ando checked his watch and said, "Here's my first command as your lieutenant. Go enjoy Christmas dinner, before all the girls get taken." We eagerly obeyed, and Ando followed with Vic Abe.

A big group of beautiful *mademoiselles* had been scheduled to come by and sing Christmas carols to our battalion, and men from each company were already taking "their share" of the ladies when we arrived at the mess tent. Replacements were joining us veteran soldiers, and my gang couldn't get near the girls, so many men swarmed around them. We focused on chow instead, and what a feast Tommy and his crew had prepared: hot turkey, cranberry sauce, mashed potatoes AND rice, and apple pie. Bottles of cognac welcomed us to the tables.

I looked over at Happi as we ate, surprised at the cloud that had come over his face.

"You okay?" I asked.

Happi shrugged. "Had a great time with the children. But right now, I just see unfamiliar faces. Didn't know there could be so many new guys. It's hard to take."

I thought for a minute, recognizing this difference in us. Me, I was dying to head over to the repple depple, to get to know all the new men as they were being processed, but not Happi. I remembered how concerned he was with the new men back in Naples, and I figured the guy had trouble getting comfortable with strangers.

"Come on, it's Christmas," Mak said. "Let's make merry."

Poi poured us all a drink. We drank and ate and celebrated.

Kat poured a second round.

"Careful now." Poi held his hand up as Kat poured. "You heard what happened to your asshole friend here?"

"Well?" I asked.

"Got loaded on cognac on our first trip into town. Tipped over his jeep just for fun," Poi said.

Kat added, "Brass don't see humor, eh. So guess what?"

I had no idea.

"I'm back in the infantry." Kat laughed.

I couldn't tell if he was really happy about it or not, but I felt good. Hell, after seeing what had happened to our chaplain's jeep, I didn't think being a driver was any safer than being a rifleman.

"Welcome back to the team," I said, and we all toasted Kat.

Lieutenant Donnelly came by as we finished our luncheon, greeting us as our company commander. We poured him the rest of the cognac and toasted him with the dregs in our glasses.

"Come on, Hiro," he called as we got up to leave. "Some things don't change."

I knew what was coming and rubbed my hands together. Donnelly just loved challenging us kotonks to sit with him plantation style, squatting while keeping our feet flat on the ground, and it was my turn.

We ran from the tent and took our positions outside.

I wobbled.

He teetered.

We fell.

"Who has to buy the beer for everyone?" Mak called, knowing the usual conditions of the challenge.

"It's Christmas. Cognac all around." Donnelly laughed and waved Happi over to give it a try, and the Buddhaheads told us we were getting the knack, at last.

With my pal's spirits restored, I visited town with him and Mak later that afternoon, when local folks invited us into their homes, kissed us on both cheeks, and treated us to yet more feasts, even ravioli and some kind of beef, probably black-market stuff. We brought them candy and cigarettes from our rations, and everyone ended up dancing together before we left. After we wrote letters home, Happi and I sat on the floor and talked late into the night, Happi sketching the whole time.

"I really miss my family," Happi said, "but I tell you, the way the people here are trying to overcome their suffering, decorating and sharing everything they have, I'm glad to be right where we are. Such a beautiful old area, such good spirits."

We talked about Ando's commission, too, and Happi handed me a letter that he'd just written his family, vowing to show our new lieutenant what a good soldier, what a good man he could be.

"He's not a 90-day wonder," he wrote of Ando, "but one of us. Started as a private. We admire the heck out of him."

I handed the letter back to Happi, feeling his emotions deeply. I knew he'd give his all once the war started up again.

But for now, Happi showed me his sketches, and I recognized a few of the children of L'Escarene and a couple of the French who had made merry with us. I could feel the mix of happiness and hunger and sadness of the little ones, the relief from the tedium and horror of war of the townspeople.

"You're real good, you know," I told him as we got ready to turn in.

"Drawing really helps clear my head, sort through things," Happi said, yawning.

"Have a sketch of your nurse?" I asked.

Happi looked through his drawings. "As a matter of fact, I do," he said and handed me the pad. "Never met a gal like this one. Funny and smart, really listens to you, and you want to hear her every word. Good sense of humor, too. Sees right through your bullshit but still likes you." He hopped up and headed to the bathroom.

I studied the picture.

Was this for real?

Did Happi have any idea?

If there ever existed a Caucasian version of Ruth, there she was. Same wavy hair to her shoulders, same smile, same glint of love and determination in her eyes, even if they were a little rounder. Her personality sounded like Ruth's, too.

I handed the sketch back to Happi when he returned. "She's a real catch," I said. I wanted to say more, but let it go for now.

As Christmas moved into Epiphany, a big holiday for the French, Ando reminded us that we always had work to do, and at the moment, we really needed to find a good supply of wood. So a few of the boys elected me to lead the way, like I automatically had lumberjack expertise because of my Seattle upbringing. What the hell, I thought. I knew enough, so we struck out on an expedition to find just the right tree, sturdy and tall. Once we'd settled on a good specimen, I directed everyone in proper cutting and felling.

"Begin on this side so it will fall away from the other trees," I said to Happi and Poi. I knew that was an impossible task, because a hell of a lot of trees rose close together all over the damned place, well above power lines. A telephone pole stood several feet away.

"Like this?" Happi took a chop with his axe.

"Yeah, make it around forty-five degrees on the upper chop and the same on the lower," I said.

I told him to stop about a third of the way through the tree and then said to Poi, "Okay, now start on your side. Start a little above where Happi cut."

Poi attacked the tree like a mad man, but before I could stop him, everyone was yelling, "Timber!" and the damned tree fell in just the opposite direction of what I wanted, and on top of another tree. Both fell on top of the electric wires, which sparked and frizzled.

"Oh, no," I muttered.

"Uh-oh," Mak said.

"Oh, *merde!*" the French called as they ran from their houses.

Everyone proved an instant expert, like me, gesturing which way to push what tree, and a community meeting broke out in which the nuances of weather and holidays and tree felling were discussed and debated and translated.

Looking around, Poi shrugged, removed his boots, and began climbing the telephone pole, saw in hand.

"Eh, *kanaka!*" Happi laughed as he called Poi the name for a native Hawaiian. There were actually a few native Hawaiians in the RCT, but Poi was as close as our squad was going to get.

"*Mon Dieu!*" called the French.

Poi raced up the pole and began sawing the top of the closest tree, which snapped off and fell hard against the pole. The pole swung around and around, and the French gathered opposite us for a better assessment.

"Hang on!" I called to Poi. He clung to the pole, his legs flying.

"Holy shit!" Poi yelled. "Son of a f—b—!"

I lost the last two words to the wind on our side, but one of the French who knew a little English began laughing and calling out, *Sainte merde!* and *Fils de pute!* as the rest joined in. The pole slowed its oscillation, and down Poi slid, to great applause and cheers. After more arguing and conversation, we worked with *nos amis* and lifted the trees from the wires, and people ran back in their houses, returning with bottles of wine. No one had lost electricity. We toasted one another, fast friends.

• • •

Over the next several days, Happi walked around our battalion area in search of more subjects to draw, and I visited the repple depple with Mak and Ando, knowing it was high time we introduce ourselves. Especially with Mak by my side, I remembered how it felt to be new, eager, and scared as hell, all at the same time. That was an eon ago, before the war had aged me, and I thought the replacements looked younger and younger with each shipment. I worked hard to make them feel comfortable.

"How do you do, Private," Ando welcomed our newest boy into the group. "I'm Tosh Ando, your platoon lieutenant." The kid's ears stuck out of his head like crock handles, and damn if they didn't remind me of my kid brother.

"Charles Wesley Morita, sirs," the young soldier said. He pointed to Ando's bandaged head. "Where did you get wounded?" Ando explained, saying he was almost healed.

Ando introduced me, his platoon sergeant, and Mak, my assistant.

Mak and I eyed each other, knowing that answered our question. Mak patted me on the back, whispering, "We're a team."

"Team," I said, knowing we would move forward together.

We turned our attention back to our men.

"Just graduate?" I asked Private Morita.

"Was handed my diploma one day and my uniform the next, sir."

"You Buddhahead, eh? I hear in your voice," Mak said.

"From Kona, sir," Morita said.

"Ah, the dry side of the Big Island," Ando said. "I'm from the wet side, home of the Hilo lullaby." He spoke of his family and plantation, explaining to me that when Hilo's ever-present rain tip-tapped the metal totan roofs in the evenings, it lulled everyone to sleep.

Morita soon became known as "Jug" as everyone pulled his ears, just begging to be yanked. He always laughed, reminding me again of Koichi and lifting all our spirits.

Looked like I had two brothers to keep my eye on.

I had to admit, it was difficult welcoming men who were replacing our friends, dead or wounded, and we attended lots of church services to remember them. Damned if Fowler didn't show up at some of them, just as I thought he might, his figure high above the soldiers who looked up to him in all ways. But me, I avoided getting near him, knowing I had to sort things out before coming to some kind of peace with the man. I gave my full attention to Chaplain Morimoto, who preached about the American Dream, how we AJAs were fighting the war for our share of it. I sure as hell wanted my portion.

Occasional skirmishes and casualties kept the war near us, even here, and Menton's residents were evacuated as shelling continued. But we made the trek down into town to grab pockets of peace and enjoy its handsome stone villas and hotels down by the sea, the bars and dance halls further in. We began calling this time the "Champagne campaign," we were enjoying the good parts of this R&R so much. Passes into Cannes were many, the French Riviera ours. Nice became a favorite place to have as good a meal as could be had, plus a bottle of wine, to see some of the ladies, and to get our pictures taken.

Saigo, that's what we thought as we posed for the camera. The end. We were hearing of progress made at Yalta, of plans for peace and a new world order, but we knew these photos could be our last.

20

Champagne Campaign

February 14-March 1945

"Come on, Hiro, when you gonna sing?" Mak tilted his glass toward me and yelled over the din of voices in the Dancing Auguste bar. It was the night of Valentine's Day, and we were celebrating like there was no tomorrow.

Which is pretty much the way we led our lives.

"Need more beer," I called back. Neon lights glowed through the smoke, and soldiers packed the tables, talking and joking. Just a couple of men sat over at the bar, where Happi stood as he drank and yakked with the bartender. The band was on a break, but the music of high spirits filled the air.

"Hey, Mak," I said. "Get that pretty little waitress over here. Just give her a pinch."

Men laughed around our long table, most all from our platoon. Vic Abe came in with a few more friends, taking up the slack, now that Kat was a rifleman again. Besides, Kat was back at camp, sick as a dog.

"Eh, we'll get Happi to sketch her." Mak motioned for the waitress. We'd all seen Happi out by himself, sketching everything in sight. Just a couple of days ago he'd written his family to ask for some cheap watercolors and more paper and pencils so he could take an Army correspondence course in art, things were in such short supply around here. He'd even found a beret and appeared every bit the French *artiste*, especially when he clenched a pipe between his teeth.

More of our buddies sat at tables next to us, and I felt momentarily content, happy that we could celebrate together after the whole damned combat team had marched through hell on earth.

Damned Bristol.

Damned Fowler.

My buddies and I were among the lucky ones. Our original squad didn't have one KIA, and a lot of us had survived our wounds well enough to enjoy this time.

"Come on, let's get the beer flowing," I said to the waitress as I pulled out some bills. "Beers all around. Have no fear! Bière! Bière!"

"Hey, Hiro, give us a chorus," Poi cried.

"Come on!" Tommy shouted, savoring some time away from the kitchen.

"Okay." I grabbed Mak's beer, drained it, and hopped up on the table. I gyrated my hips and made hula motions with my arms to accompany my singing of "Tangerine," thinking all the while of my darling Ruth and how we had danced to the song.

Caballeros sigh!
Oh my, oh my!
Lalalalala!

"Go, Hiro!" the men yelled.

"Move them hips, kotonk."

"You Buddhahead now."

I finished my performance and jumped down as applause and hoots filled our area. Mak handed me a fresh beer, but grew serious as he looked over at the bar.

"What's going on?" Mak gestured toward Happi, who was talking to a couple of MPs, gesticulating with his hands now and then.

"Better see what's up," I said.

We rushed over and asked the police officers, members of a Puerto Rican unit, if there was a problem.

"This guy one of your men?" an MP asked.

We said yes as we eyed Happi, who had a couple of beers in him and was giving everyone a piece of his mind.

"Take him with you, okay?" The MP nudged Happi toward us, studying the torch-in-hand patch on our arms.

"You guys 442nd?" he asked. "I've heard a lot about you. Keep up the good work."

"Thanks. Come on, Happi." The three of us walked back to our table.

"Gimme a beer," Happi said. "Stupid jerks, making me move. I didn't do a damned thing." We watched the MPs as they circled the bar, and I put Happi's arm in a hammerlock.

"Why you always beefing these days?" I kidded him, but was serious. Over the past couple of weeks, my buddy had started mouthing off at people at the least provocation. I figured that despite his new love, the guy was hurting pretty bad from what we'd all been through, hiding his pain with tough talk and booze.

I took a swig of beer, thinking how damned angry I felt, too, how I drank these days not just to have fun, but to let myself forget everything, if only for a few minutes. So many men had gone down in the Vosges, so much had spun out of control, I had to be ready to take matters into my own hands if I wanted things done right.

Suddenly Mak sprang up, pointing toward a soldier taking a swing at one of the MPs near the bar. Men from around the dance hall joined in the scuffle. Mak and I ran toward the bar again, followed by Happi and the rest of the platoon. The band filled the room with music, competing with our voices.

"What's going on?"

"Who is that guy?"

"Who started the fight?"

I didn't have to think. I was platoon sergeant, the senior enlisted man here, the senior EM. I reached into the melee and pulled men apart. "Damn it all, knock it off," I hollered.

Mak, the next senior EM, worked by my side. Happi got in there, too, sobering up to help take control.

"Calm down, guys," Mak bellowed.

The MPs grabbed the soldier who had socked their lieutenant and yelled at him as they pushed him outside.

Mak and I recognized Yoyo Wasuke, who looked totally bombed. I remembered the night back at Shelby when the guy had woken everyone up with his clamor, drunk and belligerent then, too, and Mak reminded me how Yoyo had curled up in his foxhole during our rescue of the T-Patchers. The guy chose the wrong times to fight.

But all that didn't matter. I did what I would have done for any man in our company. I turned to the MPs, who had their pistols drawn, and talked quietly to them, even cajoled them. Hey, they came from Puerto Rico, annexed after the Spanish-American War, so a territory of the United States, like Hawaii. It wasn't clear why Yoyo had even taken a swing, but he obviously had been drinking too much, just like a lot of soldiers. Couldn't they go easy on him?

The MPs talked it over and put their pistols away. Their lieutenant stepped forward. "Okay, tell you what, why don't we call this a misunderstanding. But I think it's best you get your men back to camp. Call it a night."

We got everyone going, and Vic said he'd get his jeep. He pulled up, and Happi, Mak, and I jumped in.

"So where's Yoyo?" Vic asked as we sped away.

"Probably hoofed it back to camp, if he's not being held somewhere," Mak said. "Asshole."

"I'm glad the MPs jawed him out," I said. "But probably in one ear and out the other. What a piece of work."

I hit the sack as soon as we returned and forgot the fracas, and I saw Happi sketching away as I fell asleep.

• • •

Happi and I made it to the beach the next day, but a frigid rain put a damper on things, with no bathing beauties in sight. We ended up grabbing a couple of bières in town. Over the second round, Happi told me he'd received a letter from his nurse a couple of weeks ago. She wanted both of them to feel free to date others until they met again. And she hoped that would be soon, when the war was over.

"Not sure how to take that," Happi said glumly.

"Chin up," I said, understanding why Happi had been belligerent recently. "Sounds like the door's still open."

"Here's hoping." Happi lifted his beer. "I'm going to run to her arms the day I get out of this damned uniform."

Kat called to us as soon as we entered the schoolhouse. "What happened last night?" he asked. "A couple of Fowler's MPs got me out of my sickbed. Told me they wanted to look around. Said something about a fight."

We told him about the scuffle, and Kat said the MPs had searched the place, rifling through clothes and papers and whatever else was lying around.

"I don't understand," I said. "The Puerto Rican MPs agreed to call it a misunderstanding. We all shook hands and left."

The mystery grew deeper the next morning.

"What the hell?" I was brushing my teeth when four MPs and the Provost Marshal from Regimental, all Caucasians, filed into our schoolhouse.

Mak, putting on his shirt, hurried toward me. He muttered, "What's going on?"

In marched Lieutenant Colonel Fowler. He stood in the center of the room, feet spread apart, commanding the space. He held a sheet of paper and consulted it as he barked orders to the MPs. Mak and I frowned as we exchanged glances.

"Take these two," he pointed to us. "And that friend of theirs, Private Ishikawa, find him." He read the paper again. "George Minoru Ishikawa."

Happi was in the bathroom, and I wished I could signal my pal to jump out the window.

Fowler walked in exaggerated strides toward two of the MPs, who were tossing things around. He pointed to the sheet and gave the names of several more men he wanted rounded up. Some of the MPs took me and Mak by the arm, pushed us outside and into a jeep, and drove us to an interior holding area, a few minutes away. It was just me and Mak at first and then Tommy, Happi, Vic, Poi—all guys who had been with us at the Dancing Auguste. A few other soldiers came in, men who had followed us into the fight. Yoyo Wasuke was the last to enter. He stood as far away from our group as he could and stared at the floor. He wouldn't meet anyone's eye.

"Think this has something to do with the fight?" I said to Mak. I was dying for a smoke but didn't have any butts with me.

Mak handed me a cigarette. "Looks like it. But why is Fowler involved? We didn't break any rules. I don't get it."

Ten or fifteen 442nd MPs were milling around, and one barked that each man would now be called in for questioning.

We drew closer together as we waited, all but Yoyo, that is. He leaned up against the wall and slid down to the floor, looking sullen and angry.

"Koga, you're up," the MP said. "Come with me."

The MP did a smart about-face, and I followed him into a room. Three more MPs sat behind tables shoved together for the occasion.

"Name, rank, and serial number," the first MP said.

I didn't know why they needed all the formality, but did as ordered. I hated this part of the Army, all the protocol used to put people in their places, too many men given too much unearned authority.

"Were you present at the Dancing Auguste in the city of Menton on February 14 sometime between the hours of 1900 and 2300?" The second MP stood up and walked around the room.

I said I was.

"And were you involved in the fistfight that ensued at the bar between men of the 2nd Platoon of I Company and the MPs from the Puerto Rican 68th Brigade?" the third MP asked, also walking around.

"I went over to break up a fight."

"Yes or no, Sergeant Koga," Number Two said.

I hesitated, recognizing the inaccuracy of a yes-or-no answer.

"Yes," I said and added in a lower, but firm voice, "but only to break up a fight. We shook hands with the MPs and agreed it was a misunderstanding."

"Did you punch the MP, Sergeant?" Number One asked.

"I didn't punch anyone," I said. "I saw a scuffle had broken out and ran over to stop it. We shook hands and agreed to call it a night. End of story."

"Did you punch the officer?" Number One persisted and walked toward me.

"I did not."

"Then who punched the officer?" The MP stuck his face in mine.

I closed my eyes and pulled my head back as I thought. Yoyo struck me as a prime asshole, but I wouldn't squeal. Men in the 442nd weren't stoolies.

"I'm not sure, and it would be unfair of me to say more." I turned my cheek.

"We will ask you again, Sergeant. Who punched the officer?" The third MP spat the words as he walked around.

"I don't know, sir."

Hell, Yoyo would be in here soon and tell these guys what happened, and then everyone could go.

"Do you realize that if you don't tell the truth, you could be on your way to a court-martial?" the second MP said.

"I am telling you what I know."

"You are dismissed. But don't think this is over." Number Three opened the door, and yet another MP took me by the arm and walked me back to the holding area. Mak and I rubbed shoulders as we passed. I rolled my eyes to the ceiling when he glanced at me.

I joined our men, and an MP called for Tommy. A few minutes ticked by, and Mak returned, and then Tommy, shaking their heads.

Then Happi was called.

And then the others.

279

As men returned, I examined their faces for clues about what they had been through, but they just frowned.

All except Yoyo. He still wouldn't meet my eyes. Or Mak's. Or Happi's. Or those of any other soldier. He just headed for his spot, alone. I knew then that he hadn't confessed.

The questioning began all over again. And again. After the umpteenth round, I had had enough.

"Okay, I'll take responsibility." I threw in the towel. I hated to do it, but what choice did I have? I couldn't let our men suffer this way. "I didn't throw the punch. But I was the senior EM there. I'll take responsibility."

"Throw him in the brig," an MP said. He hurried from the room as another MP cuffed me. When we walked out of the compound, I saw Happi being cuffed, near the stockade area. Mak and Yoyo were taken in another direction. Tommy, Poi, and Happi followed them, surrounded by MPs.

The steel handcuffs bit into my wrists, and my cheeks burned with anger and humiliation as the MPs pushed me into a jeep and drove away. My mind went haywire. After ten or fifteen minutes, we pulled in near some old buildings by the water. We entered one, and the MPs threw me into a barely lit room, just wide enough to stretch my arms and long enough to lie on the cot sitting against one wall.

They'd shoved me in solitary.

A knock at the door a while later announced the arrival of dinner, an insult of cold rations pushed into the room. Times were tough everywhere, but all the same, I imagined the tastier bits of food I might be eating, the real coffee and wonderful wine I could be tasting, the laughter with my pals. I tried to cheer up as I chewed the malted milk tablets, but the reminder of Lawson and my family just made me angrier.

Damned rations, they were the reason I was even here. Fowler was still mad about the way I had laid into him after the detail, right in front of his officer buddies. My battalion commander had grabbed the first opportunity to knock me to my knees, even if he had to twist the truth in his favor and take my own pals with it.

The thought repeated itself, day after day, and I questioned my own resolve in not exposing a private who had broken faith. The idea of going free tempted me, putting this damned un-fair imprisonment behind me and getting on with things, but no, I couldn't go against my conscience. I just couldn't. If I made an exception in this case, where would the exceptions end? Someone had to toe the line, and I had good company. All us AJAs were true blue except Yoyo, and I refused to sink to his level. I felt caught in a vise of betrayal, a private on one side and a colonel on the other.

I created every which way to pass the time.

I ran in place.

I shadowboxed.

I did push-ups.

I shadowboxed.

I thought about Ruth and how I wanted to marry her.

I shadowboxed.

I wondered how my family fared.

I shadowboxed.

I hoped my buddies were okay.

I thought about Wes Inada, how he had warned me to lie low in the Army.

I wondered if Ben Honda had been awarded his Medal of Honor.

And I cursed Fowler, still trying to figure out the son of a bitch.

I remembered how he and his fellow officers back at Shelby had banded together in their little country club, scoffing at us nisei in the name of rules.

But then he led us bravely through Italy and through France.

Had it been Bristol and his craziness that made Fowler crack? The worst in the colonel began coming out. He pulled rank on me and got my men killed.

The bastard deserved every last word I had screamed at him, even if his buddies heard me.

And now he wouldn't let up.

He sought revenge.

I wouldn't be a snitch, but from now on, damn if I wouldn't question every order from leaders I had no faith in. I had no idea what else he was capable of, but I would do whatever it took to protect my men.

My determination grew strong as the hours and days dragged on, but an MP surprised me on the fourteenth day. "Come with me," he said.

"Where we going?" I asked.

"Back to your company," he said.

I guessed I had served my sentence, and my heart lightened. I followed the MP outside.

The bright sun blinded me, but damn, it was good to be free again. I breathed in the salty air and enjoyed the ride back to camp. I spotted the 442nd torch-in-hand sign as we entered the regimental area, and the MP brought the jeep to a screeching halt in front of a big stone building and then walked me inside. A private guarding a locked room spoke with the MP and signed some papers.

"Inside," he commanded me.

"Hiro!" Happi and Mak hopped off their tiers of a bunk bed as I entered the room, dark and cramped. Tommy and Poi did the same from another bed. We shook hands and slapped each other on the back, glad to be reunited.

"So we're not free?" I asked, confused.

Everyone grumbled "no," and we shared stories of the past couple of weeks.

"Solitary for me, too," said Happi.

"When you get out?" I asked.

"I was in the calaboose for almost a week," he said. "Made it here for my birthday. You missed the party."

"I made this one memorable for him," Tommy said. "Twenty-one, eh. Big celebration."

"Cooked botulism bouillon for my special day," Happi laughed. "Cleaned out our systems, and good."

"Hey, I didn't have ingredients for a cake. I tried." Tommy smiled, shrugging.

"What about the others?" I asked.

"I guess the MPs rounded up anyone they thought was near the fight, but they've let the others go. It's just us now," Mak said.

"Where's Yoyo?" I asked.

"Don't know. We saw him being marched around the area when we got here. Haven't set eyes on him since," Poi said.

"Think they're afraid we'll beat the hell out of him if he's put in with us?" Happi said.

Mak said to me, "You know, when we all compared notes, it sounded like the MPs wanted people to turn against you, specifically. What a bunch of bullshit."

Tommy said, "We don't even know what we're accused of. Being your friend?"

I told him where he could put that one, but I knew he was right. After all these months, I explained exactly what had happened after the ration detail, my confrontation with Fowler.

We heard the metal lock on the door scrape, and a guard called Happi and Tommy outside.

"Bet they're shoveling," Mak said as Poi lit our cigarettes. Mak said all of them had been repeatedly ordered to dig six-feet-deep holes, fill them in, and dig again, as individuals and as a group, depending on who was bossing them around.

We heard the lock click once more, and another guard escorted us to an equipment storage area. We picked up shovels and walked until we caught sight of Happi and Tommy, hard at work.

"Go help them," the guard said.

"Welcome back," Happi said as we joined in. "Screw this."

Just like Mak said, we all dug a hole, filled it in, and began again.

Happi wiped sweat from his face, scowling, and dug some more.

He held his shovel still, glanced at us, and dug again.

"What?" I asked.

"Hah?" Mak said.

"Aren't you guys going to do anything?" Happi said, shovel at his side.

"What you mean?" Poi stopped digging.

"What can we do?" I said.

Happi plunged his shovel into the ground.

"What?" Mak asked.

"What?" I echoed him.

"Damn it, why don't we just speak up? No way any of us should take the fall."

"We just don't rat on our guys, Happi," Mak said.

"Maybe that's what Fowler's counting on." Tommy held his shovel steady.

"You guys really think that's right?" Happi asked.

"How the hell did he even know who was at the dance hall?" Tommy asked. "Someone must have told him."

We dug some more.

I looked at everyone and stopped. "The MPs couldn't possibly have remembered all our names. Must have been someone in our group."

"Only one I can think of is Yoyo," Happi said. "Wouldn't that make sense? Fowler hears about the trouble, and Yoyo sings like a canary to the MPs. Tweet, tweet, tweet."

We all agreed as we dug and dug, stopping again only when Happi's brother, Shig, came by to say hello. We gave the brothers space to talk by themselves.

Back in our prison, Happi told me, "Shig worked like hell to maneuver around the war zone to see me. Doesn't know how I got involved in all this hot water." The Army had jammed a cot for me into the room, and I sat on it while Happi stretched out on his bunk, doodling on Army stationery. The other guys were still out. "Shig wants me to focus on the things I can do, for myself and everyone else, no matter the trouble."

I remembered Molly's words when she was trying to lift me from a funk, and I said to him, "No one can take what's inside you, your core. You just have to act on everything you hold dear."

Happi stopped drawing and looked at me. "I promised myself I was going to be a better man for Ando, and I mean that more than ever, with all this stockade shit hanging over us."

Happi seemed to perk up after that, and he was the guy who kept up our spirits as we shoveled our way through the next several weeks, all the while wondering where Yoyo had disappeared. Good news from the Pacific helped. General MacArthur had taken command of ground forces, Admiral Nimitz of naval powers, and the Japs were falling. Allies had opened the Burma Road, invaded Iwo Jima, taken Manila,

Bataan, and Corregidor. Tokyo itself was being firebombed. Things were looking up.

Then Tommy and Poi were released to I Company, told they'd been cleared of all wrongdoing.

The Regiment was shipping out, back to the Gothic Line.

21

Second Push, Italy

March-April 5, 1945

"He's back." I heard men whisper when we rejoined the platoon.

"Isn't that Hiro?"

"Guy got shafted."

"Glad he's here."

As new jeeps and weapons and radios rolled in, we reported to Ando in our staging area of Pisa. Mak and Happi and I had been locked up in Regimental since returning to Italy, but we had just been released, happy as hell to have the whole damned ordeal behind us. The company was filling with replacements, with more on the way, and our leadership was needed.

Ando shook our hands. Mak and I stayed close by our lieutenant as Happi took off to meet new soldiers, making me hope he was finally coming into his own. Maybe Shig had lit a fire under him. Plus Happi was determined to prove himself to Ando. There was no telling where my pal would go with that kind of spirit.

We settled down to business.

Mumbles and grumbles around our encampment worried me as we walked around.

"We're returning in secret," men said. I could hear the pride in their voices. "That's how good our outfit is. Don't want to alert the Germans." Men couldn't even leave our staging area, our presence was so secret.

"But why are we getting attached to the 92nd Division?" Others sounded perplexed. The Negro division, the Buffalo soldiers, had been stuck at the Gothic Line since we left.

"Are they lousy soldiers?" men asked. "Stalled here so long."

"What gives?"

I gathered with Mak and Ando to discuss the situation with our higher ups, beginning with how the Allied focus had shifted to France over the past several months, carrying us and other troops with it. The 92nd had stayed on and fought without support, their forces depleted, with no combat-ready Negro troops available as replacements.

We swallowed hard as we listened, realizing that this division could be a challenge to work with. Their predicament could lead to men being assigned and reassigned to positions for which they weren't qualified. On top of that, rumor had it that their senior officers, all white, had had no faith in the combat abilities of Negro GIs from the outset, a dispiriting state of affairs that could not be overcome by the unit's many Negro junior officers, who themselves were constantly being rotated. Sometimes the GIs didn't even know who their leaders were.

"How can soldiers fight like that?" I said, dismissing any speculation about race and performance. We were hearing good news about other Negro units—the Tuskegee Airmen, the 333rd Artillery, the 761st Tank Battalion—and figured they'd had better organization and support.

"Good thing our brass believes in us, no matter the bumps along the way," Mak said. I knew some bumps were greater than others, but I held my tongue.

Ando agreed. "You have to have trust to instill confidence and courage, teamwork."

I recalled hearing how the 92nd men were among the only Negros to train as infantry in this war, and I hoped whatever preparation and experience they'd had would help now. We needed them. A revitalized effort was under way to break the Gothic Line and rout the Jerries, once and for all. We wanted to wrap things up and head home.

Ando gathered all of us platoon and squad leaders. "We're committed to fighting together. We'll make things work," he said to everyone. Attached to the 92nd Division, we would again fight under the command of none other than General Clark, now leading the 15th Army Group. He had begged Eisenhower for our return.

"Let's start with the big picture," Ando said, spreading out a map. "Hold your breath, men. Here is our enormous battlefield. Germans everywhere you look."

Ando pointed to our sector of the northern Apennines mountain range, which began here in the west with its highest mount, Altissimo, and moved north and further west to the massive ridge between 3,100-foot-high Mount Carchio and Mount Folgorito, only three hundred feet its junior. It then moved further north and west to Cerreta and Georgia Hill and the three Ohio mounts. The range extended west through Carrara to the mounts of Castelpoggio and Nebbione and Carbolo, ending at the vital road center of Aulla and tapering into the flat lands of the Ligurian coast, out to the naval port of Spezia, our ultimate objective.

"Holy shit," Mak muttered. "What the hell are we supposed to do?"

"Good God," someone else whispered.

Ando continued, "Colonel Carpenter has figured out a pincer move to encircle the Nazis in these mountains and drive them out. The 100th and 2nd battalions will attack the mountain ridges from the front, the south, and our 3rd Battalion will attack from the back, the north. Once we meet up, we'll march north and west, mount by mount, village by village, until the Germans are gone."

Ando explained our movements as a division. "The 92nd Division will consist of us beginning on the right flank, taking the ridges and the villages at their base. The 370th Regiment will march on the left, moving first toward the village of Massa and attacking east of Highway 1, away from the Germans' coastal guns near Spezia. The 473rd will start in reserve, in the Serchio Valley, north of Lucca. That runs parallel to the coast, just west of the Apennines." The 370th was the last Negro regiment in the 92nd and was making every effort to get beefed up. The 473rd consisted of Caucasian infantryman who had been re-trained as anti-aircraft gunners. Both units would have support from armored battalions.

Ando gave us time to take in the enormity of the situation and then continued. "Understand this. We're starting as a diversion for the Allies and will move at night. Once word escapes that we're fighting in this section of the Apennines, General Clark hopes the Nazis will shift troops from the main Allied front, in Bologna, to fight us. That will allow the Allies to push the Jerries there into the Po Valley, on the other side of the mountains. Once our mountains are cleared, the remaining Jerries will be forced through the Po Valley into the Alps, out of Italy, and back home to the Fatherland."

"I assume the Germans have built themselves into the mountains," I said.

"You bet," Ando said. "Handmade fortifications, cement fortresses, you name it. Fighting is going to be tough." He said interlocking fire could trap us. Those long-range 288-mm coastal guns over in Punta Bianca, near Spezia, would threaten us further. The Germans had already blocked area roads needed for supplies, Highway 1, Highway 61, Highway 63. "Our engineers will have their hands full." We knew we couldn't fight without those men, who worked around the clock to clear bomb-infested roads and minefields, build new routes so we could advance. Every bullet we shot, every inch we budged, every ration we ate, came by way of them.

Ando's eyes moved over us, and he said, "And don't think the mountains alone aren't a challenge. They tower over everyone at sixty-degree angles, sometimes seventy."

Ando looked down, as though searching for something to say that would encourage us, and his words were simple and clear. "Clark called us his very best. This campaign is going to demand everything we have."

Mak and I eyed each other and the men around us, apprehension growing. We were grateful for Clark's confidence in us, relieved to once more follow a leader who respected what we did. But this battlefield looked impossible.

And how would Fowler behave?

At least we would all fight under a tremendous commander, not that moron Bristol. He'd landed in Germany, and that's where he could stay.

Ando dismissed us, saying he'd know more about the specifics of our battle once we had moved to San Martino, near the ancient city of Lucca, walled to defend against enemies of yore. We would bivouac there and train for a few days before battle.

"No more rest," Ando said. "Time for combat."

Two nights later, I climbed on a battalion truck, one in a long convoy jerking alive as we headed out. The journey was no more than twelve miles, but we inched along as drivers dimmed and cut lights. We reached San Martino well before dawn and were hard at training by breakfast. Replacements old and new joined with veteran soldiers in learning how to use new weapons and in mastering battle maneuvers. The 92nd's command inspected us, and General Clark saw that we were ready.

Ando pulled our platoon together, again spreading out the map.

The land stood barren, he warned, mountain slopes steep and slippery. The Germans could see all troop movements.

Ando looked around as everyone absorbed the information.

"Now, let's focus on our part of the effort," he said. "We're heading to the Carchio-Folgorito ridge to surprise the hell out of the Jerries at the top. Tomorrow night, we move to Azzano, our assembly area. We'll rest there the following day. Then we'll climb the saddle at night and attack the top at dawn."

Ando added that Colonel Fowler had assured Carpenter we would carry out our mission flawlessly. Fowler said his experience with us dated back to D-maneuvers at Shelby and had shown him just what we were capable of.

You bet your ass it did.

We again boarded our battalion trucks in blackness, this time headed into battle. I swore I smelled fear, the fear that gripped soldiers who knew nothing of what they were getting into and the fear that gripped soldiers who knew too much. I put my hand on the shoulder of Jug Morita, who'd removed his helmet to cool his sweaty head. I felt the young boy trembling and kept my hand steady to calm him, all the while thinking, "Shit, here we go again." Far away, an occasional burst of artillery illuminated the mountains that we would fight for.

A bump in the road threw soldiers against one another. Helmets clanked helmets. Rifle butts scraped the floor. The noises echoed into the darkness. Men regained their footing and held their breath, waiting for enemy fire.

Hours slipped by as a soft rain fell, and the vehicles squealed to a halt at Pietrasanta. I jumped from the truck with everyone, landing with a soft, mushy thud, and ran around with Ando and Mak to see that our men stood ready to take on the next leg of our journey, a march up to Azzano.

"You okay?" I checked on Jug, who was having trouble just wearing his mountain of gear. I figured the kid weighed one hundred twenty pounds, just fifteen pounds above the minimum requirement. We veterans were used to the burden, but not the replacements. Kat ran over and helped shift the weight of Jug's pile and tighten his carrying straps so the load wouldn't tilt and propel him over a cliff.

"You can do this," Kat encouraged Jug. "Go for broke."

We took off, our gear clattering, and marched in tight formation before dividing ourselves into columns on either side of the road. I kept one eye on my men, the other on the ditches to the side, and I locked my mind on the cadence of the march, willing our squads to do the same. The road was hard and winding, broken only by dirt and gravel that must have been kicked up by bombs. When the platoon rested, Ando raced up and down the road, checking our men and letting them know we stood near a village called Seravezza, about four miles from where we'd started. Azzano was still miles ahead.

Marching once more, we struggled up a trail that grew rocky and narrow, its drop-offs steeper as we climbed. I thought this must be where goats walked, an easy path for them, but not for us. Men slipped here and there as drizzle fell and cold descended, but we marched quickly. We had to complete our climb to Azzano in the dark.

Clunk!

We froze, listening as a soldier tumbled down the mountain.

Would the Germans hear that?

Thud!

Good God, there went another.

Men held their breath as one, waiting for a scream or a curse, but none came.

Was the man obeying orders to keep silent, no matter what?

Or was he dead?

Silently, men grabbed hands.

A backpack in front.

A rifle.

We formed and re-formed a human chain, holding onto one another as we made our way in slippery blackness.

Whenever a man lost his footing, he let go so he didn't drag others with him.

I had just passed a small stream crossing the trail when I heard *clunk-thud-splash!* One of my men had fallen.

I peered through the black behind and below me and could make out a man crashing to a stop, thirty or forty feet down the embankment.

I looked over our men and didn't see Jug.

I motioned the squads to move on, confident that Mak and Happi, Kat and Poi were keeping an eye on the new soldiers as they followed Ando. I slid down the slope on my butt until I reached a stream.

There was Jug, lying face down in the water.

I heard a thud behind me and turned around to see Kat. Together we grabbed Jug under his armpits and around his chest and pulled him from the water. Then I smacked him back to consciousness and checked for broken bones. The boy was in one piece. We pulled him upright and carried him between us back up the mountain. He came fully awake and walked on his own, limping a bit.

I made a quick assessment. It would be foolhardy to try and catch up with our platoon, so we simply followed the men in the rear, struggling even then to keep up with the pace. We arrived in the village of Azzano sometime in the early morning. We found some of our platoon in a farmhouse, and Jug passed out on the floor. Kat and I explored several rooms until we found Happi and Mak and Poi. We slept for a few hours and awoke to fresh eggs that men had discovered in the house and around the farm.

"What bullshit you guys went through." Our men offered their sympathies to me and Mak and Happi on our stockade ordeal as everyone ate. We sat in a large kitchen with lots of wooden furniture, old and worn, with pretty dishes on the hutches and tables. A gray sink stood against the opposite wall.

What a mistake, everyone agreed.

"They don't call it 'snafu' for nothing," Happi said. He talked to everyone, much more open since our confinement.

"Glad we can put it behind us," Mak added.

"Where the hell's Yoyo, anyway?" Kat asked.

"Who cares?" another man said.

"Last we know, he was somewhere in Regimental, off by himself," Mak said. "Hope I never see him again."

Jug entered the room and hobbled over to us.

"Sergeant," Jug said. "Thank you. And you, too, Kat. Hell, I could have died."

"Forget it." I waved the thought away. "You needed a hand. We were close by."

"Well, I owe you guys one. Thanks again."

I lit a cigarette and took a swig of coffee, which tasted real good. Our buddies had found some dark brown beans in the house, espresso beans, someone said, and made a few pots. I told Jug to sit down. The boy didn't look too hot and assuredly ached with pain.

"You know, we weren't the last to get in," I told Jug as he propped himself up against a wall.

Kat added, "Something like seventy guys got lost. Followed a wire into the village. What a night."

Ando came by to check on everyone, standing quietly for a few minutes as he listened to our conversations.

"Right back in the swing, eh?" Ando said to me. He asked Jug how he felt, and Jug said someone had brought him a breakfast of fresh eggs and vegetables, plus extra rations.

"How rations even get up here?" Jug asked. "I didn't see anyone carrying the stuff."

"A whole lot of mules and Partisans lined the trail. Hauled supplies up with our kitchen crew," Ando said. The Partisans belonged to the Associazione Nazionale Paritgiani d'Italia, the ANPI, the Italian Resistance, and had begun their work during the last push. "Wouldn't have enough to eat if it weren't for them. We should have food for an extra day or two now. Some men are digging around for more vegetables."

"Kona nightingales, those mules are, eh?" Jug said.

"Yeah, yeah, yeah." Ando looked happy as he explained the term to us kotonks. "That's what we call donkeys on the Big Island. They get lonely at night and bray to donkeys on other plantations and farms."

Ando eyed the young soldier. "Morita, can you keep up? I don't know if you've looked in a mirror, but you one bruised buggah."

Jug pulled himself up. "Just need a little more rest, Lieutenant. I'll be fine."

"You have to be in good enough shape to fight," Ando said. "Listen to Sergeant Koga."

Jug returned to his sleeping spot while Ando chatted with the rest of us. "Guess what? I spotted Ben Honda in the kitchen crew." Our lieutenant's face lit up.

"He's here?" we said in chorus. "Why's he not back with us?"

"Buggah's still not in great shape," Ando said. "Raring to fight, but he's being kept in the rear, just to be safe."

"What about his medal?"

"No word," Ando said. "Guess that's another reason to keep him safe. Has to live to enjoy it, yuh."

Ando went about his business while my buddies and I talked, now and then peeking outside, where olive groves hid men from the Jerries sitting atop Altissimo, Azzano in their crosshairs. After dinner, Ando called the platoon together for final orders, and our preparation became a solemn ritual as we wiped dirt and soot on our faces, tied our dog tags together so the Germans at the top of Folgorito wouldn't hear them clinking. We vowed not to utter a sound if we fell.

We were ready.

At 2200 hours, we took off along a sinuous path, four miles down to the valley that lay between Azzano and Folgorito, down to the line of departure. Our company followed L Company, the point unit, the two of us the prime attack force. Our Heavy Weapons Company M came in as support. Men from Antitank couldn't fire their weapons in this mountainous area, much of which confounded trajectory calculations, so two of their platoons served as litter bearers and carrying parties. K Company stood in reserve in Azzano.

I concentrated as I followed Ando, negotiating dusty white paths and leading our squads across a creek, its waters swift, its boulders slippery. I felt the soldiers' fear and determination as we pushed on.

Once on the rocky valley floor, near the base of Mount Carchio, everyone breathed deep and prepared for the final climb to the enemy, up the saddle between Carchio and Folgorito. The mountains were loaded with Jerries. We would flush them out.

Ando signaled the platoon to jump off, and I waved our squads forward. But not more than fifteen minutes into the march, every last soldier realized that nothing had prepared us for this. We adjusted and readjusted our mounds of equipment and weapons as we confronted the slope, nearly vertical, like Ando said. We advanced on foot and on hands and knees, slipping and sliding on shifting shale, grabbing rocks and spindles of shrubs that had somehow eked life from stone. We grasped a buddy's hand or arm, a leg or a rifle butt, to get pulled up or to pull someone up.

I had heard that Partisans were supposed to guide us up more old goat paths, but damn if I detected even a suggestion of a trail. Probably the dumb old goats weren't so dumb after all. They knew better than to attempt the climb.

Silently, we strained our way up, freezing when we heard the clang of a helmet as someone tumbled down the slope. *Please, God*, we prayed, *don't let the Germans hear that*. I could make out relay stations along the way, set up to evacuate men who fell and injured themselves.

After five hours, just as we reached the high ground, someone tripped a wire.

We froze.

We waited.

No Jerries fired, and Ando motioned us forward. I caught sight of Happi near Mak, helping to push our men, and knew my pal was on a new course of leadership. Poi and Kat marched near him. It was close to 0600, the sky still dark, and we followed our point men closely. We were an hour behind schedule and picked up the pace before day broke.

We waited, breathlessly, as everyone assembled.

The time to attack arrived.

We ran.

We raced.

We swooped down as one.

My heart pounded as we blanketed the area with bullets.

The Carchio-Folgorito ridge was secured by 0730, barely a scratch on us.

"Gee, maybe I was stupid to be afraid," Jug whispered to himself.

"Fear's not stupid." I stopped him and the soldiers around him for a second. "Harness it. Keep alert. Germans could be anywhere."

Ando signaled the platoon forward, and we made our way toward the south slopes of Mount Carchio, intent on cutting off the Jerries who carried supplies to Mount Cerretta, where the 100th battled.

Machine guns and grenades announced the onset of fighting. A cacophony of German and American machine guns shattered the air.

Brrrrrrrrp! German fire sprayed us without mercy.

Ratatatatat! We fired back.

The Germans who had not been captured drew us into firefights and skirmishes. Artillery and mortar barrages pounded the mountains, and planes from the 57th Fighter Group flew in to support the ground fire.

Bombs tore into the earth and bullets whizzed by our ears. We hit the ground and aimed our rifles toward the source of fire.

I spotted Jug, crouched in the middle of the storm, frozen, as others rose up and ran ahead. I knew what he was going through and crawled over to him.

I pushed Jug to the ground, hard.

"Get moving!" I said, and smacked him on the butt. "You can do it, Morita. We need you. Back to our men." I belly-crawled past him as bullets kicked up storms of dust and stone, and then watched Jug re-join our platoon. I wondered if he felt that same grab to the gut I had felt so many battles ago, knowing that I was truly part of the team and one with our men, willing to give my life for them.

Every man had to acknowledge the fear and then reach beyond it, to do what had to be done.

22

Second Push, Italy

April 14-15, 1945

Carchio fell without a single one of us dying, but the Jerries, calling on small arms, artillery, Panzers, and coastal guns, slammed L Company and our weapons men as they drove toward Folgorito's peak. In support, K Company moved from Azzano in broad daylight and took a bloody beating from the Jerries on Altissimo. Our losses multiplied, and we grew somber.

Ando gathered the platoon together to give us the big picture.

As we battled from the north and east, the 100th was attacking from the south and west, setting off landmines as they routed the Germans from Cerretta, Georgia Hill, and other mounts, Ohio 1 and 2 and 3. Shu landmines were the worst, six-inch-by-six-inch wooden boxes that evaded any metal detector. When they blew, they mutilated beyond belief.

We heard the 370th reached its first objective of Castle Aghinolfi handily on April 4, surprising the awakening Nazis. Within two days our 2nd Battalion had left its reserve position to take Mount Belvedere, and we moved on their right flank, ordered to take and hold a peak in the vicinity.

Jerries hit us with everything they had, snipers, mortar, artillery.

"Can't breathe," Kat gasped, smoke thick in the air.

"Can't see which way to go." Mak muttered as the earth exploded.

Our entire company froze.

But that didn't stop Lieutenant Donnelly. He ran right into the storm, intent on determining the sources of fire.

He returned with the information, wounded in his leg and his arm, his carbine busted. Our artillery smashed the Jerries out of their positions. We took our peak.

Inspired by Donnelly's action, we battled our fatigue to forge ahead to our next objective, the supply highway to Massa, just below Mount Belvedere. The 370th, attacking the same area from Highway 1, lost three company commanders and needed more manpower as they stalled along the coast. They were being pounded by coastal guns mounted on rail cars, run out of their hillside tunnels to be fired inland. Our flanks were left exposed.

Consolidation followed. The 473rd would fight with us, and the 370th marched into the Serchio Valley to protect our flanks. Our engineers struggled against sniper fire to clear Highway 1. A bullet seared my leg as we battled for control, but I waved medics away. We routed the Jerries from the supply road, and with the 473rd, we took the village of Massa.

"Wonder when we're getting a rest," Ando said as we mopped up. "Been on line for ten straight days. Can't expect miracles from us."

"Have to admit, I'm dead tired," I said.

"Could use some good sleep," Kat said.

Someone heard us. The 3rd Battalion marched to the village of Carrara for rest while the 2nd battled on with the 100th, moving four miles further north.

. . .

Just as we were getting settled, crazy orders came in.

"What the hell?" I yelled. "We have to go up again?"

I just didn't understand it. The 3rd Battalion was now in regimental reserve in Carrara, our company in battalion reserve. But Fowler was ordering our 2nd Platoon to destroy a Jerry outpost on a hill north of the city.

I looked for Ando for advice, but he was nowhere to be found. What the hell?

In the middle of our campaign, without any warning, a Lieutenant Munroe was taking our platoon leader's place for the next few days.

Why had Ando taken off in all this chaos? He was always our rock, reliable and sane. We were used to fighting together.

Plus everyone was grieving. We'd just received word that President Roosevelt had died. Gone was the man who had ordered the formation of the 442nd and given us a chance to serve. We had been angry as hell after EO 9066, but the President had become our commander-in-chief when we donned the uniform. Now the chain of command had been shaken at the very top, and I sure as hell questioned some of my own officers.

Fowler came right to the platoon to give detailed orders and see they were executed.

Our own success had created a problem, Fowler said. Our diversionary strategy had worked well, taking snipers from the

Bologna front and allowing the Allies to push Germans into the Po valley. But where we once thought the Germans were leaving, the 4th High Mountain Battalion and the 361st Panzer Grenadier Regiment were digging in. Right here.

"They're wreaking havoc," Fowler said. "Taking prisoners. Blocking roads. Hitting our supply parties. Our left rear is exposed."

Fowler stopped talking and looked us over. Then he spread out a map of the Carrara area and gathered us round.

"There's a German operating post over on Hill 580," he said, pointing to the map, "and there's a ridge that runs between Hill 580 and Hill 574, over here, see?"

"That ridge is across from where the 100th and 2nd are fighting, isn't it? At Castelpoggio," Munroe said.

"Exactly," Fowler said. "And our men are taking vicious fire from the Germans at the top."

I knew what was coming.

What the hell?

"I want you men to climb up there, clear the ridge, and occupy Hill 574. From there you can fire on Hill 580 and alleviate pressure on the regiment's flank."

I got the picture, but didn't understand why our platoon had to do the job. Didn't commanders know they had to rest their troops so men could work their best? I rubbed my leg, still smarting from the bullet.

Enough was enough.

"We're out of energy, Colonel Fowler," I spoke up, right in front of our men. Just days before, I had felt so relieved to be out of the brig, and now I couldn't believe I had to confront the colonel like this. "My platoon doesn't have anything left to give. We've been pushed too far. We don't even have our lieutenant right now."

The colonel ignored anything I said.

Why?

Why was he being like this?

What about waiting for a few hours so we could rest?

How about help from other units?

Could we take a different route?

"Get going. Now," Fowler said.

Damn it to hell.

Our colonel reminded me of Bristol back in the Vosges, coming up with sudden orders and not listening to anyone in the field.

Hell, Fowler hadn't listened to me then, either.

I picked up my equipment and prepared to advance my men with Munroe. We had a job to do.

I shook myself fully alert and focused on my task. At least a platoon from K Company would work with us, moving to Castelpoggio and then toward the occupied hill 580. Two platoons would do the work of a whole damned company, but we had to make it work.

Mak, frazzled from fighting, ran over and talked to me, urging me to keep calm and centered. He was right. I listened to him.

Mak headed out with Poi to scout the area and discovered a higher and a lower trail up the mountain. Munroe seemed like a reasonable man and listened to what we had to say, and together, we planned the attack before jumping off.

We marched through underbrush to position our men as close to the base as possible before nightfall. Worry weighed heavy, and no one slept much. I felt for my photo of Ruth and me. Fighting would be fierce.

I figured every which way to gain an advantage over the Jerries and awakened my men early. The sun would be in the Jerries' eyes as we attacked.

Following Munroe's lead, I left one squad in reserve at the base, directed my squad into position along the higher trail, and waved Mak to advance his along the lower, with Poi bringing up the rear. Happi moved close behind me, Kat near him, both keeping their eyes on our green soldiers and teaching by example, how to maneuver this way and that, when to wait and when to move. The hill stood almost barren, with no trees and few shrubs for cover. At least the terrain didn't look too challenging for artillery to shoot a smoke screen over us.

Our 522nd Artillery had been sent to the Siegfried Line in Germany, and the 92nd's artillery was filling in. We waited in silence for the shell to fall. Weariness and tension battled with our determination to take the hill. We always fought to win, and this mission was no exception.

I heard a whoosh and a thud behind me, hit the ground, and turned my head to see what had happened.

Hell. The smoke shell had landed a good hundred yards in back of us. God knows I wanted these men to succeed, a segregated unit like us. But the 92nd's artillery was proving unreliable. I had no idea what kind of soldiers had ended up in the unit, but I didn't have time to find out. I ordered my radioman to call our own heavy weapons men to provide cover.

Within minutes, our two squads pressed forward under thick smoke. The reserve squad waited as a base of fire to support our assault, on tap if casualties mounted.

I checked the sun and figured it would still be in the Jerries' eyes, and Munroe and I led our men up the hill with Mak's squad. At the point where the trail split, Mak moved his squad to the lower left road while Munroe moved our men up to the right for a frontal assault. Kat and Happi moved our men forward while I ran to the reverse slope.

I raced up the hill with everything I had, afraid my heart would burst, I ran so damned hard. The Jerries had awakened to the attack. I reached the peak and spotted two Jerry emplacements in front of me, and let loose with my submachine gun. As I neared a brick wall, maybe a foot shorter than me, a Jerry popped up from behind and took aim. The bullet grazed the side of my head, and I rolled to the side, stunned for just a second. I shook it off and fired back. The Jerry slumped to the ground.

Sure I had killed at least two Germans, I started down the front slope, hoping the Germans at the top were cleared, at least those in our direct path.

Oh, hell, our men were under full barrage.

The Jerries attacked from three sides. SP guns, mortar, artillery, they hit us with everything they had.

I fired like a madman, spraying everything in my sight.

Men were falling.

We needed help.

I battled my way to Munroe, stuck midway up the hill. He was yelling over the bombardment for volunteers to get mortar support.

"I'll go myself," I said. "And I'm ordering the reserve squad to move up." I wanted the men to hit the German emplacements defending the top of the ridge. Munroe gave the thumbs up and got back to fighting.

As the way to victory became clear, I entered a mental area I knew well by now, growing cooler even as the fighting grew furious. It felt weird, this state, going way beyond training, instinctively knowing just how to act. I felt at the peak of my game.

I zigzagged down the hill in search of the mortar. Soldiers from all our squads lay wounded, and I spotted Poi, damn it all, his leg mangled, covered in blood. Good God, and there was Kat, cradling his arm.

I yelled for them to be strong and battled on. I dodged bullets and found our mortar section, grabbed a few makeshift litters, and led the bearers up the hill. The Germans spotted us, this time from Hill 580, and fired. I directed four men to blast the enemy and three others to carry out our casualties. Other soldiers would search for remaining wounded.

"You got a million-dollar wound," I said. I squeezed Poi's hand before he passed out.

"Don't die on me, you bastard," I told Kat as soldiers made a tourniquet for his arm.

"Wouldn't give you the pleasure." Kat gritted his teeth through the pain.

I told the men to take good care of him and ran to check on the rest of Mak's squad. The men had made it to a wooded area toward the middle of the hill before getting barraged.

We struggled on.

We took the top of 574 by late afternoon.

Jerries still lurked around the hilltop and ridgeline over to Hill 580, and I radioed Fowler for support. The Germans would surely counterattack tomorrow. We needed help.

But Fowler said no.

No support.

What did he want from us?

Why was he treating us like this?

"Is the guy trying to kill us? You?" Munroe asked. "What the hell's his problem?"

I asked the same questions, thinking this really was a suicide mission now.

I counted twenty soldiers left in our three squads, and we were supposed to dig in and defend the whole damned ridge to wherever K Company stood.

No support. No Ando. Was Fowler really out to get me?

I had to think fast and said to hell with command. I focused on how to reorganize our men and win. We made contact with the K Company platoon, which had reached Hill 580, and decided to stay up all night to hold the ridge secure.

The Jerries attacked at dawn. We were ready and fought back hard. The Germans shot from two sides, and we battled for hours. Just when we thought we'd held the enemy off, I spotted three Jerries creeping up to our position. I sprang out in the open and fired, striking two. The third high-tailed it.

Our squads inched along the ridge, and fighting drew to a close. By early afternoon an entire company from our 232nd Engineers, committed to infantry duty, relieved our two platoons, who had held losses to one KIA and one taken prisoner. How many had been wounded, we didn't know. The ridge stood secure, a safe path opened for the Allies to move weapons ahead and advance northward.

I heard the 473rd had hit the coastal guns hard. In the Serchio Valley the 370th took the German supply center of Castelnuovo and advanced toward Aulla.

Hot dang.

We had the Germans on the run.

I didn't know what to make of my own commander, but my heart swelled with pride at what our team had accomplished.

Mak and I led our men down the hill, hoping for the hot showers and fresh uniforms we had been promised.

"We're going to make it," Happi said to us as we walked. "This war's as good as over."

That night, as we wrote letters to our families and our girls, Happi cut his short. If he told them everything now, he said, he would have nothing to talk about when he got home.

23

Second Push, Italy

April 21, 1945

"Hiro, you have a call at our command post." A runner came up to me as I returned to our company from a meeting of platoon sergeants. Ando was back with us, offering no explanation for his disappearance, and we didn't ask for one. We had to focus and move on.

"Know what this is about?" I asked the runner.

"Nope," he said.

"Hey, Happi," I shouted to my buddy. "Stay with our men again, would you? Got called to CP. God knows why."

"No problem," Happi said as he pulled himself away from a couple of replacements. "Hey, maybe they're going to give you a medal for that goddamned hill." Our men were calling it 2nd Platoon Hill.

"Wouldn't that be grand," I laughed and waved as I took off, confident in Happi's abilities. Other than me and Ando, he was the oldest man in the platoon right now and was intent on filling in for Mak, who'd been ordered to take a couple days of rest. Since our suicide mission, we had hauled ass north and west with the rest of our men to finish clearing the Jerries from the coastal hills, and Happi had taken on increasing responsibilities, showing the ropes to the replacements and volunteering for more patrols. A week into our drive, hope propelled us ahead. Once we cleared the Jerries, we would make a final push toward the coast, maneuvering around Mount Nebbione to take the major road center of Aulla, northeast of Spezia. The 370th would meet us there. Once we reached Aulla, the Germans at Spezia would be cut off from escape to the Po Valley. Their only other options were the roads north of Genoa, where Partisans were gaining control, and Highway 63, through the Cisa Pass—and the 100th and 2nd battalions were fighting viciously through the mounds in the area to block the Germans. Victory was close.

The village area we were in now, Tendola-Montegrosso-Pulica-Fosdinovo, was giving us major problems. The Jerries had their backs to the wall, fighting with everything they had. Our company rested on a ridge near Tendola, pushing tension away as we gathered our strength to attack the village.

"Know where the CP is?" the runner asked me. "In a cave tonight." He pointed me to a trail, and I sprinted down the hill, wondering if my battle actions were going to be recognized, like Happi thought. I found the entrance to the cave easily.

"Hiro." Lieutenant Donnelly rose to a crouch and greeted me as soon as I walked in, hunched over. Cold permeated the cave, its ceiling so low that even Tiny Hayashi would have to double over. Donnelly usually appeared the epitome of Caucasian good looks in our eyes, with wavy copper hair and aquiline nose, but war weariness covered his face.

I watched as he checked some papers, kneeling at first and then sitting crossed legged.

I calmed my heart.

I did not sense a medal about to be awarded.

"Sorry to pull you off like this, but Lieutenant Colonel Henderson wants to talk to you," he said in his Southern drawl. "Insisted I get you right away."

"Henderson?" I was surprised. Henderson had been 2nd Battalion CO and now served as the regiment's executive officer. What would he want with me?

"We'll get him back on the line," Donnelly said.

I refocused my thoughts and took the receiver, and Donnelly leaned against the wall.

"Sergeant Koga, I consulted with your battalion command and need to talk to you about your pending court-martial," Henderson said. "The incident on February 14, as you know."

My mind raced.

What the hell?

Court-martial?

For what?

Breaking up a fight?

I'd taken responsibility as the senior EM, but I'd made it damned clear that I hadn't socked the MP.

Had Fowler planned this all along?

"I have to tell you, Sergeant Koga," Henderson said. "If you plead guilty, you'll just get a special court-martial. No dishonorable discharge. But if you don't, they'll give you a full-blown general court-martial."

I didn't have to think twice.

"Like hell I'm pleading guilty," I said. "I could die tomorrow, and this would be on my record. I didn't sock the officer. I didn't do anything wrong. I'm not pleading guilty. That's it." I remembered through my outrage who was on the other end and added, "Sir."

"What of the others?" I asked, and Henderson said Mak and Happi were in the same boat. He didn't mention any of the other men who had been rounded up.

I asked if we should keep fighting, the colonel said of course, and then the line went dead.

Donnelly asked me exactly what the trouble was—he'd heard only rumors—and I explained what had happened at the dance hall.

"I thought this was all over when we were released," I said. "I told them a million times that I didn't punch the MP. Hell, I'm back leading my men with Mak. And Happi's more than pulling his weight."

"Doesn't make a damned bit of sense," Donnelly said. He looked me over. "I've known you since training. You're a good man, a really fine soldier. I trust you with my own life. I'll help you fight this, Hiro. Don't plead guilty. Don't."

"Thank you, sir. I need all the help I can get."

"You know who did it?"

I shrugged.

"But you ain't telling, right?" Donnelly understood the code of silence that enlisted men and noncoms held dear. "You're protecting someone who isn't holding up his end of the deal, you know. Putting himself in front of others."

"I know, but we don't squeal," I said. "Two wrongs don't make a right and all that."

"Tell you what. Let this ride for a few days," Donnelly said. "Until we get ourselves out of this shithole, okay? The Jerries are shelling us to hell and back. We have too much else to focus on right now."

He looked exasperated. "Anything else you can tell me?"

I explained how I'd given Fowler hell after the detail, right in front of his fellow officers.

Donnelly looked at the ground and then at me. "Shit. I'll see if I can meet with Henderson and our other commanders. We have to get our ducks in order if we're going to convince the brass we're in the right."

I thanked Donnelly and made my way back to the platoon as I thought about what he had said. I had heard from the 2nd Battalion guys that Colonel Henderson was a good man, fair and even tempered, but I wondered just how much Fowler had twisted the story. We never knew with our higher-ups. Maybe I shouldn't have yelled at command in earshot of the boys, but it was their butts I wanted to save. I didn't have time for niceties.

What could I do? I had no qualms about being mad as hell in the Vosges, and I hadn't broken any rules in Menton. The whole case against me felt like a damned house of cards.

I wished I could sit and talk with Wes for just a few minutes. I sure would like to hear his advice now.

Dusk was descending by the time I returned to our men, and everyone was eating as they awaited orders. Vic Abe had once again risked life and limb to bring up hot chow from the kitchen, thoughtfully prepared by Tommy and crew when they could, and my men felt comforted by tonight's hot musubi, rice balls, even without the plum in the center that we all loved. I thought of Mrs. Inada, the care she had taken to keep us fed in the most dire of times. Upset as I was, I felt happy that our men's stomachs were full for a change, their souls satisfied.

"Hey, know what Vic said?" Happi told me as he finished. "Ben Honda got sent back home."

"Get hit again?" I asked, remembering the way the guy had saved my ass, the way he'd charged up that hill.

"No. Vic said he shouldn't have been put back with the troops so fast. He's headed to the hospital again. Probably the states this time."

I was really sorry to hear that. "Any word about his MOH?'

Happi said no and then asked what had happened at the CP. Had I earned a medal?

"Shit, no," I said in a low voice. I gave Happi a quick rundown.

"Hell," Happi said. He lit a match and held it to his K rations box, heating the waxed cardboard until the box caught fire, and then warmed his cup over the flames to make coffee. "That's just not fair. They released you and me and Mak to fight, right? They needed us old boys to lead the way. How can they turn around and court-martial us?"

Coffee jumped from Happi's cup.

An explosion down near the CP shook the earth and reverberated through the air.

I grabbed my rifle, waited for any sound of shelling to end, and raced down the trail.

Good God.

Our company's CP had been blasted to hell.

Men from our weapons platoon had already rushed here from their position just below the CP, and they ran in and out of the cave. Pup Ito, a young kotonk, was directing the relief effort, and men kept calling his name for guidance. Cries for "Pup! Pup!" filled the air, conjuring up thoughts of the most innocent and loving of creatures amidst unimaginable hell.

"Oh, my God!"

"No!"

"No!"

"Goddamn Jerry bastards!"

"You can barely recognize them."

I saw pages of combat journals all over the ground.

Canteens.

Love letters.

Pieces of uniforms.

Silver first lieutenant bars.

Soldiers counted the casualties. Five, six, seven wounded. Five dead. Good God. Our boys dragged the injured into the night. Mules would come up tomorrow morning for the dead. Partisans would help take the bodies down.

"What about Lieutenant Donnelly?" I asked, afraid I knew the answer.

His remains lay toward the front of the cave, his assistant's nearby.

I broke the news to my men, and we sat together in silence. The officers who had led us were gone. The heart of our company had been ripped from us.

Regiment ordered I Company into battalion reserve at Pulica, right between the fighting in Tendola and Fosdinovo. We had a few hours to regroup.

At the break of day, we marched as bombs dropped all around. The Jerries just wouldn't let up. Ando led the platoon, and I followed, just ahead of my men, every movement of our muscles an effort as we grieved.

Boom!

An explosion to our right knocked me off my feet.

"I'm okay, I'm okay," I told everyone as they ran to me. Blood ran down my forehead into my eyes, which felt irritated. My arm was gashed, my glasses gone. The pain was so overwhelming that I didn't bother to look for my extra pair. I knew I needed help. Men called for a medic, and I called for Happi. I handed him my rifle and binoculars.

"Don't let Ando down," I told him.

"I'll show him what I can do," Happi said as he took the equipment. "See you soon."

Medics pulled me to the side, and I could just make out my friend following Ando's every move.

24

Second Push, Italy

April 23-May 1945

When I heard Happi had been shot, I bolted from my bed at the field hospital.

Why the hell had I given him my equipment?

Told him to prove himself to Ando?

"You're not ready to leave," nurses called to me.

"I'm a fast healer," I protested as I dressed. "No choice. I have to find my buddy." Doctors had stitched my wounds tight, rinsed my eyes clean of debris. They made me read an eye chart to make sure I was okay before letting me sleep for the night.

"Where you going?" a doctor asked. I explained the situation.

"Look, your eye test showed just how near sighted you are. I don't know how you made it into the Army. I can send you stateside right now. And maybe I should."

"To hell with that. I can see fine. My buddy needs me."

"You sure? I know a lot of soldiers who would jump at the chance—"

"To hell with it." I began walking past soldiers laid up in cots.

"If you insist on leaving, at least let me change your bandages," a nurse scurried after me. "You'll make better progress if your arm's wrapped good and tight." I stopped and let her put a fresh dressing and bandages on.

"Can I go now?" I said.

"God bless, and have a medic change those bandages now and then," she called as I ran outside. I raced to our company, bivouacked outside the village of Tendola.

The few men who were hanging around came up to me.

"Lieutenant Ando couldn't find Happi last night," they said. "They're out there looking for him again."

They explained what had happened. Ando had taken several men on patrol, and Happi had volunteered to probe a hill with our lieutenant, leaving the others behind a wall, protected. Happi got hit within minutes.

"I want another search party to go out," I yelled, feeling strong enough to lead this action. "The more men, the better our chances. Come on."

The soldiers knew where to head, as men from Ando's patrol had described the area where Happi had fallen. We took off, reaching the fields quickly.

"You, search over there," I ordered one soldier.

"You, over there," I told another.

I raced around like a madman.

Why had I asked him to take my place?

Maybe I could have hung on and fought.

Minutes crawled into hours, and as night descended, I returned to camp with my men.

Ando's search party was already there.

"We found Happi," they said.

Their gray faces said it all.

Jug Morita came forward. "I'm sorry, Sarge."

In a whisper, Jug added, "He was stripped naked. Ando found a couple of letters from his family and a sketchpad near his body. That's all."

I fell to my knees, overcome, and the men left me to my grief, tearless in its depth.

Not until Ando walked into the area did I move.

"Why the hell did you leave him?" I screamed. I lurched toward him, my fists raised. "Maybe he was still alive."

"He got shot in the neck, Hiro," Ando said in a low voice. "The medics said there was no way he could have survived. He must have died immediately."

"But you didn't know that. Why didn't you get him and carry him back? Drag him if you had to, dead or alive."

Ando said, "I know you just lost your friend. I called and called to him, dangerous enough. I could have been killed if I'd walked around and searched for him. You know that. I'm sorry, so sorry."

Ando fleshed out the story. Yesterday afternoon, he had met a K Company officer, right off the crest of Montegrosso, which overlooked the village of Tendola. The company had established an observation post there and secured the ridge between Tendola and Pulica. No, the officer had assured him, they'd seen no enemy movement in Tendola.

"That didn't make sense," Ando said. "There was still plenty of German artillery in Pulica, and Jerries could be lurking all around the area."

Taking no chances, Ando gathered together a reconnaissance patrol to determine enemy positions. Most of the men were green, and he ordered them to take cover behind an old stone wall. He wanted to approach the hill in front of them by himself, as it might be filled with Jerries. A bell tower and other buildings stood off in the distance, also possible enemy hiding places.

"I told Happi to stay with the men," Ando said, his voice cracking. "I wanted him to guide them if they got in trouble while I was gone. But he insisted and insisted he come with me. He just wouldn't stop."

I would hear none of it. My buddy was dead, his body left to scavengers.

Raging against Ando, raging against myself, I stormed out of camp.

When I returned, I found Happi's two letters and sketchpad in my sleeping area. I put them in my pocket next to Ruth's photo, vowing to return them to his mother if I ever got out of this war alive.

That night I dreamed of Koichi for the first time in years, flailing helplessly as he lay dying. I rushed around, calling for our parents to help, tearing the house up as I searched for medicine to save him, praying for God to save him. I was powerless. Powerless.

Everyone felt hungover with grief the next morning, but we arose to do our jobs. As we got ready, news of Ben Honda came in. He had landed in a convalescent hospital in Michigan, where he'd been awarded the Distinguished Service Cross, a terrific medal to be proud of, but a significant downgrade from the Medal of Honor.

Goddamn, if anyone deserved the MOH, it was Honda.

Our men were as low as they could be.

Dazed and numb, I dug deep for every ounce of my strength to accomplish what was usually second nature. We had been ordered back on line, and I had to protect my men and do my duty. I had to go on. Orders were orders.

Under full-blown attack by K Company, Tendola fell just hours after Happi had probed for the enemy, clearing the path to Nebbione.

The Germans were trapped.

On April 24 the 473rd joined the Partisans fighting in Spezia and three days later, slammed Genoa. Together with the 370th, we cut off Germans trying to escape through the Cisa Pass between the Ligurian and Tuscan Apennines.

The war in Italy ended on May 2, eight days after Happi died.

• • •

Everyone rejoiced with the cessation of battle, but I felt little. Only news of the 522nd Field Artillery in Germany moved me. Our brothers had encountered emaciated, barely living Jews on a march from a sub-camp of Dachau. Laying down their arms, our men reached out to some of the worst of the war's victims and helped liberate the slave labor camp. Only now were its horrors fully emerging.

The whole war in Europe ended on May 8. Bells rang and people sang and danced and drank in victory and in grief. I withdrew, thinking of my family and of Ruth, how I wished we could rejoice together, even with all the bad things hanging over me. I sorrowed for the nurse waiting for Happi's next letter, for his return to her arms, and I imagined how his mother felt, losing her son so close to the return of peace, Joji-chan, Joji-chan, her beloved, sweet boy.

• • •

Two days later, on May 10, 1945, MPs delivered an official summons to me and to Mak to appear at Regimental Headquarters for our court-martials. The MPs waited in their jeeps while we packed our things for the ride to HQ.

I watched Mak fold his senninbari, stained with his blood and his sweat. "Damned thing can't protect me from my own commanders," he muttered.

We shuffled out to the jeeps.

Regimental HQ had taken over one of the many palazzos in Novi Ligure, just minutes north of Genoa and two hours north of Massa-Carrara, where Happi had died. Mak and I were confined to separate rooms before being called out individually.

"Sergeant Koga, come with me." A Caucasian lieutenant escorted me up a broad, gently curving staircase. My mind raced as I glimpsed gigantic mirrors and paintings and chandeliers around the mansion.

"Is this my trial?" I asked.

The lieutenant kept silent until we stood before a wide door that rose high to the ceiling. "In there."

I walked in to find two first lieutenants and two captains, all Caucasians, behind a table in the center of the immense room, plus an AJA second lieutenant at a table to their side. I had never set eyes on any of them, all from the legal branch of the Army, I was certain. A Caucasian warrant officer stood to my side, so I wondered if he was my legal counsel. Heavy brocade draperies adorned the windows, and gilt filled the room.

I grew more apprehensive as I looked at the officers' shiny hardware and chests of ribbons. The charge of hitting an officer was serious, no matter your color. Would I get a fair trial with these men?

I sure wished Wes Inada was here.

"This is the special court-martial of Staff Sergeant Hiroshi David Koga of the 442ⁿᵈ Regimental Combat Team," one of the captains read from a sheet of paper, "accused of violating the Sixty-third Article of War: Disrespect toward a superior officer, and the Ninety-sixth Article of War: Drunk in uniform in a public place."

What the hell? Did the guy say, "special court-martial"?

Didn't Henderson say if I pleaded guilty, that's what I'd get, with no dishonorable discharge?

The captain's voice was sonorous, making my heart and head pound. "The violations occurred on or about February 14, 1945, at the Dancing Auguste, a public bar."

What was going on?

The warrant officer remained silent.

I tried to speak.

I was told no one had recognized me.

The AJA lieutenant kept his eyes down, writing all the while.

One of the officers at the table said that Lieutenant Ando was my character witness. I looked around and didn't see him.

Could I make a statement now? Call some witnesses?

Where was the MP?

Wasn't that warrant officer supposed to help me?

"Lieutenant, take the accused into the hallway," the stony-faced captain said. The officers huddled as I was escorted out. I waited for what seemed an eternity, though my watch marked the passage of only a few minutes.

The door opened, and I was directed back in.

I stood in front of the officers.

"It is the finding of this court that the accused, Staff Sergeant Hiroshi David Koga, is guilty on all counts. You are hereby demoted to the rank of Private and are sentenced to hard labor for six months. You will forfeit $28 of pay per month for the same period."

I had no breath.

No words.

This was the worst wound I'd suffered in the whole damned war.

• • •

Two hours later, Mak and I were whisked away to Ghedi Air Base, where I Company was guarding German POWs.

Mak and I compared notes, realizing that we'd been given the same sham trial, the same damned sentence, the maximum possible, we figured.

"Verdict was in before we started," I muttered. I remembered what Colonel Henderson had told me.

"We were guilty before being proven guilty," Mak grumbled.

"What proof?" I said, and we both grimaced.

"Wonder what hard labor will be?" Mak said. "Digging more damned holes?" We had been given credit for time served and had seventy-four days left.

"At least we'll be with our men," we both said.

Once at Ghedi, we were placed in a barracks stockade, not too far from the POWs we helped to guard, which turned out to be our hard labor. Ghedi was regimented like any other Army camp, and when I stood in the guard tower, I thought how much the layout looked like Minidoka, where I had first served time as a prisoner of the U.S. government.

Had I come full circle? I didn't want to think that way. I was better than that. I simply wanted to join our men in freedom, the freedom we had fought for.

Just weeks into guard duty, Mak and I caught wind that I Company would move to Lecco for R&R as we waited to go home. We also heard that Private Chickenshit, Yoyo Wasuke, had been court-martialed, too.

We never saw him again.

25

Lecco and Florence, Italy

May-September 1945

Mak and I continued our sentences on the outskirts of Lecco, where Ando had found a perfect spot for our men. The alfalfa field was surrounded by a fieldstone wall a few feet high, forming a nice enclosure for the camp, and soon everyone was putting up pup tents and having fun, even Mak and me.

It really looked like the entire world war would be over soon. Bombing of French Indochina and fire bombings of Japanese cities had intensified since the war in Europe ended, and word came in from the Pacific that the Japanese were withdrawing from China. Japanese resistance ended in the Philippines and Okinawa, which had been invaded the previous month. The Japs still vowed to fight to the death rather than surrender unconditionally, and men grew anxious about their siblings in the MIS, wherever they fought. I was one of many who also worried about relatives who lived in Japan, and I knew others were concerned about cousins who had fought for our enemy. But for the most part, we were confident that the war in the Pacific would end soon, and the world would be at peace.

"Have a great time." Ando signed Kat Kato's pass to Milan. Kat had returned from the hospital days before, his arm in a sling. Tommy stood behind Kat, signed pass in hand. "But not too much cognac, eh?" Ando kidded, and everyone laughed.

The only people Ando didn't talk to were me and Mak. We sat in the middle of the men we had led, privates once more, ignored by our platoon lieutenant. We just didn't understand.

"Hey, no *shinpai*, eh?" Men told us not to worry about Ando as they brought goodies to us. Our brig had loosened up considerably, an end-of-the-war nod to dubious justice, just two wires running parallel around a square of maybe fifteen or twenty feet on each side. When they weren't making a show of "guarding" us, our buddies climbed over the wires eight and ten at a time to share beer and cigarettes and grub. Sam Sakura brought Lucy in to play with us, and I told him about Bou, how I couldn't wait to see him.

"Ando's just busy," men reassured us. "He's got lots of paperwork, and he's started bringing around three little girls, local girls. Says they're helping him unwind from all the killing we've done."

I recalled Ando's concern that he couldn't stop killing, and despite our falling out, I hoped those little ones were reassuring him about his own humanity.

"Here's my way of feeling better," someone said as he hand me a beer. "Drink up."

We toasted, but my heart wasn't in it.

• • •

"Howzit, brah," Jug Morita interrupted my thoughts one morning. He was making his way past the olive drab pup tents that surrounded the stockade, the smell of dirty canvas melding with something much happier, cypress and orange blossoms, I guessed.

"On your way to the lake?" I waved Jug in, thinking how much fun a swim would be.

"Of course," Jug said. He came by with treats for us every day. "So what you guys up to?"

"Maybe we'll clean our room today." I gestured around the enclosure.

Truth be told, I had thought that sitting in the brig again would be easier, now that the war in Europe was over. But I had too much time to think how Happi's body had been left for scavengers, to imagine how his family had heard of his arrest and his death, to blame Ando and myself for our part in creating the circumstances that led to his being killed. And I thought of the ten men who had died on my ration detail, vanished into thin air.

I hung an undershirt to air on the top wire, around three feet high, and lit a cigarette. "What goodies you have for us today?" I asked Jug.

I had no sooner spoken the word "goodies" than Mak crawled out from our pup tent, where he'd been writing a letter to his family. He said "hi" to Jug and took a swat at my garrison cap, which I had placed at an admittedly cocky angle behind my pompadour.

"Hey, Hiro, tell Jug our plans. We're going to the movies after chow. What's the name again?"

"*The Fleet's In*," I said. "Wouldn't miss it for the world." I let my cigarette dangle from my lips as I stood up. "That's where my song's from." I hummed "Tangerine" and danced the hula around the enclosure. Our pals took turns sitting in for us while we went to the movies some nights, and so far, no one had been caught.

"Here." Jug handed us cigarettes from his rations."Want some coffee?" Jug gave us a thermos. "And surprise, surprise, a treat from Tommy." He pulled out two doughnuts from a piece of cloth, warm and moist. "He just made a batch."

Tommy sent special grub to us whenever he could, in extra big portions, probably remembering when we were all in the brig together. We sat plantation style, and I poured coffee all around, ready to talk story.

"Oh, boy, tastes like home, yuh. Real *malasada*!" Mak took a big bite of the doughnut, a Portuguese version popular in Hawaii. He pulled off a generous piece for Jug.

"Mahalo, brah. But that's for you," Jug said.

"T'anks, eh," Mak said.

"Where did Tommy get the sugar?" I swiped sweet granules from my mouth and licked every last one from my fingers.

"Hey, can't trade everything for rice," Jug said.

"Maybe he ground up every sugar cube from our damned rations," Mak laughed.

"Find out when you're headed back?" I asked Jug as we ate.

"Don't have enough points," he said. "My dad's pretty sick, but you know the Army."

"Too well," Mak grumbled.

"What about you?" Jug asked me. "Aren't you getting married?"

"Hope so."

"What does your girl think of all this?" Jug waved his hand at the wire.

I didn't say anything. How could I tell the woman I loved that I'd been demoted and thrown in prison? Would she still want me?

I spoke as nonchalantly as I could. "Haven't said anything yet. She has enough to worry about, working at her job and feeding all the boys I'm sending to see her. Hell, this is almost behind us, anyway."

Many of the 442nd's wounded, kotonks and Buddhaheads alike, had been sent to Midwest hospitals, and I told the boys to visit Ruth and her apartment mates before they headed home. Better to have fun now, I said. Our troubles on the homefront were far from over. Quite a few issei and nisei languished in the camps, and those just released were facing horrendous problems. Given twenty-five dollars and a one-way train ticket anywhere, many had returned to the West Coast, only to get shot at or discover that their houses had been burned, windows broken, doors kicked in. Others found their farms and tools and equipment had been stolen by the very people they'd entrusted them to. A lucky few recovered what they had lost.

Frustrated at the whole situation, I refocused on Chicago, kidding Jug that he'd have to join the boys and meet Ruth. We chatted a while longer before he took off for the lake.

"Bring back some sashimi," Mak called as we watched him leave.

Mak sat on his haunches and waved me over. "So you really no tell Ruth nothing?"

I shook my head as I gave up sitting Hawaii style and sat cross-legged. "What about you?"

"I wrote my family right away. Happi, too."

"Look, it's bad enough that command is separating us from our men," I said. "I don't want to feel on the skids with my family."

"But everyone's sticking with us," Mak said. "Your family sure won't give up on you."

Welling up deep inside was a memory of the time my parents died, when my siblings, overwhelmed at the thought of caring for me, wanted to send me to our uncle in Japan. I squelched the feeling of abandonment sweeping over me again and took a drag off my cigarette.

Mak added, "We all have two *ohanas* now, two families. Our own and 442. The aloha will never die."

Mak's words calmed the panic in my gut, and I lit another cigarette while he walked over to one corner to take a leak. With all this time on my hands, I had thought a lot about Mak, too. Did he blame me for the court-martial mishmash? He was such a calm, caring guy, but sometimes he didn't speak his mind. Had it bothered him that I'd taken over the squad when he was in the hospital? Promoted to platoon sergeant?

"You know, Mak, I take a lot of the blame for our court-martials," I said when he returned. I tried to explain my thoughts. "If I hadn't lost it and laid into Fowler after the ration detail, none of this would have happened."

"You don't understand yourself, asshole," Mak said. "No way you cannot do what you did. You stick up for what's right, no matter what."

We thought as we smoked, and Mak added, "You are soldier's soldier, Hiro. Got something nobody else has. Everyone knows that. You set our pace, and guys always look to you for direction. And you never ask nobody do something you wouldn't do."

"Did you mind losing your promotions to me?" I asked. "It wasn't a matter of one of us being better than the other. Just a matter of timing. Who was in the hospital when."

"No problem, brah," Mak said. "We always a team, one day lead, one day bring up rear. Do everything to get our guys through the war."

A corporal came to the stockade and interrupted us. "You're on garbage duty. Right now."

• • •

A few days later, I wrote to Ruth.

My dearest love,
The time is passing slowly as we wait to go home, but we're making the most of our R&R. Lecco is a beautiful area, with lots of swimming and fishing and fresh air. We're all breathing easy now, drinking beer galore, and eating some real food. The boys have even set up a tent for movies, so it's fun day and night.
A couple of evenings ago, the movie was "The Fleet's In," and I sang "Tangerine" and danced the hula, the way the Buddhaheads have taught me. I'll teach you, too, when I get home, my darling wahine.
All of us are counting our points to go home, and it looks like mine have piled up. I know I will hold you in my arms soon.

In June, news came that Japan had approached the Soviets about negotiating peace with the Allies on its behalf, in return for territorial concessions. Stalin indicated interest, and the Japanese waited for further details, which weren't forthcoming. The Potsdam Conference demanded Japan's unconditional surrender, which wasn't happening. The world waited.

After several weeks, our company was transferred to Florence, where we all helped guard POWs, mostly as the Germans repaired Army vehicles in a Fiat plant nearby. The smell of horse and dairy stables around the area reminded many of us of the camps, and we shared food and supplies with a couple of young Italian boys who sort of adopted us, bringing much of the loot back to their destitute families, we were sure. Damned if we were going to forget anyone who needed help.

A few weeks into our sentinel duty, Mak and I were released, free men at last. My heart soared, but maybe too much so. Days later, I didn't bother to put on a mitt when we played baseball and busted a finger when I made a good catch. I had to ask someone to write my thoughts to Ruth every couple of days to let her know I was okay. Nobu Sakai, the Buddhahead I'd carried from the train station, volunteered the most, telling me it was his way of paying me back. I didn't even read what anyone wrote, content that Ruth knew I was alive.

We set out with renewed energy to make merry.

What's more exciting, I joked with my pals, the prospect of girls or the promise of a good hot meal? Let's have both, we said. We explored Florence, appreciating the art and the signorinas, and I thought constantly of how much Happi would have loved the architecture, of the buildings and of the girls. We searched nearby farms for vegetables and chicken so the Buddhaheads could make chicken hekka again, and even we kotonks grew fond of the stew, pretty *oishii,* we said, delicious.

Another favorite pastime was finding ways to raise money for beer, "the mora lira, the mora birra," I quipped, and we frequented one particular bar where the owner gave us credit for cigarettes and other rations that he could barter. Times were still tough, locals scrounging through garbage piles for food and women prostituting themselves for cash.

Since we'd been released from the brig, Ando had stopped avoiding Mak and me, and he frequently joined the boys at the bar for a change. Everyone knew he wasn't much of a drinker, but now that the war had ended, he was letting himself enjoy the camaraderie he always encouraged.

On one night of particularly high spirits, soldiers packed the room, and a lucky few were keeping dates with local girls, their families in tow. Others were dancing with girls who had been brought in as a group for the evening. We stood around the bar as we sang songs from Hawaii and Japan, love songs from the radio and dances. My buddies toasted everything under the sun—girls, peace, Hawaii, girls, buddies, girls—and as usual, I danced the hula and la-la-la'd my way through "Tangerine."

Just as I finished, someone raised a glass to Happi. I stopped smiling and turned on Ando.

"Why the hell did you leave him there?" I cried. "Why'd you leave him all alone?" I ran toward our lieutenant with my fists raised, propelled by every damned injustice I'd known.

It took six men, half a squad, to keep me off our lieutenant. I strained and pushed and pulled. I shoved everyone away.

"We don't leave a man behind, damn it all!" I stomped out of the bar.

Ando stood speechless, color drained from his face.

• • •

I saw little of our lieutenant after that, and the war took an unexpected turn in the following days. An atomic bomb dropped incomprehensible levels of death and destruction on Hiroshima on August 6. The Soviets fulfilled their Tehran and Yalta promise by making a three-pronged invasion of Manchukuo on August 8, three months after the German surrender. Another atomic bomb devastated Nagasaki on August 9. The bombs were an unknown beast, spreading fireballs and heat and chaos for miles, burning and maiming and killing for days and weeks after being dropped. A pall fell over camp.

"Holy shit."

"Good God."

"Is the MIS there? What about my brother?"

"Are my grandparents dead?"

"My aunt."

"My cousins."

I told of my sister and grandparents. Were they dead? We could barely voice our worries, and we pondered in silence the horror and the morality of killing the innocent to end the war against an enemy who always fought to the death, who tortured and maimed, who just wouldn't lay down its arms. Would an invasion of Japan, the only other option, have cost even more lives? Most probably. For the first time, Japanese heard the voice of their Divine Emperor on the radio as he uttered an oblique message indicating the surrender of Japan, an inconceivable idea to his subjects.

The war in the Pacific ended on September 2 with the signing of the Japanese Document of Surrender on the USS Missouri in Tokyo Bay. Several members of the MIS were in attendance.

World War II was over.

26

Chicago

1945-1946

Between time served and medals earned, I was one of the first soldiers with enough points to go home, and I grabbed the first empty space on a ship that was offered. I headed straight to Chicago, got processed at Fort Sheridan, and ran to see Ruth.

I rang the bell as I pulled our photo from my pocket.

Ruth answered.

"Will you marry me?" I asked as I held the picture next to my heart.

She pulled out her copy and held it against hers. "Yes! Yes! Yes!"

I picked Ruth up by the waist and circled around the apartment, her roommates applauding. "I love you, I love you, I love you!" I yelled. Ruth echoed me, not saying a word about my single chevron, insignia of a private. Did she not notice? Not know Army symbols? I hoped I didn't have to wear my uniform again, to give her another chance to see.

I stayed at Molly and Lawson's over the next few weeks, and when I wasn't playing with Virginia—who was growing out of her toddler stage into the prettiest and smartest young girl the world had ever seen—Ruth and I talked and kissed and made plans to wed. A lot of the boys still stopped by to see her on their way home from the hospital or from Europe, and everyone enjoyed lots of beer and food as we talked story.

The topic of my court-martial and the stockades came up from time to time, usually after the third or fourth beer, but I always managed to steer the conversation to something else. I didn't think Ruth any the wiser, but sometimes she asked me to tell her more about the war. Those eyes of hers had always said she accepted me, all of me, and I didn't know what to say. Not everything, not yet.

The time was right, though, for visiting Happi's family, and I told Ruth I needed to make this first visit alone. She said she understood, and one Saturday morning I took the letters Ando had given me and tied them gently with ribbon, keeping the sketchpad for myself. It's all I had left of my friend.

I worried what I was going to say.

Did they know Happi was in the brig with me?

Did they know of the court-martial?

Did they know how he died?

I put on my uniform and made my way over to their greystone, passing window after window displaying flags with stars, for residents' sons serving in the Army. A flag with one gold star and one blue hung in the Ishikawas' window. I knocked at their door.

"Mrs. Ishikawa?" I said as the door opened.

She looked at me, her eyes welling up.

"Hiroshi," she said softly. She took my hand and led me into the apartment. We looked at each other again, and Japanese reticence be damned, we held each other silently as tears streamed down our faces. Fumie and Sumako came up to us, and I held them, too, whispering, "I'm sorry, I'm so sorry."

"Is Mr. Ishikawa here?" I asked. "Eddie?" I knew Shig wasn't back from Europe yet.

"My husband sends apologies," Mrs. Ishikawa said. "Someone call in sick at pharmacy. He go in to help. And Eddie working, too."

I said I understood and held Happi's letters out to his mother. "Lieutenant Ando found these next to Happi." Tears rolled down her cheeks as she undid the ribbon and opened the letters that she had written to her son about making a new life in Chicago, about looking forward to Joji re-joining their family.

"So close," she said. "He almost made it. So close." She handed the letters to her daughters.

"He was a brave and good soldier," I said. "A great friend. He always gave everything he had. And he gave his all the night he died."

"How he die?" Mrs. Ishikawa asked.

"Sniper. The area was full of them, picking soldiers off." That's all I could get out.

I couldn't tell her more, and she didn't ask.

Fumie said, "He wrote us back in March that he was in the calaboose, somewhere in France. Began in solitary, he said, and then got thrown in with a bunch of his buddies."

Sumako added, "He said something about a brawl at a dance hall. Do you know anything about it?"

"Everyone was released." I thought that was a good way to leave things. "Everyone fought like hell at the Gothic Line."

"But Happi said something about waiting forever to hear about a court-martial," Fumie said. "Said the accusing officer, an MP, I think, wasn't around, so things might go easy."

"But he dropped the topic in his last letters," Sumako added. "When you started fighting again in Italy."

I remembered how Happi had cut his last letters short, thinking he'd have nothing to talk about when he got home.

And to think it actually would have been good to have the MP there, to testify that he'd told us to just call it a night and get back to our quarters.

What should I say?

I chose my words carefully. "Beats me what he was thinking, but I do know that Happi fought to the death with us. He died an honorable man. A hero."

The women looked at each other.

"You know better than we do, Hiroshi," Mrs. Ishikawa said. "I take you at your word."

I waited for a moment before I asked my next question. "Happi's remains," I said in a soft voice, "what have you done with them?"

Mrs. Ishikawa's lips trembled. "We decided to keep him with the troops he loved, in the land where he fought. He is being buried in Florence, in new American Cemetery."

"I think Happi would have liked that," I said. "And his spirit will always be with us."

Everyone agreed, and we talked more about Happi's love of art and architecture, the fun we had had, his wish to build a house for his mother, to create their new home.

Happi's family seemed to be coming to a peace of sorts by the time I left, and I grew anxious only at their last question.

"Hiroshi," Sumako said as she touched my sleeve. "Isn't that a private's chevron? I thought you were Happi's sergeant."

Shit.

"Long story," I said as I inched toward the door. "Six Purple Hearts and an Honorable Discharge, that's what I earned, and they're what matters. Who cares about the pretty stuff on a uniform."

Mrs. Ishikawa looked in my eyes. "War is awful, ne? We will never know."

The girls agreed, and as I left, my yearning for understanding battled with my guilt.

Back home, I spent the next several nights tossing and turning, worried that I had lied, or at least had not owned up to my part in the whole predicament. I wanted to tell them more, but this just wasn't the time, especially when I couldn't even tell Ruth. I had done all I could do for now.

Best to put the whole damned war behind me and get on with life.

In late November, Ruth and I took a train up to Minneapolis, where we were married by her parents' minister, in their home, on December 1. No one had much money, but Ruth's mother and father had scraped up enough cash to give us two nights at a hotel for our honeymoon. We felt like the richest people on earth.

Before we returned to Chicago, we stayed with her parents for a couple of days, and I overheard Ruth talking to her mother after breakfast one morning, as I returned from the bathroom.

"I don't know everything that happened in that darned war," Ruth said, "and I think there are things Hiroshi isn't telling me, things he's not ready to talk about."

"War is terrible," her mother said. "Unspeakable."

Ruth agreed. "I hear so many of his friends, talking over and over and over about battles and barrages and bombs. They laugh it up, but I know they're trying to make sense of it all."

"They so young still," her mother said. "War terrible way grow up. You and I never know. Give him time."

"He's a good man, Mom. Really good. He went through so much even before the war, losing his parents and all. I don't want to push him."

"Then don't. You strong-willed young lady, Ruth. No force. Like minister said, love gentle, love kind."

"I will be both," Ruth said. "I promise."

The two stopped talking, and I tiptoed back several steps and then made enough noise to let the ladies know I was on my way to the kitchen. I took my seat, wanting to hug them both. Ruth really did accept all of me, and her mother liked me, at last. I would talk when the time felt right.

Back in Chicago, Ruth's roommates left to meet their families at Bainbridge Island, so I was able to ride out their lease while we looked for a smaller apartment. We were hearing that more than twenty thousand issei and nisei from the camps were being processed in the city with help from the WRA, the largest resettlement on the mainland. We were delighted that families were coming back together and staying strong, even if their presence created competition for living space.

"Where should we move?" Ruth and I asked. The government and churches were urging everyone to assimilate fully rather than create Japantowns, which had contributed to "the Japanese problem," they said. But we all knew that view ignored the economic, cultural, and legal strictures that had kept us out of mainstream living in the first place.

"Our neighborhoods are damned shabby, and a lot of people are slamming doors in our faces," I said. "Caucasians still don't like Japanese."

"Why don't we look right around here?" Ruth said. "It's already more accepting of us than other neighborhoods." It was either this or Molly's Clark and Division area, which had begun to grow northward into Lakeview. But the South Side was familiar territory to Ruth, so we confined our search.

By the end of February, we had found a small, three-room flat at the front of a tidy brick rowhouse at 41st and Ellis, just a few blocks northeast of her old apartment and right next to the El tracks, with tree-lined boulevards and houses that were getting spruced up.

"Am I giving you enough time?" I would ask after our love-making, worried that the boys were taking too much of my attention. In the weeks after we signed our lease, they had moved their partying from Ruth's old place to our new home, some on their way to becoming residents of Chicago themselves. And when my old comrades and I weren't laughing and reminiscing about the war, we were visiting mothers and fathers, girlfriends and wives, brothers and sisters of boys who hadn't made it back, who would not enjoy the fruits of our victory. Silently, I grieved for the men on my detail, their names not known to me, and for their families, for they had no answers.

"You and I are fine," Ruth would always say. "We have our whole lives ahead of us. You men have earned this time. Besides, your friends know about jobs and schools that can help you."

I knew she was right. Some of my buddies had appealed for help to the Quakers, who were still lending a hand. Others were getting assistance from a new re-settlers committee. Jobs, housing, playing fields, social events—you name it, the committee was there to help.

Issei and nisei found employment as domestic servants and factory workers and technicians. Brave entrepreneurs began to operate all kinds of businesses—apartment buildings, hotels, grocery stores, restaurants, salons. Baseball leagues popped up. Christian and Buddhist churches sprang to life. Quietly, instinctively, we solidified Japanese neighborhoods, especially around the Lakeview area and northward, to remember our history. Assimilation with the Caucasian world was left mostly for schools, offices, and civic organizations.

"I've found something I can work with," I said after much thinking and yakking. With the help of the G. I. Bill, I began a new venture—a one-year course at the Chicago Technical School, thinking I would be good at refrigeration and air conditioning things—while Ruth continued making decent money at the milliner's. I had to admit, my poor bride spent many an evening listening for the El trains that stopped near our apartment, waiting for me to rumble in from school or from a night drinking with the boys, but we knew our lives were taking shape, and we made time for the two of us, too.

"It feels so good to be in your arms again," Ruth would say as we danced. With her salary and an internship I had started, we eked out enough so we could enjoy AJA gatherings at the YMCA/YWCA or cut the rug to swing bands at the Trianon, about twenty blocks south of us. A couple of times we even double-dated with Poi Hirano and Fumie Ishikawa at the Aragon; they had been seeing each other since Poi was released from the hospital and seemed pretty serious. We never talked about Happi's last days.

Veterans filled our home during the spring and summer, and we heard the bittersweet news that a soldier in the 100th had been posthumously awarded the MOH for saving his buddies at the Gothic Line. We knew more men deserved the medal and wondered if they would ever be recognized. In mid-July we celebrated the march down Constitution Avenue by the remaining men in the 442nd, mostly replacements who had been shipped back home en masse. The men received the RCT's seventh Distinguished Unit Citation from President Truman himself, who said that we had fought and won two battles, against the enemy and against prejudice, though we knew the latter struggle continued. As we read the newspapers, we were puzzled to learn that none other than Lieutenant Colonel Martin Edward Fowler was in command of the returning troops, but we focused on the courage and heroism shown by all. Just a few weeks later, he brought the troops home to Hawaii, too, and we enjoyed reports of the great fanfare that surrounded the returning heroes.

"You think some of the boys don't like that colonel because he was so mean to you?" Ruth said as we put down our papers.

"Why do you say that?" I was surprised.

"Oh, I hear your friends talking," Ruth said, flushing. "That's all."

I wondered how much she'd heard. The guys kept telling me how unfair things had been, how very unfair, but they talked about it when Ruth wasn't around. I would have been promoted to lieutenant if it hadn't been for that colonel, they said. Mak would have advanced, too.

I looked at Ruth again, thinking my dear wife should at least know the basics, and I finally told her about being sent out on the ration detail, having to obey the colonel's orders, and seeing my men killed. But I ended with that. I wasn't ready to talk about the rest. Even I didn't understand everything that had happened.

"War is war, and it's in the past," I concluded.

Ruth said she understood and didn't ask any further.

• • •

Molly dropped by one day near Christmas, bringing the welcome news that our grandparents and sister had survived the bombing of Hiroshima, protected from the fallout by the mountains that stood between that city and our family home in Tanna.

"Grandpa is alive only because his partner asked to switch his schedule that day," Molly said, choking back tears. Our grandfather had driven an ambulance in Hiroshima for the last several months of the war.

"Did he go into Hiroshima after?" I asked. "To help?"

"The next morning," Molly said. "You know Ji-chan. Always ready to lend a hand." She looked down as she thought and added, "He said the devastation is beyond imagination. The city is gone, just vaporized. People were totally burned, flesh hanging from their bodies. There wasn't much he could do."

Our relief mixed with sorrow, and Ruth made coffee as we talked about when Aiko might come home, when Hiroshima might start healing and rebuilding.

"War does not end easily," Molly said.

"It will be with us for years to come," I said.

Quietly, awkwardly, we moved onto holiday matters as Molly spoke of getting things ready for Virginia. She checked her watch. "I actually have to pick up a toy for her," she said, rising to go.

Ruth helped her with her coat. "Oh," Molly reached into her pocket. "Almost forgot." She handed me an envelope. "This was addressed to you at our apartment."

"Wonder why," I said as I ran my fingers over it. "Feels like a Christmas card." I was full of anticipation as I opened the envelope.

What the hell?

"What's the matter?" Ruth said. "I've never seen your face fall like that."

I held up the card. "It's from my *colonel.*" What was this all about? The card showed a snow-covered Christmas tree and wished me a Merry Christmas in print. It was signed, "Lieutenant Colonel Martin Edward Fowler," with no personal greeting.

"Don't you think that's nice?" Molly said. "I wonder if he sent cards to other men."

"That was your battalion commander, right?" Ruth remembered and sounded apprehensive. "The one the guys don't like."

"The past is past," I said as I threw the card in the trash.

I saw Molly look at Ruth, who shook her head subtly, as though to say, "Don't ask."

I said no more, and Ruth did not pursue the topic.

• • •

A couple of weeks later, Molly brought over another envelope, this one containing a New Year's card signed by Lieutenant Colonel Martin Edward Fowler, with no message. I tossed this one in the trash, too, and I wouldn't answer Ruth's occasional questions about why the colonel was sending me these greetings, other than to agree he must have felt bad about my ration detail.

A Valentine's Day card followed, and I about blew my lid. Did the man have no shred of decency? I crumpled up the card and threw it away.

By St. Patrick's Day, I was acing my classes and in high spirits.

And then another card arrived, this time in our own mailbox, signed by Lieutenant Colonel Martin Edward Fowler.

Did I look like a damned Irishman?

Out into the trash.

Another arrived at Eastertime.

Out it went.

What the hell was with the guy? How had he even found my address? Molly's?

Fowler missed my graduation, but remembered me on the 4th of July, by which time I was interviewing for several positions around town, hoping I could nab one of the many jobs that the unions had reserved for veterans. This is what we had fought for, to be part of the American Dream.

I waited to hear back.

And waited.

I was perfect for this job.

And that one.

I knew I'd get it.

I didn't.

"Do you think it's your Army record?" Ruth asked softly.

"What do you mean?" I asked. "An Honorable Discharge and a bucketful of Purple Hearts? That's good enough for any employer."

Ruth said she guessed I was right.

But I kept getting turned down.

I compared my fate with my buddies, all having the same problem.

What the hell?

The unions didn't want Japs.

"Why can't this goddamned bigotry end?" I asked Ruth. "When will people think of us as Americans first, not Japs, not AJAs, not nisei, but just Americans?" I wondered how Negro vets were faring, too, especially in the South. Not well, I was sure.

We talked about returning to Seattle, where things might be easier.

"We don't have to leave," I said. "Your boss really likes you." I paused before giving her my highest compliment. "You have the go-for-broke spirit."

Ruth said, "Look, we have to make the break at some point. We're going to have babies, and you need a job. And face it, we're both getting a little homesick."

"And Bou Bear," I reminded her. "I have to get Bou." I had written Paul soon after I returned, and his parents wrote back, saying Paul had been drafted, but they were taking good care of my dog. I could come retrieve him when the time was right.

We talked and talked over the coming days, concluding that Chicago had been a great city for us to settle in from the camps and from the war, to regain our dignity and prepare ourselves emotionally and professionally for whatever lay ahead. Sweet Home Chicago, the blues musicians called it, and so did we. We would always love it. Molly was already talking of moving, and it was time for us to forge ahead.

Together, Ruth and I visited Happi's family to say goodbye, and we gave a big hug to everyone. I had to admit, Mr. Ishikawa looked gaunt, after all he had been through, and my heart ached for him. He kept grasping and rubbing my arm as I told him what a good man Happi had been, how much I missed him.

After Ruth caught them up on news of her family, their old friends, they told us that they, too, were moving, to California. That's where many relatives had settled, including Uncle Minoru, who had moved there when he was released from camp several months ago. We promised to stay in touch.

As we inched toward the door, Mr. and Mrs. Ishikawa saw me eyeing a bunch of envelopes that they were packing, spread out on a coffee table. All were addressed to Happi's mother or siblings in Chicago, each with a beautiful watercolor painting beneath the return address. I saw a black barracks on one, a curving blue canal on another, a wildflower on yet another.

"I paint these while I wait to get out of Minidoka," Mr. Ishikawa said, pointing to the return address of his barracks number in Hunt, Idaho. "Never tried get one to Joji. Get ruined in V-mail."

He stopped, his lip trembling. "Too bad, too bad. Joji love to learn draw and paint with me, even as little boy."

I told them how much I had enjoyed Happi's sketches myself, how very talented he was. Mrs. Ishikawa's eyes welled with tears, and she cradled my face in her hands as we left.

"You take good care of her," Mr. Ishikawa said as he tilted his head toward Ruth. "We always love her."

I promised I would, and we stepped off to our future.

27

Seattle

1946-1953

As soon as we returned to Seattle, I called Paul Johnson and his parents to see if I could pick up Bou. No one answered, but after a few hours, I took a chance and ran over.

I rang the bell of their house and waited.

Mrs. Johnson opened the door.

"Oh, Hiroshi," she said in a soft voice. She hugged me, and then I felt her sobbing, her tears wetting my shirt.

"Come in, come in," she said as she pulled herself away. I could see her hands shaking.

I should have called again.

"Hiroshi." Mr. Johnson clasped my hand in both of his. Paul's father looked like he'd aged twenty years.

"Bou's out in the backyard," Mrs. Johnson said. "But before we get him, we have to tell you—"

"Paul was drafted soon after you left," Mr. Johnson said.

I braced myself.

"Ordered to France." Mrs. Johnson added.

"D-Day, you know," Mr. Johnson said, his voice cracking.

"Earned the Purple Heart."

"They said he died a hero."

"We waited to tell you in person."

"I'm so sorry," I said. I hugged them both as I choked back my own tears.

We talked for a long while, remembering what a good soul Paul was, funny and caring and smart, and then the Johnsons brought me to the back door. "I think Bou's been waiting for you." Mr. Johnson handed me Bou's leash. "You can come back in or leave by the gate, whatever you want." He held me by the shoulder.

"I-I-we don't have a place yet," I said. "Can Bou—"

"He can stay here for as long as you like," Mrs. Johnson said. "He's our family, too. And so are you. You're welcome to stay with us until you get yourself going."

I was taken aback at her offer. "If we could just stay until we get a place, find a job, that would be great."

Mr. Johnson said he'd help us with our luggage when we were ready, and he held open the door for me.

There was Bou, lying in a corner of the yard. When I stepped out, he stood up with one paw raised, his ears pricked as though he heard something.

"Bou!" I called, my heart thumping as it reached out to his. "Bou Bear!"

Bou turned, saw me, and raced over. I knelt down, and my little dog wriggled and whimpered and jumped for joy to see me again. His silver muzzle was hoary white now, but his eyes were still bright, and we played and played, repeating our reunion every day when I returned from looking for a job or for an apartment.

Until one afternoon, when Bou took one last bite of a cookie and breathed no more.

I sat on the ground and held Bou tight, knowing for sure that he had held on until I came home. He had let go now, in peace. Alone with him, rocking him, I wept openly for the first time since the war ended, grieving the losses of my family and my home, of Happi, of other friends and comrades, of Bou Bear, pure goodness and love.

The Johnsons, Ruth, and I buried old Bou in their back yard and cried together, for the love we had known and for the love we had lost.

It was time to find a way forward.

• • •

The next week, Ruth and I managed to find a tiny place to rent near Japantown, and that wife of mine somehow talked her way into handling the books for a doctor's office while I searched for a job.

Nothing here.

Not for you.

Go away.

With no union jobs to be had for us Japanese, even here, I took a position at my old sporting goods store just to make money. Our expenses were about to mount.

"Welcome, little one," we greeted our first-born. Ruth quit her job and dedicated herself to raising our family.

"Aren't you beautiful!" We burst with pride at our second.

We hoped for a third someday.

Here they were, our new *sansei* generation, and I begged for extra hours so we could make ends meet. Housing was difficult to find for nisei, even the houses reserved for veterans, but eventually we traded rent for mortgage payments when we found a little house in the Lakewood-Seward Park area, always friendly to minorities, Negroes and Jews and Buddhists among them. Molly, Lawrence, and Virginia settled about an hour away in Washington state, as did Aiko, safely back from Japan and married to another kibei. Frank opted for Los Angeles. Ruth's siblings scattered, one marrying a Japanese Canadian, one of more than twenty thousand interned during the war.

Outside our nest, our life centered almost out of necessity on AJA matters, and I became one of the first commanders of the Nisei Veterans Committee. Those who had heard about my court-martial knew it had been unfair and rarely mentioned it, though it was ever present beneath the surface, waiting to be eradicated like a cancerous growth. I helped raise funds for a seventeen-foot-high monument to Seattle's war dead, and I visited families of the men who did not return, most frequently, Mr. and Mrs. Inada.

"Miss him so," Mrs. Inada said of her son, Glenn, who had died in Italy early during the Second Push, one of seventy-three Minidoka men killed in the war.

"Hey, Hiro," Wes limped toward me. We slapped each other on the back, and he told me he and his family had been one of many not allowed to give their loved ones a proper memorial service until after the war. Japanese names were only now returning to community honor rolls.

"We still have to work for that American Dream," I said, and Wes agreed.

"So how's the leg?" I asked.

"Doing its job." Wes knocked on it. "Hard as a rock and my ticket to law school." He said he had already started at Georgetown on the GI Bill.

"And what's with you?" he asked. "Good God, six Purple Hearts, I heard? You're lucky to be alive." He drew closer and lowered his voice. "Heard you got screw—" he glanced at his mother as he scrambled for a different word, "had a spot of trouble in France."

"I did, but it's behind me. Have to go on."

28

Honolulu

1953

As 1953 approached, plans got under way in Honolulu for a first reunion of the 442nd, on the tenth anniversary of our outfit's founding.

"Aren't you going?"

"Come on, you have to attend."

"It's gonna be a once-in-a-lifetime experience."

We would honor our own patriotism and the progress made on the racial front. Truman had signed an executive order to integrate the Army in 1948. Issei everywhere had been given the right to become U.S. citizens under 1952's McCarran Act, which nullified old legislation excluding or limiting Orientals from immigration and naturalization. The head of the JACL had been instrumental to the act's passage.

Who would miss the party?

Sadly, it looked like I would. I had just lost weeks of work as I recovered first from a botched tonsillectomy and then the mumps, which our daughters had generously shared with me. No way I could afford to go.

My buddies wrote letters and made long-distance phone calls to each other.

"Could you spare a few bucks?"

"Gotta get Hiro there."

They even approached Lieutenant Ando, who said he'd be happy to help. He dug deep, saying life had been good to him.

"Lieutenant Ando sounds so nice," Ruth said, both of us touched by his generosity. She always referred to him by his rank, politely, respectfully, and I always spoke highly of him, never saying a word about what had passed between us. My boss gave his blessing, and I was on my way to two weeks of festivities. I wanted Ruth by my side, but money stretched just so far.

．　．　．

The opening day of the reunion, a bunch of us Seattle vets took an early morning Northwest Airlines flight to Honolulu, laughing and joking about old times until we approached the airport. As the plane descended, we passed over Pearl Harbor, and we made out the hull of the Arizona lying beneath the aquamarine waters, grave to more than a thousand Americans, an oil slick floating on the surface. A flagstaff stood at the protruding severed rear mast, a temporary wooden platform placed amidships as a more permanent memorial was being discussed. I recognized the circular foundations of gun turrets, where many of the victims had lost their lives defending their ship, their mates, their country, and we saluted the flag and the grave.

"Tears of the Arizona," someone whispered, pointing to the oil.

"Hallowed waters," said another.

"Reason we're here."

"Let's remember the men lost, when we remember our own."

"We're all one."

"We can never forget."

We stepped off the plane, our memory of suffering, courage, and sacrifice mixing with our desire to celebrate our achievements, and we were soon overwhelmed by the festivities awaiting us.

"Come on, guys," I said. "I don't deserve this." My buddies kept thanking me for my leadership and decorated me up to my nose in leis. They made me ride in the head car of the two-hundred-fifty-car motorcade from the Honolulu airport that was kicking off the celebration. Four Army jeeps led the way, the first occupied by Earl Finch, appointed Grand Marshall because of the many kindnesses he had shown to us during and after the war. He had not only befriended us in the Jim Crow South, but had also written to many overseas, visited our wounded in hospitals, and welcomed everyone back home.

"Mahalo!" people called out as we made our way around the city.

"Go for broke!" others cheered.

"Proud of you!" one person after another yelled.

I was amazed. The islands were still heavily populated by Nikkei—the new term embracing all generations of Japanese descent—and the exploits of the 100th/442nd had reached legendary proportions. Thousands of people jammed the streets, waving flags and calling to us.

The motorcade ended at McKinley High, and after opening ceremonies, a thousand of us lined up in the school's auditorium to register for reunion activities. Buddhaheads told me the most bigoted of haoles during wartime had called this school "Tokyo High," the school was so full of nisei.

"Good reason we stop here, eh," they said as we waited. Their principal had been one of the haoles who believed in them and demanded they stand up for their rights as Americans.

"Teachers and students did just what he asked," they said. The first Executive Officer of the 100th Battalion had taught here, and graduates filled the ranks of our team, including, sadly, the 100th's first man killed in action.

The mix of somber and happy reflection continued as men chatted, and Mak and I ended the day sharing a raucous dinner with lots of our buddies. We unwound that evening at his home. Nora, his very pretty and very pregnant wife, brought us a couple of "oyasumi" beers before excusing herself to check in on their little boy and girl, who were sleeping after a day in the care of their grandmother. "I'm turning in, too," Nora said. "Have to rest up for tomorrow's events."

Mak turned serious as we drank our next beer.

"Today's motorcade sure showed how far we've come since we took off for war," Mak said.

"How's that?"

Mak explained that several days before the 442nd shipped overseas, the city had honored the volunteer soldiers with grand festivities at Iolani Palace, the former royal home commandeered by the martial law government. After the ceremonies, the boys returned to Tent City, Schofield Barracks, to pack and prepare for what was supposed to be a secret departure from the islands, with a dignified march to their ship.

"Couple days later, when we leave Schofield, we take train into Honolulu, to Iwilei station, yuh. We looked for trucks to carry duffel bags while we march. But Army sent no trucks," Mak said.

"You're kidding." I didn't think I'd ever know everything about the Hawaii boys, the men I had fought with shoulder to shoulder.

"Bags real heavy and tall as us," Mak said. "No one told us what to take, so we'd packed everything—clothes, ukuleles, baseball bats. We had to drag bags all way to ship. Whole mile, yuh, and we out of shape. Sweated and strained, with rifles, too."

Word had spread about their departure, and men's families and friends were lined up along Ala Moana Boulevard to say goodbye. But MPs marched alongside the new citizen-soldiers like they were prisoners, pushing mothers and fathers away and ordering the men not to break ranks.

"Pretty humiliating," Mak said. "Finally made our way along waterfront to ship, where we drive along today." The SS Lurline, the pride of Matson's luxury line, newly converted for war, was waiting at Pier 11 to take them to California. From there, they caught trains to Shelby.

"Speaking of that ship," I asked in a low voice, in case Nora might hear, "what happened to that girl of yours back in Chicago?"

"Went and married another doctor," he said, his eyes distant as he remembered young love. "I knew she would. But I dated a lot when I got back and sure got lucky. Nora is wonderful."

We were quiet for a minute and then I asked, "So how you doing, really?" I knew Mak was working at Meadow Gold Dairy to make ends meet and, like all of us, wanted a better future, but employment wasn't my concern. "You know, the court-martial and everything." I lit cigarettes for us.

Mak looked down. "Tell you truth, I just try not to think of it. Just pretend it didn't happen. What about you?"

"Pretty much the same," I said. "I only told Ruth about the ration detail, how my men were killed."

"I told Nora the basics," Mak said, "but that's all. I just don't want to talk about it, and she just knows when to stop asking questions."

Mak went to the kitchen for more beer, and as he handed me one, he said, "Bad dreams, really bad, sometimes." He shrugged and took a long drink.

"No more for me these days," I said. "But I think about everything late at night, really late, when Ruth's asleep. I mean, Ruth just will never understand what we went through—no civilian can—but I've piled secrets on top of that."

"Some lies are meant to protect, ourselves and others, some meant to destroy," Mak said. "Yours aren't bad."

"Some secrets are kept out of love, others out of hate," I agreed. "Maybe mine are white lies, big fat ones, but it still bothers me to have secrets between me and my wife. She trusts me, you know."

"Nora trusts me, too," Mak said. He picked at the label on his beer bottle as he thought.

"I got an ulcer," he admitted, mumbling. "Swear it's because of this."

I confessed to going to work bleary-eyed at times, my back aching from old wounds and lack of sleep.

"Wasn't right," he added. "Damned bastard."

"Screw him," I muttered.

We soon called it a night, knowing we had an early memorial service the next morning at Punchbowl, resting place of so many of our men and of Pearl Harbor casualties, their identities known and unknown. Mak and I vowed that this reunion would be the rekindling of our friendship, one that would include our wives and children, too.

The following days were filled with patriotic speeches by some of our old commanders, all in uniform, and we veterans listened as our aloha shirts filled the room with color. During one gathering where all units intermingled, I landed in the middle of the One Puka Puka boys.

I couldn't believe it. I stood next to the 100th's battalion commander, who stood face to face with none other than General Bristol.

Bad feelings about the general had grown even stronger since the war as we learned more about the man.

Did Bristol have combat experience?

He had been a desk general under Eisenhower.

Did he really think we were robots?

Maybe, but we were also the best troops available when he called us to rescue his boys.

Why did Bristol call our men off Hill C?

He discovered it was in another commander's sector, and he didn't want to give the man credit for the win.

Why was everything rushed?

Bristol wanted to be first general into Germany.

He put himself first, in front of the men he led.

No moral courage, everyone said.

The man had no moral courage.

"Please," Bristol said as he held his hand out to be shaken.

The 100th commander saluted and stared straight over Bristol's head.

"Come on," Bristol tried again. "Let bygones be bygones."

The commander held his salute and stared ahead.

Veterans stood still as we watched the men.

Bristol tried again.

The commander stood his ground.

Bristol put his hand and his head down and pressed his way through the crowd.

"Bastard," men whispered.

"Desk general."

"Killed so many so needlessly."

"Never did court-martial anyone, did he?"

"He didn't dare."

"Knew he was in the wrong."

Every so often I'd catch sight of Fowler, too.

There he was at our big welcome, extolling our fighting virtues.

There he was again, posing for a newspaper photo with our other RCT leaders.

And there he was yet again, escorting his wife to this party and that, always surrounded by 3rd Battalion soldiers, everyone except a lot of us Itemites.

Had he spotted me at the head of the motorcade?

What was he thinking?

My heart raced anytime I'd spot him, and I held my head down so he didn't see me.

And then I'd get back to the fun.

We enjoyed luaus full of island food and drink and hula, and we yukked it up in company breakout parties, in hotels and on beaches and in yards. We visited other islands, too, to meet with the families of our comrades who hadn't made it back. Solemn ceremonies, real sad ones, were held everywhere to honor the absent men. Some of us even stopped to remember dear Lucy, who had served in her own way, giving many of us solace and warmth. After the war, soldiers sneaked Lucy into Hawaii, where she gave birth to puppies conceived in Italy. She met her Maker years ago.

"Never thought you'd be a man of the cloth," I said to Jug at our big I Company party, midway through the reunion. He was now the newly ordained Reverend Charles Wesley Morita and was helping to officiate at our services.

"Me, either," Jug said. "But the war changed me."

"How so?"

"I began understanding the meaning of God's admonition to 'fear not.' And you helped, you know. Those words are going to be the heart of my ministry." We talked about the day he had frozen and about the day I had frozen, too.

"I overcame a lot of my fear on the battlefield," I admitted, "would do anything for our men. But now, back in civilian life, I don't know. Guess I have to figure out what 'fear not' means all over again."

"Well, I'm going to do everything I can to give others the courage to live in compassion and strength and trust. We really are part of one another. What we do to the least of men—and 'least' is in the eye of the beholder—we do to the Highest. Maybe start thinking along those lines."

I promised I would, even if I wasn't much of a religious thinker or philosopher. Jug told me to be patient. We all needed time to learn.

"Hey, anyone want to slide down some mountains?" Kat came up to us.

"Can't thank you guys enough," Jug said. "When I think how many times my life was saved—"

Jug stopped talking when one of the reunion officials came to ask about a blessing he was supposed to say before dinner. He excused himself as a woman walked up to Kat.

"Hiro, meet my wife, Hisako." Kat grinned.

I had to admit, the guy had been right. Hisako was a real stunner, sharp, and a good talker. I turned to Kat, knowing it was my turn to thank someone for saving my life, and Kat drew me closer to him.

"Okay, long ago I promise to explain why I so mean back at Shelby, yuh," he said.

"Pray, tell," I said. I'd been waiting for years.

"Seem silly now," Kat said. "But you look just like my father back then, like twin, just taller. Younger. And you and me, we both drink a lot like him, yuh, just without the nasties he had. I was so damned mad at him for being mean to my mother, for walking out on us. Not a penny to our name."

He lowered his voice. "And right after you showed up at Shelby, one of sisters wrote and said he appeared at our door, tried to make up with our mother. She wanted none of it, and he got rough, yuh."

Kat looked down at the ground and then back at me. "Didn't know what to do so far away. Took it out on you."

He offered his hand, and I shook it as he added, "No excuse. Really sorry, eh."

"Sometimes I think it's easier to lose your father through death than to go through all that hurt and anger," I said.

"Think you're right," Kat said. "Glad you and me got over this, yuh."

"I'll get some plastic surgery if it'll help us along," I kidded.

"For better, eh? You one ugly buggah," Kat said as he patted my back.

A familiar voice interrupted us.

"You two sure caused me so much *shinpai*." Lieutenant Ando came up and shook our hands, smiling. "Glad to see you're still friends."

What should I say? I hadn't talked to Ando since the night I tried to sock him.

Kat began reminiscing about our trip to see Ando's sensei, and Ando said the man was back in Hilo, teaching a new generation.

Just as I began relaxing, that darned Kat and Hisako were pulled away by some jeep driver friends, leaving Ando and me alone.

My thoughts raced. I'd been madder than hell and hurt and confused at the end of the war, but Ando was my lieutenant, and I admired him for everything else he'd done.

"Thank you," I began. "The boys told me you helped me get out here."

"The least I could do, Hiro," Ando said. He drew nearer, as though he wanted to talk more. But a woman walked up to us, and he said, "Hiro, I'd like you to meet Emiko. Emmy. My wife."

"I've heard a lot about you," Emmy said in a soft voice and smiled. "You are quite the hero."

Emmy had dark brown eyes that looked right into your soul, and I thanked her. But I told her there were tons of heroes in our outfit. I had no idea what Ando had said to her, and we moved onto other topics, my mind constantly returning to the one subject that needed to be addressed.

Ando had joined the MIS after the war and found his brother in Japan.

Why did you leave Happi behind, Ando?

He was starting at the Hilo Sugar Company next week and was buying his old luna's house. Could you believe how times had changed everywhere? We were even "Asians" now, not "Orientals," the old term discarded for the history of racism it carried.

Doesn't it bother you?

We had miles to go, Emmy said. Her father, a community activist, had been interned at Gila River and was treated with disdain even by his friends when he returned home, like he was guilty of doing something wrong. He still suffered.

"Same thing happened to the Tule Lake internees," I said. She listened carefully as I told of them, and Ando nodded slowly.

Are you hurting, Lieutenant?

"Let's hope time will heal everything," Emmy said. She looked tenderly first at me and then at Ando, and I knew he'd married well.

Mak joined us, and as more veterans came over to chat, I watched Emmy, our eyes meeting a couple of times. I hoped she was right about time's restorative powers.

The topic of my court-martial inevitably came up in talks with my buddies, especially as our time together drew to a close.

"You should fight it," friend after friend said as we got ready for our farewell dinner. "You were screwed to the wall." They said the same thing to Mak, who just walked away.

"Forget it," I said. "Let's just get on with our lives. Enjoy what we fought for."

"We fought for justice," Jug joined the conversation. "And that's exactly what you didn't get."

"You gotta fight. I know how much court-martial hurts," Ben Honda said, raising his fist. "You think I save your stinkin' life for nothing?" I raised my fist, thanking him again.

"Listen to him," Poi Hirano said. "You have to fight this."

"Knock it off, guys," I said. How could I take even a first step without letting Ruth know everything that had happened? "It's ancient history."

I turned to head out to our banquet and saw Ando standing to one side, within earshot of us. We looked at each other for several seconds, silently. He made an almost imperceptible motion, like he wanted to say something, but friends pulled him toward the party. My pals began heading out.

I stood by myself, wondering if Ando and I would ever speak what was on our minds and in our hearts. It didn't seem either of us was ready.

PART IV

29

Seattle

June 1976

"I'm ready to talk now, Hiro," Ando said as I wrapped up my story. "Let's get this out in the open before the rest of my hair falls out. Are you ready?"

I ran my hand over my own thinning hair. "I better be." I turned up the volume on my hearing aid so my war-battered ears wouldn't miss a word.

I looked down and then said, "I'm sorry I tried to sock you, Ando, really I am. I was pissed at the entire world, and I'd lost my buddy."

Ando leaned his head to one side as he blinked slowly, saying, "You were in deep pain, Hiro. And there were things you didn't know that could have helped you understand what was and wasn't happening."

"Like what?" I asked.

"Well, just to start, you have to realize I didn't even know about the bar fight right away," he said.

"Vic Abe didn't tell you about driving us back?" I asked.

"No. My own friend, right?" he said. "It was like he was protecting me as a new looie, I guess. Didn't want to get me involved."

Ando went on. "And it wasn't my doing that I disappeared so many times toward the end of the war."

"No?" I asked.

"When you had to fight for that hill without me," Ando said, "I'd been pulled out on Temporary Disability without any warning. Told I needed a rest. That's it. In the middle of battle."

Ando thought for a minute and then added, "You'd been arguing more and more about the colonel's strategy, I remember, right in front of our platoon, our company. And now I wonder if that colonel of ours was trying to get rid of you any way he could. A few men told me that sometime after that battle, they saw him jumping up and down on an overhang of dirt and rock above you."

"Part of it fell on me," I remembered. "I got bruised up, that's for sure."

I thought back to the court-martial. "What about my so-called trial? You were supposed to be my character witness."

Ando groaned. "A couple of lieutenants interviewed me by myself in one of the mansions Regimental had taken over. They told me the interview was enough for the judicial folks and I shouldn't attend your trial. And later on, command told me to stay away from you when you were in the stockades."

"Damn," I muttered. "Do you know who was giving the orders?"

"Now that you've told me all this, I'd venture a guess that Fowler was behind everything. I tried to speak up, but who would listen to a new second lieutenant. You know how tight the command structure was."

I turned to Ruth. "I'm sorry, hon. I should have told you earlier. At least you know now. Everything."

Ruth said she understood as she held an envelope out to me. I took it as I turned to Shig. "And I'm sorry I never had the guts to tell you and your family how Happi died. It was just too painful."

"For me, too," Ando said.

Shig thanked us both. "You were good friends to my brother. I understand, now more than ever."

Ando added, "I never told anyone this, but since the war, I've tried to follow the Buddha and live my life for both Happi and me." His greatest effort, he said, was leading scouting projects at Hawaii's Camp Honokaia, activities like archery and riflery that would help young boys grow into men. "Buddha, Dharma, Sangha—I've tried to follow the teachings of the Buddha and act to benefit others, the community."

"You sent flowers to our mother every year on her birthday, too," Shig said. "She was so touched."

"Has all that helped you deal with everything?" I asked, putting Ruth's envelope on my lap while I listened. "Forgive yourself?"

Ando thought a minute before speaking. "I can't deny that I've had difficulty finding peace. Emmy can tell you how many nights I've spent tossing and turning, even though I've never told her why. Face it. Happi took my place in death. It would have been me who was killed if I hadn't given in and let him come with me."

"So have you been trying to repay Happi for his sacrifice?" I asked. "Like karmic debt?" I'd read a little about that, but didn't really understand.

"That's what I started to say earlier," he said. "We Buddhists do have an idea of karma, but it's not a simple matter of repaying debt. It's more like taking actions to remedy what we see as wrongs committed, to help heal people and situations, to learn from them. Once we do that, we're freed from making the same errors, and we can hope to live more fully as our true selves. It's a matter of evolving, I guess you'd say. I'm getting there, but I have more to do. What about you?"

"Oh, I've forgiven you. It's taken me years to get through this, to make sense of it all, but the night Happi died, what you did was right. I know that now," I said. "You had to live to protect our other men. You could have been shot dead if you'd searched for him."

I took a drink of water and added, "In the end, I guess, there isn't much to forgive."

"Thank you," Ando said. "That helps free me to focus and finish what I am doing. But what about you? Forgiving yourself?"

"I just can't think in terms of Happi taking my place in death," I said, "but, yeah, to this day, I feel bad about giving my equipment to him, even if I know it was the right thing to do, militarily. I have to admit, it gnaws at me deep inside."

I stopped for a minute, thinking. "When it comes down to it, I guess I feel guilty about creating the whole situation. I was the one who set the court-martial in motion and everything that followed. Maybe I should have kept my mouth shut, like my pal told me."

"I have two responses," Ando said. "One, that wouldn't have been you. You were a leader, always showing by example and standing up for our men, in thought, word, action. I sure relied on you. And two, there's something beyond just shutting up, something good to be quiet for, and that is to hear the stillness. When you're ready to go inside, be calm, and shut out the noise, you can find that stillness. It's where we know compassion, forgiveness, life."

"That's a lot to take in," I said. "I need more time to come to terms with it all." I looked down as I thought, seeing the envelope Ruth had given me. I held it up, making a "so what is this" face to her.

"I need understanding and forgiveness, too," Ruth said softly. "Why don't you read what's inside."

July 28, 1945
Florence, Italy

Aloha, Ruth,

After getting through the whole darned war, your lolo boyfriend went and busted a finger and now us buddies have to write for the dummy. My turn today. He laughs at the way us Buddhaheads talk, but I keep telling him we did go to school and learn a thing or two. And no soldiers want to admit that lots of mothers don't allow their keiki to speak pidgin at home, just English. Turns out we can write words on a page pretty well, probably better than we talk. So here it goes.

Hiro wants to let you know he's doing fine and I'd say he is. His mouth still runs like a sewing machine, just for starters. He's pilau, too, and swears like a pirate. He tries to talk Italian and French to all the pretty girls and they can't understand a word and just laugh and laugh. He's picked up some words from us Hawaii boys too. You'll see.

But he's a little different since the war started, like a lot of us, more serious sometimes. War will do that to a guy. He'll kill me if he knows I'm telling you this, but you should know so you'll be prepared for when he comes home. See, he got into a bit of a tiff with our commander back in France and got his sergeant stripes taken away and thrown in the brig. Really wasn't fair, you know. Your fellow took the fall for something he hadn't done and paid the price. But he's out now and he's bounced back and is still the fun guy you fell in love with, I'm sure so don't worry too much.

Now that I'm writing I want to say mahalo for all the goodies you sent Hiro. He sure is a generous guy and shared everything with us. Hope I can do something for you someday.

Aloha,
Nobu Sakai for Hiro

Slowly, I folded the letter and put it back in the envelope.

What the hell?

Ruth knew everything all along?

My court-martial?

My demotion?

The stockades?

"You knew?" I heard my own voice cracking. "All these years?"

"I did," she said.

"Why didn't you say something?" I felt surprised, hurt, angry, all at once.

"I knew you'd speak up when you were ready," Ruth said. "Even with everything you've told us, I'll never truly comprehend what you've been through. But I'm trying."

She came over and hugged me, and she looked as relieved as I felt, the burden of years of secrets lifting from our shoulders.

"I have more to reveal, too," Ando said.

"You're kidding." I thought I'd had enough.

"Two days after the barroom brawl, Fowler knew it was Yoyo who punched the MP."

"Really?"

"And I did, too," Ando said.

"What the hell?" I stood up, every one of my muscles tensed.

Ando said that Chaplain Morimoto had stopped by the schoolhouse after we were all taken away, telling Ando that he had been on the line when Fowler spoke with the Puerto Rican MP officer. It was clear that Yoyo had socked the man.

The chaplain visited Yoyo in the stockade and told him to own up, but nothing came of it.

"I thought you and Mak would be set free, but the chaplain said Fowler wanted to make an example of you, as the soldier who punched the officer," Ando said. "I had no idea why he had it in for you, but I do now. Heck, the MP didn't even want to press charges."

I couldn't believe what I was hearing.

"What about Morimoto?" I asked. "He was a captain, for God's sake. Why didn't he speak up?"

"Maybe he tried," Ando said, "or maybe command didn't call him to testify, knowing the truth would out. Or both. Who knows what Fowler did behind the scenes."

We focused on our current lives as we ate dinner, talking about jobs and children—Shig and Ando each had two sons—and then our friends left for their flight to O'Hare. Ruth and I finished packing for our own trip tomorrow.

I didn't know how to handle all this new information, but I'd heard Fowler might be at our reunion, and I was already figuring out ways to avoid him.

30

Chicago

July 1976

I Company had taken over three rooms for its hospitality suite at the NVR Reunion, and I couldn't have been happier as I scanned the first room, packed with veterans and wives against the backdrop of this grand dame hotel, the Sheraton. Men sported their aloha whites, which had become de rigeur wear for our reunions, the V-necked aloha shirts emblazoned with our liberty-torch-in-hand patch, the white playing now against the red damask on the walls, patterns of red squares on the carpet. Everyone was enjoying a few laughs before the reunion got under way with trips to the theater, parades, banquets, sports outings, and dancing. Lake Michigan sparkled outside.

"You hear about the Munson Report?" people were saying as we jostled through the crowd. The air was abuzz. A new book on the internment had brought to light 1941's secret Munson report to FDR. We couldn't believe it, but then again, we could. The report had stated categorically that no Japanese problem existed on the mainland or in Hawaii.

People held their reunion programs open to the page where President Ford's proclamation to the reunion appeared. After declaring that Executive Order 9066 had become defunct with the end of the war, laying to rest any fears of displacement still held by some issei, Ford said, "I call upon the American people to affirm with me this American Promise—that we have learned from the tragedy of that long-ago experience forever to treasure liberty and justice for each individual American, and resolve that this kind of action shall never again be repeated."

But Ruth and I quickly found a living reminder that there would always be difficulties in achieving that promise.

"Isn't that your favorite colonel?" Ruth pressed herself against me. She must have recognized him from photos in various publications about our outfit.

Fowler, his hair snowy white, his stature diminished with age, was making his way toward us from the back of the room, waving his hands and pressing through the crowd. "Koga. Hiro. Let's talk," he called.

I felt my back stiffen as he tried to soften me up, using the name my men have given me. How dare he. "Let's go," I whispered to Ruth.

"You sure?" she said. "We just got here."

"Let's vamoose." I clasped her elbow and led her out of the room into a large foyer, where we hung around until dinner, talking to veterans who had spilled out of the suite.

Just as we headed to the buffet, I glanced down a hallway and stopped cold in my tracks. There was Fowler, who had nabbed Ruth's younger brother, Russ, veteran of the Korean War. The colonel was gesticulating wildly as he ran on at the mouth.

Ruth and I looked at each other and continued to the banquet room, where the Nisei Ambassadors drum and bugle corps was giving everyone a big Chicago welcome. The corps had helped spread our legacy, not nearly as well known here as it was on the West Coast and in Hawaii.

Russ joined us halfway through the meal, and as festivities quieted down, our conversation turned to the colonel.

"I can't believe the guy," Russ said, finishing dessert. "How does he even know we're related? Good God, on and on he went about having some kind of disagreement with you that led to your court-martial."

Russ put his fork down. "Hiro, what court-martial was that?"

Briefly, I repeated what I had told Ruth, Ando, and Shig.

"Sounds like you were screwed to the wall, Hiro. That guy is nuts, I tell you," Russ said. "I couldn't understand half of what he was saying. He's obsessed."

"I wonder if he's told his lies so often that he really thinks they're true," I said.

"And trying to convince others," Ruth said.

"Our guys aren't falling for his BS," I said of my comrades.

"Me, either," said Russ.

Getting ready for bed, I told Ruth that I wasn't going to let the bastard ruin our time here. I lived for these get-togethers, full of my buddies and our families, even our kids getting to be friends. And Ruth and I had fond memories of Chicago.

The next day, Ruth and I visited the Auditorium Theater to remember Happi, wishing with all our hearts that he'd been able to come back and draw everything in the city and hear Chicago's symphony, even if it had long performed in a different concert hall. Quietly, reverently, we placed a few drawing pencils and a 442nd cap on a seat near where Happi, Mak, and I had stood, and after saying a short prayer, we walked away.

And then Fowler reappeared.

Ruth and I were back at the hotel, waiting for an elevator to bring us down to the hospitality suite when we saw him.

Fowler called out from the other end of the hallway and hurried toward us. "Come on, Koga. Hiro. Can't we talk?"

The elevator doors opened, and I pushed Ruth in. People shuffled to make room for us.

"Close!" I demanded of the doors. "Close, damn it all!"

People stared at me.

We escaped once more.

We walked into the hospitality suite, smiling as we made our way through the crowd, saying hello to old friends.

"Hey, Grandma and Grandpa." Sam Sakura came up and slapped me on the back, and he and his wife both kissed Ruth. We'd all seen each other at our last I Company reunion in Vegas two years before, and we assured each other of how well we still looked, even if Ruth and I had entered a new phase of life. The eldest of our three girls had just given birth to our first grandchild, start of the *yonsei* generation. We were elated.

"Sayaka taking care of your nosebleeds?" I kidded Sam. Sayaka was the nurse that he had so loved back in Minidoka, and they had married as soon as he shipped home. At the very first reunion Ruth ever attended, she had told Sam that she'd always be grateful to him. He was one of the many medics who'd patched me up during the war.

"Hope Chicago's treating you well," I said. Sam lived and worked in the northernmost Japanese area of city, which had grown from the burgeoning AJA community in the Lakeview area after the war, way up into the 5000-blocks on the Far North Side, not too far from the Aragon ballroom. That's where he'd established his dental practice.

"I'm doing great," Sam said. "Lots of nisei moved back to the West Coast, so our numbers aren't growing—"

"What are we down to, fifteen thousand or so?" Sayaka commented.

Sam said yes. "But we have a wonderful community, in different areas around the city. And almost two hundred businesses. I make a good living." He said about eighty nisei veterans lived in Chicago now, and a service committee, which had grown out of the post-war re-settlers group, offered many social and cultural programs for residents.

"Always involved with the Nisei Ambassadors, too," he said. He had helped start the drum and bugle corps after the war. "The group's more integrated these days, the way our community is. We never had a Japantown to speak of, you know, but have been more spread out, even to the suburbs lately. Kids of all races are playing together."

"So you got both your wishes," I said, remembering the day Sam left Minidoka for the Army. "Sayaka and the corps. Plus the gift of better times."

Sam hugged Sayaka around the waist, saying, "The Ambassadors still keep our motto for their own."

"Speaking of which, how about we go for broke and get a drink?" I was getting thirsty.

As we made our way through the crowd, Sayaka said, "When did you get in? We didn't see you here yesterday." A hospitality suite was always the center of socializing at our reunions, the bar in the middle of this year's three rooms.

I told them about spotting Fowler. "Why is he even here?" I asked. "He has to know how we all feel."

Sam ordered the four of us drinks and said, "I know a lot of the men in our company won't have anything to do with the guy, but

I don't think the rest of the battalion feels that way. A lot of men admire him for his leadership."

I acknowledged the fact and drifted into my own thoughts while the others talked. Tight as the men in 442nd were, it seemed to me that we had each ended up with our own war in our hearts. At our reunions, one veteran regaled old comrades with stories of combat while another couldn't utter a word. One man was haunted by an atrocity that another couldn't or wouldn't remember. We could only give one another the freedom and support to deal with our better angels and our worst demons as best we could, to come to our own resolutions about our wars, which truly knew no end.

"Did Hiroshi tell you about Fowler's cards?" Ruth brought me back to the conversation.

I told them the story—the cards had stopped after a year of holidays—and Sam suggested Fowler had obtained my address via Fort Sheridan. I had used my sister's address when I was discharged there, so Fowler must have tracked me down from that. Sam said the colonel had commanded Sheridan at some point.

Sam took a drink, adding, "Those cards are baffling. Maybe he was saying he was sorry. Maybe he was harassing you."

"Sounds like a guilty conscience to me," Ruth said. "Trying to make up for what he did."

"Yes," Sam said.

"I wish he'd just had the guts to vacate my court-martial," I said. "Not pursue it in the first place."

"Maybe the damage was done when you jawed him out in front of his fellow officers," Sam said. "Hell, I can understand the way he felt back in the Vosges, trying to maintain a semblance of order when everything was falling apart. But to frame you in a lie afterwards? Keep at it when all danger was gone? Maybe underneath it all, he was always trying to save face and protect his fragile ego."

"Could be," I muttered, thinking that made sense.

"Strange that he ended up here, along with one of your other battalion commanders, isn't it?" Sayaka said.

"How's that?" Ruth asked.

Sayaka explained that Colonel Matthews, our first battalion commander, was an Illinois native and had become Adlai Stevenson's lieutenant governor soon after the war ended.

"Sure loved that man," Sam and I said, remembering that Matthews had died just a couple of years before. Silently, I wondered how different my Army tenure, my memories, and my dreams might have been under his continued command.

We broke up to mingle with other partygoers, and as dinnertime neared, Ruth and I signaled each other that we should go freshen up.

We jostled our way back into the first room, where we got caught in the crowd of hungry celebrants trying to get near a pupu table for a snack.

And there he was.

Again.

I looked at Ruth and tilted my head in Fowler's direction. He was sitting at the table all alone, not tasting any of the tempting snacks but just hunching over his icy drink and smoking a cigarette, apart from the group that I felt so very much a part of.

People pressed in to get near the food, pushing me close enough to hear him talking into his whiskey.

"I was a son of a bitch," he muttered. "I know I was an SOB."

And then he looked up at me.

I tried to move, but I was trapped.

"Koga. Please." Fowler extended his hand. "Come on, huh? After all these years."

My heart beat hard. I didn't want to shake hands, no less get close to the man. But good manners had been ingrained in me. I clasped Fowler's hand quickly and released it.

"You his wife?" The colonel turned to Ruth and again offered his hand.

Before Ruth could say, "Howdy-do," Fowler said, "Well, tell me, Mrs. Koga, how the hell can you stand to be married to a man like this?"

I didn't know if Fowler meant his words as a conciliatory joke, tacit agreement that I had been a good soldier, or an opening volley to justify his actions once more. I glanced at Ruth, who looked like she might explode, and I looked at Fowler, who sat with his mouth open, waiting for someone to say something.

And then things clicked.

They just clicked.

I had not realized until this moment what a small man my battalion commander was, what a thin-skinned, hurting, and insecure bully hid behind that uniform and those lies of his, still caught up in pressing the rules and the appearances to absurdity. Even Bristol had admitted his failings in a cowardly way, never following through on his threats of court-martial. But Fowler, this man would talk himself in circles until the day he died, and I refused to be glad-handed or listen to his drivel. I didn't know if I wanted to sock the guy in the kisser or put my hand on his shoulder in pity.

The man may have braved the worst on the battlefield, but he had no moral courage to do what was right in the face of overwhelming adversity, to swallow his pride and put all his men first.

"I'm sorry you feel like you have to keep talking to people about what happened." I opted for simple words. "But I'm not going to take this or expose my wife to it."

"My husband is the kindest, most decent man I know." Ruth came to my defense. "His comrades have the utmost respect for him. He is a hero. A soldier's soldier, they call him."

I turned to go, spotting Ando, Shig, and their wives nearby, looking on in silence. They nodded to us as Ruth hitched her arm in mine, and we walked away.

31

Honolulu and Seattle

1983-1996

I felt like I'd been released from prison after that, freed from sec-
ond-guessing and misgivings and bitterness about the colonel,
and when Fowler died just a few years later, I thought my story
with him was finished, at last.

I went about my work—I'd finally broken into the unions as
a car salesman, and a damned good one at that—while Ruth kept
at hers, as a legal secretary. Retirement was looming, but Ruth's
boss wanted to keep her, she was so sharp and accurate, and I
needed to sock away a few more rainy-day funds. We had four
grandchildren now, so we had lots of presents to buy.

And then Ruth and I attended yet another reunion, this one at
Honolulu's Pagoda Hotel.

"Hey, you the one in the stockade or what?"

A veteran from M Company yelled at me over the party din.
He stood on one of the bridges spanning the ponds outside, part

of an elegant Japanese garden that encircled the hotel's Floating Restaurant and teahouses.

"Back in Italy," he yelled. "You, you sit behind the wire, eh? Bad boy, rascal, you!" Orangey-red roofs echoed the colors of the pond's koi and the man's florid face. A waterfall splashed just beyond him, but not loudly enough for me.

He gulped his beer and shook a finger at me. "Snafu guy. You the snafu guy."

"Ah, go to hell," I muttered and glanced at Ando and Emmy, who were trying to carry on a conversation with me and Ruth. Ben Honda and his wife were with us, too. Our old lieutenant frowned.

The man wagged his finger again and guffawed, throwing an hors d'oeuvre into the water, which splashed in exuberant wriggles of orange.

"I can't believe men are still kidding you," Ando said to me.

"Once an asshole, always an asshole," Ben Honda grumbled. "I knew that guy before I transferred to I Company."

"Seems you got all us snafu men," I kidded Ando, trying to make light of the matter.

"That's the last straw," Ando said. "We have to get this off your record. Mak's too."

Surprised by Ando's response, I took a moment to breathe and closed my eyes, inhaling the unique fragrance of Hawaii, the perfume of leis full of plumeria and ginger and tuberose and I didn't know what else, and I opened them to the sight of colorful muumuus and aloha whites. God, I just loved our ohana, even if an occasional idiot raised his head.

"Forget about it," I said. "Like the ponds here, water under the bridge. What can you do?"

"A heck of a lot, that's what we can do," Ando said, sounding indignant. The timing was perfect, he said. The drive for AJA justice had picked up steam since our bicentennial reunion, and AJAs had taken power in Hawaii. He recited his list.

- Petitions for writs of error *coram nobis* cases had been filed in the cases of Korematsu, Yasui, and Hirabayashi, with newly discovered documents showing that the government had lied about issei and nisei disloyalty and the military necessity of the evacuation.
- Korematsu's conviction had already been overturned.
- Hirabayashi and Yasui were hopeful they would be cleared.
- A commission first appointed by President Carter had acknowledged that the government had interned us with no proof of sabotage or espionage, acting out of racial prejudice, war hysteria, and failed leadership.

"Let's not let this ride until it's too late," Ando said. "Veterans are beginning to die, you know." Kat had dropped dead from a massive heart attack only last year, and Ando told of his most recent deathbed vigil, for Kat's brother, of all people. The guy had developed a close friendship with one of Ando's cousins, who asked Ando to sit with them. Kat's brother had suffered nightmares about Company B's assault on Cassino ever since the war, uncontrollably pulling his hair out, and he needed comfort in his final moments. In true Hawaii fashion, a native kahuna also stopped by, to summon spirits to escort the Buddhist to the other side. Ando sensed the specters of parents and siblings and soldiers around the bed, he said, lending solace and guidance to the living and the dying.

"Let's get these court-martials off your records before we're the ones lying there," Ando said.

I knew then that Ando needed this as much as we did. We were his last boys he wouldn't leave behind, and he was still working toward some kind of peace about Happi. I had to admit, I was also struggling with the revelations he'd shared before our Chicago reunion, about knowing that Yoyo had pulled the punch, and I didn't think I'd ever stop feeling bad about how I had dragged Happi and Mak down. Maybe Ando's efforts would help me in more ways than I expected.

Forgiveness sure was a bitch, and self-forgiveness was the bitchiest.

. . .

Ando immediately contacted Hawaii's senators, both nisei veterans, asking for their help. The senior senator, from the 100th Battalion, already had his hands full fighting illness, but Senator Bert Noritake, from E Company, took point, sending us the proper form to complete while he researched our records.

I recalled Noritake's kindness to Happi back at Shelby, and the senator told Ando he remembered our friend with fondness. Noritake had received a field commission after Wes headed stateside, but his dreams of becoming a physician vanished when he lost an arm at the Gothic Line, around the same time Happi was killed. Back home, he threw himself into law school. Politics beckoned once Hawaii became a state.

I stared at DD149, Application for Correction of Military Record, lying on my desk. Should I make the effort, if only in Happi's memory? For my lieutenant?

I called Wes Inada to ask what he thought of our prospects.

"What can I tell, you, Hiro. There aren't any guarantees, but you have to fight this," Wes said. "Lying and deception are what got Hitler to power, how fascism and authoritarianism thrive. They have no place in our democracy, in our system of justice."

390

He added that even Supreme Court Chief Justice Earl Warren, former attorney general and governor of California, had lived to regret his own early racism, noting the internment was not in keeping with the American concept of freedom and the rights of citizens. In the end, not one issei or nisei was found guilty of espionage or sabotage.

"And get this, Hiro," Wes said. "Hugo Black was the justice who wrote the majority opinion in the Korematsu case back in '44. I heard that years ago he admitted privately that his decision was the biggest mistake of his career. How about that?"

Wes went silent for a few seconds and added, "You're lucky to live where you are and have Hawaii folks helping, you know. Aside from the courts, there aren't too many people out here on the East Coast who have a clue about the internment and our fighting. But I'm one of them. I'll see if I can pull some strings."

I buckled down to work.

I completed the form in September of 1985, giving a rundown of everything—my war service, the ration detail and the MP incident in Menton, the way Lieutenant Donnelly offered to help me before he died, my trial six months after the incident, with no counsel and no witnesses, the stockades, Ando's wish to help me and Mak this many years later.

Ando called me a week later, disgruntled. "Mak's given up," he said. "Says he still has nightmares about the court-martial. Doesn't want to dredge up the past."

"Sensitive guy, Mak is," I said, "much more introspective than me." I could understand his feelings.

"Well, I say *poho*, yuh," Ando said. "He's wasting a chance for justice."

And thus began the Noritake Campaign. I lost track of how many times I filed and refiled that damned application, always told that my papers had been destroyed by a fire back in 1973, at the National Personnel Records Center in St. Louis.

That, or the passage of time had been too great to obtain a record.

Months passed.

Years passed.

Hirabayashi's convictions were overturned.

Yasui died fighting.

I heard nothing.

Ruth kept up my spirits with her *"Kodomo no tame ni"* pleas, for the sake of the children. That's why she herself was pursuing redress for our internment, even talking about her experiences in public reparations meetings and teaching others about what we'd been through, to help right the wrong and make sure others did not suffer like we had. "If you don't do it for yourself," she said, "do it for the children's sake."

Our daughters echoed her, as did my siblings. Our grandchildren began piping up.

Did I really want "PFC" chiseled into my tombstone?

I dug in, vowing to stay in the battle.

Time marched on.

President Reagan signed HR 442, the Civil Liberties Act, offering an apology for the relocation camps and a restitution payment to each survivor of the camps, which had held one hundred twenty thousand people, seventy percent of us American citizens. Noritake, the JACL, and Yasui had been instrumental in getting the act passed.

With other internees, Ruth and I received $20,000 reparations checks and formal letters of apology from President Bush.

And still, I heard nothing about my application.

I dug in further.

I grew weary.

Ando asked Senator Noritake's assistant for an update on my case. Noritake replied that everything possible had been done to help. End of story.

"You can stop now," I said to Ando when he called with the news. "I really appreciate all you've done. Maybe it's just not meant to be—"

"No way I'm giving up," Ando said.

"You don't have to earn my forgiveness, you know," I said, wondering if I was right in my assessment of Ando's motivation.

"What do you mean?" Ando asked.

"Well, back in Chicago, you told me about Yoyo, the way you knew he punched the MP. That threw me for a loop."

"I still struggle with my own feelings, Hiro," Ando said.

"But I've forgiven you for that, really I have," I said. "What a dilemma that was. You don't have to keep working for my blessing."

"Maybe working is the only way I can see my way to forgiving myself, Hiro, to find the resolution to put things behind me, once and for all," Ando said.

I knew I'd shoved a lot of things aside in the name of getting on with life, but I'd tried to be good to everyone, too. "I've always tried my best," I said, "even if my actions weren't conscious efforts to forgive myself, visiting families of dead comrades, talking with Happi's family, apologizing and making amends if I've upset Ruth or our girls."

We fell silent for a few seconds, and Ando said, "I wish more people took that kind of action, to do good, especially some of our leaders."

"Fowler, you mean?"

Ando said yes. "That man couldn't admit a wrong or forgive, that's for sure. Didn't have the guts." He thought for a moment before adding, "I don't know why, but maybe deep down, he couldn't really love. Forgiveness is an act of love, after all, sometimes a daring, courageous act of surrender, letting go of your ego in empathy, compassion."

The truth of Ando's words touched my heart, words that few tough old soldiers would have the guts to speak, and I added, "Appearances were more important to him than what was inside, what really matters, truth and integrity, just for starters. He grasped tight to his lies to the bitter end. He didn't know when to stop pressing the rules beyond their limits."

"He never followed the Middle Way, to put it in Buddhist terms," Ando said. "He just took the extreme and never let go."

We were quiet as we thought, and then Ando said, "What's left to us is to control our actions and responses. We can't just shove our anger, our recriminations, in the back of our minds to fester. We can't rehash and rehash what has happened. We can't keep the past alive with what-ifs, wondering how things could have been different. Those are all ways of giving our power away. If we let someone or something else control our feelings, our reactions, our lives aren't our own. We have to act, mentally, spiritually, physically, and break with the past. If we don't, we can't be fully present to our own lives."

I knew Ando was right, and I knew I had to work more on my feelings about Fowler, about Yoyo. But I wondered if Ando heard his own words, if he was being careful not to get eaten up and worn down by his own work. I decided not to say more for now and asked him what his next move was.

"I have no idea what takes place in the hallowed halls of Washington, but I'll think of something." He promised to send me a copy of the senator's letter.

When I read it, I saw Ando's annotation in the margin.

"Fooey!" he had written. I was taken with the directness of his spirit and his spelling, just as the word sounded.

"Fooey!"

Ando's new battle cry announced the Wilson Campaign, led
by Hawaii's U.S. Representative Betty Ikeda Wilson, herself no
stranger to fighting discrimination and inequality. Changing tact,
she and Ando focused on obtaining hard evidence of my court-
martial, to give us the ammo of facts, the details of exactly what
had happened. We had to get the government's attention.

Just as Wilson went into high gear, I fell low.

Cancer.

I had cancer of the vertebrae.

Chemo and radiation treatments made me miserable, unable to
work, but Ando and Wilson didn't miss a beat. The Special Court-
Martial document itself was beyond our reach; if a court-martial
didn't involve a bad conduct discharge, the records were routinely
destroyed within ten years after review by the Judge Advocate
General. But the Special Court-Martial *order* was still available.

Within two years, we had it in hand.

. . .

"I can't believe this." I showed Ruth the packet, which included Special Court-Martial Order No. 18, my honorable discharge,
and papers in support of a couple of the medals that I'd won. "One
fat lie after another."

I felt too agitated to sit, so stood up and looked over Ruth's
shoulder, spewing things out as she read. "The first charge says
that I acted disrespectfully to the MP. Look, his name is right
here, Carlos Ramos. Can you believe it? It says that he was my
superior officer. Good grief."

"And the second charge accuses you of being drunk in uniform in a public place," Ruth read, "'to wit, 'Dancing Auguste,' a public bar.'"

"But that's stupid," I said. "We were allowed to go to bars then. We weren't on line. And I hadn't been drinking so much that I didn't know I was the senior enlisted man there and did my duty. I broke up the fight."

I pointed to the text. "And read this. It says I pleaded guilty, pleaded guilty to both charges." I sat down. "Not true. Not true. It's just like Mak and I said back then. We were guilty before being proven guilty, with no proof."

Ruth pointed to the bottom of the page. "Did you see this? It says that you, you as 'the accused,' were on the distribution list for this order."

"What?" I took the documents back. I had to give Ruth credit. She had an eye for detail that I didn't, plus the patience to go through documents methodically.

"I never received a thing. Not a damned thing." The only accurate words in the whole damned document were the notations that I had been demoted to private and had been given a sentence of six months of confinement and forfeiture of six months' pay.

"I really was framed," I said, "judged without trial and thrown in the slammer. And given the maximum sentence, too. It was a done deal before it even began."

"Kangaroo court," Ruth said. "What a travesty."

She returned to the document. "Who is this Ogawa fellow? A nisei?" Someone named H.S. Ogawa, Second Lieutenant Infantry, Assistant Adjutant, had signed off on the document, which had been approved "by order of Colonel Carpenter."

"Probably some clerk," I said. "But Colonel Carpenter? That surprises me. He was regimental commander at that point, I think. Everyone thought he was a good egg. I really wonder what Fowler did behind the scenes."

I read more. Even the write-up for my Silver Star at the Gothic Line, on 2nd Platoon Hill, referred to me as "S/Sgt. Koga, then private. "That's just not true."

At least we found one happy surprise. The executive officer on the awards panel had recommended that my Silver Star be upgraded to a Distinguished Service Cross.

"But you never received it?" Ruth asked.

I reminded her about the top brass downgrading awards of men they didn't know. But I was tickled, and Ando, who had earned his own Silver Star in the last days of the Vosges campaign, sounded jubilant when I shared the news.

Ando suggested I file another DD149 with the new evidence in hand. I obliged, but Christmas, my birthday, Valentine's Day—all passed with little news of progress in my case, other than word from the secretary of the Board for Correction of Military Records. They couldn't take action on my application, because, yes, my files had been destroyed by fire.

"I'm not getting any better," I confided in Ando in our next phone call. I was in and out of remission. We had been fighting for thirteen years now.

"Remember the words of Martin Luther King," Ando said. "The moral arc of the universe is long, but bends toward justice."

"I just don't know how much longer I can hold on," I said.

"Try, Hiro, please try," Ando said. "I have one more ace up my sleeve. Will you join me in my battle cry?"

"Fooey!" we called.

32

Honolulu and Seattle

1997

A ndo's battle cry announced the MacAlister Campaign, and I hoped it was the last. My body ached like hell, and I was weaker than I thought humanly possible.

Ando told me that Hank MacAlister was a friend from Hilo and a veteran of 2nd Battalion Headquarters Company. A hapa haole, rare for our generation, he was the man to get us out of the rut, and fast. He had the brains and organization skills of an engineer and connections we could use. Hank was already lining up everyone in a kind of tag team effort, from Noritake to Wilson to Ando and Ruth and me. We had to circle the wagons once and for all and bring this home.

"I'm thinking of a two-pronged attack," Hank said. "So let's focus on the first. We need to determine every which way you were wronged."

With the help of Wes Inada, Hank discovered that my case would have been ruled by the 1928 edition of the Army's Manual for Courts-Martial, which was updated in 1943, including the Articles of War appended to it. He cut right to the chase in a letter to me.

Damned if I didn't find the document right here at the University of Hawaii. I've read every last word and I'm coming up with a list of rules that were violated. Writing down a list helps me think things through. Here are just a few of the wrongs committed against you.

- *You should have experienced the minimum restraint and time possible before and during the trial, as well as in the final action of the case.*
- *You should have been tried immediately after your arrest and confinement—or the charges should have been dropped.*
- *You should have been given a court-appointed trial judge advocate and defense counsel.*
- *You should have been able to attend your proceedings in an open court.*

When we spoke on the phone, I laughed as I thanked Hank for letting me know the correct plural of our judicial messes—they were courts-martial, not court-martials, as I'd been calling them for years—and then asked the question for which we had never really found a satisfactory answer. "How the hell did Fowler even know we were at the bar? The MPs wouldn't have known us in a sea of nisei."

"We also have to question the very morality of sending men into battle from the stockade and then locking them up again," Hank said. We understood that a case might be made for military expediency, given the state of the RCT after the Vosges campaign, when leaders were needed desperately, but we called into question the morality, nonetheless.

Over the coming days, everyone reviewed the evidence in hand, making phone calls and writing notes.

"We have the stories of Donnelly's support and Chaplain Morimoto's knowledge of who had thrown the punch," Ando offered, "plus reports of the barroom fight and the stockades."

"But the stories are all hearsay. We need proof. We need sworn affidavits," Hank said. He gathered them from Ando and me, Mak and Tommy. I reviewed the affidavits with Ruth and found the documents agreed on the important essentials: one, that no one had been arrested or charged at the bar; two, that Mak and I had broken up the fight; and three, that the MPs had shaken hands with us and said no hard feelings.

Hank also asked for help from the 2nd Battalion's Colonel Henderson, with whom he had become friends after the war. Henderson didn't recall phoning me about the court-martial, though offered to write a character reference for me. I found it strange that an officer would forget something so unusual, but I had to take him at his word.

Betty Wilson wrote in mid-April, saying that she'd sent my personnel records onto the Board for Correction of Military Records. She'd also reread the letter I received from the secretary of that board, who pointed out that as applicant, I was responsible for giving evidence, that I had to show the existence of an error or injustice important enough to warrant action by the board. The secretary suggested I talk to Chaplain Morimoto or Yoyo Wasuke and get a statement, and that's what Wilson asked of me now.

I updated her on Morimoto, who had died years ago, and told her my latest news from Ando, who planned to visit Yoyo around our 53rd reunion. I didn't mention that I held little hope for his efforts.

And then the miracle happened.

At long last, the single holdout came through.

Yoshiharu "Yoyo" Wasuke owned up to starting the fight.

"Took two visits, a pot of honey from my bees, and a lot of persuading from his wife," Ando said in his next phone call. But all the effort was worth it. Yoyo heaved a sigh of relief after his confession, like a weight had been lifted from him, and the guy talked uninterrupted when Ando took him for coffee.

It wasn't clear if Yoyo had squealed our names, Ando said, but in all his unloading, Yoyo mentioned that the MPs had asked for a pass and had drawn their pistols, which no one had remembered. But we did know this: In a war zone, soldiers didn't need passes. And the MPs shouldn't have drawn their pistols.

It took some research to confirm that we really stood in a war zone, but Hank dug up that fact in the 442nd archives. "I found maps and records that show exactly where we landed."

"And Happi, son of a gun, Happi has helped us after all these years," Ando said.

"What do you mean?"

"His brother Shig heard about us trying to overturn the court-martial, and he just sent some letters that Happi had written to his family. Hoped the information in them could help us. Wanted to know, too, if Happi had been court-martialed."

"What did they say?"

"In one, Happi mentioned that he was having trouble seeing Shig in the Menton area," Ando said, "because, yes, we were in a war zone." I got choked up, grateful for my friend's voice beyond the grave, and Ando was glad to give Shig the news that Happi had not been court-martialed. His record was clean.

The new information was included in my application, yet another "edition" of DD149, and this time even I got my hopes up.

Weeks and weeks passed as we waited for a response, giving us time to ponder the irony that Yoyo had actually been innocent all these years. That was not to say that what he had done was right, punching the MP and dragging everyone down with him, but it sounded as if the MPs had made the first misstep. For years, Yoyo must have felt aggrieved, and he had never once attended a reunion. Between thinking about the MPs and the way he'd hurt his comrades, we wondered how the guy slept at night.

And then we received the news we had been waiting for.

"I have my sergeant stripes back!" I yelled in triumph. "I have my stripes!"

I knew this victory was partial—my court-martial still held—but I felt some of the burden of the past had been taken from my shoulders. And the news could not have come at a better time.

My back had been killing me, and I consulted the doctor.

The cancer was spreading.

"Look what I brought you." Ruth handed me Happi's sketchpad as I stretched out on the sofa one afternoon. Treatments were laying me low once more. "Thought looking through these might make you feel a little better."

"Thank you. You know me well, " I said, grateful for her care. I thumbed through Happi's old sketches of Nice and Menton, remembering our friend and all the good times we had.

Ruth looked on and stopped me at one. "That's the brawl you were in, right?"

"Yes," I said, scanning the page.

I studied the images closely.

"Look," I pointed to the MPs, growing excited. "They have their pistols drawn. I have to tell Ando and Hank. Another confirmation. Happi's helping us again."

I turned to the individual sketches in back of the bar scene. "See, that's me. Mak. Poi." Ruth pointed as I turned to images of other men she'd met over the years.

I told Ruth again about Fowler and his MPs coming into our schoolhouse, tossing things around, and rounding us up after the fight.

I looked at the drawings.

What the hell.

"What is it?" Ruth asked.

"You know, Kat told me that those MPs had come in the day after the brawl, searching all over our quarters and taking things back with them," I said. "I just wonder—"

"What?"

"Happi finished the sketches that morning. I wonder if the MPs took them when they left and brought them back the next day."

"And that's how they knew who was in the bar," Ruth said.

"That's how they knew," I said. "Could be that Yoyo sang like a canary, and these drawings sealed our fate."

I laughed. "Happi had been intent on making his sketches realistic. Noritake himself had helped him. And look what happened." We couldn't win for losing.

Ando called shortly before dinner. We told him about Happi's sketches, and he said that now I had my stripes back, Hank was setting his sights on the Judge Advocate General for the final appeal to set aside my court-martial. Noritake's secretary had discovered that we were way past any deadline for filing an appeal, which boiled down to either October 1, 1983, or the last day of a two-year period beginning with the date of sentence approval, according to an amendment to court-martial rules. But if we could establish a "good cause" for not filing, we might be heard.

"This is becoming your own *coram nobis* case," Hank wrote. "We need to find the good cause, the something new that now sits before us. And that is the second prong of my attack." He said that Article 69 (b) of the Uniform Code of Military Justice outlined that "good cause" amounted to

- Evidence that had just come to light
- Discovery of wayward court proceedings, something known as fraud on the court
- Revelation that there was no authority over the accused or the offense, something called lack of jurisdiction
- Discovery of an error in the proceedings that harmed me—something known as error prejudicial to the substantial rights of the accused
- Judgment of inappropriate sentence

"Face it," Hank said. "You're asking the government to forgive your tardiness, your delay in filing. You have to show up with the goods to convince them you're in the right. You have to prove you have good cause. Let's see if there's anything else we can find."

We got down to work.

First came a search for Ogawa, the man who had signed off on my court-martial order. We wanted his recollection of what had happened at the trial. We received lots of help on this one, but it turned out Ogawa had dementia.

Another dead end.

Our next goal, and it was a big one, was to find the MP himself, Carlos Ramos. Chaplain Morimoto had told Ando that the MP didn't want to press charges. To find Ramos would be a coup.

As coincidence would have it, in the middle of our search, Hank addressed a meeting of Item chapter in Honolulu to update everyone.

"Hey, I'm going to Puerto Rico next week for a bankers' meeting," Mitsuru Oyama spoke up. "Why don't I look for Ramos." Mits was the clerk who had to take over I Company after the Lost Battalion rescue.

Within days, Mits did himself even better. He actually bumped into an associate who knew the MP. We couldn't believe it.

Ando knew we were on the right path.

Ramos had become a colonel, and he had a terrific memory. In an interview with Mits, he swore that no arrests had been made at the time of the incident, that he had requested charges be dropped, and that he had not been called to testify at the court-martial.

"So Ramos is your new evidence. That justifies a review of your case," Hank said. "His absence from the proceedings was, in legal terms, an 'error prejudicial to the substantial rights of the accused.'"

Hank and Mits wrote an affidavit for Ramos to sign and mailed it off. Mits called to touch base and told me that he'd written many citations for medals for me during the war, but had been forced by Colonel Fowler to rip them up. I thanked Mits and told him that nothing, just nothing, would surprise me any longer.

Hank had my next application in my hands within a week, enumerating every last wrong made against me, and there were thirty or more items. He showed what defense counsel could have done to help, concluding that I had not been tried in an open court.

And would anyone be interested in this finding: any officer who caused a delay in a court-martial was liable for court-martial himself?

I sure as hell was, even if we were a day late and a dollar shy.

The clock ticked loudly, and I was admitted to the hospital as everyone waited for Ramos's affidavit. The final application couldn't be filed without it. I sensed my end was near, and as soon as I was hospitalized, I said to Ruth, "Ask Jug if he'll do the honors when the time comes."

That afternoon, Ruth phoned Jug, who said yes, of course he would, and he called back the next day to say that Nobu Sakai had offered to help and would bring candies, too. Ruth and I smiled at the sweetness of friendship in war and in peace. Molly and Lawson, Aiko and Frank made the trek to see me, as did Virginia, now about the age at which Haha had died, and her spitting image. I told them all that I was sorry I'd be the first to leave our party. Koichi and our parents were calling.

And then that wife of mine brought it all together, acting on instructions about what documents to sign, what papers to have notarized, what exhibits to place in which order, what to mail back to Hawaii, what to mail to JAG. In the middle of this, I asked her to bring my photo of us in Chicago.

"And here's mine," she said. We each pressed our copy to the other's heart. She brought Happi's drawing of us, too, which Shig had given to us, and quietly, we remembered our youth and our friends. I looked at her, even more beautiful than the day we met, her hair shorter and her looks much more content with age than mine. I asked her to bring me Happi's sketchpad again, and when she was gone, I flipped through the pages, found the drawing of Happi's nurse, and tore it into little pieces. Combined with my moving to the Great Beyond, I imagined the burden of knowing Happi had adored her right to the end might be too much for Ruth to bear.

Some secrets were kept out of love.

Ruth helped me sign Form 3499, my JAG application testimony, on Memorial Day.

She leaned over and kissed my forehead. "I'll see this to the end, no matter what," she promised.

I prayed for just a little more time.

I began counting the days.

Where was Ramos's affidavit?

On June 7, my doctors gave me a new cancer drug, which helped, and I rallied.

Two days later, word came that Ramos had mailed the document. It arrived in Hawaii on the thirteenth.

"Here's our copy." Ruth brought the affidavit into my hospital room as soon as she received it and read it to me. We kissed, hoping the document would seal the deal.

I returned home a few days later, happier than I'd been in months.

"Dad, this is going to do it," our daughters called. Our grandchildren joined in their chorus.

"Don't write me off just yet," I said.

Letters flew between everyone who'd been involved in the fight. We mailed Ramos thank you notes and gifts, he mailed me a get well card, and Mak, himself fighting stomach cancer, said he was willing to give justice a chance. I was soon sitting up in bed, and then spending a few hours on our sofa each day.

Six weeks later, Yoyo Wasuke died from lung cancer.

I felt bad for the guy, even if he'd wronged me. I was having bad days again and had an idea of what he'd suffered. At least I knew we were close to victory.

I decided now was a good time to speak with Ando. With the overturning process this far advanced and me so sick, I wanted to

come to some kind of resolution about our guilt, our recriminations, our letting go.

"I tried to talk to Yoyo's wife," Ando began our conversation.
"I want to seek justice for him, too, but she'll hear none of it."

"I feel bad he's gone, really I do. But what you're doing takes
a kind of forgiveness that is beyond me." I broached the topic
immediately.

"I'm not condoning his lies," Ando said. "Let's be clear about
that. But what's done is done. He owned up to his mistake, and I
give him credit for that, even at this late stage. And now we know
he'd been wronged, too. He was one of my boys, and I wanted to
help."

I was having a hell of a time letting go of this one, but continued to listen as Ando talked. "I know you Christians have an
idea of grace," he said, "that God's grace can absolve a repentant
sinner. We don't have that notion of an outside power, but I think
at this point, we can both understand that forgiveness has everything to do with compassion, and that has to include yourself to
be true, to free yourself from the past and live fully."

I saw his point. "I guess that's why we ask God to forgive ourselves as we forgive others, why we're commanded to love our
neighbor as ourselves. It's a two-way street. Can't have one without the other."

Ando was quiet and then added, "Taking compassionate action to right wrongs and help others is good for everyone. We
never left a man behind in combat. We came back for Happi and
other men we'd lost on the field when we could, and we can't leave
ourselves behind now."

I took a deep breath, seeing my way to peace more clearly. "I
don't have much time left, Ando. And at this juncture, I just have
to accept things for what they were, with no judgment. We can't

change the past. We did our best under the fire of war and under a couple of commanders who sometimes could have been our enemy. We were true to our comrades and ourselves. And that's the way we've led the rest of our lives."

I thought way back to our visit with Ando's sensei, about words I didn't understand then. "Maybe that's what your teacher meant when he said we had to forgive when we got home. He was telling us not to rehash the horrors of war, but to keep the fear, the bloodshed, the suffering where they belong, in the past. We can learn from even the worst of what's happened, but we can't wallow in it. Otherwise we can never really live again." I felt lighter now, knowing that a heart full of forgiveness and love had no room for fear, vengeance, recrimination, and I thought of Jug, what he'd said years ago at our first reunion. Living courageously in compassion and trust and strength was what it was all about.

"It's the only way to truly get home, to rediscover your center, after all you've lived, the joys, the sorrows. If we're fortunate, the wounds heal and make us stronger," Ando said. "Sensei reminded us of the Golden Rule, which is in every religion and philosophy. And his teachings reflected our Eightfold Path and Middle Way, to serve others and end the suffering. I've tried my best to live my life that way."

"Have you finally hit the forgiveness jackpot?" I asked. "With all the work you've done?"

Ando laughed softly. "Once you and Mak win your cases—and you will—I have just one thing left."

"And what's that?"

"During the war, I couldn't consecrate the ground that Happi fell on," he said, "and I vowed that I would go back and do that. I'm going to take one of those veterans' tours someday and visit not just his grave, but the spot where he died. Once I have purified that ground, my life will be complete."

Veterans and their families were taking tours of our battlefields as we opened up about the war. We sought healing on the grounds that had wounded us in so many ways, on the fields that had killed so many of our friends, that had killed so much inside us.

Ando added, "And then I can die."

"And live," I said. "You can live."

"I've had great joy in my life, Hiro," Ando said. "Please understand that. Emmy, our sons and grandchildren, our friends, all have filled me with happiness. But this one action will give me final peace."

We chatted a little bit longer, about how many were now forgiving the JACL for its actions during the war, not condoning, but doing away with the bitterness. Some were even seeing our protestors not as loud-mouthed turncoats, but as conscientious objectors.

Ando said, "I've saved a bit of good news for last."

"What's that?"

"Tak Nishida is a friend of mine from K Company," Ando said. "A Buddhist professor, in New York state. You're not going to believe this, but it turns out he was on your ration detail."

"What the hell?" I said. I knew of only one survivor, the man I had carried to safety.

"Tak just wrote an article for the GFB," Ando said. That was the *Go for Broke Bulletin,* like the alumni magazines my daughters read from their colleges, except for us old soldiers. I used to read mine as soon as it came into the house, but hadn't kept up of late. "Turns out Tak brought up the rear of your detail with one other man. After the barrage, they found an aid station together. Tak wanted to know if anyone else survived."

"You're kidding me," I said.

"Tak swears his wristwatch protected him, saved his arm from being blown off," Ando said, and I wondered if he was the young soldier I'd seen checking the time when he volunteered that night.

Ando continued, "When I told him about you and the other man, Tak said the barrage must have hit the middle of your detail, so the two men at either end survived."

"How about that," I said, amazed.

"Tak's already working with Pup Ito to find the names of your other men," Ando said. I recalled Pup had led the rescue and recovery mission for our command post. "Pup's been compiling a directory of soldiers' names, hometowns, and death places and dates."

I couldn't believe it, and I thanked Ando for sharing the information. It meant the world to me.

Ando said he knew Tak and Pup and was sure they'd find the names. "And one more thing," he said. "Tak told me that he just read the collected letters of Reverend Morimoto in our archives here. Turns out the chaplain kept in contact with Colonel Matthews—"

"Our first battalion commander," I said.

"Right. Well, the chaplain wrote that after Colonel Fowler led the troops home, he was sent on TD, except it wasn't so temporary. Captain Grand came back as battalion commander."

"I didn't know that," I said, remembering how we had all loved Captain Grand.

"And this is where it gets interesting. Matthews wrote back that Grand had much aloha for us men and that we'd preserve our dignity and self-respect under him," Ando said, drawing out the sentence. "His exact words. Curious, eh?"

"Sounds like command was onto Fowler, at last," I said.

"Maybe a bit of good old *bachi* came into play," Ando said, "and Fowler got a little of what he deserved right then and there. And who knows what's in store in the Great Beyond. That guy may have to live many lifetimes, many incarnations, to learn his lessons."

I told Ando I hoped he was right, and he told me to rest well. After we hung up, I slipped into a new stillness, with all the busy-ness of life behind me, sensing, knowing for the first time my true home and my center for the precious jewels that they were, the things that even Molly had told me years and years ago would always be with me.

Be still and know I am God. The lessons I had heard in church came back to me in a new way.

Then I took a nap, dreaming vividly of my parents and Koichi, of Happi and all the men I had lost, of Yoyo, too, even of the German I had killed in the foxhole, all dancing and swaying together in one big bon odori as they visited me. There was no need to say goodbye, I told them. I'd be joining them soon.

I gained a little strength from Ando's story, and Ruth and I supported each other when we got hit with the next piece of news.

Betty Wilson reported that a Colonel Patrick Darwin at JAG had written that it would take ninety days to process my application, perhaps even longer, given its complexity.

Hank had a kitten when he read Darwin's comment that the process entailed "securing the original court-martial record of trial and allied papers."

Didn't they know the original record was destroyed in a case such as mine?

And just days later, we received word that JAG had turned my case down.

We hadn't filed the application by the deadline.

Were they serious? Had they even read my file?

I tried to help, but the new medicine had stopped working, and I returned to bed. My doctors said they had run out of options. I should get my house in order.

I told them we were working on that, believe me.

Over the next couple of weeks, Hank worked with Ruth to boost her spirits and draft a letter of appeal, which she signed and mailed on October 7. In the first three pages, she reviewed the history of my case and provided the names and addresses of the main people we had contacted. Then she went for broke, like all good 442nd soldiers, using her legal smarts to pound home our discovery of newly found evidence, of Ramos' affidavit, of the unfairness and prejudicial errors of my trial. She closed with a final plea.

Please review again my husband's Application for Relief. He is nearing death, and I will not stop fighting this last battle for justice and vindication.

Halloween passed. Betty Wilson wrote a letter in support of Ruth's appeal. Thanksgiving passed. And then, just before Christmas, we received the best present ever, a letter on the stationery of the Office of the Judge Advocate General, 2200 Army Pentagon, Washington, D.C.

Ruth whispered to me as our daughters stood around her, our grandchildren at the corners of our bed, where I lay. What a great country we lived in, she said, to admit its mistake and rectify its error. She held my hand as she read through her tears.

December 9, 1997
Dear Mrs. Koga:

This responds to your October 7, 1997 request that I reconsider my action on your husband's application for relief under Article 69 (b), Uniform Code of Military Justice.

Based on careful consideration of the entire file and the information provided in all documents submitted, I have determined that in the interest of justice, there is, indeed, "good cause" to consider this appeal even though it was not filed within the statute of limitations. Mr. Koga's appeal is granted and his court-martial is set aside.

Your husband has been understandably concerned over this event in his life, and your letter eloquently details his extraordinary efforts to erase the court-martial conviction from his record. I am particularly impressed by your husband's gallantry and the six Purple Hearts he earned during World War II. I express my deepest sympathy over his illness and wish you the very best in the future.

Sincerely,
Chester D. Houghton
Major General, U.S. Army
The Judge Advocate General

And to the side of his signature, the general had written in his own hand,

Your husband is an American Hero—and that is how he should be remembered. CDH

Coda

Tendola, Italy

Several years later

"He took my bullet." Ando spoke just above a whisper as he searched for the spot where Happi had fallen. "It was meant for me."

The old lieutenant had asked just a few people from his battlefield tour to join him, this task was so tender, and he walked ahead with the vigor of a young man, cutting a path through the grass, deep green and overgrown in its springtime lushness of peace.

He came to a halt in front of a knee-high stone wall, part of a dilapidated, ancient building. "This has to be it," he said softly. Ando pointed to a bell tower and other buildings in the distance. "I'll conduct my ceremony here."

Holding himself with military comportment, he opened his satchel as tour members drew near. He wore a red polo shirt embossed with the emblem of Camp Honokaia, and his bald head shone in the early morning sun.

A dark-haired Italian soldier, veteran of a more recent war, helped Ando take out his *senko* and place it on the crumbling wall. With reverence, Ando lit the incense and then found his ojuzu, inserting his hands and placing them together in *gassho*, in gratitude for the life of George Minoru "Happi" Ishikawa.

Bowing and closing his eyes, Ando murmured, *Namu Amida Butsu. Namu Amida Butsu. Namu Amida Butsu.* Buddha of Infinite Light. A monarch butterfly landed lightly on the stones and spread its wings in the warmth of the sun.

Ando straightened up, cupped his hands around his mouth, and called loudly.

"Happi!"

"Happi!"

"Happi, I'm here!"

His voice cracked, and he wiped his eyes with a handkerchief.

Ando told his story, how, even during the war, he had wanted to consecrate the ground where Happi fell, how he promised himself that he would return. He thanked the Italian soldier for arranging his visit, for this chance to fulfill his vow.

Ando bowed his head and placed his hands together again before leaving.

"Mission accomplished," he whispered.

Namu Amida Butsu.

Acknowledgments

Hiro's War is a work of fiction rooted in history, and the author discourages speculation about the personalities and events that served as a springboard for the story. Characters, dialogues, and situations have been created to meet the demands of storytelling, and the novel stands on its own as a universal tribute to the indomitable spirit and accomplishments of the nisei soldiers and their families, as a call for the continued pursuit of equal justice in this country. I stand deeply indebted to the armies of 442nd aficionados living in flesh and in spirit who helped in my labor of love, including Dr. Victor Izui, Junwo "Jim" Yamashita, William Y. Thompson, my veterans' tour of the nisei battlefields of Italy and Europe, Dr. James McIlwain, Dr. Robert Foote, Dr. Kenneth Inada, Louise Kashino Takisaki, Debbie Kashino, Beverly Kashino, Sadaichi Kubota, Amy Kubota, Alan Kubota, Debbie Kubota, Claire Mitani, Joji Watanabe, Pierre Moulin, Colonel Bert Nishimura, Andrew Ono, Eddie Yamasaki, George Morihiro, André Freminet, Claude Freminet, Bernard Hans, Karen Kanemoto/Legacy Center Manager, Japanese American Service Committee of Chicago, Dr. Masue Taniguchi, Jan Taniguchi, Sandra Ishikawa, Kazuyo Tennant, Vincent

Matsudaira, Shig Doi, Sakae "Andy" Yamashiro, Davide del Giudice, Clarence Tamayori, Robert Nagata, Masa Kobashigawa, Barbara Horiuchi, Fred Miller, Ken Shiokawa, Geary Mizuno, Beth Mizuno, Dr. Kim Sichel, Judge Toshimi Sodetani, Diana Freeman Harris, Latoya Hathorn Norman, Katherine Baishiki, Michael Harris, Dana Nolan and the West Valley Graphics team, Terry Nakagawa, Nathan Huxtable, Richard Izui, Marc Rupp, and Michael Antonello, General Counsel, Lynn University. For editorial guidance and encouragement, I extend my thanks to Dawn Raffel, Heidi Bell, Sheryl Johnston, Barbara D'Amato, John Silbersack, and Emily Victorson. I am also grateful for the use of the archives of the 442nd Club, the digital archives of Densho: the Japanese American Legacy Project; the digital archives of the Go For Broke National Education Center; the African American Military Museum, Hattiesburg, Mississippi; 442nd RCT battle journals and soldier biographies; and numerous books, pieces of correspondence, and DVDs about the internment and the 100th Battalion/442nd RCT. Tami Boyce honored the text with fitting interior design.

Made in the USA
Monee, IL
19 July 2021